Living
Large

Living Large

Rochelle Alers

Donna Hill

Brenda Jackson

Francis Ray

A SIGNET BOOK

SIGNET
Published by New American Library, a division of
Penguin Putnam Inc., 375 Hudson Street,
New York, New York 10014, U.S.A.
Penguin Books Ltd, 80 Strand,
London WC2R 0RL, England
Penguin Books Australia Ltd, 250 Camberwell Road,
Camberwell, Victoria 3124, Australia
Penguin Books Canada Ltd, 10 Alcorn Avenue,
Toronto, Ontario, Canada M4V 3B2
Penguin Books (N.Z.) Ltd, Cnr Rosedale and Airborne Roads,
Albany, Auckland 1310, New Zealand

Penguin Books Ltd, Registered Offices:
Harmondsworth, Middlesex, England

First published by Signet, an imprint of New American Library,
a division of Penguin Putnam Inc.

First Printing, January 2003
10 9 8 7 6 5 4 3 2

Ⓟ REGISTERED TRADEMARK—MARCA REGISTRADA

Printed in the United States of America

PUBLISHER'S NOTE
These are works of fiction. Names, characters, places, and incidents either
are the product of the author's imagination or are used fictitiously, and any
resemblance to actual persons, living or dead, business establishments, events,
or locales is entirely coincidental.

Contents

Reunion

Rochelle Alers

This novella celebrates
the three divas—
Francis Ray, Brenda Jackson, and Donna Hill—
"Let's do it again." Gwendolyn Seay—for
Roosevelt High School, Long Island, and my editor,
Genny Ostertag—thank you for believing in
Living Large.

How hard it is to find a capable wife! She is worth more
than jewels!
—Proverbs 31:30
Good News Bible, Today's English Version

One

Heads turned, gazes shifted, jaws dropped, and lips parted in muted whispers as Elaine Jackson's statuesque figure moved with fluid grace, leaving trailing in her wake the subtle scent of a classic perfume.

She followed the maître d' to a table, where her best friends awaited her arrival. The three women had a standing quarterly appointment to meet at the Bayou, Harlem's finest New Orleans–style Creole restaurant and bar.

She felt good, and she knew she looked good—from her professionally coiffed hair and makeup, to her tailored navy blue linen suit piped in white, down to her groomed feet shod in a pair of blue-and-white spectator pumps.

The beginnings of a smile tipped the corners of her mouth when she saw Meredith Endicott lean over to whisper in Brenda Gaskin's ear. The first cousins were inseparable. They looked enough alike to be mistaken for sisters. The fact was that their mothers were sisters. Both women claimed gold-brown complexions, sandy-brown hair, dark eyes, and a liberal sprinkling of freckles over pert, upturned noses.

Elaine, Brenda, and Meredith had grown up in the

same Long Island neighborhood, and then had gone on to attend New York University as business school majors. Their friendship had spanned more than four decades of birthdays, engagements, marriages, child-births, tears of pain, joy, and a divorce.

She had half expected to see a man sitting at the table with the cousins, only because her two well-meaning friends had begun hinting that it was time she began dating again. What they failed to understand was that she had adjusted quite well to her current marital status. Elaine wasn't the first woman whose "perfect marriage" had ended without warning, and she certainly would not be the last.

A waiter paused at the table, pulling out a chair and seating Elaine as her dining partners exchanged mysterious glances. Smiling and flashing two matching dimples, she thanked the man as he pushed the chair in.

"Sorry about being late. The train was delayed just outside of Penn Station." She had made it a habit never to drive into Manhattan from the suburbs, preferring instead to ride the Long Island Railroad. Peering closely at her friends, she asked, "What are you two grinning about?"

Meredith, the older cousin by a mere three weeks, said, "Where is he?"

Elaine's expression mirrored puzzlement. "What are you talking about?"

"Don't play the innocent, Lainie," Brenda said, her large dark eyes fixed on Elaine's shortened glossy raven curls.

Since she'd known Elaine Stewart née Jackson, Brenda had never seen her wear her hair above the nape of her neck. Now, seeing the shorter hairdo was as startling as the light cover of makeup on Elaine's flawless mahogany face. The last time she saw Elaine wear makeup was before her divorce two years ago. It was the night Brenda had driven from her home in Cherry Hill, New Jersey, to Old Brookville, Long Island, to comfort her best friend, who'd tearfully informed Brenda that Dwight Stewart had decided to abruptly end their marriage.

Reaching for a goblet of sparkling water near her place setting, Elaine took a sip. "Have you two ordered?"

Brenda studied Elaine's impassive expression, silently admiring the slanting eyes that afforded her an exotic look, her short, straight nose, and her full, curvy mouth outlined in a shimmering vermilion-red shade that was the perfect complement to her velvety dark complexion. She had always thought Elaine pretty when they were growing up together, but the ensuing years had been more than kind to her friend, because now at age forty-two Elaine was stunningly beautiful.

"Oh, now, you're being evasive?" Meredith drawled sarcastically in a low, sultry voice reminiscent of the sensual sounds from a muted horn.

A slight frown marred Elaine's smooth forehead. "Will someone please tell me what's going on?"

"No, *you* tell us," Brenda countered.

"You saunter in here looking like a diva, and you don't expect a reaction from your two best friends?" Meredith added in a hushed whisper.

Several men sitting at a nearby table were still gawking at Elaine. They stared, slack-jawed and seemingly frozen in place, their gazes lingering on the soft swell of breasts rising above the décolletage of the white silk vest under the blue jacket. A single strand of perfectly matched ten-millimeter pearls shimmered with a pink hue, as if warmed by the heat of her lush bosom.

"All I did was cut my hair," she said in defense of her new look.

Meredith sucked her teeth. "You cut your hair, waxed your eyebrows, and you're wearing makeup. What's up with that?"

"It was time for a change."

"What brought on this epiphany?" Brenda asked.

A mysterious smile softened Elaine's mouth. "I want to experiment with several different styles before our twenty-fifth reunion."

Everyone in their high school graduating class had received an invitation to attend a celebration at a Long Island hotel to commemorate a quarter of a century of changes and maturity. It was now mid-May, and in another six months Elaine would be reunited with former classmates she hadn't seen in years.

Meredith smiled. "You do look fabulous."

Elaine's smile widened. "Thanks."

"Do you plan on coming with someone?" Brenda asked.

"I don't know," Elaine answered. And she didn't. She'd married her high school sweetheart, Dwight Stewart, at eighteen, and after twenty-two years of marriage he'd wanted out. His claims that he'd married too young, that he needed to spread his wings, that he had to find himself, had shattered her fairy-tale world wherein she'd believed they would live happily ever after.

She'd survived the shocking disclosure like thousands of other women, going on with her life, while not embarking on self-destructive behaviors like overeating, starving, or medicating her occasional bouts of depression with alcohol or pills. Providing emotional support for her teenage daughter had become a top priority, followed by making certain her real estate enterprise remained solvent.

What she hadn't done since her marriage ended was date. And it wasn't as if she hadn't had offers. It was just that she wasn't interested in most of the men who'd approached her. She'd accepted one invitation of dinner after her divorce was final, and she'd spent the night grappling with a man who should've auditioned for the World Wrestling Federation. He'd persisted in curving an arm around her neck, putting her in a headlock rather than holding her hand or arm. She'd ended the evening when she excused herself, walked out of the restaurant where they were scheduled to share dinner, and called a taxi, aborting the date less than half an hour after it had begun.

All conversation halted as the three women decided to share a bottle of wine along with their entrées. Elaine selected shrimp étouffée, Meredith jambalaya, and Brenda a classic gumbo.

Elaine lingered over dinner with Brenda and Meredith, catching up on what had been going on in their lives over the past three months. She told them she'd facilitated the sale of a home on the North Shore of Long Island in which the price tag approached three million dollars, while Brenda and Meredith related the escapades of some of the employees of their home–health aide business.

The trio had earned undergraduate degrees in business. Elaine had returned to college once her daughter entered school to add an MBA, while Brenda and Meredith earned Masters in public health and social

welfare respectively. The cousins had married law and
medical school graduates, and each was the mother of
a son and daughter. Both claimed solid marriages—
Brenda recently celebrated her fifteenth wedding anni-
versary and Meredith her sixteenth.

Their Saturday outing ended with the usual hugs,
kisses, and a promise to do it again in three months.
Elaine declined Brenda's offer to drive her back to
Pennsylvania Station, saying she wanted to linger in
Harlem to survey the changes in the historic neighborhood. What she didn't say was that she'd thought
about moving from the suburbs into Manhattan. Her
daughter, Zoë, had left home for college, making Virginia her permanent residence, and Elaine did not
need a four-bedroom, five-bath house set on five acres
in an exclusive Long Island community.

She'd never wanted the house, but had conceded
to Dwight because he claimed it was necessary for
entertaining their clients. And during her marriage,
she and her husband had done a lot of entertaining.
Dwight owned and operated the largest foreign-car
dealership in Westchester County, while her Long Island real estate office was consistently ranked among
the top three in home sales among independent companies. They'd hosted holiday parties, outdoor cook-
outs, and family celebrations.

Now there was only her, and Elaine had to decide
whether she wanted to continue to live in what once
had been the showplace of one of Long Island's
African-American power couples.

She strolled up and down streets along the Mount
Morris Historical District, admiring the restored
brownstones and ignoring the stares from men who
admired her voluptuous figure as she walked.

A young man sidled up to her, his pants falling

down around his narrow hips. She purposely ignored him as he flexed overdeveloped biceps under a revealing tank top. She counted off the seconds, waiting for the light to change at Malcolm X Boulevard. He whistled softly under his breath, garnering her attention. He looked no older than her eighteen-year-old daughter.

Licking his lips, he winked at her. "Oooh, M*ama*, you look like a Hershey's bar with all the nuts in the right places," he drawled lasciviously.

The light changed and Elaine stepped off the curb, biting back a smile. She knew she was an imposing figure standing five-seven in her bare feet, and three inches of heels only added to the effect. That coupled with 160 solid pounds on a size-sixteen frame was certain to turn at least a few heads. She'd expected mature men to look at her full figure, but not adolescent boys.

She was never what she'd thought of as *cute*. Brenda and Meredith were petite and claimed single-numeral dress sizes. They were cute. She'd approached adolescence wearing a ten, and when she'd married Dwight at eighteen she'd been a perfect size twelve with a thirty-six-C bra size. She had recently celebrated her forty-second birthday and she was now a sixteen and a thirty-eight-D.

Elaine had always been comfortable with her full-figured body as a young woman, and since entering middle age she was extremely confident about her appearance. Most of the women in her mother's family were tall and full-figured. For generations they'd been sternly lectured to stand tall, pull their shoulders back to show off their ample bosoms, and watch what they put in their mouths.

She worked out every other day in her in-home gym

and followed a diet a nutritionist had set up for her at the insistence of her internist after he had documented a slight elevation in her blood pressure. She'd informed the young doctor that the stress of going through a divorce was responsible for the rise. He'd ignored her explanation, recommending she modify her diet. The exercise, coupled with a daily increase of fruits, vegetables, and water, along with lean portions of broiled meat and fish helped her feel better than she had in years. The high-protein, low-fat, low-sodium diet increased her energy level so that she now worked longer hours than she had in the past.

She completed her walking tour, hailed a taxi, and headed downtown. Ninety minutes later she parked the car she'd left in the commuter lot at the railroad station in the four-car garage attached to her sprawling split-level ranch home.

Yes, she thought, turning off the engine of the elegant black BMW—a fortieth-birthday gift from Dwight. He'd given her the car two weeks before he informed her that he wanted a divorce. She'd begun to think of it as his guilt gift.

She was going to sell the house and move into the city. What she had to decide was whether she would sell her real estate business, or attempt to set up a new one in Harlem. Relocating to Harlem would be somewhat like going home. Her parents had lived there before they relocated to Roosevelt, Long Island.

Shrugging a shoulder, Elaine opened the car door and stepped out into the coolness of the garage. Pressing a button on a remote, she deactivated a sophisticated security system and a made her way through a door that led directly into the kitchen. She knew she had time to make a decision. She'd give herself until

the end of the year. It was now summer and six
months was enough time to determine whether she
wanted to continue a lifestyle she'd shared with
Dwight Stewart or begin anew.

Two

Elaine deactivated the alarm, opened the door to EJ
Realty, flicked on the lights, locked the front door,
and then made her way to her private office. It was
nine-thirty on Sunday morning; the real estate office's
weekend staff wasn't scheduled to arrive until eleven.

She preferred coming in early to check voice-mail
messages and scheduled house tours. Even though her
office was on Long Island's South Shore, and in a
predominantly African-American community, her reputation of matching families and couples from every
race and ethnic group with homes in communities that
fit their personal profiles had become legendary. EJ
Realty's computers claimed a database with the latest
demographics gathered on every town, village, city,
and hamlet in Nassau and Suffolk Counties.

She had retrieved all of the messages from the voice
mail and had put up a pot of gourmet-flavored coffee
when the soft chiming of the doorbell echoed throughout the one-story storefront situated in a strip mall
with law, insurance, tax, and medical offices.

Glancing at the clock on her desk, she noted the
time. It was a little after ten. She walked out of her
office, through an expansive room set up with four

desks, and into a spacious reception area. Staring through the glass door with *EJ Realty,* the address, phone number, and Web site URL emblazoned with gold gothic lettering, she saw a tall, bespectacled black man smiling at her.

A slight frown furrowed her smooth forehead. There was something about the man that was familiar, but what it was escaped her for the moment. She was certain she'd seen him before—*But where?* she asked herself.

He was dressed in a pair of tan slacks and a light blue cotton shirt. Despite the warm weather, he had on a navy blue linen jacket and a matching blue silk tie knotted under the collar of the button-down shirt. His shoes were imported black slip-ons. Her right eyebrow arched. The man's shoes were very, very expensive. She usually could judge a customer's worth by his or her choice in attire, make of car, and occupation. There were instances when she misjudged, but that was less than ten percent of the time.

Unlocking the door, she opened it slightly. "We're not open until eleven, sir."

His smile widened. "I'm aware of that, but I thought I'd get here early to reminiscence with you."

Her frown deepened. "'Do I know you?"

"You should, Elaine," he said cryptically.

Opening the door wider, she peered up at him, searching her memory. The man was tall, an inch or two over six feet, and slender. His skin was a clear gold-brown, reminding her of the color of a pecan. A lean face, high cheekbones, and a dimpled chin made him a very attractive man. Her gaze narrowed slightly as she met the large, dark brown, deep-set eyes behind a pair of black, oval, wire-rimmed glasses. His cropped black hair showed slight traces of gray at the temples. Not even the deep voice was familiar.

She bit down on her lower lip, shaking hear head. "I'm sorry," she apologized, "but you seem to have the advantage. I don't think I know you."

His smile faded as he stared down at her, extending his right hand. "I know it hasn't been *that* long, Elaine. Reuben Whitfield."

Ignoring his gesture, Elaine covered her mouth with her hand. "No!" she gasped through her fingers. Within seconds she found herself in the strong embrace of a man with whom she'd gone to high school.

The boy everyone had called the Scientist had changed remarkably—and for the better. He was taller and had gained weight, his face had filled out, and he looked nothing like the former bespectacled *über*-nerd who'd responded to everyone's teasing with a shy smile.

Intellectually gifted, Reuben had grown up very secure. His parents had doted upon their only child, exposing him to a lifestyle many of his peers fantasized about. Every summer his parents took a month off from their medical practices and traveled the world. By the time Reuben had entered high school he'd visited every country in Europe and several in Africa and Asia.

Elaine felt the solid wall of his chest against her breasts. A slow heat built up in her face as she eased back in his embrace. Not only did Reuben look good, but he also smelled wonderfully masculine. She inhaled the scent of lime on his smooth jaw, finding it sensual and hypnotic.

Her slanting eyes tilted upward as she took his hand, pulling him into the office. "Please come in."

Turning slightly, she closed the door with her shoulder.

Reuben Whitfield stepped into the tastefully designed modern office. Track lighting, cream-colored miniblinds, and bleached oak tables and chairs added a touch of sophistication. He'd wanted to surprise Elaine, and it was apparent he'd been successful. She hadn't remembered him, even though he would've known her anywhere in the world.

She was beautiful—but no more beautiful than she'd been in high school. He didn't know why, but he missed not seeing the loosely curling hair flowing around her shoulders and down her back. The shorter hairstyle made her look chic—very fashionable. He and Elaine Jackson had shared several classes during their four-year stint at Roosevelt High School. Not only had she been smart, but she also had been liked by everyone.

And it was apparent she'd done well for herself: marrying her high school sweetheart, graduating college, and establishing and operating a flourishing real estate business. His gaze lingered on chairs and a love seat in the reception area covered with a beige, black, and brown mudcloth pattern. A Ghanaian mask hung on one wall, and several woven baskets were positioned on a two-shelf bookcase filled with books, pamphlets, and magazines.

Elaine led Reuben into her private office, directing him to a beige leather love seat. She sat, pulling him down to sit beside her. It was good to see another face from her childhood. She, Brenda, and Meredith got together four times a year, but since moving away from Roosevelt she rarely ran into anyone she knew from school or her old neighborhood. As she stared at Reuben, a secret smile curved her lush mouth.

How could she have forgotten his dimpled chin or his sensual mouth? He might have been labeled a nerd in high school, but she had always liked his mouth. His lower lip was slightly fuller than the upper one, making him look as if he were always pouting.

"It's good seeing you again, Reuben." She'd missed him at their ten-year reunion. "I must say time has been very good to you."

Reuben's penetrating gaze took in everything about Elaine in one sweeping glance. She'd put on weight—but in all the right places. A white man-tailored shirt and a slim khaki skirt failed to conceal or minimize the full curves of what he'd always thought of as a fabulous body. Whenever Elaine Jackson had walked the halls of Roosevelt High every boy turned around to stare at her. And he had been no exception. Except that he had been more surreptitious—less blatant.

Attractive lines crinkled around his eyes. "Time has blessed you," he countered softly. "You look fantastic. I always thought Dwight Stewart was one of the luckiest brothers on the face of the earth. He married a woman whose looks matched her brains."

Elaine turned her head, moving restlessly on the love seat. She stood up, Reuben rising with her. "Please don't get up. Would you like some coffee? I just brewed a fresh pot," she said, the words rushing out. She knew she was speaking too quickly. What she did not want was to talk about her ex-husband.

Reuben arched an eyebrow, sinking down to the plush comfort of the love seat and crossing one leg over his opposite knee. Had he said something wrong? Before Elaine had jumped up as if she'd been burned, he had seen an expression of wariness cross her lovely face.

His gaze narrowed when he noticed her bare fingers. On the day the seniors at their high school had received their class rings, Dwight had presented Elaine with a diamond engagement ring. It was rumored that a collective groan had gone up all over the building once the buzz was confirmed that Elaine had accepted Dwight's marriage proposal.

Reuben hadn't been exempt from the moaning, groaning, and gnashing of teeth; it was just that he preferred to do it in private—in the cloistered confines of his bedroom.

He watched as she withdrew two delicate cups and saucers from a breakfront, placing them on a small round table with seating for two. Her movements were smooth and executed without any wasted motion as she removed a carafe filled with brewed coffee from an automatic coffeemaker in a corner of the private office. Here, as in the reception area, the African-inspired theme was repeated in pieces of art and the fabrics covering several chairs.

She glanced at him. "Cream and sugar?" Opening a small refrigerator, she removed a container of cream.

He nodded, uncrossing his legs and coming to his feet. "Please."

Closing the distance between them, Reuben again stared at her bare, professionally manicured fingers. Resting his hands on the back of a black wrought-iron chair, he studied his former classmate. He was less than a year younger than Elaine. He'd been the youngest in their graduating class at fifteen, and Elaine was next at sixteen. He'd skipped two grades and she one. And because they were younger than the other incoming freshmen, they'd formed a strong bond with each other. But at that time Elaine wasn't interested in him. She much preferred the older boys—one in particular: Dwight Stewart.

Dwight was handsome, bright, athletic, and the highest-scoring running back on their football team, the Rough Riders. Most of the teenage girls in the predominantly African-American community had had a crush on Dwight, but Elaine was luckier than the others because she'd become Mrs. Dwight Stewart.

Elaine offered Reuben a dimpled smile after she'd placed a small china dish of almond-studded biscotti on the table. "Enjoy."

Circling the table, he pulled out a chair, seating her before he sat down. There was only the distinctive sound of spoons blending cream in porcelain cups as Reuben and Elaine stared at each other over the small space separating them.

Reuben took a sip of coffee, savoring its warmth and the flavor on his palate. Nodding, he said, "Now, that's good coffee."

Elaine cradled her cup between her palms, her gaze fixed on her ex-classmate's even features. How had she forgotten his penetrating eyes?

"What's been going on in your life, Dr. Whitfield?"

His gaze widened as he lowered his cup to the saucer. It was apparent she'd known of the changes in his life since they'd graduated high school. "Who told you I was a doctor?"

She smiled. "Are you or aren't you a doctor?"

He angled his head. "I am a dentist."

"That makes you a doctor, Dr. Reuben Whitfield. It would stand to reason that you would consider a medical career, because both your parents were doc-

tors." The elder Whitfields, both pediatricians, had retired the year Reuben graduated college, and
subsequently moved back to Nashville, Tennessee.
"And," she continued, smiling, "when we got our
yearbooks everyone laughed because you'd indicated
'Undecided' as a career choice."

"I was undecided at that time," Reuben confirmed.
"I'd entered Columbia not knowing what I wanted to
study. The first two years I loaded up on science
courses because I was certain I could pull A's. Six
months before graduation I decided to become a dentist. My parents had retired and were planning to
move back to Nashville, so I went with them, enrolling
in Meharry Medical College's School of Dentistry."

"How are your folks?"

His expresion closed, as if he were guarding a secret. "My dad passed away six years ago, and my
mother last year."

His father had been forty-three and his mother
forty-one when he'd been born. They'd thought they
would be childless, but what his mother had thought
to be premature menopause resulted in an unexpected pregnancy.

Elaine digested this information, choosing her words
careful. "I'm truly sorry, Reuben. Your folks were
exceptional."

She still had her parents. They were retired, in good
health, and had moved from Long Island to a retire-
ment community hear Hilton Head, South Carolina.
Her younger brother, Melvin, lived in Charlotte,
North Carolina, with his wife and children. Zoë, who
had elected to become a Virginia resident, spent her
free time visiting her grandparents, uncle, aunt, and
cousins in the Carolinas.

Reuben managed a sad smile. "Even though I know they lived full lives, had remarkable careers, and fulfilled most of their dreams, I still miss them."

What he didn't say was that his parents would've given up everything for a child. His mother had confessed to him that he'd become as precious to her as her next breath.

His expression changed, the beginnings of a smile tipping the corners of his mouth. "How are you and Dwight doing?"

Waiting a beat, Elaine said through stiff lips, "We're not."

Leaning forward, Reuben squinted behind the lenses of his glasses, a gesture he hadn't affected in years. "What happened?"

Elaine sat up straighter, pulling her shoulders back, unaware that the motion brought Reuben's gaze to linger on the outline of her full breasts pushing against the cotton fabric of her shirt.

"We are divorced." The three words came out so glibly that she even surprised herself. "Dwight claimed we married too young and that he needed to spread his wings to find himself before he got too old. We share a daughter. Zoë is finishing up her freshman year at Norfolk State."

Propping an elbow on the table, Reuben rested his chin in his cupped hand. It was all he could do not to snort in disgust. Dwight Stewart had come down with the middle-age crazies. There were quite a few of his colleagues who'd succumbed to the same malady, and usually with disastrous results. They'd lost their wives, homes, day-to-day interaction with their children, and a social coterie that had taken years, if not decades, to cultivate.

"What a fool!" he spat out.

Amusement flickered in Elaine's eyes. She'd also called Dwight a fool along with a few other colorful adjectives. "What about you, Reuben?"

He sobered. "What about me?" he asked, answering her question with one of his own.

"Are you married? How many children do you have?" She watched, transfixed, as Dr. Reuben Whitfield's expression changed from surprise to desire, his gaze lingering on her lips.

"No and none."

Her delicate jaw dropped. "You never married?"

Removing his glasses, he pinched the bridge of his nose with a thumb and forefinger. "No. I never found a woman who held my interest long enough for me to consider spending the rest of my life with her."

Resting her elbows on the table, Elaine laced her fingers together. "I never thought you'd become a finicky bachelor."

He replaced his glasses, smiling. "I'm not finicky, just particular." He'd stressed the last word.

Elaine kept her features deceptively composed. "Why have you come to see me?"

She wondered why Reuben Whitfield had shown up after a twenty-five-year separation. Even though they'd been good friends in high school, once they graduated she'd lost touch with him. Both had attended college in Manhattan, living in dormitories, but hadn't sought the other out whenever they returned home to Long Island during semester breaks or holidays. And when she wasn't studying she spent all of her free time with Dwight, who had also attended a college in one of the five boroughs of New York City.

"I got your name from a colleague. You handled the sale of a house for him in Huntington Station earlier in the year."

She searched her memory for a client who was a dentist. "You know Paul Schneider?"

Reuben nodded. "We were at Columbia at the same time."

She shook her head. "Talk about hard to please. The man was more peculiar than his wife."

Reuben laughed aloud, the sound deep, warm, and rich. "I wonder what you're going to say about me after I close on my property?"

"You're looking to buy a house?"

"I'm moving my practice from Manhattan to Long Island next spring. I've already listed my condominium apartment with another Realtor. It's in the heart of Lincoln Center, so it shouldn't be difficult to sell."

In spite of herself, Elaine chuckled. "Talk about irony. I'm thinking about selling my house and moving into Manhattan, while you're considering the reverse."

"Where in Manhattan?"

"Harlem."

Nodding slowly, Reuben bit down on his lower lip, and she stared at his strong, masculine mouth. "I'd thought about Harlem several years ago, but decided against it because I now want a slower, quieter pace. I'd like to work three days a week instead of four," he added.

He'd planned to set up a partnership with an oral surgeon and an orthodontist in a newly constructed medical building in a predominantly African-American section of Amityville.

"Are you thinking of retiring?"

He winked at Elaine. "Not yet. I'll probably hang

up my instruments when I'm sixty and do some traveling. Right now I need a house."

"Where?"

"I don't know, Miss Jackson. That's why I'm here."

Elaine noticed he'd called her by her maiden name, and that suited her just fine. She referred to herself as Elaine Stewart only when it concerned her daughter Zoë.

"But you grew up here on Long Island. You know the communities," she argued softly.

"And you forget that I've lived in Manhattan for fifteen years. After my parents moved I rarely came out here. Besides, a lot has changed since we graduated high school."

I've changed, and you certainly have changed, Elaine thought. Their gazes met, fusing as she studied Reuben through lowered lashes. "I'm booked solid today. Leave me a number or numbers where I can reach you and I'll set up an appointment for us to get together and talk."

Reaching into the breast pocket of his jacket, he withdrew a brass case and handed her a business card. "Are you free this week?"

She took the card. "Let me check my appointment book."

She left the table and walked to her desk. Reuben stood up, moving over to stand behind her. She felt his warm, moist breath feather over the nape of her neck. He leaned closer, and the heat of his body eased into hers, bringing with it a layer of moisture that settled between the valley of her breasts. She wanted to tell him to move back—that he was too close. Instead she studied the appointment book too intently.

"I'm free Wednesday afternoon."

Reuben smiled. "Perfect. I don't have office hours on Wednesdays."

He knew he'd invaded Elaine's personal space, yet he did not move. There was something about this older, more mature Elaine Jackson that wove a spell over him from which he did not want to escape.

As she shifted to face him, her chest brushed his, rendering them both motionless. Clamping her jaw, Elaine stared while Reuben's sensual mouth curved into an unconscious smile.

"How's three-thirty?" he heard himself mumble.

"Three-thirty is okay."

Lowering his head, he kissed her cheek. "I'll see you Wednesday."

Turning on his heel, Reuben walked out of Elaine's office and into the reception area, meeting a young woman as she unlocked the front door. He smiled, nodding as he brushed past her. The door hadn't closed behind his departing figure when he began whistling a nameless tune. It wasn't until he was seated behind the wheel of his sports car that he recognized it as a song that had been popular when he was in high school. He was still smiling as he headed for the parkway and drove west for his return trip to Manhattan.

Elaine Jackson was a free woman!

And that meant he had been given a second chance. As a high school student Reuben had been too young and too easily intimidated by the older male students to make his feelings known to Elaine or any other girl who'd captured his attention. And there had been no way he could've challenged Dwight Stewart for Elaine's affection.

But time had changed him. At forty-one he was

nothing like the nerdy boy everyone had called the Scientist.

He hadn't been ready for Elaine twenty-five years ago, but he was more than ready now.

Three

Elaine was ready for Dr. Reuben Whitfield when he was shown into her office Wednesday afternoon at exactly three-thirty—or at least she thought she was until he pulled her close, brushing a light kiss over her parted lips. In that instant everything about him was magnified tenfold.

Seeing him again made her aware that he was no longer the short, skinny, bespectacled boy from high school. The tall man cradling her in a loose embrace projected an air of authority and self-confidence not even her salesman extraordinaire ex-husband had. Reuben was attractive and virile, and had acquired a polished veneer of sophistication a lot of men spent years refining. The tantalizing smell of his aftershave stayed with her even after he'd put several feet between them.

Reuben's gaze lingered on Elaine's upturned face, silently admiring the healthy glow of her clear complexion. He successfully concealed a smile when he noticed a tiny mole at the corner of her left eye positioned high on her cheekbone. The shorter hairstyle offered him an unobstructed view of her entire face.

He remembered when her height had eclipsed his

until their senior year. It was then that he'd begun to grow. He grew three inches that year, while his hormones had kicked into high gear. It was also the year he'd developed a serious crush on one girl, and that girl just happened to be his best friend, Elaine Jackson.

There had been other women in his past—during his days as an undergraduate and after he'd entered dental school—but none of them had ever affected him like his best friend from high school. And he hadn't lied to Elaine when he revealed that any woman he'd been involved with hadn't been able to keep him interested for more than six months.

There were droughts between his relationships, but he did not mind the solitude. He much preferred his own company rather than wasting his time with inane chatter or boring gatherings. He'd learned to like himself well enough to spend time alone doing what he liked to do: preparing gourmet meals and listening to jazz.

"Are you ready, Elaine?"

"Excuse me?" she said, baffled.

"We can discuss my specifications over an early dinner."

Her eyes narrowed slightly. It was a look he'd remembered whenever Elaine did not approve of something or someone.

She smiled at him, her mood shifting abruptly. "Is this a date-date or a business-date?" There was a tiny bit of laughter in her voice.

Reaching for her hand, Reuben folded it in the crook of his elbow. "Both. I'd like to reminiscence about 'back in the day,' as the kids say, and to let you know what I'm looking for in a house."

"Where do you want to go?"

Angling his head, he winked at her. "We're going to my place. I want you to see how I live so that perhaps you can find a house where I can incorporate my individual style without it looking too staid."

It was apparent Paul Schneider had told Reuben of her ritual for matching buyers with the homes of their choice. Whenever possible, she visited clients, cataloging the contents of their homes or apartments. This practice made it easier for her when she set up appointments to show a particular house. Young professional couples usually preferred newer, more contemporary designs, while older ones favored more traditional structures. She wondered about Reuben. Would his taste be modern or conventional?

He released her hand, and Elaine missed the warmth and strength in his strong fingers. "Give me a few minutes to tidy up my desk and I'll be right with you."

Waiting until he walked out of her office, she made her way into her small private bathroom, flipping on an overhead light. Peering into a mirror over the vanity, she stared at her reflection. The heavy lashes shadowing her eyes flew up. What she saw shocked her. Excitement and anticipation shimmered in her slanting eyes. It had been two years since she'd felt blissfully happy, fully alive.

"Not the Scientist," she whispered to her reflection. Not her good buddy from high school.

But she had to remind herself that Roosevelt High School's Reuben Whitfield looked nothing like Reuben Whitfield, D.D.S. The Scientist had been quiet, timid, and almost self-effacing, while Dr. Whitfield was compelling and self-assured, and over two decades had acquired an aura of virility that was in no way offset by his bookish appearance.

It had taken twenty-five years for their roles to reverse. Years before it had been Reuben who had been shy, and now it was she who was anxious and tense. What she had to ask herself was, Would she feel this way if she'd still been married to Dwight?

Pushing the question to the farthest recesses of her mind, she picked up a sable brush from a tray, dipped the bristles in an enamel compact filled with loose bronzer, blew off the excess, and then dusted the shine off her nose.

She touched up her lipstick, then brushed her curly hair off her face and over her ears, smoothing the shorter, straighter strands down the nape of her neck. After washing and drying her hands, she returned to her office, retrieving her handbag.

She informed the office manager she would be out with a client and that if she needed her then she could page her. Elaine had issued pagers and cell phones to all of the brokers at EJ Realty. Of the four brokers, two were full-time, one was part-time, and the remaining broker worked on an as-needed basis.

Walking out into the bright sunlight, she spied Reuben leaning against the door to a gleaming silver Audi TT. She did not know what she'd expected him to drive, but it wasn't the low-slung two-seater. It appeared he wasn't as staid as he appeared.

Smiling, he bent over and opened the passenger-side door for her. Waiting until she was comfortably seated, he rounded the sports car and slipped behind the wheel. He'd removed the jacket to his light gray suit, and the navy and silver tie that had graced his neck lay atop the jacket in the small space behind the two seats.

Turning on the engine, Reuben checked his mirrors, then pulled away from the curb with a smooth burst of power. Cooling air from vents swept over his moist face as he attempted to concentrate on his driving and not on the woman sitting beside him—and failed.

Seeing Elaine Jackson again after twenty-five years had been so startling and shocking that he hadn't been able to concentrate on too much since he'd stood at the door to her real estate office, staring at her looking back at him. Her soft, comforting voice, the curly hair framing her exquisite face, and the lush body that had been the envy of most high school girls had remained with him for years, and whenever he dated a woman she was physically Elaine's prototype.

Stopping at a red light, he paused, then made a right turn onto the street leading to the parkway before taking a quick glance at his passenger's profile.

"Have you kept in touch with some of the others who graduated with us?" he asked as he maneuvered smoothly into the fast-moving parkway traffic.

Elaine's dimples showed as she smiled. "Do you remember Brenda and Meredith?"

Vertical lines appeared between his eyes. "Weren't they cousins?"

"Yes. Well, we've kept in touch because we all went to NYU. Brenda's married, has a son and a daughter, and lives in Cherry Hill, New Jersey, with her cardiologist husband. Meredith is also married, lives in New Rochelle, and also has a son and daughter. Her husband is a lawyer. We get together every three months and have lunch at a restaurant in Harlem."

She, Meredith, Brenda, and their husbands used to meet in Manhattan on a Friday during the Christmas season and check into a midtown hotel. The three couples would take in a Saturday matinee, and then share dinner at one of the restaurants in the theater district. They usually would split up Saturday night, doing whatever piqued their interests, reunite Sunday morning for brunch, exchange gifts, and then depart for their respective homes, with a promise to repeat the ritual the following year. It had been more than two years since Elaine had accompanied the cousins and their husbands for what had become a Christmas tradition. Brenda and Meredith continued the custom, stating they were just waiting for Elaine to get over the anguish of losing Dwight.

What her two best friends hadn't realized was that she'd gotten over Dwight a month after he'd moved out of their home. It had taken twelve therapy sessions—three times a week for four weeks—to confirm their marriage was over a year before Dwight Stewart verbalized his intent to officially end it.

"I've run into a few of our classmates over the years. Do you remember Carl Henry? Everyone called him Bunky?"

Reuben nodded. "I remember Bunky, and I'm certain back then every cop in Nassau County knew of him. Whenever there was trouble in the neighborhood the police always showed up at the Henry house. They were always so frustrated because they could never charge him with anything."

"That's because Bunky was too slick for them."

"What's he doing now? Or should I say where is he?"

"He's an assistant principal at a middle school."

"No! I don't believe it. My mother swore Bunky was going to spend time in an upstate prison. She didn't know how he did it, but whenever Mrs. Henry brought Bunky for an annual exam my mother invariably discovered something missing from her office. One time it was a jar of tongue depressors, and another time it was half a box of latex examining gloves. He was the best when it came to sleight of hand.''

"Believe it or not, Bunky did reform himself.'' There was a comfortable silence, Elaine studying her former classmate's impassive expression. "How about you, Reuben? Whom have you kept up with?''

"To be truthful, no one. I found high school to be a very traumatic experience. There were times when I hated it so much that I thought of dropping out. That's the reason why I didn't attend the ten-year reunion.''

Elaine stared at him as if he'd lost his mind. "What are you talking about? We had a wonderful time together. You graduated valedictorian.''

"*We,* Lainie,'' he said, stressing the pronoun. "You and I shared some good times. You forget that I was two to three years younger than our peers when I entered high school. And that meant I was physically smaller and socially less mature. When the other boys were seniors they were driving while I was still pedaling a bike.

"My grades were the only thing that allowed me to fit in—made me acceptable. And I studied much harder than I needed to because I wanted to prove a point—that I was smarter than everyone. I wasn't content to earn a ninety. I had to have perfect scores.'' He'd graduated with a perfect 4.0 average.

Elaine stared at him, stunned by this disclosure. She knew Reuben had been something of a loner, but she never suspected he'd been so tormented.

"What happened in college?" Her voice was a hushed whisper.

Her question elicited a smile from Reuben. He gave her a quick glance, grinning from ear to ear. "It was great. Living on campus in Manhattan opened up a brand-new world for me. I discovered wonderful restaurants, museums, the theater, and jazz clubs in the Village."

She peered closely at him. "How about girls?"

His expression stilled, becoming sober. "I never found time for girls, Lainie. I much preferred interacting with *women*."

"Are you saying you like older women?" Elaine noticed a frown settling into his even features.

"What I like," he said after a pregnant pause, "is a woman who's not into playing head games, a woman who is open and truthful, and most of all a woman who isn't afraid to speak her mind regardless of what others might think of her."

"I take it you haven't found that woman?"

"I found her," he admitted, "but that was a long time ago."

"What happened to her, Reuben?"

He smiled again, tiny lines appearing around his dark, deep-set eyes. "I lost her to another man."

Reaching over, Elaine placed her left hand over his right resting on the gearshift. "You're still young. It's not too late for you to marry Miss Right and have children."

Reuben enjoyed the soft pressure of Elaine's hand on his. It was comforting and sensual. He curbed the urge to kiss each finger before drawing one into his mouth to make her feel what he was feeling—what he always felt whenever they were together.

When they were in school together he'd thought his feelings for Elaine were just adolescent adulation—a boy lusting after a girl who would never see him as a romantic counterpart.

He shrugged a broad shoulder under his crisply starched white shirt. "I'm little old to think about fathering a child."

It was Elaine's turn to lift her shoulders. A lot of men in their early forties were becoming fathers for the first time. "Are you too old to marry, or have you decided on perpetual bachelorhood?" she teased.

Reuben shook his head, smiling. "No and no. If I met the right woman, then I'd be more than willing to marry her before the end of the year. But first I need a house, Miss Jackson."

"I'm certain I can find something for you that will meet your specifications, Dr. Whitfield."

"That's what I want to hear," he countered, chuckling deep in his throat. He would buy his dream house, and if fate allowed it, then he would have a special woman with whom he would share it.

Four

Reuben pushed a button on the dashboard, activating the CD player and filling the confines of the car with the soft, haunting sound of a muted trumpet. Elaine relaxed against the supple leather seat, closing her eyes. All of her senses were heightened: she took in the intoxicating scent of the leather, which lent it a new-car smell, the soothing jazz flowing through the speakers, and the heat and fragrance from the body so close to hers.

Elaine wasn't certain why she'd touched Reuben's

hand, but the innocent gesture made her feel something she hadn't felt in years: desire. It was that moment that she'd had to fight her own personal battle of physical restraint.

Her marriage to Dwight had been filled with passion, and it was only the passion that had kept them together—had righted the wrongs. After most arguments or disagreements, they usually apologized to each other—in bed. And it had been more than two years since she'd slept with a man or shared the intimacy that served to fill a lingering void far beyond the physical act itself.

She knew she was a passionate woman, capable of holding nothing back. Dwight had been her first and only lover, but she was mature and liberated enough to admit he probably would not be her last.

Opening her eyes, she stole a glance at Reuben's profile through lowered lids, visually examining the long, slender, well-groomed fingers curving around the steering wheel. She admired the firm set of his chin, the fullness of the lower lip she found so alluring, and the sharp angle of cheekbones that afforded the lean face its distinctive character.

Studying the adult Reuben Whitfield reminded Elaine of his father. She remembered Dr. Daniel Whitfield as a tall, spare, white-haired man with warm dark eyes that literally sparkled behind a pair of rimless glasses. Chief of pediatrics, the elder Dr. Whitfield had been the first African-American to hold that position at one of the leading teaching hospitals on Long Island.

The Whitfields had occupied a large house on a corner property, and both Drs. Whitfield owned matching black-and-white Jaguars. Roosevelt residents had whispered about the Whitfields being the wealthiest black family in the community, and if true it did not affect who they were: generous, friendly, and fair-minded in a close-knit, family-oriented neighborhood.

Reuben had spent as much time under the Jacksons' roof as Elaine had at his house. He'd tutored her in chemistry and physics, resulting in her passing the state Regents with a score in the low nineties. Her parents were teachers, and she and her brother, Melvin, always spent their summer vacations in South Carolina with their grandparents and countless cousins. These were the times when Elaine had missed Roosevelt, Long Island, and her best friend more than her boyfriend.

And now, twenty-five years after graduating high school, seeing Reuben again she realized she'd missed him. She'd missed his intelligence, dry wit, gentleness, and honesty. With him she could always be herself, but it was different with Dwight. She would smile when she hadn't wanted to, appear gracious to Dwight's corporate clients—those whom he depended upon for the rental of fleets of luxury foreign cars for CEOs and elite customers. It had taken years for her to garner the nerve to refuse her husband's every request. And the more she challenged him the more their marital bliss dissipated.

She'd been forewarned that her marriage was in jeopardy, yet she'd refused to accept the inevitable, and the result was that she was left stunned and off balance when it ended. Intensive, short-term therapy helped her accept her new status: for the first time in her life she'd become an independent woman—and she loved it.

*　　*　　*

Reuben parked his car in an indoor garage near West Sixty-eighth Street, and after putting on his tie and jacket he escorted Elaine out to the street, holding her hand protectively as they skirted pedestrians rushing along the crowded sidewalks.

"Where do you live?"

"On Sixty-fifth and West End Avenue." Squeezing her fingers gently, he winked at her when she glanced up at him. "We'll eat first; then I'll take you to my apartment," he said, adjusting his longer stride to stroll at a leisurely pace.

Elaine peered into a store's showcase window, admiring an assortment of gems and crystals in offbeat settings. Slowing her pace even more, she lingered in front of a shop featuring vintage clothing.

Staring up at Reuben, she said, "I never realize how much I miss the city until I'm here."

He nodded. "I forgot that you lived here while you went to NYU."

"Isn't it strange that we attended college in Manhattan, yet we never ran into each other?"

Reuben wanted to tell Elaine that even if he'd contacted her she probably wouldn't have had time for him because of her involvement with her courses and with Dwight. He'd thought about her a lot whenever he returned to Long Island during school holidays, but had never taken the initiative to visit her. He'd received an invitation from her parents inviting him to attend their daughter's wedding, but had declined with the excuse that he would be summering in Europe. Elaine Jackson had married her high school sweetheart on June thirtieth—the same day she celebrated her eighteenth birthday.

He arched an eyebrow. "We grew up in the same

town, attended colleges in the same borough, yet it has taken us twenty-five years to meet again."

A soft smile of enchantment touched her lips. "You're right. Now that we've met again, let's try not to lose contact with each other."

"I agree," he said, returning her smile. *I don't intend to lose you a second time,* he added silently.

Reuben turned westward on Seventieth Street, escorting Elaine into one of his favorite French restaurants—Café Luxembourg. It was just the beginning of the dinner hour, and the small, intimate restaurant was half-filled. More people sat at the bar than at tables.

Elaine went completely still when Reuben curved an arm around her waist, then forced herself to relax. Her gaze swept around the space. "It's charming."

"That it is," he said close to her ear.

A casually dressed young man with longish brown hair came over to greet them. "Good evening, Dr. Whitfield. Two for dinner?"

"Yes, please."

Reuben's hold on Elaine's waist tightened as they followed the maître d' to a table for two in a far corner. A bud vase with a lily sat on the table along with a lighted candle. Reuben seated her before sitting down opposite her.

The maître d' placed two menus on the table in front of them. "Your server will be with you shortly. Enjoy."

Smiling, Elaine nodded. Her gaze shifted, coming to rest on Reuben's handsome face. "I assume you must eat here quite often if they know you by name."

He shrugged a broad shoulder in his expertly tailored charcoal gray lightweight silk-and-wool suit. "I try to eat here at least twice a month. They serve some of the finest French cuisine in the city." He picked up his menu, studying it despite knowing every selection. "What do you say we share a drink to celebrate our reunion?"

She stared at him through her lashes, unaware of the seductive gesture. "I'd like that very much. What are you drinking?"

He gave her a direct stare, his gaze taking in the lushness of her face and body. "How about a manhattan?"

"Excellent choice." She glanced down at the menu. "What do you recommend?"

"I always order their country salad. It's made with endive, goat cheese, and *lardons*—diced fried bacon. But the salmon and chicken are also good choices."

"What is *côelettes d'agneau grillées*?

"Grilled lamb chops with fresh thyme."

"That sounds wonderful." Her gaze lingered on another selection. "What's in the *choucroute garnie*?"

"Sauerkraut with pork, sausages, and potatoes."

Elaine shook her head. "Too heavy for this weather. I think I'll have the baked chicken."

Throwing back his head, Reuben laughed. "You had me translate the menu, and then you decide on chicken."

Placing her hands on her ample hips, she glared at him, and then stuck out her tongue in a childish gesture.

His smile faded. "Don't do that," he warned softly.

"Do what?"

"Stick your tongue out at me."

"Why not? I always used to do that to you."

He stared at her, unblinking. "That was okay when

we were kids, Elaine," he said in a soft tone. Lowering his chin, he continued to stare at her. "But now it's very, very sexual."

She emitted a nervous laugh. "Don't be so serious, Reuben. There's never been anything sexual between us."

He blinked once. "That's only because you were promised to someone else. Correct me if I'm being presumptuous, but I don't think there's a man in your life right now."

Elaine was caught off guard by Reuben's statement and the flash of desire in his penetrating eyes. She stared wordlessly at him, her heart pounding so loud she was certain he could hear it.

"What are you saying?" she whispered, recovering her voice.

Resting an elbow on the table, he cradled his chin on a fist. "I like you, Elaine. I've always liked you."

She forced an uneasy smile. "Of course you like me, because I like you. We've always liked each other," she continued.

Shaking his head slowly, Reuben lowered his arm and leaned forward. "You don't understand, Lainie. I *like* you a lot," he said, stressing the word. "In the way a man likes a woman."

More surprised than frightened, Elaine bit down hard on her lower lip as an unexpected warmth swept over her. She'd always thought of Reuben as a friend. But time had changed him into an attractive, confident man who could turn any woman's head just by entering a room. He was charming, apparently very successful, and had acquired a quiet sensuality that was deceiving when meeting him for the first time. What, she asked herself, was there not to like?

Leaning back in her chair, she regarded him closely, looking for a hint of guile. "Where are you going with this?"

He squinted at her. "Nowhere. Where *we* go will depend on you."

Elaine lifted a perfectly arched eyebrow. "Why me, Reuben?"

"Why not you? I know how I feel about you."

"And that is?"

Crossing his arms over his chest, he angled his head. "I've liked you for so long that I can't remember when I didn't. Of all of the girls in Roosevelt you were always very special to me because you treated me as an equal. You never teased me or laughed at me. If you'd asked I would've attempted to walk on water for you, because everyone else treated me like some kind of freak. Even my teachers saw me as a laboratory experiment when they'd put advanced mathematical equations on the board to try to stump me."

Closing her eyes, Elaine let out her breath slowly. "I had no idea what you went through in high school," she said softly as she opened her eyes. It was the second time he'd talked about feeling alienated.

Reaching out, he caught her fingers, holding them in a firm grip. "I'd promised myself I wouldn't talk about those days, and here I am getting maudlin."

"I'm sorry I made you break your promise."

"It's okay. Confession is usually good for the soul," he said, smiling.

"You're so right."

Reuben had revealed his feelings, while Elaine wasn't quite ready to let him know how meeting him again had affected her. The young boy from her youth was safe, predictable, but the older, more confident man sharing her space made her feel what she did not want to feel—a rising desire, a need to lower her defenses to enjoy whatever it was Reuben Whitfield was willing to offer her.

A waiter approached their table, taking their beverage order. Within minutes he returned with two chilled glasses containing cherries in a red liquid.

Reuben gave the waiter their entrée selections, and then raised his glass when the man walked away to place their orders with the chef. "A toast to our reunion."

Elaine touched her glass to his. "Here's hoping it will not take another twenty-five years for our next reunion."

"Hear, hear."

She took a sip of the cocktail, closing her eyes when the icy sensation settled in her chest before detonating in a fiery, quickly spreading heat. Placing a hand over her breasts, she blew out her breath.

"Whoa!" She gasped, her eyes filling with moisture.

Reuben flashed a wicked grin. "What's the matter, country girl? Can't hang?"

She glared at her dining partner, blinking back tears. "For your information, city boy, I can hang as well as you can."

He reached for her glass. "I don't think so. I'll have the waiter take it back and bring you a white wine."

Elaine slapped at his hand, pulling her glass out of his reach. "If you touch my glass you'll find yourself drawing back a nub."

His eyes widened behind his lenses. "I thought it was too strong for you."

"You thought wrong, Reuben Whitfield." She'd recovered from the burning sensation, savoring the warmth flowing through her body. A slow smile parted her lips, displaying the deep dimples in her flawless cheeks. She felt more relaxed than she had in a long time, and she knew it was because of her childhood friend.

Reuben smiled at Elaine over the rim of his glass, staring intently as she took tentative sips. They sat watching each other, hoping to identify what it was that had drawn them together, made them friends, and as a man and woman why the invisible bond was till evident.

The hypnotic spell was broken when the waiter placed their salads on the table. In unison, Elaine and Reuben picked up their forks and began eating.

Reuben settled the bill, escorting Elaine out of Café Luxembourg at the same time a large group of well-dressed older men and women crowded the entrance. He and Elaine had barely touched their entrées. They'd spent the better part of ninety minutes talking about what they'd been involved in since graduating high school.

Cradling her hand in the bend of his elbow, he pulled her closer to his side. "Let's go down this block," he urged softly. The sidewalks were teeming with people pouring out of subway stations, off buses, and out of stores and office buildings.

Elaine noted young schoolchildren and adolescents dressed in the latest fashions, dusky-hued nannies with crisp Caribbean accents pushing pink-checked babies in strollers, and several older, classically attired couples strolling along the sidewalk arm in arm. She'd spent four years living in Manhattan while attending college, and she had almost forgotten the constant hum of noise and excitement that made the Big Apple so vibrant and hypnotic.

Pressing her body closer to Reuben's, she smiled up at him. "I'd forgotten how electrifying Manhattan can be."

Reuben successfully hid a frown. He wanted to leave Manhattan, while Elaine was contemplating moving back. And he'd told her the truth when he confessed he wanted a slower pace. He wanted to wake up to trees and green lawns; he didn't want to be jolted from sleep by the screams of sirens and honking horns; and he had tired of jostling for space whenever he stood on the sidewalk waiting for a traffic light to change.

He'd spent more than half his life traveling and studying, and now he wanted a change in lifestyle. He hadn't dated a woman in three months, hadn't slept with one in nearly four, and had found himself at a crossroads. When the clock had struck twelve, signaling the beginning of a new year, Reuben mentally made two New Year's resolutions: to change his residence and move his practice. He hadn't consciously thought of seeking out a wife, because all of his life he'd resisted the pull of matrimony; he'd scoffed at most of his colleagues, some who were now on their second and third marriages. Those who hadn't remarried juggled girlfriends between weekend visits with their children.

Reuben craved order in his life—personal and professional. There had been a time when he wanted to marry and father several children, but that time had passed. His parents had had him in their forties; however, he hadn't wanted that for his children. There were occasions when he'd felt uncomfortable because his parents were so much older than those of his contemporaries, the times when people mistook his parents for his grandparents.

At the moment he wondered what turn his life would have taken if he had married Elaine. Would she have had more than one child? Would they still be married? She'd talked about her daughter, whose independence and strong personality were evident from birth. Zoë hadn't wanted to be held, had walked at eight months, spoke in full sentences at eighteen months, and preferred playing alone to joining other children. When Elaine had described Zoë, Reuben thought of himself. Ironically, her personality sounded more like his than Elaine's or Dwight's.

"Where is your practice?"

Elaine's query broke into his musings. "I have an office in a building a block from Rockefeller Center."

"How many patients do you treat?"

"At times, too many. There are days when it's like an assembly line. I open at seven for those who have to be at their offices by nine o'clock." His staff included a hygienist and two dental assistants.

"What time do you close?"

"I take my last patient at six. Tuesdays are my late nights. We're open until eight."

"You must work an average of twelve hours a day."

"I'm sure you do, too," he said, turning a corner at West End Avenue.

"Only at certain times of the year. I have other brokers, and an office manager who can cover for me."

Meeting her gaze, he smiled. "I plan to change the office hours after I relocate."

"Won't you lose patients?"

He shook his head. "Actually, no. Most of my patients are Long Island commuters." He wasn't concerned with losing patients or income. He'd established a very successful practice, and as his parents' only heir he'd inherited everything they'd amassed during their lifetimes.

"I live here," he said, directing Elaine toward a modern high-rise apartment building. A maroon-liveried doorman, standing under a matching canopy, touched the shiny brim of his hat.

"Good evening, Dr. Whitfield, ma'am." He flashed a friendly white-toothed smile.

Reuben returned his smile. "Good evening, Raoul."

Elaine mumbled a soft greeting, noticing the dark eyes sweeping over her body before she and Reuben crossed the carpeted entrance. She tried not to think of the number of women Reuben must have brought to his apartment. She had to come to the realization that this man was different from the boy she'd grown up with.

The furnishings in the vestibule were exquisite. Massive, hand-painted vases were filled with a profusion of fresh flowers in every variety. Textured wallpaper matched the design of the plush carpeting underfoot. She waited near a bank of elevators while Reuben retrieved his mail. The doors opened as he closed the distance between them. She entered the empty car, Reuben following and pressing a button for the nineteenth floor. The elevator ascended quickly, coming smoothly to a stop at nineteen.

As they exited, their footsteps were muffled in the plush carpeting lining the hallway. Reuben stopped in front of apartment 19H, unlocked the door, and pushed it open. Streams of waning daylight poured into an entryway that led into a huge living room with wall-to-wall windows. Even at that distance Elaine could see the shoreline of New Jersey across the Hudson River.

Reuben dropped a stack of letters, magazines, and catalogs on a table in the entryway. "Come in," he urged, taking her elbow and leading her into the living room.

The panorama unfolding before her stunned gaze rendered her motionless and speechless. Reuben had decorated his apartment in an eclectic mix of styles: Russian cubist, art deco, and Oriental. A black marble fireplace, facing the wall of glass, was the room's focal point, while priceless area rugs covered the highly polished parquet floor. The colors of copper, black, and gold predominated. It was wholly masculine and unabashedly elegant. A freestanding wall separated the living room from a dining area, where a vintage chandelier was suspended above an oval rosewood-topped mahogany table and six chairs covered in gold suede.

Turning around slowly, she took in everything with a sweeping gaze. "I can't believe it." Her voice was filled with awe.

Reuben moved closer, standing behind her. "What can't you believe?"

"It's beautiful, magnificent. Why would you want to leave this?"

"I need change in my life. There's been too much sameness for a long time."

Shifting slightly, she stared up at him looking down at her, his eyes studying her with a curious intensity. There was something lazily seductive in his gaze. A quiver surged through her veins, heating her blood and eliciting a tingling in her breasts.

No, she implored Reuben silently. She did not want him to look at her like that; inhaling deeply, she let out her breath slowly, bringing his gaze to linger on her chest. His gaze shifted upward, their eyes locking as their breathing came in unison.

He came closer without moving. "I never would've believed one could improve on perfection, but you have." His hand came up, a forefinger tracing the outline of her jaw as he lowered his head and pressed a kiss to one corner of her mouth.

Elaine felt his heat, inhaling the natural masculine scent of his body mingling with citrus aftershave. "Reuben." His name was a breathless whisper.

"Yes," he whispered back, angling his head and moving his mouth over hers. He increased the pressure until she kissed him back, her lips parting, Reuben swallowing her breath.

He kissed Elaine without touching her. His only contact with her was his mouth slowly, methodically devouring hers. Kissing her was what he'd wanted since reuniting with her.

"Reuben?"

He smiled. "Yes, Lainie?"

"We shouldn't be doing this." Her lips brushed his, tasting him.

Curving an arm around her waist, Reuben pulled her flush against his flat belly. "Why not?"

"Because we're friends."

"Haven't you known friends to kiss each other?" he crooned, placing soft, nibbling kisses at the corners of her mouth.

Placing her hands on his chest, she pushed him gently. "Not like this, *friend.*"

He chuckled deep in his throat. "Perhaps we can give a whole new meaning to *friend*."

Elaine rested her forehead on his shoulder. "Not now."

Nuzzling her ear, Reuben placed a kiss along the column of her long neck. "When?"

"After you buy your house. I never mix business with pleasure." She couldn't believe she'd just said that. It sounded so clichéd, trite.

"What if I switch brokers?"

She stepped back, easing out of his loose embrace. "Are you serious?"

Inclining his head, Reuben said, "Very serious."

Elaine was totally bewildered by his behavior. "Do you or don't you want to buy a house?"

"I do."

"And you want to date me?"

"I do."

"Because you like me?"

"Yes."

Her lids fluttered wildly. "Can we do this?"

"I believe we can."

Mixed feelings surged through her. She'd changed, Reuben had changed. Her mind reeled in confusion as she tried sorting out her emotions. Would becoming involved with Reuben be an easy transition from friends to lovers, or would it be fraught with insecurities from their past?

"I need time to adjust to this revelation."

Reuben took two steps, pulling her into a passionate embrace. "I'll allow you all the time you'll need. Just make certain it doesn't exceed twenty-five years."

Elaine couldn't help laughing. Throwing her arms around his neck, she kissed his chin. They held each other for a full minute before Reuben led her out of the living room and into a smaller room he'd set up as a den.

She quickly cataloged the contents of each room, making notes on the pad she carried in her purse, while Reuben put up a pot of coffee in the narrow utility kitchen. They sat in the living room, drinking coffee and watching the setting sun cast its fiery rays over the Hudson River.

It was close to ten o'clock when Elaine pulled into the driveway of her home, waving at Reuben through the open window. He had driven her back to her office, insisting on following her car to Old Brookville to make certain she arrived safely.

Waiting until he approached her car, she smiled up at him. "Thanks for dinner."

Leaning down, he kissed her forehead. "It was my pleasure. I'll call you."

She nodded, smiling. "Good night, Reuben."

"Good night, Lainie."

She pressed a button and the garage door slid up, and she maneuvered into the lighted space, deactivating the security system to the house. Two minutes later she walked up the staircase leading to her bedroom, a satisfied smile tilting the corners of her mouth.

It was apparent the Scientist was ready for her, but the question remained, Was she ready for him?

Five

Elaine stood in front of a full-length mirror, staring at her reflection. She wrinkled her nose. A pair of black capri slacks hugged her hips and thighs like second skin, and a yellow vee-necked sleeveless cotton pullover clung to her chest like the peel on a banana.

"It's too tight," she mumbled under her breath.

The outfit she'd chosen to wear for her Sunday outing with Reuben was definitely too revealing. Knowing he was physically attracted to her, she did not want to exacerbate the situation by appearing too seductive. She hadn't completely recovered from this grown-up version of Reuben Whitfield. The former image of a short, thin, shy, gifted, eyeglass-wearing adolescent boy still lingered along the fringes of her memory.

Her hands went to the waistband of her slacks and she undid the button. The melodic chiming of the downstairs bell interrupted her musings and she quickly buttoned the pants. Reuben had arrived, and it was too late to change. Slipping her bare feet into a pair of low-heeled woven black leather mules, she made her way out of her bedroom and down the staircase to answer the door.

Peering through the security eye, she saw the distorted image of Reuben staring at the door. She opened it, coming face-to-face with the man whose presence had haunted her dreams for the past two nights.

She'd tossed restlessly whenever she recalled his kissing her, awakening several times to the scent of a lime-based aftershave wafting in her nostrils. After a while she left her bed to recline on the chaise in her sitting room, where she finally fell asleep without the disturbing erotic dreams jolting her into wakefulness.

A bright smile lit up her face when Reuben's firm mouth curved into a slow smile. "Good morning." Her voice was low, unwittingly provocative.

"Good morning." He winked at her. "You look marvelous in that outfit."

He would think so. She groaned inwardly, opening the door wider to permit him access to her home for the first time. Her outfit was so tight she felt exposed. When she saw a flicker of lust in his dark eyes, she again berated herself for choosing the slacks and top. She could've worn a dress, thereby leaving something to his imagination.

Elaine forced a smile. "Thank you. Please come in."

Reuben stepped into a yawning foyer, awed by the white marble floor with black accents. A massive black-lacquered credenza with engraved gold Asian-inspired hardware was the space's focal point. Extending the hand he'd concealed behind his back, he offered her a large bouquet of delicate white calla lilies.

A soft gasp escaped Elaine. "How did you know?"

Tilting his head, he regarded her for several seconds. "I remember your telling me a long time ago that lilies were your favorite flowers."

A glossy vermilion-red lipstick shimmered on her full lips. "I can't believe you remembered that."

Moving closer, Reuben curved his free arm around her waist, bringing her into contact with his wide chest. His custom-made shirts and tailored suits had masked a solidly muscled physique. His casual attire of a black cotton golf shirt, double-pleated tan linen gabardine slacks, and black loafers failed to conceal a pair of broad shoulders, a slim waist and hips, and muscled arms and strong wrists. The forty-one-year-old dentist appeared to be as physically fit as any man half his age.

During their return drive to Long Island the other night, he'd revealed a lot about himself. He wanted a house with enough space to set up an in-home gym because he disliked having to wait for exercise machines at the overcrowded sports club where he had his membership. He also wanted a large kitchen where he could cook his favorite dishes. He'd confessed to taking the month of July off every year wherein he traveled to different countries to participate in gourmet cooking classes. Reluctantly, he admitted the *New York Times* had profiled him in their Home section, referring to him as "The Big Apple's Gourmet Dentist." One of his friends had given his name to an editor at the newspaper.

Elaine took the flowers, rising on tiptoe to kiss Reuben's smooth cheek. "Thank you. They're beautiful. Please make yourself comfortable while I put these in water."

He followed her through the foyer and into a living room that could easily hold two of his. Bleached pine floors, walls covered with a pale wheat-colored fabric, chairs, a sofa, and two facing love seats in varying shades of beige, tan, and peach were dwarfed by towering ceilings and floor-to-ceiling windows. The modern seating pieces, set on a priceless Persian rug, provided a unique contrast to antique tables, lamps, and vases.

Reuben had contacted Elaine at her office, setting

up a day and time when he could take a driving tour of several Long Island communities. And because he did not have children, school districts had not become a determining factor in where he would reside. She had suggested two along the North Shore, and one on the South Shore before she set up an appointment for him to meet her at her home Sunday morning for brunch.

Reuben groaned under his breath as his gaze lingered on the rounded curves of Elaine's swaying hips as she walked across the room. A film of moisture beaded his upper lip at the same time his body reacted violently to the image of her lush body. Everything about her tantalized: high, full breasts, firm thighs, curvy calves, and hips. Sweet heaven, he did not want to think of her hips. Moving over to a chair on shaky knees, he sat praying the evidence of his arousal would ease before she returned.

Removing his glasses, he buried his face in his hands, taking deep breaths. The throbbing in his groin continued unabated. *Down, boy. Easy, easy,* he continued in his silent monologue to his swollen flesh.

"Reuben. Is something wrong?"

He dropped his hands, opened his eyes, and attempted to jump to his feet when he heard Elaine's voice, but the fire raging in his loins refused to go out. She stood less than a foot away from him, and he hadn't heard her approach. He crossed his legs, forcing a plastic smile.

"Oh, no," he said too quickly. "I was just meditating." It was only a half lie, because he had willed his body to follow the dictates of his mind.

Lifting an eyebrow, she gave him a puzzled look. "I'm going to start the coffee."

The tense lines in Reuben's face eased. "I won't be long." He hoped he was telling the truth, while praying Elaine hadn't noticed his erection. Why had he waited to become a middle-aged man to react to a woman like an adolescent boy with little or no control over his sexually awakening body?

He knew the answer to his question at the same time it formed in his mind—Elaine Jackson. He'd watched her mature. It began with her height, then her body blossoming and filling out with womanly curves. He was aware when her voice had changed to a deeper register the sound of it sweeping over him like velvet. As her face and body changed, so did she. Her interest in boys—boys older than he was—had become the most startling revelation for Reuben. Even though he and Lainie were only a year apart, she had preferred boys two or three years older than herself.

Slowly the hardness in his flesh eased, permitting him to stand without embarrassing himself. He walked over to a massive stone fireplace and stared at the photographs lining the mantel. His gaze lingered on a photograph of Elaine dressed in a delicate white dress, reclining on a chaise with a small child on her chest, both of them facing the camera. A curtain of curly hair flowed over the side of the floral cushion. The expression on Elaine's bare face was one of supreme satisfaction. The child cuddled to her breasts had inherited her mother's curly hair and slanting eyes. Zoë Stewart was as stunning as her beautiful mother. They were mother and daughter—Madonna and child.

He studied several other photographs of Elaine and Zoë, noting the changes in each of them. There was only one picture with Dwight. It was taken the day

Zoë had graduated high school. Clad in a cap and gown, she stood between her parents, smiling broadly. Reuben leaned closer, staring at Dwight. He hadn't changed much except to put on weight. Unconsciously the man had been his nemesis, winning the heart of the woman he'd always wanted.

Reuben froze. The realization hit him hard, swiftly. He was in love with Elaine Jackson! He'd unknowingly fallen in love with her a long time ago, and after reuniting with her he knew he still loved her.

Pushing his hands into the pockets of his slacks, he whistled softly. His step was light, his body relaxed. He could envision another photograph on the mantel of a fireplace—one of him and Elaine on their wedding day.

He walked past a space set up as a family room. A large flat-screen television was mounted on one wall, while the latest state-of-the-art stereo system graced another. Light colors and French doors letting in an abundance of sunlight beckoned one to come and stay awhile.

He found Elaine in a kitchen of enormous proportions. This was his kind of kitchen! It was the perfect design of practicality and functionality. A cooking island abutted a long table with a butcher-block surface. The island also included double sinks. The burners and grill were in addition to a built-in cooking range with two oversize ovens, a microwave, a grill, and six flameless burners. The stainless steel was repeated in a large refrigerator/freezer, dishwasher, and compactor. Bleached-wood cabinets matched the butcher-block preparation table.

Elaine wanted to sell her house and he was looking for a house. Reuben would've offered for the property on the spot if she hadn't shared it with Dwight, because when he took her to bed he did not want the memory of another man who'd slept under the same roof to come between them.

He was more than aware of his personality characteristics—and one thing he was was selfish. As an only child he had never had to compete or share, and at forty-one he wasn't willing to change.

"How many rooms do you have?"

Elaine's head came up as she stared at Reuben standing under the arched entrance to the kitchen. "Four bedrooms and five bathrooms. The house has six thousand square feet, set on a little over five acres."

"Will you be able to sell it quickly?"

She smiled as she turned her attention back to cutting up strawberries for a fruit salad. "I'm certain I can. I know someone about half a mile up the road who has been asking about it."

"Do you think you'll get your asking price?"

"Probably."

"What do properties in this area go for?"

"High six figures to low seven." And if she did sell the house she would not have to split the proceeds with Dwight. She'd gotten the house and a generous sum of cash, stocks, and bonds in her divorce settlement. She would put her house up for sale, but first she had to research properties in Harlem. A restored town house or brownstone would be perfect. She would live on one floor, use the street-level space for her real estate office, and possibly rent out the remaining floors.

"What can I help you with?" Reuben asked, walking into the kitchen.

"Please take this bowl out to the patio. Since the

weather is so beautiful, I decided we would take our meal there."

Reuben sat in the enclosed patio with Elaine, admiring the profusion of color in her walled garden. Brunch had been fresh seasonal fruit, scones with imported jellies and jams, fresh-squeezed orange juice, and a carafe of brewed Irish cream–flavored coffee.

He'd eaten three scones while Elaine had eaten only one. "I don't want to move from this spot." He groaned, patting his flat belly.

Elaine set down her coffee cup. "We can cancel our outing. It's not as if you were scheduled to take a house tour."

"We cancel and do what?" There was an open invitation in the burning depths of his dark eyes behind the lenses of the oval glasses.

She waved a hand. "You can hang out here and read the paper or take a walk. Even though I hadn't planned to go into the office, I still have work to do around the house. I need to put up a few loads of laundry and weed my garden."

"Are you sure you don't mind company?"

"Of course not." There was a hint of laughter in her voice. "Ever since Zoë left for Virginia I find myself talking aloud just to hear the sound of a voice."

"Are you lonely, Lainie?"

Sighing audibly, she closed her eyes for a few seconds. "Not really. I have my business and my friends. And my family isn't that far away."

"Do you miss Dwight?"

"Hell, no," she blurted out.

Lowering his head, Reuben successfully hid a smile. He'd thought she was pining for her ex-husband. "I saw the photographs of you and your daughter. She's quite beautiful."

Elaine flashed a dimpled smile. "Thank you. She's a lot of fun, despite being Miss Independence."

"Had you decided to have only one child?"

She glanced away, staring at a rosebush climbing along a flagstone wall separating her property line from her neighbors'. "Zoë had just celebrated her third birthday when I found myself pregnant again. I knew there was something wrong from the very beginning because of the pain. It continued for the first three months before I began bleeding. My doctor recommended complete bed rest. At the end of my fifth month I began hemorrhaging. I fainted while trying to get to the bathroom; when I woke up in the hospital Dwight told me that the baby was gone and we would never have another."

Reuben's expression was like that of someone who had been punched in the face. She had lost a baby, a part of herself, while he selfishly had avoided having children because of his own childhood insecurities.

Pushing back his chair, he stood up and rounded the table. He touched her elbow, pulling her up gently. Cradling her face between his palms, he lowered his head and brushed his mouth over her parted lips. The kiss was meant to denote an apology, a gesture of healing, but somehow that message was not communicated.

His fingers curved around her neck, stroking the soft hair on her nape as Reuben deepened the kiss. He moaned softly when she pressed closer, the fullness of her breasts burning his chest.

Elaine felt the heat from Reuben's mouth ignite a passion she had forgotten. Raising her arms, she pulled his head down. It was her turn to moan as his tongue slipped between her lips, testing, tasting, and teasing.

Her hands were as busy as his. Her fingertips grazed the close-cropped hair, traced the outline of his clean-shaven jaw, massaged the muscles in his strong neck before splaying over his pectorals. His body was hard, unyielding.

Tightening his hold on her waist, Reuben tried absorbing Elaine into himself. He wanted her naked, his hardness inside her, her flesh fusing with his. A familiar heaviness settled in his groin, but this time he made no attempt to conceal it by pulling out of her scented embrace.

He wanted her to know that he wanted her—had wanted her for years. He had wanted her even after she'd committed to marrying another man, and unknowingly he had wanted her when he found himself drawn to women who'd reminded him of her.

Some of his friends had teased him about dating full-figured women, but he'd always ignored their disparaging remarks about more than a handful or a mouthful. The only person who'd known what lay in his heart had been his mother, who'd asked him to delay his trip to Europe with several older cousins to attend Elaine's wedding. He'd tearfully confessed that he thought he was in love with Elaine, and because she was lost to him he would never marry. He never spoke Elaine's name in his mother's presence again, but suspected she was disappointed in him because he'd refused to let go of an adolescent fantasy. His parents died without seeing him married or his giving them grandchildren.

"I want you, Lainie," he whispered close to her ear. "I've wanted you for so long that I can't remember when I didn't want you."

Elaine couldn't think straight—not when his hands were searching under her top. Not with his hands on her breasts. "Reuben?"

"Yes, darling?"

"Can we do this?"

He smiled. She sounded so young, so unsure. "Of course we can. We can do and be anything we want. And I want to be your lover and anything else you want me to be."

Easing back, she stared at him, their gazes fusing and locking. His steady gaze bore into her in silent expectation, and Elaine knew he was waiting—waiting for her to tell him they could take their friendship to another level.

Reuben radiated a virility that appealed to her femininity. Something in his manner called out to her, telling her that what she'd share with him would be new, different from what she'd shared with Dwight.

There was something about the adult Reuben Whitfield that she was powerless to resist. He was her friend, had been her confidant, and if she consented he would become her lover.

Was she ready?

Was she ready to take off her clothes and lie with someone from her past? Someone who'd always been special to her?

As she closed her eyes, a sweep of lashes brushed her cheekbones. Reuben stared at the rapidly beating pulse in her throat. He did not want to rush her, but he wasn't certain how long he could wait.

"Yes, friend."

He lowered his head, bringing his mouth mere inches from hers. "Yes, what, Lainie?"

Her eyes opened slowly, desire shimmering in their

depths. "Yes, you can become my lover, but only if you let me become yours."

Bending slightly, he picked her up as if she were a small child, cradling her to his chest. Adjusting her weight, he headed for the staircase leading to the upper level of the house. His stride was determined, his footsteps muffled in the deep pile of carpeting on the stairs. Stopping at the top, he glanced down a wide hallway. He didn't want to sleep in the bed Elaine and Dwight had shared during their marriage.

Sensing his hesitation, Elaine said, "The first bedroom on the left." It was one of two bedrooms she'd set up for houseguests.

Reuben didn't notice the carefully chosen furnishings in the sunny yellow and periwinkle-blue room as he lowered the woman in his arms to the firmness of a brass bed. His gaze never strayed from her face as he reached into the pocket of his slacks, taking out a condom. There was no risk of his getting Elaine pregnant, but he wanted her to feel comfortable sleeping with him if he protected her the first time. He'd never slept with a woman without using a condom.

He removed his glasses. Reaching up, he pulled his shirt over his head, revealing a broad, smooth chest and a flat belly. He kicked off his loafers, unbuckled his belt, and then pushed his slacks and boxers down his hips and legs.

Elaine was certain Reuben heard her gasp of awe when she saw his hardened flesh jutting between his thighs. Never in her wildest dreams would she have thought the skinny boy would grow up to be so masculine, so very virile. She watched as he opened the packet and rolled the latex sheath down the length of his sex.

Her body ached for his touch, his complete possession. Holding out her arms, she smiled. "Come."

The single word galvanized Reuben into action. Sitting down on the side of the bed, he slowly and methodically undressed Elaine, lingering to admire her body with each article of clothing he removed. He started with her shoes, then her blouse, easing it over her head. Reaching around her back, he unsnapped her bra, freeing her breasts.

His heart thundered in his chest. Her breasts were large, but firm, with dark brown areolas and prominent nipples. Lowering his head, he suckled her. Her soft moans fired his blood as he suckled one breast before giving equal attention to the other.

Moving slowly down her body, he placed tender kisses over her belly as he unbuttoned her pants and slid them down her legs. The only barrier that remained was a pair of black lace panties. He placed his hand over the mound between her thighs, feeling her feminine heat.

Shamelessly Elaine writhed under his hand, her hips moving in an untutored rhythm that had passed through the ages from Eve. She did not think about the fact that it was only the second time she'd seen Reuben since they were reunited a week ago. What mattered was that they had a history, a childhood filled with memories that would never fade.

Reuben removed her panties and then moved over her, kissing her gently on the lips. She stiffened as his straining flesh brushed her inner thigh. He kissed her mouth, her throat. Continuing his downward journey, he touched his lips to her breasts, circling the areolae with his tongue. Her breath was coming faster, harder, as he moved to her belly and still lower to the tangled curls between her legs.

Gasping, she attempted to extract herself as he held her hips firmly and staked his claim on the throbbing flesh at the entrance to her femininity. This was a type of lovemaking she had never experienced before. Dwight had balked at putting his face there.

His mouth burned her, leaving her struggling and laboring for her next breath. She wanted to move, writhe, twist, but was prevented when he held her hips fast. The throbbing grew stronger, threatening to explode. Elaine wanted to share her climax with Reuben, wanted him inside her at that moment. The blood roared in her head and the shudders shaking her legs traveled upward. Just when she thought it was going to be over, he moved over her, easing his hardness into her body, swallowing her cry of shock.

Elaine wanted to tell him to stop, that she hadn't slept with a man in two years, that he was so much larger than her ex-husband, but bit back her protests once her newly awakened flesh cradled the length and width of his engorged sex.

Reuben let his hands roam intimately over Elaine's breasts, loving the silken flesh. She was a lush ripe fruit, bursting with sweet juices. He loved touching her flesh, smelling her fragrant body, and above all tasting her hot, wet femininity.

He loved her wholly—in and out of bed. They were friends, had become lovers, and their bodies found an exquisite rhythm that promised forever.

Elaine's eager response matched Reuben's, her hips meeting his powerful thrusts. Moaning in erotic pleasure, she rubbed her distended nipples against his chest, striving to get closer. The heat from his body coursed down the entire length of hers, incinerating her mind and her body.

Her whole being was electrified with a passion she had never known or experienced. The little tremors started up again, growing stronger with each thrust of Reuben's powerful hips.

"Reuben!" She couldn't keep the dismay out of her voice. She was frightened, frightened that she would lose herself in the passion rising and spreading through her like wildfire.

The fireball exploded, and she abandoned herself to the whirl of ecstasy; her body stiffened, bucked uncontrollably, then stilled as her chest rose and fell heavily.

Reuben felt her pulsing flesh squeezing his hardness as he pressed his face to Elaine's neck, surrendering to the passion that taken him beyond himself. Struggling for his next breath, he lay heavily on her body. The awesome climax had left him weak as a newborn baby.

Tightening his hold on her body, he pressed his mouth to her ear and whispered, "I love you, Lainie."

Six

Elaine lay in the protective warmth of Reuben's arms, staring up at the ceiling. His admission of love had chilled her to the bone despite the heat coming from his body.

"I think we're moving too quickly."

Shifting slightly, he frowned at her. "Why would you say that?"

"I met you exactly one week ago, and we're in bed together. I'm adult enough to accept that, but I think it's too soon for declarations of love."

Reuben released Elaine, rising on an elbow to glare at her. Without his glasses she was able to see the intensity in his deep-set eyes—eyes that flashed anger.

"We've had more than twenty-five years to get used to each other."

Sitting up, she reached for a sheet to cover her naked breasts. "Not we, Reuben. It's *you*. You forget that I was in love with another boy and that I married him."

Raw hurt glittered in his gaze. "If that's the case, then why did you let me make love to you?" She raised her hand to touch his cheek, but he captured her wrist, stopping the gesture. "Answer my question, Lainie."

Her temper flared. "How dare you—"

"I dare," he spat out, interrupting her. "I dare," he repeated, his voice softer, calmer, "because now I realize I've been in love with you all my life. Every woman I've ever been involved with looked like you."

Her anger evaporated, leaving her confused. "Me?"

"Well, not exactly like you. They were built like you. You know what I mean."

A frown furrowed her forehead. "No, I don't know what you mean, Reuben."

He swallowed, searching his brain for the right words. What he didn't want to do was insult Elaine. "I happen to like women with breasts and hips," he explained sheepishly. "Full breasts and full hips."

"If you tell me you're attracted to me because of my breasts and hips, then I'm going to make you sorry you ever drew breath, Reuben Whitfield."

"No," he said, laughing.

"Oh, now it's funny?"

"Wait, Elaine. It's not what you think."

Her gaze narrowed. "You'd better explain yourself."

Easing his hold on her wrist, Reuben sat up, pulling Elaine up effortlessly to sit between his outstretched legs. Cradling his arms under her breasts, he told her how he'd fallen in love with her in high school, disclosing his intense dislike for Dwight Stewart.

"He didn't deserve you. He only dated you because he regarded you as a trophy."

"How do you know that?" A lump had settled in her chest, making it difficult for her to breathe as she recalled the number of times Dwight told her to make certain she looked good for his clients. Was that what she'd been to him for twenty-plus years—a trophy wife?

"Dwight was one way when he wasn't with you, and an entirely different person with you. He seemed to stand a little taller, swagger more whenever the two of you were together. It was so obvious that I was surprised you didn't notice it."

"It was obvious, Reuben; it's just that I chose not to acknowledge it. Whenever Dwight and I went out or entertained at home he always insisted I buy a new outfit. I have so many clothes I can open my own boutique."

Closing her eyes, she sighed audibly. "One man marries me to enhance his image, and you tell me you love me because of my breasts and hips."

"Don't put words in my mouth, Lainie. I said I was attracted to women with your body type because it made it easier to fantasize that it was you I was with."

"That's not fair to those women."

"It wouldn't have been fair if I'd deceived them."

"Why does it sound so adult, Reuben?"

He chuckled softly, pressing a kiss to her hair. "Because it is."

Twisting in his embrace, she lay on his chest, placing light kisses around his flat nipples. She rested her head on his shoulder, feeling the steady, strong beat of his heart under her cheek. "Can we go a little slower?"

Reuben combed his fingers through her short, curly hair, smiling. "Of course, sweetheart. I told you we have at least twenty-five years to get it right."

Elaine opened the door leading from the garage to the kitchen. She dropped her handbag on a countertop, kicked off her shoes, and was heading for the bathroom off the pantry when the telephone rang.

Picking up a wall phone, she answered the call. "Hello?"

"Hi, Mom."

Sitting down on a tall stool, Elaine settled down to talk to her daughter. "How's it going?"

"Okay."

"Just okay, Zoë?"

"Only half okay."

Elaine felt the hair on the back of her neck stand up. "What's going on, Zoë?"

"It's Daddy.'

"What about him?"

"I saw him this weekend. He drove down with a woman—a woman he introduced as his fiancée."

"What's wrong with that?"

"She's twenty-three! That's half his age, Mom. She says she's a *model*."

"So?"

"So? How can you say 'so'?"

"Because I can," Elaine retorted. "Your father and

I are divorced, which means he can see or marry anyone he chooses. And the same goes for me."

There was a moment of silence before Zoë's voice
came through the earpiece again. "Are you seeing
someone?"

Elaine's smile was as dazzling as a brilliant sunrise.
It was the first week in July, and she Reuben had
planned to go away for a week with the onset of the
July Fourth holiday weekend. They'd continued to see
each other on an average of one day a week, but
hadn't shared a bed since their initial encounter. Not
sleeping with him had permitted her to have objectiv-
ity with regard to their relationship.

They'd recaptured the easy camaraderie from their
youth. When Reuben wasn't house hunting, they went
to the movies, attended a New York Knicks NBA
championship game and a raucous Yankees–Mets in-
terleague baseball game, and whenever their favorite
restaurants overflowed with out-of-town tourists, he
prepared exquisite gourmet meals in his apartment or
at her home. He ended each encounter with a passionate kiss and a declaration of love.

She had yet to tell him that she loved him, knowing
it was only a matter of time before she confessed what
lay in her heart. Gentle and incredibly patient, Reuben had eased her fears and had gotten her to fall in
love with him.

"Yes, I am, sweetheart." A loud squeal came
through the earpiece, and Elaine jerked the receiver
away from her ear.

"That's fabulous. Who is he?"

"Someone I grew up with." She and her daughter
had always had an open dialogue with each other.

"Does Daddy know him?"

"Yes, he does."

"What does he do?"

"He's a dentist. Not that it matters all that much."

"Hooking up with a doctor is a whole lot better than an anorexic chickenhead. She's just marrying Daddy for his money. I'm willing to bet she'll squeeze out one knucklehead baby, then bleed him dry."

"It's not for you to question your father's lifestyle."

"I just don't want him crying and souping snot after she pimps him, that's all. By the way, for my birthday he offered me the car he drove down here." Zoë would celebrate her nineteenth birthday in October.

"I hope you took it," Elaine said.

"My mama didn't raise no fool. Of course I took it. How many eighteen-year-olds do you know who own a Porsche?"

"That's my girl."

"I'm driving down to visit Grandma and Grandpa this weekend. Grandma told me that Uncle Melvin arrived last night with his family."

"Promise me you'll drive carefully."

"I promise. Are you still coming down in August for the family reunion?"

"I wouldn't miss it."

"How's business?"

"Slow, but it'll pick up in the fall."

"I gotta go, Mom. My break just ended."

"Love you, Zoë."

"Love you back, Mom."

Elaine hung up, smiling. Her daughter had elected not to live on campus. She'd rented an apartment in a three-family house owned by an elderly Norfolk couple. Even though Dwight deposited money in an account in her name at a Virginia bank each month, Zoë worked part-time at Victoria's Secret in a large mall. Every month Zoë mailed her a gift from the store. Elaine's lingerie drawers were filled with frilly bras and panties, all of them with the tags still attached.

She hadn't had much use for the sexy garments—until now. Reuben had made a reservation to spend a week at a seaside cottage on Cape Cod. It would be the first July in eight years that he wouldn't spend the month abroad at a cooking institute. She had rearranged her own work schedule to spend more time with him.

Reuben was scheduled pick her up at five the next morning. She had to pack enough clothes for a week's stay. A sensual smile softened her delicate features; she would make certain some of the minuscule garments her daughter had sent her would join her more conservative undergarments.

Reuben arrived at four-ten instead of five, casually dressed in a pair of walking shorts, running shoes, and a T-shirt. Elaine rushed to the door to answer his ring, a towel wrapped around her body.

Opening the door, she glared at him. "You're early. I just got out of the shower."

He closed the door, grinning from ear to ear. "That was my intent."

Backpedaling, Elaine held up a hand. "No, Reuben!"

Ignoring her plea, he stalked her until her back was pressed against a wall. Anchoring his hands over her head, he leaned forward, making her his prisoner. The diamond bracelet on her right wrist, a gift from Reuben for her birthday, gave off blue and white sparks of fire.

Removing his glasses, he placed them on a table.

"You've teased me for weeks, and I don't think I can take it any longer. I'm not a monk, Elaine, so why do you make me do penance? I may as well become a eunuch."

She wanted to tell him that she planned to end the drought this weekend, but was never given the opportunity when he took her mouth in a burning kiss that left her knees weak and trembling. Elaine raised her arms, and the towel fell to the floor at their feet.

Bending slightly, he swept her up in his arms, his eyes glittering dangerously. "Tell me where, or I swear I'll take you right here."

"Upstairs," she whispered. Reuben took the stairs two at a time, cradling her 160 pounds to his chest as if she weighed half that amount. She felt his tension as surely as if it were her own.

He carried her into the bedroom where they'd made love for the first time, placing her gently on the bed. She watched as he practically ripped off his clothes, and when he came to her and parted her knees she was more than ready for him. His urgency had her wet before he slipped on a condom and entered her.

They came together like two freight trains in a head-on collision, straining and attempting to absorb one into the other. A loud sigh of satisfaction escaped her parted lips as Reuben began to move in her. She had missed him, missed their being one.

A lingering frustration and a runaway passion merged, making it impossible for Reuben to engage in a prolonged session of lovemaking. Withdrawing, he let his mouth worship her body. He'd asked himself over and over why he'd agreed not to sleep with Elaine and could conclude only that he loved her enough to adhere to her wishes and needs.

What about his needs? He wanted and needed her; needed her the way a man needed a woman and wanted her for his wife.

Yes, wife.

He wanted to marry Elaine Jackson and spend the rest of his life with her.

Elaine felt the heat at the base of her spine spread until she was mindless with the shivers of delight shaking her body like a leaf in the wind. She gasped, moaned, groaned, and then screamed aloud when Reuben reentered her with a single swift thrust of his hips. Her fingers curled into tight fists on his damp back. His hardness electrified her, and she couldn't disguise her body's reaction as she soared and then shattered into a thousand pieces, floating back down to earth in a climax that left her weeping and clinging to her lover's neck.

Reuben's soaring ecstasy overlapped Elaine's as he caught her chin, holding her gently, and breathed out the last of his passion into her mouth. The runaway pumping of his heart continued long after the throbbing in his groin subsided. It was only when the vestiges of a lingering passion were swept away that he realized the enormity of what he'd done. He had broken his promise to Elaine not to make love to her unless she consented.

"I'm sorry, Lainie."

Holding his head to her breasts, Elaine kissed his graying hair. "For what?" Her voice was heavy with sated passion.

"For making love to you."

She laughed softly. "I'm not."

His head came up and he stared at her as if she'd taken leave of her senses. "You're not?"

"No, my darling. Did you really think I'd spend a week with you and not share a bed with you?"

Reuben closed his eyes, mumbling a silent prayer of thanks as he kissed her gently on the lips. His mouth moved to the side of her neck and lower to her heaving chest.

"You are so beautiful—so perfect." They lay together, savoring each other's warmth, the scent of their bodies mingling with their lovemaking.

Elaine stirred in his embrace. "I have to get up. I need another shower."

"Would you like company?"

She nipped the area between his shoulder and neck with her teeth. "I'd thought you'd never ask."

Reuben moved off the bed, extending his hand. She placed her hand in his, and together they made their way to the bathroom, sharing a secret smile reserved for lovers.

Seven

Reuben sat on the beach, watching Elaine as she frolicked in the waves coming off Nantucket Sound. It was their third day in Craigville, and the first day the sun had put in an appearance. He had made the trip from Long Island to Massachusetts in record time. They'd stopped at a supermarket to stock up on basic staples before settling into the charming one-bedroom beachfront cabin.

He'd opened all of the windows to let in the salt-filled air while Elaine had busied herself making up the bed with the linens they had brought with them. Their first night on the island they'd eaten in a restaurant not far from the ancient Native American village of Mashpee. Elaine ate authentic New England clam chowder for the first time, and was pleasantly surprised to find it filled with large pieces of clam. They enjoyed a leisurely seafood dinner with side dishes of sweet corn on the cob and cole slaw. They returned to the cabin, too full to do anything except shower and fall into bed. Both were asleep as soon as their heads touched the pillows.

Pulling his knees to his chest, he contemplated broaching the subject of marriage to Elaine. He had been tempted, but decided against it because she still hadn't told him that she loved him. And no matter how much he loved her, he would not marry a woman who did not return his affection.

He'd gone through the motions of looking for a house, but he knew his heart wasn't in the exercise. Elaine had shown him beautiful homes in picture-perfect upscale communities, but he had yet to commit to purchasing one. When he selected a home he wanted one that would suit Elaine's taste and needs. She hadn't spoken of moving to Harlem again, so he thought perhaps she'd changed her mind.

His gaze narrowed behind the lenses of his sunglasses as she walked out of the water, coming toward him. Her full figure was clearly outlined in a black maillot. And it was not for the first time that he marveled at the firmness of her body. He stared at the curve of her calves as she lay down on the towel beside him. Droplets of salt water clung to her short curls.

Leaning over, he kissed her mouth, tasting salt and brine on her lips. "Has the water warmed up?"

Slipping on a pair of sunglasses, she smiled up at him. "It's still a little chilly, but it's invigorating."

"I'm going back in for a final swim of the day." The sun had passed overhead and the air was growing cooler.

Elaine nodded, then turned over on her belly and rested her head on folded arms. The summer sun felt good on her exposed body. She couldn't remember the last time she'd been this relaxed. She'd called Zoë, informing her that she was spending the week on Cape Cod, and if she needed to reach her she should call her on her cell phone.

She hadn't bothered to call her office. If there was an emergency she was certain the office manager and the supervising broker would handle it.

Reuben returned to lie beside her, reaching for one of her hands. "Did you put sunblock on your back?"

"Yeah," she mumbled, not opening her eyes. "I don't want to get up."

"You can't sleep out here in the sun."

Turning her head, she smiled at him. "Can we sleep out here tonight?"

Reuben lifted his eyebrows. "It gets cold at night."

Her smile widened, dimples winking at him. "You can keep me warm."

"Have you ever made love on the beach?"

"No." She managed to look insulted.

He wrinkled his nose. "Neither have I."

"Want to try it?"

"You're a wicked woman, Lainie Jackson."

"I'm just curious."

"Okay," he said, dropping a kiss on the end of her nose. "We'll try it tonight."

* * *

Elaine sat across the table from Reuben, the flickering light from a candle highlighting the alluring slant of her dark eyes. A cherry-red linen sheath with a square neckline was flattering to her dark skin. They had selected a restaurant that featured karaoke along with dinner, and several patrons had gotten up to sing.

Reuben leaned over the table. "Do you want to try it?"

Elaine rolled her eyes at him. "Are you kidding? If I had to sing for my food I'd die of starvation."

"Do you think the other people who got up there can sing?"

"I'm not about to make a fool of myself, Reuben Whitfield."

Pushing back his chair, Reuben stood up. "I'm going to try it."

Covering her face with her hands, Elaine smothered her laughter as Reuben wove his way through the closely positioned tables to the stage. A smattering of applause followed him.

A beige linen shirt and matching slacks showed off the richness of his tan. The summer sun had darkened his skin to a deep chestnut brown. Several women at a nearby table stood up and whistled as he stepped up onto the stage.

Lowering her hands, Elaine stared at a blond woman who looked as if she were ready to audition for a role on *Baywatch*. Her white spandex dress was pasted on her body like a postage stamp.

Reuben exchanged words with the deejay, shaking his head. It appeared as if they'd finally settled on a song when he took the microphone.

Clearing his throat, he spoke into the mike. "I'd

like to dedicate this song to a very special woman. Lainie, this one is for you."

Everyone in the restaurant turned to stare at her as she struggled to maintain her composure. Heat swept over her face and she glared at Reuben for making her the center of attention.

The music began and words appeared on a large screen. A catchy reggae beat had most clapping and swaying as Reuben sang along with Maxi Priest crooning Bob Marley's "Waiting in Vain."

Closing his eyes, he sang the lyrics without looking at the screen. He substituted "twenty-five years" for "three years," eliciting shouts and raised fists from everyone in the restaurant.

Reuben had a wonderful singing voice. He'd captured the spirit of unrequited love with just enough passion to have everyone on their feet applauding wildly. He bowed from the waist, and then blew a kiss at Elaine, who had once again covered her face. He left the stage, swaggering like a superstar, his teeth showing white in his deeply tanned brown face.

"If you don't want to marry him, then I'll take him!" shouted the buxom blonde. The entire place erupted in laughter.

Elaine stood up, waiting for Reuben as he returned to their table. Raising her arms, she curved them around his neck and pulled his head down. She kissed him flush on the mouth amid whistles and hooting.

Pulling back, she stared at the shocked expression on his face. "You don't have to wait anymore," she crooned softly. "I love you, Reuben. Now let's get out of here so I can show you."

Reaching into the pocket of his slacks, Reuben left a large bill on the table and followed Elaine as she led him out of the restaurant. Just before they reached the door, she turned and gave a thumbs-up sign to those staring at them.

"Let's go, lover," she said to Reuben as he held back. "Either you're going to put up or shut up."

Releasing her hand, he cradled her face between his palms. He made love to her with his eyes. "Tell me again."

"What?"

"What you said to me inside the restaurant."

"About loving you?"

"Yes."

It was her turn to make love to him with her heated gaze. "I love you, Reuben. Is that what you want to hear?"

A triumphant smile crossed his face. "Yes!"

His hand rested on the small of her back as he led her to his car. He opened the passenger-side door, waiting until she was seated and buckled in before he took his seat behind the steering wheel.

The setting sun turned the ocean a bright red-orange as the fiery ball sank lower, disappearing beyond the horizon. A sprinkling of stars had littered the navy blue sky by the time they returned to the cabin. They'd completed the return trip without exchanging a word. They had said enough back at the restaurant.

Elaine did not follow Reuben into the cabin, electing to sit out on the porch and stare at the beach. She heard the gentle lapping of the incoming tide but could not see the water in the darkness. Kicking off her sandals, she pulled her feet up under her on the cushioned wicker chair, rocking gently.

Her head had fallen at an odd angle by the time

Reuben came out onto the porch wearing a pair of cotton pajama pants. Moving silently, he stood beside her and touched her shoulder. Her head slipped lower. She was asleep.

Hunkering down, he studied her delicate face in the light coming through the window from a lamp in the front room. He loved her, and she'd confessed to loving him.

Gathering Elaine from the chair, Reuben held her close to his heart. He felt complete; for the first time in his life he had everything that he'd ever wanted.

Reuben waited in LaGuardia Airport for Elaine to come through the gate for arrivals. He hadn't thought he would miss her as much as he did. She'd flown to South Carolina to spend a week with her family, asking that he accompany her; he had to refuse because of a backlog of patients. He always closed his practice in July; therefore, August became an unusually busy month for him and his staff.

He spied her as he held up a sign with her name printed above the words *WHITFIELD CAR SERVICE*. She wagged her finger while shaking her head.

"What am I going to do with you?" She laughed as Reuben picked her up and swung her around.

"I don't know." Lowering her to the floor, he kissed her.

She kissed him back. "I think I'll keep you." Her expression grew serious. "I missed you, Reuben."

He winked at her. "I missed you, too, darling. Let's get out of here." He reached for her single piece of luggage.

Elaine waited at the curb while Reuben went to

retrieve his car from the short-term parking lot. She had spent a wonderful week with her family, re-connecting with her parents, brother, and daughter. Her teenage niece and nephew had spent most of their time with cousins their own age, watching music videos or listening to CDs.

Zoë had questioned her relentlessly about Reuben, and Elaine was forthcoming when she told her daughter she'd fallen in love again. She had sworn Zoë to secrecy, saying that when she felt the time was right she would tell the rest of the family.

She had no idea where her relationship with Reuben was going, despite their declarations of love. He seemed to have lost interest in relocating, and she didn't press him. After all, it was his money, his life, and his future. She refused to set herself up for heart-ache. Once was enough.

Eight

Elaine sat in the Bayou, waiting for Brenda and Meredith to arrive. She'd spent Friday night in the city with Reuben. He'd picked her up at her office and driven to Manhattan, where they ate dinner at a restaurant in Greenwich Village. They spent two hours walking the narrow, winding streets before stopping at a Starbucks for lattes. It was minutes past midnight when they walked into his apartment, shared a shower, and crawled into bed without making love.

Her week had begun slowly, but ended with a flurry

of activity. She had attended the closing on two houses in one day, and two of the brokers had gone to contract on a total of three properties. It was late summer, and business was gearing up for the fall.

The cousins arrived together, waving and smiling as they approached her table. After hugs and a round of kisses, the three sat down for their quarterly reunion.

Brenda gave Elaine a sidelong stare. "Well, look at Miss Lainie. Don't you think she's looks rather content, Merry?"

A becoming tan had concealed the spray of freckles on Meredith Endicott's nose. "Who is he?" she crooned in her distinctively seductive voice.

"You'll find out soon enough."

"I knew it!" Brenda crowed. Diners from nearby tables turned to stare at them. "Sorry," she apologized, flashing a quick smile.

"When will we meet him?" Meredith asked Elaine, continuing with her interrogation.

"At the reunion."

Brenda waved the waiter away from the table. "You're really going to bring him with you to the twenty-fifth reunion?"

Elaine smiled at her two best friends. "Yes."

"How serious is this?" Meredith questioned.

Elaine's eyebrows rose slightly. "How do you define serious?"

"Sleeping together is serious."

"Marriage is serious."

The cousins had spoken in unison.

"Not marriage-serious," Elaine said.

Meredith leaned closer. "Are you at least getting some?"

She smiled, but didn't answer.

"Of course she is," Brenda countered, frowning at Meredith. "Is he good, Lainie?" she whispered conspiratorially.

Elaine hesitated, a smile touching her mouth. "Sometimes he's so good that I want to holler for my mama to make him stop."

The cousins' mouths dropped as they stared at each other. "Damn," Brenda whispered.

"Can I get an amen?" Meredith crooned.

"Amen," Elaine answered. "Drinks are on me this time."

The three women ordered glasses of champagne, toasting each other and a quarter century of love and friendship. They ended dinner two hours later, promising to do it again. They would see one another at their high school reunion celebration in November. A week later they would meet again at the Bayou.

Elaine sat on a cushioned wrought-iron love seat in her garden as the leaves on an overhead tree floated down around her, settling on the manicured lawn. She hadn't turned a page in the book resting on her lap since she'd opened it. Her gaze lingered on the tall, slender frame of the man with whom she'd fallen in love.

Reuben strolled around her garden, hands clasped behind his back. Every once in a while he would lean over and pluck a withered petal or dead leaf off a bush.

He had gotten a buyer for his apartment, and December sixth was tentatively established as the date for closing. He had four weeks to choose a place to live, or be forced to put his belongings in storage and live in a hotel or sublet an apartment on a month-to-month basis.

Running a hand over his graying head, he turned and walked back to Elaine, sitting down next to her. Placing an arm over the back of the love seat, he smiled at her.

"I have to buy a house."

Resting her head on his shoulder, she inhaled the familiar scent of his cologne clinging to the fibers of a wool sweater. "You've been saying that for months."

"I know."

"If you know, then why aren't you doing something about it?"

Reuben ran his fingers through Elaine's curls. Her hair was growing out. "I'm not certain where I want to live."

"Didn't you tell me you liked Oyster Bay?"

"Yes. But do you like Oyster Bay?"

She sat up, staring at his profile. "What does my liking Oyster Bay have to do with you buying a home there?"

"Will you come visit me?"

"Of course I'll visit you. What's going on with you, Reuben? I've never known you to be so indecisive."

Shifting on the love seat, he gave her a direct stare. "Where I decide to live will depend upon you."

"Why me?"

"Because I want you to live with me."

Elaine shook her head. "I'm sorry, Reuben. I'm liberal, but not so liberal that I would elect to live with a man."

A grin curved his mouth and crinkled his eyes. "Would you live with a man if you were married to him?"

She wrinkled her nose. "Of course I would. What kind of question is that?"

"Marry me, Lainie."

"Why? So you can have a legal roommate?"

"Stop it!"

Her temper rose to meet his. "You stop it, Reuben! Stop talking in riddles."

Moving off the love seat, he went to his knees in front of her. Reaching for her hands, he tightened his grip when she attempted to pull away.

"I love you, Elaine Jackson, and I want you to marry me. I want you to be my wife and live with me, and I want to spend the rest of my life with you." He saw her shocked expression, unable to believe she didn't know he wanted her to share his life, his future. "I've never said these words to another woman, Lainie," he continued passionately.

Hot tears filled Elaine's eyes as she leaned forward and pressed her forehead to Reuben's. "I want so much to marry you but I'm afraid."

Rubbing a thumb over her cheek, he wiped away a fat tear. "Afraid of what, darling?"

"I can't go through another divorce."

"Who said anything about divorce?"

She couldn't stop her hands from shaking. Fears she'd put to rest had surfaced without warning. After her marriage ended, she'd told herself that she was an independent woman who could take care of herself, that she didn't need a man—not for anything. But then Reuben Whitfield had come back into her life and had proved her wrong. She did need him. He made her laugh and helped her experience the joy of being born female. He had become lover as well as friend. Now he was offering her his name and his protection. He was offering her a second chance at love.

But did she love him enough to risk marrying again? Could she trust enough to share her life with him?

"Reuben?"

"Yes, darling?"

"When do you want to do this?"

"Anytime before we move into our new home."

"Do you want to marry before I sell this house?"

"No," he said softly. "I will not live in this house with you. We're going to start anew and create our own memories."

She flashed a brilliant smile. "I think I'll like living in Oyster Bay." The property Reuben had looked at was in a new development, overlooking the water. "Do you think we're going to need more than three bedrooms?"

He shrugged a shoulder. "Maybe we should get the one with four bedrooms. There's always the possibility that Zoë will get married and drop by with a grandchild or two."

She giggled like a child. "Imagine me, a grandmother."

"You'll be a helluva sexy grandmother."

Elaine touched her mouth to Reuben's. "I suppose we should walk down and talk to the guy who wants to buy this place."

Rising to his feet, Reuben pulled Elaine from the love seat. He wrapped an arm around her shoulders, offering his body's heat as they set off down a narrow path flanked by towering trees that nearly shut out the sunlight. It was a lovely fall day for a walk in the country.

Reuben had left Long Island twenty-five years ago. He'd returned because he'd felt an urgency to come home.

He was coming home to Long Island.

The single word may have represented a place, but to him it was more than that. It was a person.

Elaine Jackson had become his home.

Nine

Reuben flipped the top on a velvet-covered rectangular box. A set of studs and matching cuff links set with black and white diamonds winked back at him under the recessed lights in his dressing room. The precious stones set in white gold had been a gift from his mother when he'd graduated dental school.

His gaze shifted to an assortment of rings and bracelets in a larger velvet-lined box, and he smiled. Several antique pieces, some dating back to the eighteenth century, lay among more modern settings. Picking up a ring with a vibrant blue sapphire flanked by two brilliant blue-white diamond baguettes set in platinum, he slipped it into the pocket of his dress trousers.

This night was to become one he would remember all of his life: the ring would establish his official engagement to Elaine Jackson and commemorate the twenty-fifth reunion of their high school graduating class.

The rooms in his apartment replicated those at Elaine's house—they were crowded with labeled corrugated boxes. The date for closing the sale of his apartment had been pushed up to December eighteenth—a day before he closed on the Oyster Bay property. He and Elaine were to be married in a Christmas Eve candlelight ceremony. The following morning they would fly to Saint Thomas for a weeklong honeymoon, returning New Year's Day to begin a new life together in a new home.

Elaine had continued to amaze Reuben since agreeing to marry him. She was less guarded, less tense, and much more affectionate. It was as if she'd regained the confidence she'd exhibited when attending high school. She was once again the princess all of the other girls had tried to emulate or wanted to be. The days when he didn't see Elaine they communicated by telephone, ending every conversation with passionate declarations of love.

Even their lovemaking had changed, becoming less intense. Their coming together was deeper, more tender. The last time he lay in her scented embrace, overwhelmed by emotions he could not identify, Reuben had felt the pull of paternity for the first time in his life. He wanted a child—a child who would continue the Whitfields into perpetuity.

He recovered quickly from the startling revelation, knowing it was selfish of him to think about fathering a child with Elaine, even if she had been able to conceive, because she'd already raised and nurtured a child, and to ask that she start motherhood again with teething, toilet training, and dealing with the angst of an adolescent would be selfish on his part. The notion of wanting to be a father lingered for a day, then dissipated as quickly as it had come.

Reuben inserted the studs and cuff links in his wingcollar dress shirt. A black-and-white pin-striped tie and cummerbund completed his formal dress. Glancing at the gold watch below the French cuff on his shirt, he noted the time. It was five-thirty. He'd planned to pick Elaine up at six-thirty. A cocktail hour was scheduled for seven o'clock and a sit-down dinner at eight.

He reached for his jacket from a hanger in his walk-in closet, and headed out of the dressing room.

Elaine glanced at her reflection in a full-length mirror for the last time, then turned and made her way out of her bedroom and down the staircase to answer the door. It had taken her three days to select an outfit for the very special gathering. She had finally decided on a sheer black dress in shimmering silk with a matching underslip. The garment had long sleeves with banded silk cuffs and was embroidered from the scooped neck to the slightly flaring hem with delicate flowers and shimmering bugle beads. The toes of her black silk pumps were visible only when she took a step. The heels on her shoes were three inches high, making her appear more statuesque than she actually was. She liked wearing high heels with Reuben, because they presented a striking couple.

Smiling, she opened the door. If she had doubts about her appearance, they were quickly put to rest when she saw the flicker of approval in her fiancé's dark eyes.

Reuben stared at the woman he planned to marry in a month, his breath catching in his chest. She was stunning, from the coiffed curly hair, carefully made-up face, down to the swell of breasts rising and falling about a shimmering black dress that fell in soft gathers around her feet. The delicate bracelet dotted with bezel-set diamonds on her right wrist and a pair of diamond studs in her lobes were her only jewelry. The precious gems paled in comparison to the woman standing before him. To him she'd become the most precious jewel in his universe.

Elaine opened the door wider, admiring the man who had captured her heart. "You look wonderful." Reuben was heart-stopping, drop-dead gorgeous in formal dress. Pressing her cheek to his, she said, "I just have to get my coat."

"Not yet, darling," Reuben said quietly, holding her hand. Reaching into the pocket of his dress trousers, he withdrew the ring and slipped it on the third finger of her left hand. Light from a chandelier in the foyer caught the fire of the baguettes, and Elaine gasped in surprise. "My great-grandfather gave it to his beloved upon their engagement. Her middle name was Elaine, so I thought it fitting that another beautiful woman bearing the same name should wear it."

Holding out her hand, Elaine shook her head in wonderment. "It's beautiful, Reuben." She smiled up at him, her eyes filling with tears. "Thank you."

Cradling her to his chest, Reuben kissed her fragrant curly hair. "You're beautiful. And I should be the one doing the thanking—thanking you for accepting me to share your life."

"If you don't stop you're going to have me bawling like a baby." Pulling back, she touched a fingertip to the corners of her eyes. "Let me check my makeup; then we can go."

Elaine walked into the Marriott, her hand enveloped in the warmth of Reuben's, grinning from ear to ear. She recognized some of her former classmates, who looked genuinely surprised not to see her with Dwight Stewart. What she suspected was that most of them hadn't recognized Reuben Whitfield as her escort for the affair.

She spied Meredith Endicott and her husband beckoning to her as she waited for Reuben to check her floor-length silk coat and retrieve their name badges. Meredith looked speculator in a copper satin pantsuit with a black blouse in the same fabric. The deep vee in her top revealed more flesh than Elaine had ever seen Meredith show since knowing her.

Elaine pressed her scented cheek to Meredith's. "I see you came to show off a bit," she teased.

"It's a Wonderbra," Meredith whispered. "Praise the saints for Victoria's Secret."

"Can I get an amen from the choir," Elaine countered.

Meredith's jaw dropped and she folded her hands on her hips. She glared at Elaine's chest. "Now, you know you don't need no Wonderbra, girlfriend."

"I wasn't referring to a bra. I meant panties. A thong, to be precise."

Meredith's eyes nearly popped out of her head. "You wear thongs?"

Elaine sucked her teeth and rolled her eyes. "Don't knock it until you try one. It's guaranteed to spark up your marriage."

Her last night on Cape Cod, Elaine had worked up enough nerve to wear one of the thongs Zoë had sent her, and when she had undressed in front of Reuben and he saw the tiny triangle of lace and the narrow strip of silk between her bare buttocks once she turned and presented him with her back, the man had nearly fainted in shock. He recovered quickly and they shared the hottest, most mind-blowing, brain-sucking sex either had ever experienced in their lives.

She'd returned to New York, called her daughter, and requested she send an assortment of thongs in various colors and fabrics. Tonight she wore one in a sheer black nylon that barely covered what should've been concealed.

Reuben returned with his name tag attached to the lapel of his tuxedo, and Meredith let out an ear-piercing scream. "Scientist!"

Those milling around the lobby of the hotel turned and stared numbly at Reuben Whitfield hugging Meredith Endicott née Benson.

Meredith recovered quickly, pointing a finger at Elaine. "Don't tell me you've been seeing the Scientist?"

Elaine extended her left hand. "Seeing and marrying Christmas Eve."

Meredith let out another ear-piercing scream when she saw the exquisite estate piece on her friend's finger. "I don't believe it. I can't believe it," she said over and over until her husband returned with their name tags.

Elaine hugged Meredith's husband, asking briefly about their children before she introduced him to Reuben. The two men shook hands, smiling.

Reuben curved an arm around Elaine's waist, pulling her against his length at the same time Dwight Stewart walked in with a tall, thin woman clinging to his arm, wearing what appeared to be a spandex slip. The diamond ring on her left hand was as big as a headlight.

Lowering her head, Reuben pressed his mouth to Elaine's ear. "Let's go in and mingle."

"Okay." She'd spied Dwight at the same time Reuben had. Zoë was right: her father's fiancée did appear to be anorexic.

Elaine followed Reuben into a large room ablaze
with lights from several chandeliers, where tables
were set up for a buffet cocktail hour. Reuben did
not let go of her hand as he ordered glasses of wine
for them.

Brenda arrived with her husband, and the screaming
and congratulating started all over again. Brenda clung
to Reuben's neck, declaring she couldn't believe he
had grown up to be so fine. When he revealed he had
become a dentist, she admitted to admiring a little
silver sports car bearing DDS plates.

Pulling Elaine to one side, she said between
clenched teeth, "I'm going to pay you back for holding
out on me, girlfriend. Who would've thought that the
school nerd would turn into Prince Charming? Damn,
but he's one fine brother-man!"

Meredith came over, joining them. "So he's the one
who makes you holler for your mama? I can see why,
Lainie." She shook her head in a gesture that mirrored
her disbelief. "Even with the glasses he's hot!"

Elaine affected a serious expression. "You should
be ashamed of yourselves, drooling over another sister's man. And what makes it worse is that you're
both married."

"I may be married, but I ain't blind, crippled, or
crazy," Meredith drawled in her deep, seductive voice.

"You deserve all happiness, Lainie," Brenda added.
"Especially after what Dwight did to you."

"Did you see that scrawny chickenhead he had
hanging on his arm?" Meredith said. "She'd better
hold on, because those pipe cleaners she has masqu-
erading as legs would never hold her up. I'm willing to
bet her hair weave weighs more than her entire body."

Elaine frowned at her two best friends. "Don't be
catty, girlfriends."

Brenda sucked her teeth loudly. "You wouldn't be saying that if you didn't have Reuben."

"Even if I didn't have Reuben, I still would wish Dwight well. I believe we all get what we deserve. It's just that right now I'm a little more deserving than Dwight Stewart," she added smugly.

The three women exchanged high fives before they returned to their men.

Roosevelt High School's twenty-fifth reunion had become a family reunion as everyone danced under streamers of gold and blue, the colors of the Rough Riders. Disco music, which had been popular at that time, blared from speakers as Elaine danced with Rueben to Donna Summer's "Love to Love You, Baby."

Reuben pressed his hips closer to hers. "I've waited twenty-five years for this," he whispered in her ear.

"Has the wait been worth it?"

"More than worth it, Lainie."

The song ended, and when they parted, Elaine found Dwight standing only a few feet away. He nodded to Reuben. "Excuse me, man. You wouldn't mind if I have a few words with Elaine?"

Reuben stared at Dwight Stewart for a long moment. "That would depend on Elaine."

She looked at her ex-husband, noting changes that hadn't been obvious when she had seen him at their daughter's high school graduation. He'd put on more weight, his chin had begun to sag, and there was puffiness under his eyes that meant either he wasn't getting enough sleep or he was retaining fluid.

She smiled at Reuben. "I'll be right back, darling."

Reuben nodded, watching Elaine with her ex-husband as he rested a hand in the small of her back. There had been a time when he almost couldn't control his envy and jealousy when he saw Elaine and Dwight together. But those times had passed. In another six weeks he would claim Elaine as wife and partner. And in another seven weeks it would be Elaine he would come home to—every night.

Elaine followed Dwight outside the hotel to an adjacent parking lot, shivering against the evening chill. "If we're going to stand out here and talk, then I'm going to need your jacket."

Dwight took off his jacket, placing it over her shoulders. The familiar scent of his ex-wife's perfume conjured up memories from their past. He'd made a mistake. He never should've left her.

"What do you want to talk about?" She sounded bored, annoyed.

Pushing his hands into the pockets of his trousers, Dwight stared at the toes of his patent leather dress shoes, permitting Elaine to view the thinning hair on the crown of his head.

His head came up and the gray eyes most girls found so appealing were dull, lifeless. "I've done a lot of thinking, Lainie."

"About what?" she drawled.

"You and me."

Her eyebrows rose in surprise. "You're kidding me, aren't you?"

"No, I'm not."

Elaine should've been flattered that her first love hadn't gotten over her and wanted her back, but Dwight was too late. Even if she had not been involved with Reuben Whitfield, she still would not consider reconciling with her ex-husband. She could not trust him.

"It's too late, Dwight."

"It's not too late, Lainie. We're both single."

"I don't believe you're old enough to be senile, but have you forgotten that there's a woman sitting inside this hotel who's wearing your ring? You're committed to someone, and so am I."

Dwight shook his head. "You can't marry the Scientist."

She smiled for the first time since coming face-to-face with her daughter's father. "Oh, that's where you're wrong, Dwight Alan Stewart. I will marry Reuben Whitfield, and I intend to spend the rest of my life loving him as much as he loves me."

Reaching out, Dwight caught her upper arm in a punishing grip. "No, Lainie. Don't do it."

She stared at his hand until he released her. "I am going to marry Reuben, and I suggest you marry your model. But let me give you some advice—feed the girl."

Dwight managed to look contrite. "She says she has to stay thin for her modeling jobs."

"She looks like a dog's mess. Everyone's talking about her."

"She looks heavier in her photographs," Dwight said in defense of his intended.

"She looks unhealthy," Elaine countered.

Shrugging off his jacket, she handed it back to him. Lifting the skirt of her dress, she pulled it up to her knees, giving Dwight an unobstructed view of her shapely legs. Lifting it even higher, she heard him gasp as she displayed lace-trimmed, thigh-high sheer black hose.

"This is healthy, Dwight, " she crooned. Turning around, she completed her exhibition when she displayed her firm buttocks in the thong. "And this is what you're going to miss for the rest of your natural life," she drawled seconds before yards of silk floated down around her feet.

Turning on her heels, she walked over to a side door of the hotel, head held high as she tried holding back screams of laughter. The look on Dwight's face when she'd showed him her behind was priceless. It was a look she would never forget. And she was willing to bet Dwight Stewart would never forget how his ex-wife looked—from behind!

She found Reuben standing outside the ballroom, waiting for her. Smiling, she leaned close and kissed his mouth. "I love you, Dr. Reuben Whitfield."

Deepening the kiss, he let his tongue slip behind her parted lips, his arms going around her waist. "Are you ready to leave?"

"Yes," she murmured against his mouth.

"Your place or mine?"

"We won't be saying that in another month."

"You're right, Lainie. Where do you want to sleep tonight?"

Her eyes sparkled. "What if we stay here tonight?"

He kissed her again. "That's a wonderful idea. Why didn't I think of that myself?"

"Because you're in love, and you know those in love aren't always practical."

Reuben laughed. "Let's tell Meredith and Brenda that we're going to get a suite, and if they want to they can hang out with us."

"I take it back about your not being practical."

"I can assure you that I'm full of surprises, Lainie.

I . . ." He didn't finish his statement when he spied Dwight coming in their direction. "What's wrong with Dwight? He looks as if he's in shock."

Turning, Elaine noted Dwight's expression. He appeared old, defeated. Curving her arm through Reuben's, she smiled up at him. "I'll tell you about it later. Better yet, I'll show you."

Reuben winked at her. "Promise?"

She gave him a sensual smile. "Promise."

Arm in arm, they returned to the ballroom to rejoin the celebration of their twenty-fifth high school reunion.

It was to become a reunion of friends from a most glorious time in their lives. It would also become a reunion of hearts and dreams.

Elaine and Reuben were blessed to have found it all as they looked forward to many more reunions to come.

SURPRISE!

Donna Hill

One

Elizabeth Howell sighed as she gazed out of the tiny airplane window. In less than an hour she would be back in New York, returning from her two-week stay at a health spa in Arizona.

Home. Oh, Lawd, she thought, anxiety causing her stomach to knot. How . . . what was she going to tell her husband, Vincent? What was she going to tell her two grown children and her granddaughter, for heaven's sake?

She'd gone to Arizona to try to get her body back on track, get her health in order, and regain some of the sexiness she used to feel. The sexiness that had been replaced by the extra twenty-plus pounds she'd put on over the years, not to mention the extra five she couldn't seem to shake over the past month. She'd gone because she wanted to see that spark in Vincent's eyes again, she wanted to look at her profile and not hang her head in shame. She wanted to be the sexy, head-turning woman she'd once been. Never in a million years would she have thought . . . imagined . . . "Oh, Lawd."

"Hmm? Did you say something?" her seatmate asked.

Elizabeth's face flushed hot as a lit match. Had she actually spoken out loud? She sniffled hard and shook her head. "Uh, no. Not really. I mean . . . I'm sorry if I disturbed you. Just thinking out loud." She chuckled lightly.

The woman looked her over for a moment, then turned back to the magazine laid out on her tray.

Elizabeth, mortified, returned to stare out of the window, nearly pressing her face into the glass. But this time the tears refused to stay in check and slowly slid down her cheeks, clouding her vision.

She felt a gentle touch on her shoulder and the softness of a tissue being placed in her hand.

"Sometimes it helps if you talk," the woman said.

Elizabeth sniffed harder as the tears fell fast and furious. She dabbed at her eyes, then her nose. "I'm so sorry," she apologized over shuddering sobs. "I'm not usually like this."

"It's all right," the woman said. "Crying is good for the soul. Let it out. You'll feel better."

Elizabeth looked across at her companion through her tears, quickly taking her in. She was slender and elegantly dressed in a pantsuit of pale cinnamon that did incredible things to her smooth pecan complexion. She wore only a hint of makeup, just enough to accent her full mouth and expressive doe-shaped eyes. Her soft brown hair was simply coiffed in an easy-to-manage bob. Elizabeth's eyes trailed down to her delicate hands and long fingers with nails devoid of polish but neatly manicured. The woman wore little jewelry: gold studs at her ears, a matching bracelet on her right wrist, and a simple gold band on her wedding finger.

Upon first blush, one would easily chart her age as late thirties to early forties, but with closer inspection the fine lines of life touching her eyes and her mouth were evident, along with the telltale streaks of gray that made her hair glisten.

This was a woman who had herself together, a woman confident in who she was and proud of it. The kind of woman Elizabeth had once been.

"My name is Helen. Helen Monroe," the woman offered. "And yours?"

"Elizabeth Howell. Most people call me Liz."

"I hate traveling," Helen said. "Especially by plane. The only reason on earth why I bother is to see my son and daughter-in-law, but especially my grandson, Matthew. What a doll. Would you like to see a picture?"

Before Liz had a chance to respond, Helen pulled her wallet from her purse and flipped to the plastic-encased photo of her grandson.

"He's three," she said proudly. "Isn't he just the cutest thing?"

Liz smiled. "Yes, he is."

Helen sighed. "I always wished I'd had more children. But . . . between careers and finances . . . time just got away from us." She turned in her seat and leaned closer to Liz. Her voice lowered to a whisper. "Last year my husband, Cliff, and I thought about fertility drugs, or maybe in vitro." She chuckled. "I know you're probably thinking I must be crazy to want a brand-new baby at my age. But I guess that old spark was still there." She put her wallet back into her purse. "Do you have children, Liz?"

Liz swallowed. "Yes, Carolyn and Mark. We—my husband and I—adopted. Carolyn and her husband, Steven, have a daughter, Desiree."

"That's so wonderful. Isn't family just a wonderful thing," she stated more than asked.

Liz nodded.

"You have to excuse me if I gab too much," she said, patting Liz's hand. "My friends and family always tell me that I talk too much, get into everyone's business. And I don't doubt that it's true." She laughed, totally at ease with herself. "But if you don't, how will anyone know what you think about anything? I'm a firm believer in getting things out in the open." She looked meaningfully at Liz. "No matter what the consequences. Sometimes they're not as bad as they seem."

Liz got the strangest feeling that Helen saw right through her, saw right into her soul.

The sound of the pilot's voice crackled through the speakers, announcing that they would be landing shortly. The stewardess walked up and down the aisle, checking that seat belts were securely fastened.

Much too soon—at least, too soon for Liz—the passengers were disembarking and seeking out the friendly faces of family and friends who awaited their return.

Liz tiptoed, peeking over the heads of the passengers to catch a glimpse of Helen. She caught up with her in the waiting area.

Breathless from the exertion of hurrying, she tapped Helen on the shoulder. She turned, a ready smile on her face.

"Oh, Liz," she said as if they were the best of friends. "Is your husband here to meet you? I'm sure I could give you a lift . . ."

"No, that's fine. I'm sure he'll be here soon, if he's not already. I . . . I just wanted to say thank-you . . . for talking to me." She smiled weakly.

"It's perfectly all right. I hope it helped?" she asked.

"Yes, I think it did."

"Good." Helen looked at Liz for a moment, wondering whether or not she should be so bold, then decided, Why not? "Tell him," she said gently. "He'll understand."

Liz's brows rose in shock. Heaven only knew what this woman must think her problem was. "I beg your pardon?"

"Tell him. It won't be as bad as you think. He'll be shocked at first, but he'll get used to it . . . and so will everyone else."

"But—"

Helen placed a hand on Liz's arm. "I've been an OB/GYN nurse for twenty-five years." She smiled mischievously. "I'd know 'that look' in the dark. Take my advice and tell him." She kissed Liz's cheek, then dug in her jacket pocket and pulled out a business card. "Here. If you ever need someone to talk to— not that I would give you much of a chance—give me a call."

For the first time in weeks, Liz actually felt better, hopeful. Maybe it would be all right after all. She took the card. "Thanks. I really mean that."

"Well, I've got to run. I know my husband must be waiting. Take care of yourself, Liz." She started to walk away, then stopped and turned. "Good luck."

Liz waved until Helen was out of sight. *Good luck.* Yes, she would need plenty of it when she told her fifty-five-year-old husband that his fifty-two-year-old wife was pregnant for the first time in their thirty-year marriage.

Two

Each step toward the baggage claim area fortified Elizabeth in her resolve. *"Vincent, I'm pregnant."* No. *"Vincent, we're going to have a baby."* *"Uh, Vincent, I know you're not going to believe this, but guess what, sweetheart. Surprise!"*

But when the crowd parted and Vincent stood before her waving and smiling with a huge bouquet of red roses in his hands, all of her determination evaporated like dew beneath the morning sun.

She fixed a smile on her face, took a breath, and lost herself in Vincent's embrace.

"Welcome back, baby," he whispered against her hair, then tenderly brushed her lips with his. "You have no idea how much I missed you."

"I missed you, too."

Vincent stepped back and held her at arm's length. Elizabeth's heart began to race.

He tilted his head to the right and drew her closer. "You look . . . great." A smile broke out across his face. "There's this . . . glow about you." He chuckled, then stroked her cheek. "I can't wait to get you home. I have a surprise for you."

Surprise! Elizabeth almost choked. "Really?" she said in a squeak. She slipped her arm through his. "Well, first we have to get my bags."

"And then home." He leaned closer. "I can't wait to see this new you totally unwrapped."

106

A surge of heat rushed through her body. Under other circumstances she would have thought it was a hot flash, but now she knew better. It was the hormones that had finally kicked into overdrive, revved her internal engine, and had her as hot and bothered as an eighteen-year-old without good sense. All the ingredients that had landed her in this unimaginable situation.

"Here's your bag," Vincent said, snatching a paisley suitcase with *Surprise!* emblazoned in mauve letters along the side.

"Yep, and the two right behind it."

Vincent took the bags with ease, although Elizabeth was sure she'd packed everything she owned.

"The car is out this way." He headed toward the exit. "I can't get over how great you look, Liz. Maybe I need to take a trip out there."

Elizabeth sputtered a nervous laugh.

"Were there any men there?" Vincent asked as he opened the trunk and deposited the suitcases.

"There were a few."

"Really?" He walked around to the side of the car and opened the door for her. "So it was coed. I didn't know that when you left." He shut her door with a thud. He got in and started the engine. His lips were pressed together into a tight, thin line.

Elizabeth looked at him. "Vincent Howell, are you jealous?" She bit back a smile.

His jaw flexed as he pulled out and headed for the highway. "I didn't say anything about being jealous," he grumbled, barely moving his lips. "I'm just not all that crazy about other men looking at you in those . . . workout outfits, and whatever else goes on in those places."

He was almost pouting, and Elizabeth couldn't stop the laughter that bubbled up from her stomach.

"Oh, so you think it's funny?" He dared to snatch a look in her direction, and she saw the sincerity in his eyes.

She reached out and put a hand on his arm. "No, I don't think it's funny. I think it's wonderful. I haven't seen you act like this since we were dating— back in the day."

Vincent took a breath. "I don't know what it is, Liz, but lately . . . it's as if I've fallen in love with you all over again. All I want to do is be with you, inside you, like some young fool. I'm fifty-five years old." He chuckled. "But I feel like I'm twenty every time I think about you."

Her eyes filled. "Funny thing is, Vince, I feel the very same way," she said softly.

He turned toward her, and the heat of desire that lit his eyes was unmistakable. Elizabeth felt that hot rush again.

"I think it's just the idea that we are finally alone, just us," he said. "The kids are out, settled, and doing well. The business is thriving. All we have to concentrate on for the first time in more than twenty years is us. Me and you, babe. We can do what we want, where we want, and when."

Elizabeth's heart thumped. *Just us,* she thought. *Not hardly.*

Three

That night Elizabeth and Vincent shared an intimate dinner for two. With both of them being certified chefs, often in the Howell kitchen it was the duel of the titans—seeing who could outdo the other with a new twist on an old recipe. But tonight was Vincent's night. He laid out a fare fit for a princess—blackened salmon, saffron rice sprinkled with parsley, steamed zucchini and baby carrots. Of course, it was presented with a flourish, and Elizabeth savored every mouth-watering bite.

Elizabeth's love of food and cooking began at her grandmother Margaret's house in North Carolina. As soon as Elizabeth was tall enough to peek above the tabletop, she was learning how to make homemade pie crusts so light that they nearly evaporated in your mouth. She learned to can fruits and use homegrown herbs and vegetables to spice up a meal or decorate a table.

She learned all the tricks from her grandmother, who was by no means what would be considered a small woman. Margaret Winston was big-boned, brassy, and loved life. Elizabeth's parents always said Liz took after her grandmother in size and attitude.

"Living large," Margaret used to say, even before the young hip-hoppers coined the phrase. "That's what you have to do, girl. Live large, and not just in size, but in attitude. Take life by the horns and shake it," she'd say, then laugh in that big way of hers. "You're always going to be a big girl; you take after me. But you keep yourself together, keep that pretty smile on your face and a hot meal on the table, and you'll have any man you want."

Elizabeth grew up living and believing in her grand-mother's golden rules, combined with her parents' adamant insistence on education.

She took the two dictums and went to culinary school, where she ultimately met the young, arrogant, and incredibly fine Vincent Howell. Together they pooled their resources and their skills and opened Surprise!, the hottest sit-down restaurant and catering business in the borough of Brooklyn. Folks came from as far away as Staten Island and New Jersey for meals created by the dynamic duo.

Thirty years. A long time to be with someone, build a life with them. Elizabeth looked across the island counter, watching the roped lines of her husband's back contract and release as he opened cabinets, took out champagne glasses, and filled them. He was still so incredibly handsome, she thought. His body was still hard in all the right places. To Vincent, the sprinkles of gray in his hair and mustache added character, not age. But Elizabeth and Lady Clairol's Off Black had become very good friends over the years. Where the few extra pounds on Vincent made him look mature, she, on the other hand, *looked* like a fifty-two-year-old, overweight woman who needed her roots done. And was pregnant.

"For you," Vincent said, handing her a flute of champagne, cutting into her thoughts. He touched his glass to hers. "To us, sweetheart, and to our future— just me . . . and you."

Elizabeth's heart pounded as she forced a smile. She took a tiny sip of the champagne and set her glass down on the counter.

"I still can't get over how radiant you look," he said. He refilled his glass.

"Must have been the air," she muttered.

"I guess so."

She reached across the counter and covered his hand with hers. "Enough about me," she said, needing to change the subject. "Catch me up on what's been going on with the business and the kids. These two weeks seemed like forever." And she meant it. In her thirty years of marriage, she'd never been away from her family for more than one night. "I missed you terribly."

Vincent put down his glass. "Not as much as I missed you, baby. It was pure torture."

She smiled, feeling that warm glow flood her body. Lately just his touch, the wicked look in his eyes, or the sound of his voice was enough to get her tingling all over.

He took another sip from his flute. "Well, to be truthful, I hope you did get some rest."

Her right brow rose. "Why? What's going on?"

"We got an urgent request from the New York chapter of the Deltas to cater their annual awards dinner."

Elizabeth released the breath she'd held, and her expression bloomed with delight. "That's wonderful. You made it sound like something awful had happened." She chuckled and shook her head. "So when is it, next month?" She was already planning what she was going to prepare.

"This weekend," Vincent said. "That was the surprise." He grinned sheepishly.

Elizabeth's hand flew to her chest. "This weekend! Five days from now?"

"Four, actually. It's Friday night."

"Oh, my goodness." She jumped up from her perch on the stool and began to pace. "We need to get busy. We have to plan a menu, get enough serving staff, check out the venue. . . ."

Vincent came around the island and blocked her pacing trail with his body. He placed his hands on her shoulders. "We will, baby. We'll get everything done, and it will be fabulous. Tomorrow." He stroked her cheek. "Not tonight. Tonight is for us." He leaned down and kissed her lips. "I want to show you how much you've been missed."

Elizabeth felt herself go limp as Vincent's arms wrapped around her body and pulled her close. She eased back and looked into his eyes. A smile of invitation that said, *Whatever you want,* spread across her mouth.

It was pure instinct that led them to their bedroom. All the while they headed up the stairs they shared kisses, gentle touches, and laughter.

When they finally stripped away each other's clothes and fell onto their king-size water bed, they made love with intense, passion-filled abandon. Comfortable in the familiarity of each other's bodies, they somehow discovered a newness that heightened their desire for and pleasure in each other.

"I don't ever remember it being like this." Vincent groaned as he moved slowly within her.

"It's better than the first time," Elizabeth whispered arching her back to meet his thrusts. "I love you so much." Her arms wrapped around him and she buried her face in the hollow of his neck.

"Just us, baby," Vincent said as his body shuddered on the verge of release. "Always."

Elizabeth closed her eyes as tears of joy and confusion spilled over her closed lids. Her body gave way to the exquisite sensations that Vincent stirred within her as she gave all of her love to him, and he to her.

Elizabeth listened to Vincent's steady breathing, the beating of his heart as he lay spooned against her. She had to tell him. He needed to know. She'd rehearsed the lines over and over again in her head. Everything would be fine. It had to be.

She'd tell him tomorrow. For now she simply wanted to relish in the joy of their rekindled love.

Four

"Liz, you look fabulous, girl," her best friend, Lena Hawthorne, enthused, wrapping Liz in a tight hug. She stepped back to assess her friend, and shook her head in amazement. "I need to take my old self to a health spa if it's going to make me look like you."

Lena and Elizabeth had been best friends since their girlhood days in their old neighborhood of Bedford-Stuyvesant. They'd grown up on the same street, attended the same school, and shared the same friends. But where Elizabeth was diplomatic and tactful, Lena was "out there," as they playfully acknowledged. She said what she thought, when she wanted, and didn't blink an eye at anyone's startled reaction. Where Elizabeth was big-boned and wide-hipped, Lena was a size eight on a bad day, with a flawless cinnamon-toned complexion that Elizabeth always envied. She never had trouble finding her size, or had to buy dark colors to camouflage her shape. Although Elizabeth had come to accept "the me that I'm in," there was always a part of her that wished she could be more like Lena.

"I know Vinny must be happy as a kid at Christmas to have you home, girl," Lena said, tossing her purse on the couch. "If he didn't call me every other day moaning about how he missed you, he didn't call once." She laughed again and plopped down on the couch. "You would think he was a young stud in love. What did you whip on that poor man before you hopped on the plane?"

Elizabeth took a seat in the recliner, and folded her hands in her lap.

"What's wrong?"

Elizabeth took a breath, leaned forward, and looked into her friend's dark brown eyes. "I'm pregnant," she blurted out.

Lena's polished mouth dropped open, and for the first time in all the years Elizabeth had known her, Lena was speechless.

"Did you hear what I said?" Elizabeth asked after several moments of silence.

Lena finally closed her mouth, reached in her purse for a cigarette, then stopped. "You're kidding me, right?" she finally muttered.

"No. I'm not."

"Look, it's probably 'the change,' girl. Pregnant!" She waved her hand in dismissal. "Don't be silly—at your age and after all this time?"

"I'm pregnant. It's *not* the change. It's a *baby*."

Lena frowned and shook her head to clear it. "But, Liz, honey, the doctors . . . all these years . . ."

"I know, I know. I can hardly believe it myself," she said, the realization and a surge of excitement hitting her at once.

Lena crossed her long legs and impatiently tapped her manicured nails against her thigh. "Women our age don't have babies. What in the world are you going to do with a baby now?"

Elizabeth's neck snapped back. "What are you saying?"

"I'm saying you can't be thinking of going through with this. What about the risks, abnormalities—your blood pressure was already sky-high. Giving birth could kill you. Have you considered that?"

Elizabeth took an exasperated breath and stood. "You're the last person I ever expected to hear this from. You of all people know how much I've always wanted my own child, a child that I carried."

"But, Liz, for heaven's sake, be realistic."

"Realistic! Don't you think I know how serious, how life-altering this is going to be for all of us?"

"And you're still willing to take that chance?" Lena challenged.

"Yes, damn it, I am."

"What does Vincent have to say?"

Suddenly the wind went out of her sails. "I . . . haven't told him yet."

Lena simply arched a perfect brow.

"But I will."

"Hmmm."

"I'm going through with this, Lena. And if you were my friend you'd be happy for me."

"Your friend! You're damned right I'm your friend.

And as a friend I'm telling you, you're crazy. You're
fifty-two years old, Liz. You have a granddaughter and
two grown children." She was beside herself with frustration. "What is on your mind?"

Elizabeth simply looked at her friend, her heart so
heavy with hurt she could barely feel its beat. Her
eyes welled with tears, but through sheer force of will
she held them back.

"I've got to get ready to go to work," Elizabeth
said, almost to herself. "We have a big job this weekend and we need all the help we can get." She forced
a tremulous smile and felt as if she were going to snap
in two. "I'm sure Vincent is wondering what's taking
me so long." She turned away, giving Lena her back.

Lena collected her purse. "Liz, honey, please think
this through. For your own health. Talk it over with
Vincent."

Elizabeth remained motionless, her body framed by
the bay window.

Lena released a breath. "I'll call you."

"Don't bother." Liz wrapped her arms around her
waist. When she heard the door softly close, she finally
let the tears fall.

By the time Elizabeth arrived at Surprise!, the restaurant was bustling with early lunchgoer activity, and
Vince had the cooking staff hopping in preparation
for the big weekend event.

His face lit up when she pushed through the swinging doors into the kitchen. The staff of eight chorused
their hellos and welcome-backs, all echoing how radiant she looked.

"Hey, babe." Vincent wiped flour from his hands
onto his white apron and came around the counter to
hug her.

She clung to him as if he were a life preserver, and all she wanted to do at that moment was remain forever protected in his embrace.

"Sorry I'm so late. Lena stopped by."

Vincent stepped back and looked at her. "I told you to take today off. It's your first day back."

She shooed away his concern, and put her hand on her ample, forty-six-inch hip. "Now, you know I couldn't hardly sit at home when we have all this going on." She reached for the hook and pulled down her own apron with her name stitched across the front in mauve letters. "Now let's get busy. You go back to what you were doing while I take a look around and make sure everything is everything."

"The general is back, y'all," Vincent announced with a chuckle.

The staff feigned groans of protest, and Elizabeth sucked her teeth and began her inspection of the troops and the barracks.

Her penchant for order and perfection were legendary at Surprise! She accepted no excuses for sloppiness, poor service, or lack of inventory. She may have been a hard taskmaster, but her staff and her customers loved her sincerely because she didn't accept anything less than the best from herself either. She never considered herself above her staff, but a part of it. Her motto was, "If we succeed or fail, we do it together."

Lawd, Lawd, she thought as she reviewed the elaborate meal plan that Vincent had outlined. *No good deed goes unpunished*, she thought, remembering her grandmother's favorite expression.

She turned toward Vincent, maybe a bit too fast, because her head spun and she had to grab the edge of the stainless-steel sink to gain her balance. She took a deep breath to clear her head and was infinitely thankful that Vincent had missed that episode, as he was engaged in instructing one of the new cooks on how to cut the fresh peaches for cobbler.

Her stomach did a little flip, then settled down. She walked toward the huge refrigerator and took out a bottle of water.

She was going to have to tell Vincent, and soon, she thought, taking a long, slow swallow. But at the same time, Lena's words of recrimination and caution danced in her head.

Five

"I'll be in around noon," Elizabeth said to Vincent as he prepared for work the following morning.

He turned from the mirror and looked curiously at her. "You, coming in late? I thought it was full steam ahead? Must be something important to keep you away. Feeling okay?"

Elizabeth kept her gaze focused on her toenails as they dried. "I, uh, wanted to take a quick run by the hotel to check out the setup for Friday night."

"Oh, sure." He chuckled. "Things were happening so fast I totally forgot you haven't seen the place. Look, why don't I drive you over? Then we can go into work together."

Her head snapped up. "No, sweetie, that's okay. You need to be at Surprise! We have more than enough to do—I won't take long."

"If you're sure . . ."

"Absolutely. I'll be in and out."

He crossed the room, leaned down, and planted a kiss on her forehead. "Okay. Then I'll see you this afternoon. I'm expecting some orders anyway."

Elizabeth watched her husband walk out of their bedroom, then heard the front door open and close and the car engine start up, then fade in the distance.

She lowered her head, right about to where her spirits were. She hated lying to Vincent. She'd never done so in all of her thirty years of marriage.

She reached for her purse and pulled out Helen's card. She'd made an appointment for nine A.M. Helen had squeezed her in, hearing the note of panic in Elizabeth's voice.

"Just take it easy," Helen had said. "Everything will be fine. Dr. Richards is one of the best high-risk OB/GYN doctors on the East Coast. You'll be in good hands."

Good hands, Elizabeth thought as she weaved in and out of the morning traffic. *I sure hope so.*

Two hours later, after every test and exam known to man, Elizabeth sat in Dr. Richards's office to await the verdict. She gazed around the small space, its walls plastered with framed photos of bouncing baby boys and girls and beaming parents. She pressed her hand to her stomach and shut her eyes. She could almost see the angelic face of her own baby, hear its happy gurgles, smell its innocence.

"I hope those are tears of joy," Dr. Richards said, surprising Elizabeth with his silent entry.

Elizabeth sniffed and quickly wiped her eyes. She looked up at him. "I'm sorry. I've been doing a lot of that lately."

"Perfectly understandable," he said, pulling a tissue from the box on his desk and handing it to her.

"Thanks."

Dr. Richards flipped open the folder with her name on it. He slid on his glasses and glanced at the pages.

"Fifty-two, hmmm, incredible." He snatched his glasses from the bridge of his nose and stuck them in the top pocket of his lab coat. "Do you have any other children, Mrs. Howell?"

"Yes . . . well, no, not naturally. We . . . I could never conceive, so we adopted."

"I see. Any miscarriages?"

"No."

"Hmmm. And you've never been pregnant?"

"No."

"Amazing. Are you taking any kind of fertility medication?"

"No."

He nodded his head, scribbled some notes on the pages, and snapped the folder shut.

"Mrs. Howell, you're probably as close as they come to a medical miracle." He chuckled lightly and shook his head. "What has happened to you is extremely rare, especially in women of your age who have never had children before. You're a very lucky lady."

Elizabeth beamed.

He flipped the folder open again and put his glasses back on. He made several noises deep in his throat and an assortment of facial expressions. He snapped the folder shut again.

"From what I can see, you're actually in pretty good shape. Your blood pressure is a little high but easily managed with diet and exercise. You're a bit overweight, but not too much, and nothing that can't be worked on. I'll wait for the rest of the tests to come back, but I don't foresee any major obstacles, and from my exam I would say you're about ten weeks along."

"Yes, that's about right," she murmured. Then what the doctor said began to sink into her consciousness. *I don't foresee any major obstacles.* "Are you saying that I'm in good health . . . that the baby is okay?"

He raised his hands as if to clarify. "From what I see so far, things look fine. However, a woman your age and your size—pregnant for the first time—it's not going to be a cakewalk."

"But basically I'm okay?" she asked again, her hopes and excitement building.

Dr. Richards offered her a smile. "Yes, basically. But I'm going to put you on a very strict diet and exercise program. You're going to have to have some genetic testing done as well. And I'll need to see you every two weeks through the first trimester, more if necessary."

He lowered his head and scribbled on his prescription pad. He handed her a sheet and then two more. "Those are for vitamins. Be sure you take them. Speak with the receptionist on your way out and she'll give you the date for your next appointment. Your tests should be back next week. If there are any problems, I'll call. If not, I'll see you in two weeks." He stood, smiling. "Congratulations, Mrs. Howell. You're going to have a baby."

Elizabeth practically floated out of the office, her face glowing with delight.

Helen was in the corridor when Elizabeth emerged. She put her hand on her hip and smiled. "Now, don't you look happy. Must be good news."

Elizabeth clasped Helen's arms. "It's all good," she

said, then hugged Helen as though she never wanted to let her go. "Thank you so much."

"You just take care of yourself and follow the doctor's orders."

"Believe me, I will."

Helen's expression turned serious. "Have you told your husband?"

"No, but I will. Tonight. For sure. I needed to know I was going to be okay. I know Vincent; he would panic and worry. And I didn't need that. At least now I can explain that everything will be fine. We can do this."

"Of course you can."

And then like a cup overflowing, rows of tears streamed down Elizabeth's face.

"Oh, Helen, this is something I prayed for, prayed so hard for. We'd given up and just accepted that we would never have any natural children. Over the years it got easier. I think Vincent may have put it out of his mind. But there was a part of me that was always empty, a part of me that believed I'd failed somehow." She wiped the tears from her eyes and sniffed. "But He answered my prayers."

"Well, Liz, as my grandma always used to say, He may not come when you call Him, but He's always on time!" She slapped her thigh and they laughed.

Elizabeth smiled and laughed with joy all the way to work. Today would be a good day.

Six

"What are you so happy about?" Vincent asked, nuzzling Elizabeth's neck and holding her close as she stepped out of the bathroom. Scented steam followed her.

She didn't answer; she only smiled.

"Hmmm. I love how you smell when you step out of the shower," he murmured into her ear, while his hand sensuously stroked her hip.

Her body shivered with pleasure. She could feel the wetness build between her thighs and the heat that engorged the tiny bud, causing it to beat like a heart. God, she wanted this man—ached for him like an addiction.

"You've been humming and smiling all day. I haven't seen you this happy in a long time." He kissed her neck, then eased down to plant teasing kisses across the crests of her full breasts.

Elizabeth moaned. "You made me happy, Vince," she whispered huskily as her nimble fingers gently caressed the hardening bulge between his thighs.

"Agggh." He sucked in air between his teeth. "Woman . . . don't start nothing and there won't be nothing."

"Oh, I plan to finish what I start," she crooned with all the sultry allure she thought she'd lost twenty pounds and a decade ago.

"Is that right?" He eased his hands beneath her

nearly sheer nightgown and raised it above her hips.
"You might have a bit of trouble with all these clothes
in the way. Let me see if I can help you." He raised
the gown further and lifted it over her head, then
stepped back.

Elizabeth immediately became self-conscious in her
nakedness. She and Vincent hadn't made love with
the light on in longer than she could remember.

"You, why don't you . . . turn the light off?"

Vincent stood there staring at her and shook his
head. "Your body is so beautiful. Exquisite. I think
you're more incredible and more of a woman now
than when I married you." He stepped closer and let
his fingers trace her body. His thumbs grazed her taut
nipples, and he felt her tremble. "You bring me nothing but joy, baby. Nothing but joy."

He lowered his head and gently caught her bottom
lip between his teeth before stroking it with his
tongue.

Elizabeth was certain that her knees were going to
give way. She clung to him, and her heart and spirits
soared. He wanted to look at her, really look. He said
her body was beautiful, exquisite. How desperately
she needed to hear that.

Inch by inch, she felt herself being lured toward the
bed and eased down.

"I know I'm not what I was in my twenties, but I'm
gonna try damned hard to make you holler."

Vincent started at her lips, then her neck, then her
breasts, paying each area its due homage. He lingered
over her belly, taunting the satin-smooth skin with his
mouth. Wickedly he explored the buttery softness of
her inner thighs until they began to tremble beneath
the flicks of his agile tongue. But when his mouth

sought out the core of her sex, gently rotating around the hardened bud with his tongue, finding the G-spot, A-, B-, and C-spots, Liz swore she saw heaven. And the song of praise that climbed up her throat was as sweet as an angels' choir to Vincent's ears.

Shaken, sated, damp from the afterglow of their loving, Elizabeth and Vincent lay nestled in each other's arms, almost as if the feel of the other's heartbeat, flesh against flesh, would assure them that the ecstasy they'd just shared was no illusion.

"Baby . . ." Vincent said.

"Hmmm."

"I don't know about you but as the godfather of soul, James Brown, would say, I feel good! Almost wanna click my heels."

Elizabeth giggled like a schoolgirl. "So do I, baby. So do I."

Vincent tried to get closer, but he couldn't unless he was back inside her again. So that was what he did, moving slowly, with the patience and skill that came only with maturity and experience.

Elizabeth felt him swell within her as he rotated his hips against her, and she cried out when he hit her spot.

If the loving lasted two minutes or two hours, it didn't matter. It was marvelous beyond words.

Vincent's warm breath brushed against the back of her neck. His leg was casually draped across hers. Absently he stroked the lines of her body, nearly lulling her to sleep.

"Guess we're not as old as we thought," Vincent said softly while his fingertips toyed with her nipples.

"Hmmm. Well, we're gonna be not old but dead if we keep this up," she said, laughter underscoring her words.

"But I'd go out with a Kool-Aid smile on my face. That's for sure."

Everything was so perfect, Elizabeth mused. Better than perfect, better than it had ever been between them.

"Vince . . ."

"Hmmm."

She drew in a nervous breath. "I'm . . . pregnant."

"Hmmm. What? Stop playing, Liz."

"I'm not, Vince." She turned so that she could face him. "We're going to have a baby."

He stared at her for what seemed like an eternity, then suddenly jumped up out of the bed as if he'd discovered a snake on the mattress. He crossed the room in long strides, ran his hand through his hair, and then spun toward her. His expression was a mixture of disbelief and joy.

"How? When?"

"About ten weeks ago, according to the doctor."

"They told us we couldn't have any kids. So how did this happen?"

Elizabeth sat straight up in bed. "What are you implying, Vincent?"

"I'm implying that it's mighty hard to believe that you suddenly pop up pregnant after thirty years of marriage. That's what I'm implying."

"I'm just as shocked as you are."

"Are you?"

"What!"

He turned away, grabbed some clothes from the closet, and stomped out. Elizabeth heard the rush of the water in the shower. A few minutes later, Vincent emerged fully dressed.

"I'm going out," he mumbled angrily, heading for the door.

"Out where? Why?"

"Out to think." He didn't even look back at her.

"Vincent—"

"Not now, Liz. Not now." He walked off, shutting the door behind him.

Elizabeth sat still as a stone. The last scenes between them flashed like snapshots in her head. She couldn't believe his reaction, his insinuations. She didn't even want to put words to what he *didn't* say. God, this was not how she had pictured it would be at all. She expected shock, she even expected silence, but to all but accuse her of doing something behind his back to get pregnant hurt her to the core of her soul.

"How could he?" she cried out to the empty room. She covered her face with her hands and wept.

Seven

Vincent drove around for hours, aimlessly, his mind spinning like a top. *A baby. How? After all this time? How could it be?*

He didn't know what he was feeling: confusion, hurt, elation, or apprehension. *A baby.* He shook his head and slowly a smile began to spread across his mouth. *A baby.* He and Liz were going to have their very own baby. *Oh, man. Unbelievable.* They were grandparents, for God's sake.

Liz! Damn. He was so wrapped up in his own head, he didn't even think about her feelings, what was she going through, how scared she must be.

How selfish was that? When he heard the words, words he'd longed to hear since the early days of their marriage, all he could think about was himself and his feelings. He knew how desperately she'd always wanted a child, and instead of being joyous about this miracle, he'd all but accused her of having an affair. *Idiot!* That was just his own male ego kicking in. For years he had believed it was him, that maybe he didn't have what it took and that he'd deprived Liz of motherhood. None of the countless doctors they'd gone to in those early years had any answers. No magic pill or potion. All they could offer was adoption. So that was what they did. Carolyn and Mark, their adopted children, were their joy.

He'd convinced himself over the years that Liz's need to have a child had vanished with the arrival of Carolyn and Mark. He told himself that their presence in their lives had filled the void in her, that her obsession with having a child had evaporated with all of the mothering and care she'd put into raising them. At least, that was what he tried to trick himself into believing. It made it easier for him to accept that *he* may have been the reason they never had children.

To be truthful, he thought, as he turned the car around and headed home, the idea of just the two of them alone had become quite pleasant and very comfortable. But this baby thing would change all of that. *A baby.* He stepped on the gas. He needed to get home to his wife, get down on his knees and beg her to forgive him for being such a fool—and then wait on her hand and foot until the blessed day arrived. He'd earn her forgiveness with deeds and actions, rather than words.

A baby! Hot damn!

When Vincent pulled up in front of his house, the lights in the four-story brownstone were out. The muscles of his stomach tightened, and he could just kick himself for being so insensitive. He wouldn't be surprised if the bedroom door was locked. And he would deserve that for what he'd done. Quietly he closed the door and practically tiptoed up the stairs.

He turned the knob on the bedroom door, and a rush of relief washed over him when he heard the click and it opened.

Nervously he stood in the doorway, the faint light from the hall outlining the sleeping form of his wife.

For a moment he could do no more than stare. This was his wife, the woman he'd loved and been faithful to for thirty years. The woman who made living easier with just a smile. He knew things had not been all they could have been between them. They'd let life get in the way and were usually too tired to find time for each other. Their sex life had suffered from that neglect over the years, but something had happened during the past couple of months to relight the fire between them, that sensual flame that had diminished to flickering embers. He was determined that he wouldn't let the fire die out ever again. He loved his wife, he loved being married. And he was going to prove it to her.

Vincent stepped farther into the room. He watched the steady rise and fall of the light blanket that Liz

had tossed over herself. Suddenly she looked so innocent and helpless. She wasn't the superwoman who
could run his life and hers with her eyes closed. She
seemed mortal somehow now, vulnerable. She was
simply Liz, his wife, his lover, his best friend—the
mother of his child. God, how he loved this woman,
and he'd broken her heart and his in the process.

He sat on the edge of the bed and she stirred. Slowly
she opened her eyes, and he knew in that instant that
he would spend the rest of his life making her happy.

"Baby." He gently brushed her hair away from her
face. "I'm an idiot, a thoughtless idiot. If you can ever
find it in your heart to forgive me, I swear I'll make
it up to you. I love you, Liz. Please believe that. I
guess I got scared—terrified—and I wasn't thinking.
Please forgive me."

Elizabeth reached up and cupped his face with her
hands. "I'm scared too," she whispered. "Scared and
so terrified I can't think straight."

Vincent's eyes caressed her face. "We'll get through
this—together. I know how much you wanted this."
His voice broke and he lowered his head. "I always
thought it was me—that I couldn't give you a child."
He swallowed hard. "That I had failed you as a husband—as a man."

"Vincent, no. You could never fail me. I always
thought it was *me*, that I had failed *you*. Not being
able to have a baby made me feel less of a woman."
She laughed sadly. "Look at us, all these years together, loving each other, living with each other, and
silently carrying around all this guilt and not saying
a word."

"Aw, baby, no more secrets, no more trying to think
we can read each other's minds. Talk, plain talk. No
matter how much it hurts."

Elizabeth nodded. "From this day forward."

He leaned closer and gently kissed her lips, then sat back and looked her over as if seeing her for the very first time. "You know, you are just as fine as the day I met you. Beautiful on the inside and out. I know I don't say it much, but I love you, Liz. Love you more than life itself. And I'm happy about this baby. Blown away would be a better description." He laughed. "Guess we still got it, huh?"

Elizabeth giggled. "Yes, I guess we do."

"A baby," he whispered in awe, and shook his head as he reached out and touched her stomach.

A smile bloomed across Elizabeth's mouth. "Yeah . . . a baby."

Vincent plopped down on the bed spread-eagled. "I'll flip you to see who's going to spoil it the most."

Elizabeth covered his body with hers. "How 'bout I flip you for who's going to walk the floors at night?"

He locked his hand behind her head and pulled her mouth toward his. "How 'bout I flip *you* and we practice a little on how we got in this predicament?"

"Vincent Alexander Howell, you are one crazy man," she cooed as she felt his fingers slowly lifting her gown above her hips.

Eight

After a hearty breakfast, Elizabeth returned to the bedroom to get ready for work.

"What are you doing?" Vincent asked, striding into the room.

Elizabeth turned from the dressing table mirror as she fastened her earrings.

"I'm getting ready for work. What do you think I'm doing?"

"Oh, no, you're not." He shook his head, frowning while he crossed the room to her. "That's out. No more working for you."

Elizabeth sprang up from her chair. "Vincent, don't be ridiculous. Of course I'm going to work."

"Look, I'll put in extra hours if I have to but—"

She stepped up to him, silencing him with a tender kiss. She wrapped her arms around his waist.

"Listen, sweetheart, I'm going to be fine. I'm used to working. I want to work. I'd go out of my natural mind sitting around this house all day with nothing to do except watch Court TV and the soaps." She watched the line between his brows deepen, so she tried another tactic. "Baby, listen, the doctor said I was okay. If he sees some reason why I should stop working, then I swear I will."

He looked at her for a long moment. "All right," he finally conceded. "But I'm driving and that's that." He turned and hurried back downstairs before she had a chance to protest.

Elizabeth tossed her head and roared with laughter. The next seven months were going to be a real trip!

When they arrived at Surprise!, Vincent commanded the staff to gather around.

"Vincent," Elizabeth hissed between her teeth. "Don't you dare."

"It'll be fine," he whispered back. "Listen up, everyone, we have a big event happening in just a few days. I'm going to need everyone to pull their weight and then some. There's no time for slacking off. If there are any conflicts or questions, please let me know immediately. Everybody cool with that?"

Murmurs of agreement and head nodding filled the room. "Tomorrow morning we're going to have a site visit to the Marriott Hotel, where the event is being held. For those of you who have not been there, it's just beyond the courthouses in downtown Brooklyn. I figured we could all meet around eight. That would give us time to check the place out and get back here to set up for lunch. How does that sound?"

"I might have a problem," Jeannette, the senior waitress, said. "My son's day care doesn't open until seven-forty-five. After I catch the bus across town, I would never get there in time."

"We'll work something out," Elizabeth piped in. "Don't worry about it. Maybe you and I can take a run over there later in the day."

"Thanks, Mrs. Howell, that would help a lot."

Elizabeth nodded, but as the questions and comments continued to flow around her she thought about Jeanette's dilemma—a dilemma that would one day be her own. She'd grown accustomed to coming and going as she pleased, sleeping late if she chose, working overtime if the mood hit her. It had been years since she'd had to worry about diapers, day care, sleepless nights, teething, and childhood illnesses. She took a breath. Yes, things were certainly going to be different.

After the staff meeting adjourned, Elizabeth went out front to check on the arriving customers to ensure that all was well and everyone was happy. As she pushed through the swinging doors, a wave of nausea swept through her, and her head seemed to spin in a complete circle. She reached for a table to steady herself just as Vincent caught her around the waist.

He quickly ushered her to an available seat, then darted behind the counter and poured her a glass of water.

"Here, drink this." He held the glass to her lips as she took slow swallows. "Are you okay?" The concern in his eyes and in his voice touched her heart.

She nodded and took a deep breath to clear her head. "Yes, I think so."

"What happened?"

"I just felt kind of dizzy all of a sudden."

Vincent stood. "I'm taking you to the doctor right now."

She looked up at him. "Don't be ridiculous. I'm fine. This is normal."

"Almost falling on your face is normal?"

"Vincent, calm down. I'm okay."

"You didn't look okay a minute ago."

"I'm better. It passed." She took another sip of water, then looked at him. "Thanks for not saying anything."

"As much as I want to shout our miracle from the mountaintops, I figured I could at least wait until we tell the kids. Which we're going to have to do soon."

"I know. I thought we could invite them over for Sunday dinner and tell them then."

Vincent nodded in agreement. "Sounds like a plan. This Sunday?"

"Sure. It will give me a day to prepare after Friday night." She stood. "Speaking of which, we have work to do." She started for the kitchen.

"Just where do you think you're going?"

"Back to work. Where do you think?"

"Oh, no, you're not. I'm not having you pass out in my gumbo."

She laughed. "I have no intention of passing out in your gumbo."

"Nonetheless, you're not going back in that kitchen. End of story. And if you won't let me take you to the doctor, then I'm taking you home. You're going to put your feet up and relax this afternoon. I have everything under control around here."

As much as she hated to admit it, the thought of taking a nap sounded really good all of a sudden. "What are you going to tell the staff? I can't just leave. They'll know something is wrong. I'm always here," she offered weakly, and yawned.

"You let me worry about the staff. You know," he said in a pseudo whisper, "we own this joint and can do anything we damned well please."

He gave her his heart-stopping smile, and between that and the sudden fatigue that had claimed her body, she couldn't resist. "Fine," she conceded, then yawned again. "But I'm taking a cab. There's no need for you to take me home. You have enough to do."

He looked at her suspiciously for a moment. "You promise to go straight home, right? No detours?"

She crossed her heart and grinned. "Promise."

"Okay. I'll call a car service." He started for the phone, then stopped and turned back toward her, pointing a warning finger in her direction. "And don't you dare move. Got it?"

"Yes, sir!" She gave him a mock salute.

She leaned back in her seat. Hmmm, taking a nap in the middle of the day, she thought as she watched her husband dial the car service. A nap might not be such a bad thing after all.

* * *

When Vincent came home that night, earlier than usual, he doted on her hand and foot. Every ten minutes he asked if she needed something, if there was anything he could get for her, did she need her feet or her back rubbed. Quite frankly, he was driving her out of her mind!

"Vincent, you know I love you," she said after his fifteenth inquiry into her needs, "but if you don't quit asking me if I'm okay, I'm going to head straight down to the precinct and get an order of protection!"

Vincent's dark eyes widened in surprise. "I only want to help. You scared me today."

"I know that, sugar. But you're not helping me if every move I make I'm practically tripping over you. Weren't you supposed to go to Kyle's house to watch the basketball game tonight?"

"Yeah, but I can watch it here, with you."

She twisted her lips into a frown, and her right eyebrow rose to a high angle. "Now, you know that me and those Knicks have a real problem."

"Hey, don't down my boys. They're gonna come back."

"Sure. That's what you said last year and the year before that and the one before that. Platform shoes will come back before the Knicks."

He laughed and waved his hand in dismissal. "Traitor."

"I call 'em like I see 'em. Go on," she said, shooing him away. "You deserve a night out. Seriously. You've been working like a fiend while I was away, carrying my load since I've been back, and worrying about me every other minute. Go. Enjoy yourself. I'll be fine. Your friends will be glad to see you, and you know you don't want to watch a Knicks game on this little seventeen-inch TV."

Vincent and four of the neighborhood guys who'd dubbed themselves "the crew" were diehard sports fans. Kyle, the ringleader, as all the wives called him, had installed a theater in his basement for the sole purpose of watching whatever game was in season.

Vincent studied her a minute, and she could almost see the delight light up his eyes.

"If you're sure."

"Trust me, I'm sure. Now go."

He checked his watch. "If I leave now, I can just make it in time for the tip-off."

"Then you should hurry," she said with a sarcastic grin.

Vincent walked over to the hall closet and pulled out his black leather jacket. "You have the number to Kyle's house, and you have my cell phone number."

"Yes, dear," she singsonged.

"You call me if you need anything."

"Yes, dear."

"I mean it, Liz. Don't play with me."

"Yes, dear," she said again, knowing she was getting to him.

"We might stop by Joe's Pub after the game for a couple of beers."

He dug in his back pocket and pulled out his worn brown wallet. He riffled through a few cards and pulled out a crumbled, badly stained business card that had seen better days and handed it to her.

She frowned and plucked it from his hand with the tips of her fingers.

"That's the number to Joe's . . . just in case."

"In case of what?"

"In case of anything. I can be home in five minutes. You have all the numbers, and I can call and check on you—"

Elizabeth sprang up from the couch and whirled on him. "VincentAlexanderHowell!"

He threw his hands up in defeat. Whenever she strung his name together like a runaway train he knew two things: Either she was in the throes of passion or ready to throw him out of the door. He suspected the latter.

"I'm going, I'm going." He kissed her quickly on the forehead. "Now don't forget what I—"

She stretched her arm ramrod straight toward the door. "Go. Now. Immediately. And take your time coming back. 'Bye. Later. See ya."

He chuckled, saluted, and headed out.

Elizabeth expelled a big sigh of relief as she locked the door behind him. "Let the choir say amen."

Now that she had some peace and quiet she was going to make use of her time. She moved from room to room lighting her aromatic candles, put some Luther Vandross on the CD player, and hummed along to "Power of Love." In no time the house was filled with the comforting scent of jasmine and the sultry voice of Luther.

"Perfect," she said aloud. "Alone at last." From the moment Vincent had accepted his impending fatherhood, he'd been on her like white on rice. Although she loved his thoughtfulness, she needed some breathing room, and she intended to take it tonight—at least for the next few hours. By then she'd be fortified for his next assault.

She went into the kitchen and poured herself a glass of sparkling cider, then headed upstairs. A nice, luxurious bubble bath was definitely in order.

But no sooner had she planted her foot on the first step than the doorbell rang. "VincentAlexander-Howell!"

She marched back toward the door and flung it open, ready to snatch him up by his collar and physically return him to Kyle's house.

"Lena . . ."

"Hi."

Elizabeth planted her body in front of the door and her hand on her ample hip. "What can I do for you?"

"I came to apologize in person, since you won't return any of my calls."

She shifted her weight. "Didn't think we had anything to talk about. You said what you thought, and that's that."

"I was wrong, Liz. Terribly wrong." She lowered her head, then looked into her friend's eyes. "I had no right to push my narrow opinions on you. I know how deeply you wanted a child . . . and I guess it was fear that had me talking."

Elizabeth frowned. "Fear? What do you have to be afraid of?"

"I was scared for you, your health, and . . . I know this is going to sound infantile . . . but I was scared for our friendship."

"What?"

Lena nodded. "Yeah, our friendship. Since our kids have been grown, it's been me and you—sisters—hanging out, laughing, and doing what we wanted. I knew that once the baby came all of that would change. And I . . . would go back to being alone again."

"Alone? What about Earl?"

Lena gave a sad laugh. "Earl! Ha. Earl is so busy 'working for our future,' he barely notices me."

"Oh, Lena." She stepped aside, put her arm around her friend, and ushered her inside. "Come in and sit down."

"You never told me," Elizabeth said once they were seated.

Lena shrugged. "Just putting up a good front, girl. Things are not what they once were; that's for sure."

"Have you talked to him?"

"I try, and he nods, and things stay the same." She looked across at her friend. "To be honest, I was and probably always have been a little jealous of you, Liz—you and Vincent."

"You've got to be kidding."

"No, you were always so confident in everything that you did. And Vincent adores you just the way you are. I always figured I had to keep making myself over to get and keep Earl's attention. But nothing really works."

Elizabeth sat back and mulled over her friend's confession. For years she'd wished that she were more like Lena, looked like Lena, had Lena's body and shoulder-length "good hair." And all this time Lena was hoping for all the things that Elizabeth already had and didn't realize—acceptance of who she was, and being loved for it. Her eyes suddenly lit up as a plan began to form in her mind.

"I have just the thing," Elizabeth said in a conspiratorial whisper. "We're going to rock these men back on their heels."

"What is it? I'm game."

Elizabeth leaned forward. "Well . . ."

Nine

The following morning Liz was awakened by the aroma of fresh-baked biscuits, instead of having her husband beside her. Slowly she opened her eyes and peeked at the bedside clock. Six A.M.

"Six A.M.! This man has lost his mind." She pulled herself to a sitting position, reached for her robe at the foot of the bed, and headed for the kitchen.

"Vincent, what in the world are you doing up at this hour?" She surveyed her kitchen and saw a feast laid out for a princess: biscuits, hand-squeezed orange juice, a bowl of fresh fruit, whole-grain wheat toast, and a piping pot of coffee.

She shook her head in amazement and smiled. "What time did you get up to do all of this?"

"About four. I didn't want to wake you. But I figured I'd fix you a wonderful breakfast before I headed out. I wanted to get an early start."

"An early start on what?" She yawned.

"We have to go over to the hotel this morning."

"Oh, my goodness! I'd totally forgotten."

"I know you don't want to hear this, but why don't you relax today? I can give them the grand tour. Come in later if you want."

"Hmmm." She thought about her options and realized that Vincent had unwittingly given her the perfect opportunity to hatch her plan with Lena. "You know what, I think I'll take you up on that."

Vincent beamed as if he'd hit the lottery. "Great. I was hoping you'd say that, so I fixed your lunch too."

Slowly, with her hips swaying, she approached him. She reached out and caressed his cheek. "VincentAlexanderHowell, you are one incredible man, and I am one lucky woman."

He wrapped his arms around her waist. "Finally we agree on something," he whispered against her mouth an instant before covering it with his own.

After Vincent was safely out of the house and breakfast was finished, Elizabeth cleaned up the kitchen, then darted upstairs for a quick shower. In less than a half hour she was dressed and ready to go. She checked the time. She'd give herself five hours, plenty of time to do what she had in mind and get back before Vincent returned.

She retrieved her purse from the closet, checked her wallet, then dialed Lena.

"Today's the day, girlfriend," Elizabeth said into the phone. "I have five hours."

"I'll be there in a heartbeat."

"I'll wait for you out front."

They'd decided on the Kings Plaza shopping mall. Since its renovations, the mall had every store imaginable all under one roof, and they intended to hit as many of them as possible.

Lena maneuvered her Lexus into an available parking space in the garage. She turned to Elizabeth and grinned. "Well, like Custer said to the troops, 'Charge!'"

They gave high fives and headed for the shops. The first stop was Victoria's Secret, where between them they spent well over five hundred dollars on slinky lingerie and nightwear in an assortment of bold colors and styles. Then it was on to Macy's, where they selected designer perfumes and got full-facial makeovers, and of course the new makeup to go along with it. After that they hit two designer boutiques and collected an armload of dresses and pantsuits. The next stop was Bath and Body Works. Elizabeth selected her favorite aromatic candles, bath oils, soaps, and scrubs and convinced Lena to do likewise. They made a pit stop in Bed, Bath and Beyond to stock up on satin sheets before returning to the car to drop off the first load of shopping bags.

"This has got to be the most fun I've had in ages," Elizabeth confessed as she stowed the last bag in the trunk. "I've been so busy taking care of business, worrying about the kids, staying behind Vincent for one thing or the other, I've totally neglected myself. But no more. With a new baby on the way, I plan to be a new Elizabeth Prescott Howell. New and improved."

"I hear ya, sis. And with some of these outfits and my own new attitude, I know I can get my husband back."

"Now, that's the Lena I know." She hugged her friend, then widened her eyes in question. "Ready?"

"Charge!"

They laughed all the way back inside the mall.

"I want to stop by Maternally Yours and see what they have. These outfits are fine for now, but in a few months . . ."

"Tell you what: It's my treat. Whatever you want."

"No, Lena, I couldn't let you do that."

"Of course you can, and you will. Let me do this . . . to say thanks."

"Thanks for what?"

"For being what a real friend is—there in the other one's corner, no matter what stupid things they say and do, and having the heart to forgive. That's rare, Liz."

Elizabeth's eyes filled. "Hey, you've been there for me, too, girl."

"So . . . is it a deal?"

Elizabeth sniffed back tears. "Anything I want?" she asked in a childlike voice.

"Anything."

"In that case . . . charge!"

They slapped five and headed for the store.

More than an hour later, Elizabeth had furnished a maternity wardrobe to rival those of the supermodels.

"Who would have ever thought that maternity outfits came in leather?" Elizabeth said, chuckling all the way back to the car.

"Gurrl, when Vincent sees you in that he might not let you out of the house! And I'd love to be a fly on the wall when you get in that little hot pink number from Victoria's Secret. And if I can't get Earl to turn up the heat in my little see-through number I'm turning in my diva card."

Elizabeth giggled. "I know, I know." She checked her watch. "I hate to cut this spree short, but I need to head back before he gets in from work."

"I hear ya. Have you back in no time." Lena slid in behind the wheel. "This was really fun."

"It sure was," Elizabeth said, adjusting one of the bags on her lap, as the trunk was full, along with the backseat. "We definitely have to do this more often."

"Next time we'll baby shop."

"Oooh, chile . . . did you see some of those adorable little outfits?"

"I know. They sure didn't have clothes like that when our kids were growing up. By the time we're done that baby of yours is gonna be the best-dressed child on the East Coast."

They both laughed at the image and chatted just like old times all the way home.

When Elizabeth put her key in the door and pushed it open, Vincent was on her in a flash.

"Where in the world have you been?"

"I—"

"Don't give me a story, Elizabeth."

She knew she was in trouble now. He never called her Elizabeth unless he was really pissed off.

"I've been calling here since this morning. Do you know I was going out of my mind with worry?

"Honey, I—"

"Don't you dare 'honey' me. You scared me to death. I didn't know what happened. I started calling hospitals," he ranted as he ran his hands across his head and paced in front of her.

"Here's some of your— Oops. Hi, Vince," Lena squeaked when she walked in on the scene.

He turned hard eyes on her. I should have known." He looked at her armload of packages. "Shopping," he said in a male-misunderstanding-the-concept tone.

Elizabeth tried to look innocent.

"Uh, be right back . . . with the rest."

"The rest!" he boomed.

Lena scurried out the door.

Elizabeth stepped up to him. "I'm sorry for worrying you, sweetheart. It was so wrong of me not to call."

"Don't try that cuddling-up stuff with me, Elizabeth. I'm too mad," he said, not sounding very convincing as Elizabeth stroked his back and placed delicate kisses on his lips.

"I wanted to surprise you, baby," she cooed into his ear, pressing her body flush against his.

"By what, giving me a heart attack, woman?"

"I'm sorry, sugah." She ran her finger along the hollow of his ear and felt him shudder. "But I think you're really going to like the things that I bought."

"You do, huh?" he murmured, looking into her eyes with a hunger that was borderline erotic. "What makes you think that?" He cupped her behind and pulled her close.

She smiled wickedly. "I can tell already, Vincent-AlexanderHowell."

"Hmmm. I like the sound of that."

Lena cleared her throat. "Uh, I'll just leave the rest of these here."

"I'll call you tomorrow, girl," Elizabeth said without ever turning around.

"If you can," Lena said with a chuckle. "Take care, you two. Don't hurt each other, now." She closed the door gently behind her.

"So, you want to, say . . . model some of those outfits?" Vincent asked once they were alone.

"It would be my pleasure."

By the time Elizabeth sashayed around the bedroom in the hot-pink halter top and tap pants, Vincent was beside himself with desire.

"Okay, enough, enough. I give up." He jumped up from the bed and grabbed her in his arms. "You're making me crazy, woman," he said deep in his throat.

"That's the whole idea."

"Is that right? Well, I feel like doing something about it. What do you say?"

She pressed her body against his. "Let the games begin."

"Hmmm, sounds like a plan I could go for." He eased her toward the bed and slipped one strap from her shoulder and then the other.

Elizabeth reached for the light.

Vincent grabbed her hand. "No. I want to see you."

"But—"

He pushed the top further down, exposing the crests of her breasts. "Ssssh. Tonight I want to see you, all of you. No darkness to hide behind."

Elizabeth swallowed hard. It was still hard for her to get used to making love with the lights on again. As she'd gotten heavier she convinced herself that Vincent didn't need to see her. She wanted him to remember her as she'd once been. But . . . whatever it took to make her man happy, she was willing to try.

He pushed the pants down over her hips and helped her to step out of them. He eased back. "Take your top off," he commanded, and a shudder of desire ran through her.

She did as she was told and stood, big, bold, and beautiful before him.

His eyes filled with awe and appreciation for her womanly form. "You're gorgeous, Liz. Absolutely gorgeous."

"Do you truly mean that?"

"Without a doubt." He stepped up to her and

kneaded her distended nipples. "Without a doubt," he whispered.

They made slow, deep love that night, finding a renewed joy in each other, reconfirming their love and commitment.

"I know I don't tell you often enough," Vincent murmured in her ear as he moved with consummate skill inside her, "but I think you are the most incredible woman I've ever known." He looked down into her eyes. "You give me joy, baby."

Tears of elation filled her eyes and spilled down her cheeks. She clung to him, her man, her husband, the father of the child she carried within. "I love you, too," she cried out as the first wave of ecstasy roared through her—and she hadn't even had to break out the satin sheets.

Ten

The week flew by with lightning speed, and Friday was upon them. But the staff of Surprise! handled everything with the professionalism that had made them renowned.

The ballroom of the Marriott Hotel was filled with more than two hundred guests dressed in all their finery. Women were in floor-length gowns, jewelry glittering at their throats and on fingers and wrists, and the men were beyond handsome decked out in the latest tuxedos and after-hours suits.

Elizabeth looked around and was suitably impressed. They'd decided on serving drinks only and removing empty plates, opting for a buffet-style dinner, as they were limited in terms of wait staff. The buffet tables on either side of the enormous hall were ten feet in length, with everything from smothered pork chops to baby veal sautéed in Vincent's special sauce. There were six vegetables to choose from, along with potatoes, white and yellow rice, and yams. And the dessert table was a sugar fiend's heaven on earth.

Elizabeth shook her head, amazed at what they had been able to pull off in such a short amount of time.

Vincent slipped up behind her. "How are you holding up, babe?"

"Pretty good." She covered her mouth and yawned.

"Yeah, right. Why don't you sit down for a while? You've been on your feet most of the day."

"I'll be okay. Really."

"When do you go back to the doctor?"

"Tomorrow at eleven."

"Well, I'm going with you. I want to hear what he has to say for myself. Now promise me that if you start feeling funny or tired you'll let me know. We can leave."

"I promise."

"Yeah, you promise. But I know you, Liz; you'll wait until they have to wheel you out of here."

She playfully tapped his arm, then looked over his shoulder. "Oh, my goodness, it's Helen."

He turned. "Helen who?"

She took his arm and maneuvered him around the tables and guests toward Helen. "Remember the woman I told you I met on the plane? She's the nurse at Dr. Richards' office."

"Oh, right."

"Liz," Helen cried in delight. "I didn't know you were a Delta." She wrapped her in a warm embrace.

"I'm not. We're catering the event."

"Then I know everything is going to be fabulous." She turned to Vincent. "You must be Vincent," she said, extending her hand.

"Pleasure to meet you. Liz has said only wonderful things about you."

"She's the wonderful one." Helen turned to the beyond-handsome man on her arm. "This is my husband, Cliff. Cliff, Vincent and Elizabeth Howell."

Cliff extended his hand to Elizabeth and to Vincent. "Glad to meet you both." He looked around. "You all did a great job. Everything looks fabulous."

"Thank you," they said in unison, then laughed.

"Is she taking care of herself, Vincent? I know she wants to be superwoman."

Vincent looked at his wife, feeling fully vindicated. "I try to tell her, but she has a mind of her own."

"Well, you have more than yourself to think about now," Helen admonished, looking at Elizabeth.

"Thank you," Vincent chimed in, and received a nudge in his ribs from his wife.

"Why don't I get us something to drink, Helen, and you ladies can catch up," Cliff said.

"Yes, and maybe you can get her to sit down for a minute while I get back to work," Vincent added.

"I feel like I'm being conspired against," Elizabeth grumbled.

Helen took her arm. "You are." She looked around and spotted an empty table on the far side of the ballroom. "Come, I see a vacancy. Let's grab it."

Once they were seated, Helen launched right into her. "You look tired, Liz. How do you feel?"

"Honestly?"

"Yes, honestly."

"Tired." She laughed lightly.

"Then why are you here?"

"I need to be. I couldn't just leave Vincent to handle all this by himself. It's a partnership."

"I understand that, but from the looks of Vincent, I'd say he could handle anything that comes his way. Who you need to be concerned about is you and that baby. You're not twenty and pregnant for the first time, Liz."

"I know, I know. But it's just that I'm so used to doing, being a part of things."

"And you don't want to take a backseat, right?"

"Right."

"But you owe it to yourself and your baby. Vincent is concerned about you. I could see it in his eyes. It's long past the time that you let someone take care of you for a change. Let him," she said, taking Elizabeth's hands between her own. "Let him shower you with love and attention. Let him treat you like the queen that you are. He wants to, and you deserve it. And so does that baby you're carrying."

Elizabeth looked around at all the glitter and the food, listened to the cacophony of music and voices. She yawned as a sudden wave of fatigue swept through her.

"You know what, Helen, you're absolutely right."

By the time Vincent and Elizabeth pulled up in front of their brownstone, it was nearly midnight. Although there was still plenty to do, Vincent insisted that Jeannette could handle the staff and ensure that everything was taken care of. Elizabeth didn't have the strength or the inclination to resist.

"I'm going to run a bubble bath and soak," Eliza-

beth said over a yawn as she pulled herself up the
stairs.

"Sounds great. I may join you. Why don't I fix us
a couple of cups of cocoa? It will relax you, help you
to sleep." He rubbed her back.

"Sure." She yawned again and continued up the
stairs.

Wearily she stripped out of her clothes and tossed
them on the chaise longue beneath the window. Heading for the bathroom, she turned on the taps full blast
and added her newly purchased vanilla-scented bath
oil.

"Ummm," she sighed as the soft scent slowly filled
the room. She went to sit on the side of the bed until
the tub filled.

By the time Vincent returned with the cocoa, he
found Elizabeth curled up on the bed, fast asleep. He
put down the mugs on the dresser, turned off the bath,
and tiptoed across the room, knowing that if he woke
her, she would swear she wasn't tired. Gingerly he
lifted her tired limbs and tucked her in for the night.
Kissing her tenderly on the lips, he whispered his love
and was surprised when she replied, "I love you, too."

Eleven

"As I told your wife during her first visit, overall she
is in good shape," Dr. Richards said. "Her blood pressure is a bit higher than I would like, and I want her
to keep her weight under control, especially in the

coming months." He pulled open her folder and took out a set of papers. "Our nutritionist went over your file and your test results. The questionnaire that you filled out regarding your eating habits, favorite foods, et cetera, was helpful in developing a plan for you." He handed the documents to Elizabeth. "It's important for your health and the health of the baby that you follow these instructions and the diet plan. We would also like to put you on a moderated exercise program as well. The wellness center is affiliated with the hospital where you will deliver, and the women who go there love it. Many of them continue even after they've had their babies."

"What can I do, Doctor?" Vincent asked.

"Your role in all of this is just as important as your wife's, if not more so. You have to be the keeper of the keys, so to speak, her support system when she wants to cheat a little." He looked Vincent over. "It would probably help a great deal if you participated in the diet and exercise program as well."

"You're kidding."

Dr. Richards chuckled. "I'm very serious." He folded his hands on the desktop and leaned forward. "This is a team effort. Your wife is going to need all of your support. It always helps when the husband takes an active part in the process. And it couldn't hurt you."

"Hey, if it's going to help my babies"—he looked at his wife—"I'm game. Even if I do have to get into some tights in front of a bunch of strange women."

Elizabeth popped him on the thigh.

Vincent chuckled, then cleared his throat. "Uh, Doctor . . . what about . . . sex? I mean, is it okay?"

Elizabeth could feel her face heat with embarrassment. She'd always been pretty closemouthed when it came to her sex life. When her girlfriends would talk about their men, she kept her limited experiences to herself. And never in her natural life had she discussed sex with her doctor. She'd always been slightly self-conscious about her sexuality. She'd been the brunt of "big girl" jokes and myths since her teens. Even in her marriage she'd been somewhat inhibited when it came to expressing her desires and fantasies to her husband. But something had definitely changed in that regard. Those baby hormones were on a rampage. She only hoped that she'd still be craving her husband's loving after her little bundle arrived.

"Sex is one of the best exercises I can recommend," Dr. Richards said, bringing Elizabeth back from her musings. "I wouldn't suggest swinging from chandeliers or anything, but of course, enjoy it as much as you can, as often as you want. It will help in the delivery as well." He looked from one to the other. "Do either of you have any other questions that I can answer?"

"No, I don't think so," Elizabeth replied.

"Great. Then I will see you in two weeks. I want you to begin the diet today. And you can start the exercise program next week." He stood and extended his hand to Vincent. "You're a lucky man," he said.

Vincent turned to his wife. "I know."

Elizabeth read over the "menu" of dos and don'ts on the ride back home. " 'No sugar, no salt, no hot sauces, no spicy food, nothing fried,' " she grumbled. "Everything is going to taste like paper."

Vincent chuckled and patted her thigh. "I know it sounds awful, but are we the baddest chefs in Brooklyn or what? We can make wood taste like filet mignon. We'll just go back to basics, babe: natural herbs for seasoning, sherbet for dessert instead of pies and cakes, fruit for snacks. It will be fine. And who knows, we might just be onto something."

"What do you mean?"

"With so many people being health conscious nowadays, let's just suppose we created the best-tasting healthy-choice menu in Brooklyn. We'd have folks coming from all over."

"You might just have something," Elizabeth said, her mind already planning and cooking.

"We could test it out on ourselves, come up with some great recipes, and see if we can take them to the public."

"I like it. Matter of fact, I love it! It would give me something to do at home, and still keep my hand in the business while I take care of the baby." She turned and kissed him on the cheek. "We can make this work."

"Of course we can. Listen, if we can make babies in our fifties, we can do damn near anything."

Elizabeth broke out laughing. "You got that right."

Elizabeth looked at the clock. She'd spoken to Carolyn earlier that morning and her daughter had said she would be over after church service. Mark had promised to be there as well. That gave her all of one hour to make sure that everything was perfect.

"Are you going to stop fussing?" Vincent asked, coming up behind her to halt her pacing.

"I'm not fussing," she said, rearranging for the fifth time the centerpiece on the dining room table. "I just want to make sure that everything is—"

"Perfect. I know. Babe, these aren't new clients you're trying to impress. They're our children. They've eaten at our table since they were toddlers." He gave her a warm hug, then whispered, "It's going to be okay."

Elizabeth heaved a sigh. "You can't know that for sure. There's no telling how they will respond to the news." She started to feel weepy again. "Look at how it hit you and Lena. Imagine our two grown children being told that their fifty-two-year-old mother is pregnant." Her eyes filled and a fat tear plopped on her cheek. "Damn, most kids don't even believe that their parents have sex."

Vincent laughed and brushed the tear away with the pad of his thumb. "Well, we certainly can nix that myth."

She popped him on his arm with the dishtowel and laughed. "You need to stop."

"Not until I'm too old and decrepit to do anything else but stare."

"VincentAlexanderHowell, don't you dare embarrass me and talk like that in front of our children."

He threw his hands up in mock defeat. "Whatever you say, babe. The secret is safe with me."

"The secret may be, but I'm not," she muttered good-naturedly.

"I heard that."

She sniffed back the last of what seemed to be unending tears these days. "Well, in the meantime, try to make yourself useful and check the chicken."

He gave her a mock salute. "Yes, ma'am."

She just shook her head and laughed. She really did love that man. She really did.

*   *   *

Carolyn was the first to arrive, with Desiree, her three-year-old daughter, in tow. Carolyn and Mark's natural parents had been tragically killed in a car accident, leaving the two siblings orphans. What was most miraculous was that both of the children were in the car at the time of the accident, strapped into their car seats, and had survived without a scratch.

By the time the adoption agency notified Elizabeth and Vincent that they had a child for them, the couple had pretty much given up hope of getting a child through adoption and had resigned themselves to being childless.

They'd adopted Carolyn when she was three, and she'd been a delight from the moment she'd become a part of their lives. Bureaucratic red tape kept them from getting her two-year-old brother, Mark, for nearly a year. He'd given them nothing but joy since his arrival. They were children that any parent would be proud of.

Carolyn had her teaching degree and taught second grade in one of the most economically disadvantaged areas in Brooklyn. Simply because you didn't have money and lived in the "wrong neighborhood" didn't mean that your children didn't have the right to the best education possible, she professed. She'd married Steven, her high school sweetheart, five years earlier, and she took her role as wife and mother as seriously as she took her profession. She was definitely the more focused of the siblings. From the time she could talk, Carolyn always had a plan.

Mark was "still looking," he always said, and thoroughly enjoyed all the rights and privileges of being a bachelor. His stunning good looks, warm personality, and position as promotions manager at an entertainment company in Manhattan lent themselves perfectly to the array of women who seemed bent on making him settle down.

"Grandma!" Desiree squealed as she darted through the door and into Elizabeth's waiting arms.

"How's my girl?"

"I'm three," she said proudly.

Elizabeth put on a serious face. "Yes, I know. A very important age, too."

"Not two, Grandma, three!"

"I stand corrected. Three."

"Hey, little bit, come give Grandpa some sugar," Vincent said, stepping into the living room.

Desiree wiggled away from Elizabeth and dashed to her grandfather.

"She never slows down," Carolyn said with a smile, stepping in and shutting the door behind her.

"You were just like her at that age, full of fire, energy, and questions."

"Good thing I'm still young and healthy or she would wear me out. She has more energy than my entire second-grade class put together."

Elizabeth got a nervous twinge.

"You look great, Mom," Carolyn said, kissing her cheek. " 'Glowing' might be a better word. Almost how pregnant women look."

Elizabeth nearly choked.

"That spa must really be something." She took her mother's arm as they walked farther into the house. "You'll have to tell me all about it. Steven sends his apologies. He's out of town on business, and won't be back until Friday."

"Here's my girl," Vincent said, opening his arms to Carolyn. She walked up to him, pressing her head against his chest.

"Hi, Daddy," she whispered.

Elizabeth watched the exchange. Carolyn and Vincent shared a special bond that Elizabeth was never able to compete with. From the time she was an infant, it was Vincent whom Carolyn craved when she was hurt, tired, sick, or scared. When she bloomed into a beautiful teen, it was from Vincent that she sought advice.

But Elizabeth didn't mind. Mark was to her what Vincent was to Carolyn. It was always to her that he came running whenever he was in trouble or needed someone to talk to. He was no mama's boy by any means, but the closeness that they shared was truly a blessing.

"And how late is my dashing brother going to be?" she asked, stepping out of her father's arms.

"He promised he'd be here by three," Elizabeth said.

"That means four," Carolyn teased. "Is he bringing one of his many girlfriends?"

"Not today," Vincent said. "Today is family day."

Carolyn looked from one parent to the other. "Is something wrong? Is one of you sick?"

"Nothing like that, baby girl," Vincent said, putting his arm around her shoulder. "Just family, that's all."

The bell rang, breaking the momentary tension.

"It's Uncle Mark. Uncle Mark," Desiree shouted, racing for the door.

"Slow down, little girl, and ask who it is first," her mother admonished.

Desiree put on her best grown-up voice. "Who is it?"

"Santa Claus," came the voice from the other side of the door.

Desiree's eyes widened and her mouth made a perfect O. "It's Uncle!" She pulled the door open and leaped up into his arms. "You tried to twick me, Uncle Mark."

"Can't fool you," he said, chuckling. "Hey, folks." He walked in with Desiree in his arms. He kissed his mother's cheek and gave his dad a one-armed hug. "Everyone is looking good—even you Carol-o."

"Very funny. You wish you could look this good."

"If I did, I'd have to change my whole agenda." He laughed and hugged his sister.

She hugged him back, grinning all the while. "I don't know why we put up with you."

" 'Cause ya love me." He put Desiree down, then looked at his mother and then his father, his tone and expression becoming serious. "So . . . why the big powwow?"

Twelve

"A baby!" Carolyn wailed. "Mom, you're kidding." She dropped her fork onto her dessert plate.

Mark looked at his father and grinned. "Go, Dad."

"You can't be serious. Have you been to the doctor?"

"Yes, and yes," Elizabeth said, not at all pleased with her daughter's condescending tone.

"So when's the big day?" Mark chimed in, totally fascinated with the idea.

"Dad, you can't be thinking about going through with this," Carolyn said, turning her angst on her father.

"And why not?" he asked, taking Elizabeth's hand. "This is something we've always wanted."

"Oh, I see," she said, standing and tossing her napkin on the plate. "So me and Mark were just something to keep you occupied in the meantime, substitutes for the real thing."

"Carolyn!" Vincent boomed. "You know better than that."

"Do I?" Her voice cracked. "You said it yourself. This is something you've always wanted." She swallowed. "Well, I hope you both are very happy. I think it's disgusting. What are you going to tell your friends? What am I going to tell my friends—Desiree? Has either of you thought about that?" she demanded, her voice rising by an octave. "You'll be in your seventies by the time it gets into high school."

"Carolyn, get a grip," Mark said. "You act like something is being done to you."

"Just shut up, Mark. What do you know about anything? If you had your way you'd be chasing skirts for the rest of your life. You don't have a responsible bone in your body." She scowled at her parents. "And neither do the two of you!"

With that she stormed out of the dining room, snatched up Desiree, who was sprawled in front of the television, and walked out of the house without so much as a backward glance.

"Go after her, Vincent," Elizabeth implored.

He started to get up.

"Leave her be, Dad, Mom. Give her a chance to cool off and see how silly and selfish she's being. You know how stubborn Carolyn can be. You won't be able to get through to her now, anyway."

Vincent heaved a sigh. "Maybe you're right. Damn, I figured it would come as a shock and that there might be some resistance, but not an outright assault on me and your mother. Doubting our love for the two of you?"

"Hey, I know better. She's just shaken, that's all. Carolyn, for as much as she loves you and seems like she has it together, is really insecure. She always has been."

"Carolyn?" Vincent and Elizabeth said in unison.

Mark nodded. "Ever since we were little she was always terrified that one day you would get tired of us and send us back, or that you would leave and we'd be alone. Why do you think she tries so hard at everything? She wants to be perfect, no flaws and no kinks. She doesn't ever want you two or anyone else to think that she's less than worthy of being loved and cared about."

Elizabeth pressed her hand to her chest. "Oh, my poor baby," she said, looking out toward the closed door. "I never knew, never suspected."

"We've never done anything to make either of you think that you weren't wanted or loved or that anyone or anything could take your places," Vincent said.

"I know that, but Carolyn just hasn't put that piece of the puzzle together yet."

"So what do we do?" Elizabeth asked her son.

"Give her some time. A couple of days. I'll talk to her. As much as she pretends that she thinks I'm a lamebrain, she listens to me."

"I'd appreciate that, son," Vincent said, clapping Mark on the shoulder. "We have enough things to worry about without having our family turn on each other."

"I, for one, think it's great. Congrats! I'm gonna be a brother again." He nodded and looked from one parent to the other. "Hey, I didn't think you two . . . you know . . . were still . . . kicking it like that." He grinned.

Elizabeth sprang up from her seat, her body flushed hot with embarrassment. "MarkAllenHowell!"

Both of the men roared with laughter, while Elizabeth stomped her way upstairs, chuckling quietly to herself. "Men!"

"She had a fit, Lena," Elizabeth confessed to her friend the next day as they lunched on tuna salad at an outdoor café. "I swear, I never expected her to act that way." She explained what Mark had said about Carolyn's insecurities.

"Oh, Liz, I'm so sorry. I know how hard that must have been for you. And to think that I was so self-absorbed I did the same thing. I can never apologize enough. Mark is okay with it?"

"Mark thinks it's wonderful. 'Didn't know you still had it in you, Dad,'" she said, mocking her son's deep voice.

Lena laughed, just imagining her godson's expression.

"Mark said I should give her some time to cool off and think about it. But the mother in me wants to run over to her house and just hug her, tell her it's going to be all right."

"Then maybe that's what you should do, hon."

Elizabeth looked at Lena for confirmation. "You really think I should?"

"Yes. Carolyn needs reassurance now more than ever. Even though she's all grown-up and seemingly independent, deep down inside is a little girl who's afraid of losing her mother again."

*   *   *

Elizabeth wasn't too particular about being in this part of Brooklyn. But she'd go up against Satan himself if she had to in order to get Carolyn to understand. She was parked out in front of the school where Carolyn worked. She only hoped she was at the right exit and hadn't missed her.

She checked her watch. Three o'clock. She'd give her a half hour. Elizabeth sat back to wait . . . and wait. Forty-five minutes later, Carolyn still had not appeared, and Elizabeth felt totally ridiculous for having done something like this without planning ahead. Suppose Carolyn hadn't even come to work today, or took another exit out of the building?

She took a resigned breath and started the engine. Just as she was pulling off, she caught a glance of the classic Carolyn Alyse Howell Taylor walk—"I am here; I am proud,"—the one that used to have men stopping in their cars to get a second look. Elizabeth always wondered if Carolyn realized how beautiful she was inside and out. She had delicate features, finely sculpted brows that only nature could accomplish, a copper complexion that never needed makeup, and a mane of wavy jet-black hair to die for. For the most part, she and Mark could pass for twins, except that Mark towered over his five-foot, five-inch sister by nearly a foot.

Elizabeth opened the car door just as Carolyn approached the street, ready to cross.

"Carolyn . . ."

She turned with a start. "Mom?" She frowned in confusion; then concern masked her face. She hurried over to where her mother stood. "Is everything all right? Did something happen to Dad?"

"Everything is fine. Your dad is at work. But I want to talk to you."

Carolyn's expression clouded. Her shoulders stiffened. "About what?"

"I think you know. And whatever it's going to be between us, Carolyn, it's not going to be out on a street corner."

Carolyn tugged in a breath. "I guess we could go by my house. I have until six to pick up Desi."

"Fine. I'll follow you in my car."

"Can I get you anything?" Carolyn asked the instant they stepped across the threshold of her two-story home in the Canarsie section of Brooklyn.

"Some cold water would be fine." She followed her into the kitchen and took a seat at the table that she and Vincent had purchased as one of their many wedding gifts. "The place looks nice," she offered, looking around.

"Thanks." She poured a tall glass of water from the pitcher and handed it to her mother without really looking at her, then began puttering around the kitchen in search of something to do.

"But you always kept everything nice and neat from the time you were big enough to put your own toys away." She laughed lightly. "I remember one day you decided you were going to 'clean up behind Mark.' And you took all of his action figures, his trucks, and his favorite stuffed animal and dumped them in the washing machine. Mind you, you didn't have a clue as to how to turn it on, so you just poured detergent on them and walked away. When Mark got up from his nap he was hysterical because he couldn't find any of his toys."

Carolyn laughed at the memory. "The room was clean, though." She shook her head. "That boy was always a slob. Still is."

"He's gotten better. At least, the last time I visited him at his apartment he didn't have week-old dishes stashed under his bed."

"Ma, don't tell me you still look under his bed."

Elizabeth was undone. "Of course I do. I've been looking under you-all's beds for as long as I can remember. Give me half a minute; I might just check under you and Steven's bed."

Carolyn reared back, put her hands on her hips in pure Elizabeth style, and said, "Not on my watch, ElizabethJeanHowell!"

Elizabeth slapped her palm on the table and roared with laughter. "You got me down, girl. You sure do."

Still laughing, Carolyn took a seat opposite her mother. "I had good training," she said, seriousness returning to her voice.

Elizabeth reached out and covered her hand. "Sweetheart, don't you know that you were my very first gift, my blessing? You filled a space in my heart that was empty when you came into my life. That can't be duplicated or replaced. I loved you from the moment I looked into your sparkling eyes and you called me Mama. I swore to your father the day we took you home that I would do everything in my power to make sure that you knew you were loved, wanted, and safe. Always, Carolyn."

Carolyn lowered her head and let the tears fall. "It was always easier for Mark, somehow. I've always had this fear that this was all going to go away, that it wouldn't last, that I would disappoint you somehow and you wouldn't love me anymore."

"Oh, Carolyn. That could never happen."

She drew in a breath. "I know being adopted is great." She looked into her mother's eyes. "But I'll never really be *yours*. One of my greatest fears growing up was that one day you would have a baby of your own and you would love it better than me and Mark. When it didn't happen, a part of me was relieved."

"And now?" Elizabeth gently coaxed.

"And now . . . I'm happy for you. When I came home Sunday night and tucked Desi into bed, I realized how precious she was and how incredible I felt carrying her, giving her life. That's a power that is too awesome to miss. And you did, for so many years. Until now." She squeezed her mother's hands. "If you can be half the mom you've been to me and Mark, that kid is going to be one lucky soul." She smiled.

"Why didn't you come to me and tell me all this?"

Carolyn pursed her lips. "Didn't Mark tell you how stubborn I am?" she teased. "I'm sure that was the first thing out of his big mouth the minute I left. Plus I had to let him badger me first. He enjoys that almost as much as I hate it."

Elizabeth grinned. "You two sure have each other pegged."

"So . . . do you know what you're going to have? I hope it's a girl. I'm tired of my younger brother! And what about clothes; you know they have to be fly. And you, too, Mom."

"Girl, Lena and I went to Kings Plaza and racked up! Your father almost passed out when I started modeling some of my outfits. Had the man sweating." She slapped her palm on the table.

"Ma! You are too fresh for your age."

"And you know what, baby girl? I'm really starting to like it."

Thirteen

Now that the news was out in the world, Elizabeth embraced her impending motherhood with the same fervor she did in every other aspect of her life. She kept each and every doctor's appointment and found new and interesting ways to prepare appetizing meals. But what she really enjoyed was her blooming belly and the life that started kicking inside. After the first trimester the waves of nausea and dizziness had passed, and she really got into her exercise classes on Wednesdays and Fridays, where Vincent joined her religiously. And truth be told, between the diet and exercise she felt better than she had since she was in her teens.

Her skin glowed, she felt invigorated, and her once-short hair grew like wild. She'd actually lost weight and knew she looked good in her array of form-flattering outfits—a fact that Vincent constantly reminded her of, although he took great pleasure in seeing her out of them.

When she reached her seventh month, she took a leave from work to devote her time to honing the new healthy-choice recipes that she and Vincent had discussed months earlier, and actually enjoyed being the center of his world, being treated like a queen.

"Are you still going to be this sweet to me when the baby comes?" she asked him one night as they lay in bed together.

He gently massaged her feet, a treat she'd come to

look forward to each night. "Well, if he or she is as good-looking as you are, you might have some competition," he teased.

She feigned hurt. "I can see myself cast aside for a younger woman already."

"It might be a boy," he said.

"Would it matter?"

He looked into her eyes. "Not one bit. As long as it's healthy and I have you by my side, nothing else matters, Liz."

"You're the best," she whispered, as he caressed her swollen belly.

"I want to be the best man I can be for you. Always. Whatever that takes." He took a breath. "This whole experience has changed me. Made me look at life differently, with more reverence."

"Me, too," she admitted. "I can't say enough thanks to the Man above for finally giving us this chance."

"He knew when the time was right. It brought us closer when we really needed it."

She sighed in contentment as his fingers gently massaged her breasts. "That it did," she agreed.

"How are the recipes coming?" he asked, then took a nipple into his mouth.

"Oooh . . . great. I have six that I want to add to the menu at Surprise!," she said a bit breathlessly.

"Tell me all about them," he urged as he continued to taunt her with his mouth.

"Two meat dishes, vegetables . . . oooh . . . a wonderful soup and a dessert."

"When do you want to try them out?" He stroked her hip and lifted her gown.

"I should be ready . . . real, real soon. I want to try one more thing with the veggies."

"Can I get a taste first?" He slid down between her thighs. "You've been so secretive about it." He stroked her with his tongue.

She moaned as her body shuddered. "That's part of the fun. I want you to be surprised, too. See your reaction with everyone else's."

"Now, that's not fair," he complained, easing up alongside of her and lifting her leg over his waist. "I don't keep anything from you," he murmured, finding her moist and ready. "Nothing at all . . ."

"VincentAlexanderHowell!"

His name bouncing off the walls of his bedroom was music to his ears.

"Well, Mrs. Howell, everything looks fine," Dr. Richards said after his examination. "The baby is growing well; your blood pressure is excellent. Your weight is good. I'd say in about three weeks you're going to be holding a very healthy baby in your arms."

Elizabeth smiled with delight. "I can't wait. This is just so incredible. Sometimes when I look at myself I still can't believe it."

"How is your husband making out with the diet and exercise?"

"He actually loves it. He's been wonderful."

"Good, good. Now, you have all of my contact information in the event labor comes sooner than expected. You have to realize that it could be any day now. So I advise you not to take any long trips."

"I understand."

"You're all registered at the hospital, so that won't be a problem."

She nodded.

"If there are no changes, I'll see you next week. If so, I'll see you in the delivery room." He chuckled.

Elizabeth smiled and stood with a bit of effort. "Thanks, Doctor."

After much badgering by Vincent, she'd finally agreed to try out her recipes at the restaurant. She promised she'd stop by after her doctor appointment to see how things were going. But when she arrived she was stunned to find the place locked up tight. It was only six o'clock.

She shook her head in confusion, then concern. What could have happened? She tried the door again. Locked. She looked up and down the street trying to spot Vincent's car. Nothing.

Digging into her purse she pulled out the keys and opened the door. The instant she stepped inside she knew something was wrong. But before she could get her bearings, balloons started floating up from beneath the tables, followed by her staff, Lena, Helen, her children, and her customers, who all popped out from various hiding places, singing "She's Having a Baby."

"Surprise!" Vincent sang, wheeling out the most gorgeous cake she'd ever seen.

Elizabeth covered her face with her hands and wept. Vincent put his arm around her and ushered her to her place of honor, right in the center of the room. Then the presents appeared, everything imaginable, from cases of infant Pampers and bottle warmers, to clothes, a stroller, a portable crib, teething rings, and even a child's computer!

"This is all so wonderful," Elizabeth murmured in awe, looking around at all the people who loved her.

"You deserve it and more," Carolyn said, kneeling down beside her.

"The rest of the things are at the house," Mark said. "We ran out of room."

"You've got to be kidding. When did you all do this?"

"It wasn't easy," Lena piped in. "Helen helped out. She gave us all of the times you had your doctor appointments, so we'd know exactly when you would be out of the house."

"And out of our hair," Vincent said.

Everyone laughed.

"Now, if you all would give the mother of my children some breathing room, we can all eat. We have a special unveiling tonight: Lizzie's De-lites."

On cue, Jeannette pushed out the buffet table that was laden with all of Elizabeth's healthy-choice recipes. The aroma was truly tantalizing.

A round of oohs and aahs filled the room.

Elizabeth stood and walked into her husband's waiting arms. "VincentAlexanderHowell," she whispered.

"Surprise, baby."

"Thank you," she murmured against his mouth.

"No, thank you."

"We'll need a moving van to get all of the gifts home," Elizabeth said as she prepared for bed. "What an incredible day. I can't believe I didn't catch on long before now."

"It took some doing; that's for sure," Vincent said as he rubbed lotion on her stomach. "Your new recipes were a hit. Everyone loved them."

"I know," she said, delight lighting her eyes. "I have some other ideas I want to— Auggg . . ."

Her entire body tensed.

"Baby, what's wrong?"

"I don't feel so . . . good." She inhaled deeply.

"What is it?"

"I think . . ." She looked down as a puddle of water filled the sheets. "We need to get to the hospital."

Vincent jumped up as if he'd been hit with a stun gun. "Hospital! Oh, man." He turned around in a complete circle.

Elizabeth had to laugh. "Vince, calm down. Just call Dr. Richards and tell him my water broke and we're on our way."

"Right, right. Okay. Dr. Richards. Right." He picked up the phone, dropped it, picked it back up, and dropped it again before he could get his hands to cooperate.

"I'd better get dressed," Elizabeth said, realizing she was in a short nightie while trying to contain her delight. "We have a baby coming."

Her labor lasted all of four hours, and Vincent was with her every step of the way, breathing, coaching, and wiping the sweat from her brow.

"I think it's time to go into the delivery room," Dr. Richards said after a brief exam. "Are you ready to bring your baby into the world, Mrs. Howell?"

"I've been ready for thirty years," she said with a calm that surprised her.

"Then let's go."

Fourteen

Elizabeth stared down at the bundle in her arms, awash with a joy that she could not explain.

Vincent leaned over the bed and slipped his finger inside the tiny balled fist. Tears filled his eyes. "You did it, baby."

"We did it together."

"She's perfect," he murmured.

"All eight pounds, six ounces of her."

"A big, beautiful baby girl, just like her mama," he said, and tenderly kissed his wife.

"I want to name her Joy, 'cause that's what she's brought us."

"That she did, sweetheart."

"And I'm going to teach you everything I know, little one," Elizabeth whispered, kissing the tip of her daughter's nose. "From hairstyles to cooking to keeping your man happy. And most of all, being proud of who you are, no matter what shape that takes."

"Can we come in?" Carolyn asked, peeking her head in the door.

Vincent straightened up, the look of a proud papa on his face. "Come on in and visit with your little sister."

Carolyn stepped in with Steven and Desiree, followed by Mark, Lena, and Helen. They all gathered around to look at the little miracle, knowing that she was destined to change all of their lives.

"Meet your new auntie," Steven said to his daughter, lifting her up to take a peek.

"She's a little auntie," Desiree announced.

Everyone roared with laughter.

Epilogue

One year later

Elizabeth dropped her suitcase on the living room floor and dashed upstairs. She'd been gone for two weeks and it felt like forever. She would have never gone back to Arizona if Vincent hadn't insisted that she could use some time off, and that he could handle Joy by himself for two weeks. She had to admit that she felt wonderful. She was in the best shape of her life, having dropped from a size eighteen to a fourteen, and she was looking good.

She pushed open the bedroom door and found Vincent sprawled out across the bed, sound asleep, with Joy cradled in his arms, her eyes wide open as if she were awaiting her mother's return.

Elizabeth tiptoed to the bed and eased Joy out of her father's arms, nuzzling the sweet-smelling body against her.

"Hi, sweetheart. Mommy missed you. Did you miss me?" she cooed to her daughter.

"Mama." Joy wiggled in her mother's arms and reached for her earrings.

"I bet you gave your daddy a fit," she said, laughing.

She gazed down at her sleeping husband, realizing just how much she'd missed him, and she couldn't wait for nightfall to slip between the sheets with her sexy husband.

That is, if they could get Joy to sleep through the night!

BARE ESSENTIALS

Y Brenda Jackson

Bare Essentials is dedicated to every woman who knows that SEXY doesn't have a dress size.

Stay Blessed,
Brenda Jackson

He hath made everything beautiful in his time . . .
—Ecclesiastes 3:11

One

Dominique Kincaid tried, without very much success, not to stare at the man who had just jogged past her. This was the second time she had seen him this week, and she wondered how much more her heart could take seeing such an impressive display of masculine perfection. He was dressed in running shorts and a sleeveless jersey, his muscles flexing with every foot he placed in front of him, running at a pace he evidently found to his liking.

He had smiled a greeting when he had passed, and she waited until he had gotten a safe distance ahead before allowing her gaze to drink in the sight of him. And she had greedily gotten her fill. His butt alone gave him very good marks, because it definitely rated a high five.

Since she had lived in the neighborhood for three years and had been frequenting the park for just that long, she figured he must be someone new to the area. Inhaling a deep breath, she thought the last thing the women who came to Simon Park at six in the morning needed was another fine specimen of a man stimulating their heart rate. At the age of twenty-nine she'd thought she had seen it all, but evidently she hadn't.

Dominique glanced longingly ahead, disappointed that he was no longer in sight and wondering if she would see him again the next time she came to the park to jog. That very question was on her mind as she slowed her pace, rounded the corner, and headed back toward home.

"And you have absolutely no idea who he is?"

Dominique smiled as she met her sister Michelle's stare. Although separated in age by only two years, they were actually many more years apart in their way of thinking. Michelle was a rebel—always had been and always would be. While growing up she had enjoyed making waves and resisting authority, which had caused their parents many sleepless nights. Owning a travel agency was the best thing, since she would never be able to tolerate having a boss.

Unlike Michelle, who took defying orders to heart, for Dominique following rules and regulations had been easy. She had been unresisting and manageable, and she strongly believed in and respected authority. Deciding on a career in law had been a natural for her.

"No, I have no idea who he is, since we haven't been introduced. I've only seen him while out jogging."

"Well, he can't stay in motion forever. He has to come to a standstill at some point in time. And when he does, make sure you're there and find out everything there is about him."

"Are you suggesting that I follow him around the park waiting for this grand opportunity?"

Michelle grinned. "Yes, that's exactly what I'm suggesting, if that's what it's going to take. Heaven forbid, but if I got up at six in the morning to go running around some park, I would definitely use my time running behind something worth my while. And from what you've told me, this brother is to die for. However, instead of dying I'd much rather you go after a piece of him instead. But you'll never come close to even claiming a pinch if you don't make the first move."

Dominique raised her eyes to the ceiling. Sometimes it was hard to believe that Michelle was the youngest. "And why do I have to make the first move?"

"Because some men don't know what's good for them, and it's up to us to show them."

"So I'm supposed to come on to him?"

"Yes, I've done it several times."

Dominique didn't find that hard to believe. Michelle went after whatever it was she wanted, and consequences be damned. "I have to really think about using that approach, Michelle. Whereas it might work for you, it may not work for me."

"Suit yourself. I'm just trying to help by giving you sound, workable advice. This is the first time you've mentioned anything about a man since Kenneth, and that gives me hope. I can't wait to tell the folks and Gramma and Grampa. They'll be so thrilled."

Dominique wished Michelle had not brought up her former fiancé. The last thing she wanted to remember was the man who had confessed—a mere week before their wedding—that another woman was having his baby. Although that had been over a year ago, the pain of his betrayal was still there. And she knew her parents, grandparents, and Michelle had been concerned that she hadn't dated since then. "Don't get everyone's hopes up too high, Michelle. I merely mentioned that I happened to notice this guy."

"Yeah, but at least you're back to noticing, and that's good. I suggest the next time you see him that you do more than just notice him. If I were you I would do something, just about anything, to get his attention and to let him know you're interested. Some men are too dense to figure these things out on their own. You have to give them a clue."

Dominique shook her head, smiling. "I'll think about it."

"Do more than think, Dom. This guy might be one you don't want to get away."

Dominique inhaled and decided not to tell Michelle she had thought the very same thing about Kenneth when she had first met him, and boy had she been wrong. So wrong that she wondered if she would ever get it right again. She glanced at her watch. "Lunch was great, but I have to go. I'm due back in court at one."

"Then by all means scat, *Your Honor*. It definitely wouldn't do to have your humble servants waiting."

"So you saw her again today?"

Jordan Pescott folded his arms across his broad chest and smiled up at the man standing at his desk looking down at him. Royce Parker was someone he had known since his high school days, and was the person instrumental in his relocating to Florida. Tired of doing little more than shuffling papers and handling minuscule cases the senior attorneys hadn't wanted to be bothered with, Jordan had taken Royce up on his offer to leave New York and move to Orlando and work for the prestigious law firm of Smith, Hammond, and Rowe. So far he had not regretted the move, and after this past week it seemed things were definitely beginning to look even better.

"Yes, I saw her again."

"And?"

"And she was jogging, which didn't provide me with any time to hold a conversation."

"But you did check out her hand?"

Jordan's smile widened. He decided not to tell Royce that her hand hadn't been the only thing he had checked out. "Yes, I checked out her hand, and there wasn't an engagement ring or a wedding band."

"Good. So now it sounds like the coast is clear and it's okay to move ahead and plan your next strategy. When do you go jogging again?"

Jordan shook his head. Royce made it sound like meeting the woman was some sort of military maneuver. "I jog every day, but I think she only jogs twice a week."

"Umm, so chances are you probably won't be seeing her any more this week."

"Probably not."

"But if she's noticed you like you've noticed her, then there's a possibility she might add an additional day to her jogging schedule."

"Yes, there is that possibility." Jordan grinned at the way Royce thought he had everything figured out. And chances were he had. The same age as he was, thirty-five, Royce was a die-hard bachelor and an expert on dating, since he had been doing the dating thing a lot longer than Jordan had. Jordan had gotten out of commission—for four years, to be exact—when he had fallen in love with and married another attorney. It might have worked with some folks, but for him marrying another person with the same demanding profession had been a huge mistake, one he would never make again. He didn't see another marriage in his future, but was interested in meeting someone and entering a solid and exclusive relationship. The risk of AIDS made the thought of having multiple bed partners a bit scary, to say the least. Besides, he didn't need several bed partners to keep him happy. All he needed was one really good one. And he had a feeling that the woman who'd caught his eye while he was out jogging was capable of setting his body on fire. He was burning up just thinking about her.

"Well, I'd better get back to work. I have a date with Kincaid this week, and I'd best be prepared."

"Who?"

"Judge Kincaid. She's the sistah I was telling you about who found favor in the governor's eyes, and was appointed to fill the spot of an older judge who retired early due to health reasons."

"Oh, yeah." Jordan remembered how Royce had sung the woman's praises by saying she was tough but fair. She also expected a lawyer to have his stuff together when he entered her courtroom. And, according to Royce, the way she had handled the more experienced good-old-boy attorneys as well as the up and coming, wanna-make-a-name-for-themselves hotshots had earned most people's respect. Being the youngest woman on the bench—and an African-American too—definitely had not been easy for her. But now, three years and a landslide victory later, she was doing the job the taxpayers had elected her to do.

"You'll have your day in court with her, Prescott," Royce was saying. "If I'm not mistaken, she's the one who'll be hearing the Masons' case."

When Royce walked off, Jordan was left alone with his thoughts. They moved away from Judge Kincaid and immediately went back to the woman who'd been jogging. Would she modify her schedule and show up another day this week, as Royce thought she would? The thought of seeing her again sent a surge of adrenaline flowing through him. He shook his head. Over the years he had seen his share of beautiful women, and it surprised him that any woman could have that much of an effect on him. Especially a woman whose name he didn't even know. But the one thing he did know was that there was something about her that had given him a voracious sexual appetite. The very thought appalled him, because until now he'd never known such a need could exist. He tried convincing himself that the reason he was in such a state was because he hadn't slept with a woman in over six months. But a certain part of him throbbed against such a notion. He knew exactly what had him in such a bad way, and could not place the blame on anything or anyone else.

He looked forward to going jogging in the morning, and hoped that his sexy mystery lady didn't disappoint him.

Two

Dominique leaned over to tighten the strings on her shoes, appalled that she was actually taking Michelle's advice and running behind a man. She checked her watch. She was a little early, but already other joggers had begun arriving. She tried not to look nervous or anxious as she began doing her stretches.

What if he doesn't show up today? What if . . . Before that second thought could formulate in her mind she caught a movement out of the corner of her eye, and when she turned, she saw him. He seemed to suddenly emerge out of the shadows of the predawn morning. At one point she could see him clearly; then, when sensual heat drifted over her, her vision became somewhat hazy. Even from a distance of thirty or more feet he was eliciting an extreme reaction from her.

She thought it would be best to try to ignore him for now. Not feeling capable of standing on wobbly legs any longer, she eased her body down to the thick, grassy surface to do some additional stretches. Sitting on her bottom and bending her body to touch her toes, she tried dismissing him from her mind and found she couldn't. Especially when he was the main reason she had gotten out of bed to be here at this hour. She loved coming to the park and did so often, walking around, feeding the pigeons, sitting on a bench to appreciate the things around her and to stay connected with the normal side of life that she didn't often find in her courtroom. Tuesday and Thursday mornings were her normal days to job. She had never jogged on a Friday morning before. Instead she much preferred taking advantage of getting a little extra sleep before going to work. She made it a point never to schedule her first case on Fridays before ten.

As she continued to do her stretches, her body got tense instead of relaxed. She inhaled and then exhaled but didn't have a chance against the pulsating heat throbbing fast and furious through every part of her body.

*   *   *

Jordan sucked in a deep rush of mid-September air when primal recognition made his breath catch. Royce had been right: It seemed his mystery lady had modified her schedule. He had spent a good majority of the night and that morning thinking about her and hoping that he would see her today. And now she was here and wasn't in motion, which gave him a chance to make his move before she got on her feet and took off jogging.

He walked toward her with determination, hoping she would be receptive to getting to know him the way he wanted to get to know her. Although his movement toward her had been quiet, when he got within five feet of her she turned and looked his way. Their gazes caught, locked, and held with an incredible force. He could have gotten hit by a bolt of lightning and doubted he would have felt it. The only thing he felt was desire, so deep within his body it was almost painful. He halted for an earthshaking moment and shook his head to clear it. And when he started walking again, closing the remaining distance separating them, his breath froze in his lungs and every muscle in his body tightened. When he discovered he could breathe again, he took in a deep gulp of air and came to a stop in front of her. Her scent—sweet, warm, and sensual— surrounded him in the early morning air, causing his nostrils to flare in deep male regard.

The only thing he could do was look down at her as he struggled to collect himself. That effort took him a few seconds, and then he said, "Hello. I'm Jordan."

He watched as she sat up from leaning back on her arms to slowly extend her hand to him. "Hello, Jordan. I'm Dominique."

*   *   *

Dominique inhaled slowly as she allowed her eyes to drink in the sight of the man standing over her, up close and personal. Just as she'd thought the very first time she had seen him, he was an impressive display of masculine perfection. Besides jogging, whatever else the brother was doing in the way of physical fitness was well worth the effort, because he was definitely built.

Her gaze moved slowly down his broad shoulders and solid chest toward a very flat abdomen. The athletic shirt he wore stopped just above his navel, and she felt goose bumps forming on her arms when her attention was drawn to the thin line of dark, curly hair that ran from his navel and dipped low into his running shorts. Then there were his muscular thighs that looked hard as steel, and legs that appeared solid and strong. She suddenly felt her head spinning in female admiration as she darted her eyes back to his face.

His features were just as pleasing. His hair was cut short and his skin was the color of rich, dark chocolate. In her line of work she was used to seeing handsome men come into her courtroom, mostly attorneys dressed in tailored, name-brand, fashionable clothes. But she had never seen a man so striking and so incredibly sexy. The bones of his face were lean and angular, and he had dark eyes fringed with sinfully long lashes. His nose was a perfect size, and his mouth had a shape that made her think of doing something like kissing it.

The roar of a truck's engine reminded Dominique where they were. It also made her take note of the fact that he was still holding her hand.

A blatantly male smile curled that kissable mouth of his and quickly spread to his eyes. "Are you ready to get up?"

She came close to telling him no, because she wanted to check out his body some more. Instead she nodded and he gently tugged on her hand and pulled her to her feet, bringing her body close to his. She suddenly found his chest pressed against her breasts and his thighs touching hers.

Dominique stared at him, blinking slowly as she tried to get her bearings when he released her hand and took a step back. She could tell from the expression on his face that their closeness had affected him as much as it had her.

"Do you want to jog with me?"

The words had been spoken in the sexiest voice she had ever heard. There was an incredible huskiness to it. "I've see the pace at which you jog," she answered softly, still looking at him. "I doubt I'll be able to keep up."

"Then I'll adjust my stride to match yours."

She nodded and they began jogging, but to Dominique her legs weren't working right. They felt heavy, weak, still in shock. She forced herself to move at her normal pace and noticed that Jordan had slowed his movements to keep up with her. There was no conversation between them, just deep breaths. By the time they made the one-mile mark, Dominique noticed her movements were less awkward and her pace had steadily increased. But he was still letting her set their rate of speed, and she wondered if she ran hard and fast enough if she would be able to rid herself of the heated desire still flowing through her body.

A half hour had passed, and Dominique knew it was time to slow down and do her cool-downs. She had switched from brisk walking to jogging only recently, and she didn't want to overdo it. Besides, her body could take only so much trauma in one day, and being so close to Jordan had definitely been a major impact.

When she slowed her pace to a stop, so did Jordan. Bending over, she rested her hands on her knees and began taking deep, slow breaths—for more reasons than the obvious one. Out of the corner of her eye she saw Jordan bending as well, breathing in and out in a way that made his biceps bulge and his muscles flex. Although he didn't appear nearly as exhausted as she did, he did look hot and sweaty in a very sexy way. She couldn't help wondering if that was how he looked after making vigorous love to a woman.

She inhaled sharply. She shouldn't be having such thoughts about this man whom she really didn't know. Although he had introduced himself, he was still a virtual stranger. For all she knew he could be a mass murderer, a rapist, or a serial killer. She quickly glanced around, thankful the park was full and numerous people were about. But still, over the years she had heard enough court cases that involved rape in which the victim had had no idea of the trouble she'd been headed for until it had been too late.

She straightened her body and looked over at him. He had also straightened his body and was staring at her. The intensity in his eyes was heated. Her heart rate accelerated when it felt as if he were actually touching her with his gaze. Nothing like this had ever happened to her before, and she found herself taking a step back. "I have to go."

"Now?" he asked, taking the towel that was wrapped around his neck and tucking it into the waistband of his shorts.

"Yes."

"Can I see you again?"

Dominique wanted to see him again, but her cautious nature kicked in. She had to be sure of him, especially after what had just transpired. Until she knew more about him and felt comfortable with him, he certainly wouldn't be coming to dinner. "Yes, I'll be back to jog again Tuesday."

"Damn," was the only word Jordan could think of saying as he leaned against the oak tree and watched as Dominique sprinted away as fast as she could. Thanks to his coming on so strong, he had pretty much-botched things up. The way she had looked at him had let him know she wasn't used to guys getting turned on just by looking at her. Hell, he usually didn't get this turned on just by looking at a woman either. But the sexual chemistry between them was too strong, too explosive, and too volatile. Even now he felt the stirrings of desire so deep he would have to keep the towel around his waist until he got home.

Rubbing his neck, Jordan tried to relieve his body of some of the tension he felt. He couldn't get Dominique out of his mind. Her body was just the way he liked—full-size and stacked. Some men preferred slender, petite women but he had a thing for a voluptuous woman who had an abundance of everything in all the right places. There was just something about a woman with enough breasts to hold in his hands and enough hips and thighs to cushion a good hard ride. The last thing he wanted to be concerned with when he mounted a woman was breaking something because she didn't have enough meat on her bones. To some men thin was in, but in his book thick was definitely it. And he thought that she had the best shaped behind he had ever seen. It was thick, tight and pretty damn tempting. Even the large T-shirt she had pulled down over well-toned childbearing hips hadn't been able to hide that from his view. And her legs were definitely a gorgeous looking pair.

He smiled thinking that he was beginning to appreciate his move to Florida after all. As he began walking away from the park and back toward the condos where he lived, he hoped Dominique would keep her word and show up on Tuesday. Then he would let her know he was an okay guy, a law-abiding citizen with a pretty good job who even went to church most Sundays.

He didn't want to think about the possibility that he had scared her off for good and wouldn't be seeing her again. He knew she lived somewhere in the neighborhood and if he had to, he would start asking around and knocking on doors. There was no way he would let her get away.

As he crossed the street it suddenly dawned on him that he didn't even know her last name.

Three

Michelle Kincaid's expression was one of disbelief. "What do you mean, you're not going back to the park on Tuesday?"

Dominique turned away from the sink, where she had been busy washing a head of lettuce, to meet her sister's astonished features. "I've decided not to let anything develop between me and that guy. It's for the best."

It had been a hard decision to make, but she couldn't see the point in starting something that likely wouldn't go anywhere. At least anywhere she was ready to go. She needed to enter into a relationship that started off slow and easy. There had been too much sexual chemistry, too much spontaneous combustion, and too much plain old lust flowing between her and Jordan that morning. After she had gotten home and had thought about it, she had decided the last thing she needed was to be that overwhelmed by any man. It had been bad enough how she had felt about Kenneth and the way he had ended up hurting her. Even if Jordan turned out to be a nice guy, she still wasn't ready to indulge in any type of relationship with a man.

"Dom, you can't be serious. Do you know the ratio of men to women? When you find one as good-looking as you claim this man is, you don't jog away."

Dominique raised her brow. "I don't see you knocking yourself out trying to find a man."

"Only because I have issues."

"What issues?"

"I have an extreme domineering complex, which is something I have to work on. I hate being told what to do, especially by a man."

Michelle sounded so sincere Dominique couldn't help but grin. And the sad thing about it was that what she'd said was true. "Okay, you do have issues," she agreed. She had seen Michelle in action before and pitied any man who had fallen under her spell. Most men automatically flocked to Michelle because of her gorgeous looks and perfect, petite figure. She was one of those women males couldn't help but drool over. Yet she hadn't found a man willing to put up with her domineering ways.

"Enough about me, Dom. You're the one everyone is worried about."

"Well, they shouldn't be. I'm fine. I have plenty of cases to keep me busy, and—"

"But you don't have a man. Of the two of us, you're the one who always wanted to get married and have a family. I don't want you to let what Kenneth did turn you against all men and make you not want to take another chance at love."

Dominique hadn't turned against all men in general, but there was a man she planned to avoid in particular. And he was the only one who had piqued her interest since Kenneth. After calling off her wedding, she had gotten a number of offers from interested males wanting to give her their shoulders to cry on and their beds to make love in to help her forget her troubles.

"I will give love another chance one day, but not now."

"So you're letting Mr. Hunk slip through your fingers?"

"Yes, that's about it."

Michelle shook her head. "I hope you don't live to regret that, Dom."

Dominique turned back around to the sink. She hoped she didn't live to regret it either.

"I take it your lady didn't show up this morning."

Without commenting on Royce's statement, Jordan pushed himself away from his desk and leaned back in his chair. He felt frustrated, disappointed, and madder than hell. "No, she didn't show," he finally answered.

"I can tell you're pissed about it."

"Yeah, I'm pissed. But I'm more pissed off with myself than with her."

Royce raised a dark brow. "Why?"

"I'm to blame for her not showing up. I came on too strong Friday and scared her off."

Royce took the chair across from Jordan's desk. "So what's your next move?"

"Wait it out. I doubt she'll avoid coming to the park forever. And when I do see her again, I'm going to handle things differently." Even while saying the words, Jordan wondered just how he would downplay his attraction to Dominique if he did see her again, when just thinking about her made him hard.

"Well, I've got just the thing to take your mind off your troubles for a while."

"What?"

"The Fairchild case starts tomorrow. Why don't you drop by the courthouse as an observer? It's time you see Judge Kincaid in action so you'll know how to handle her whenever your turn comes. It will be a good idea, especially now."

Jordan's forehead bunched in confusion. "Why especially now?"

"Because yesterday during jury selections she was in rare form, and according to Mack, who was in her courtroom this morning, she's still acting strange."

"Strange in what way?"

"Hard. She's not giving any slack. There used to be a soft side to her, but yesterday she all but chewed me up and spit me out."

Jordan chuckled. Royce always had a way with women, and he found it amusing that any woman, even a judge, hadn't fallen under his spell. "I thought you said she was tough but fair."

"She is. I guess she's entitled to PMS days like other women, but she wasn't this bad even after her fiancé dogged her out."

"Dogged her out in what way?"

"According to the newspapers, he told her a week before the wedding that another woman was having his baby."

"Ouch."

"Yeah, man, can you imagine?"

Actually, Jordan couldn't imagine it. He had a problem with any man who mistreated a woman and he considered what Judge Kincaid's fiancé had done mistreatment of the worst kind because it involved a violation of trust. And to think it had gotten printed in the papers for everyone to read. How humiliating that must have been for her. "Like you said, maybe it's a PMS thing."

"Man, I hope so. Another day like yesterday and I'm liable to develop a drinking problem."

Jordan's smile widened. Although he had a full caseload, he decided to stop by the courtroom tomorrow and check out the proceedings for just a little while. As Royce said, it would probably take his mind off his troubles for a while.

She was having a bad day, Dominique thought as she glanced around her courtroom and saw all the bored faces. Milton Harper, an attorney who should have retired a century ago, was rambling on and on, citing precedent that was no longer good case law. But because he'd been somewhat of a legend in his day, none of the opposing counsel dared to object.

After enduring what she felt was more than enough, Dominique had no other choice but to be the one to

object. She then gave Harper, as well as the other
attorneys, a look that dared them to question her
authority.

Less than an hour later she was back in her chambers with a splitting headache that wouldn't go away.
Her next case was a high-profile one, and since it was
the first day, the courtroom would be crowded. No
doubt news reporters would be plastered from wall
to wall.

"Here's something for your headache."

Dominique looked up into the concerned face of
her secretary. Ruth Fowler, at seventy, was old enough
to be her grandmother and should have retired five
years ago. But since the woman never married and
didn't have any family, she had spent her last fifty
years at this particular courthouse as a dedicated secretary. And she was a good one. Besides being a secretary, she occasionally acted on Dominique's behalf as
a guard dog, protecting Dominique's privacy against
attorneys and city officials who didn't have anything
better to do with their time than to want to talk poli-
tics. Ruth had also been instrumental in keeping the
news reporters at bay when word had gotten out about
her aborted wedding last year. Dominique thought the
world of Ruth and didn't know what she would do
without her.

"I'll be fine, Ruth, once I eat something."

"You've ordered in?"

"No, Michelle is bringing me something."

Ruth nodded. "I guess like everyone else she'll be
at the circus today."

Dominique couldn't help but smile. That was exactly what the proceedings today would be like—a circus. Danah Fairchild had been charged with the

murder of her husband, billionaire Lee Fairchild. Mrs. Fairchild's attorneys claimed that she was innocent of the charges. Today both the prosecution and the defense would be presenting opening arguments.

"Yes, she'll be there," Dominique finally answered. "I expect we'll be tired up with this case for several months."

Ruth nodded. "This may not be a good time to tell you, but you got a call this morning."

Dominique raised a brow. "A call from who?"

"Kenneth Reynolds."

Dominique didn't say anything for the longest while; then she said quietly, "I wonder why he's calling me."

"Probably because he's heard that you're still pining over him."

"I don't know why he would believe that."

"I do. You haven't dated anyone since the two of you split. So quite naturally, with that big ego of his, he figures that he's the reason. He probably also figures that you've forgiven him for his sin and will take him back."

"Not while there's still breath in my body."

Ruth chuckled. "That's what I figured, but I didn't think I should be the one to tell him that."

Dominique inhaled deeply. If the truth were known, the only man she was pining over was Jordan. She had been thinking about him constantly, and although she felt she'd made the right decision by not showing up yesterday morning at the park, she'd discovered that a part of her wasn't completely happy about it.

"You should have a special man in your life, Dominique."

Dominique raised a brow. "You're beginning to sound like Michelle, Ruth."

"Constance is worried about you, too."

Dominique shook her head. Her grandmother and Ruth had become bosom buddies since Ruth became Dominique's secretary three year ago. "Gramma worries about everyone, Ruth. Last night she called me concerned that the president was giving a press conference on the front lawn of the White House and wasn't wearing a jacket. Since it was in the fifties in D.C., she thought he was all but asking for pneumonia."

"This isn't funny, Dominique."

"What isn't? The president catching pneumonia or everyone thinking I need a man?"

"We don't think you *need* a man; we just think you should start dating again."

"And I will, sooner or later."

Ruth frowned. "We're hoping it will be sooner rather than later. Constance and I would like some little ones to spoil while we still can."

Dominique couldn't help but grin as she shook her head. "Yes, ma'am, I'll keep that in mind."

Four

The first thing Jordan noticed when he entered the courtroom was that the place was packed. It seemed everyone wanted to be present at what some labeled the trial of the year.

An atmosphere of anticipation hung in the air. There was also an ambience of doubt, Jordan thought. Royce and the other members of the firm's defense team were going to have a hard time convincing the jury of Danah Fairchild's innocence when the media had already painted her as the manipulating, greedy, and conniving wife.

Taking one of the few available seats in the back, Jordan settled into a comfortable position. He planned to remain only long enough to hear Royce present his opening arguments.

Moments later, the bailiff's strong voice started the proceedings. "All rise. The Honorable D. Kincaid's court is now in session. . . ."

Jordan, like everyone else in the courtroom, stood and focused his attention toward the front when the judge entered. He blinked when recognition hit—right below the gut—and his breath got lodged deep in his throat.

He blinked again, thinking he must be seeing things, but when the judge took her place behind the bench he knew he was seeing clearly. The Honorable D. Kincaid was Dominique. Even wearing a black robe and with her hair twisted into a knot on top of her head, he recognized her.

"Everyone may be seated."

As the bailiff instructed, he took his seat and watched spellbound as Judge Kincaid began speaking with all the authority she possessed, holding everyone's rapt attention.

Everyone's but his.

His entire body was tinged with awareness as his mind drifted to the first time he had seen her jogging. He continued to stare, mesmerized, unable to pull his gaze away. He then remembered the morning they had jogged together in companionable silence for three solid miles, and how he had wanted to ask her out but hadn't gotten the chance before she'd taken off. His hands curled into fists and he wondered what fast fix he could use to keep his body under control when it was getting hard already. He shifted positions in the seat, not wanting to make his predicament obvious to those around him. Placing his briefcase in his lap seemed to be a pretty good solution.

Settling back in his seat, he wondered what her reaction would be when she saw him. Would she immediately recognize him as he had recognized her? Her attention was on the occupants at the defense and prosecution tables, as well as on those individuals sitting in the jury box. He couldn't wait for the moment when he could capture her gaze with his.

He didn't have to wait long. Wayne Martin, a member of the prosecution, stood to address the jurors in opening remarks. It was then that Judge Kincaid allowed her gaze to scan the scope of her courtroom.

Jordan slowly inhaled a deep breath the moment their gazes met. Her eyes glittered in surprise. Then it happened. Across the span of the courtroom he felt the connection, an electrifying sexual charge. It galvanized a solid link between them with a force that nearly took his breath away.

He knew that he wasn't alone in this dilemma when he noticed a shudder touch Dominique that was so lightning fast, if he hadn't been watching her so intently he would have missed it.

When Royce stood to present the opening argument for the defense, Jordan shifted the briefcase in his lap, feeling his body getting harder. He couldn't help but wonder what Her Honor was thinking at this very moment.

*   *   *

Dominique released a shuddering breath and forced her gaze to move on, away from Jordan. But that didn't stop a feeling of unrestrained warmth from flooding her insides. She mentally shook herself and returned her attention to the attorney who was speaking to the jurors, and not the man sitting in the audience. But still, she couldn't help but search her mind for answers. Was he a member of the press? A curious spectator? A family member of the accused or the victim?

She forced her attention back to the proceedings. A while later, opening arguments for both sides had been completed and the first witness was being called and sworn in.

Moments later Dominique found herself looking back in the audience at Jordan. He was still staring at her. She wondered if perhaps his being here was no coincidence. Had he intentionally sought her out?

"I object, Your Honor!"

Dominique's attention was drawn back to the front of the courtroom. The defense attorney had stood, not agreeing with something the prosecutor had asked the witness. She racked her brain, wondering just what the defense attorney was objecting to, and felt annoyed for letting Jordan be a distraction. Everyone in the courtroom was looking at her, waiting for her to respond. Since Wayne Martin was known for using underhanded tactics at times, she decided to play it safe and asked, "On what grounds, Counselor?"

"The prosecution is arguing facts not entered into evidence, Your Honor."

She nodded, then said, "Objection sustained."

Martin looked agitated. The defense attorney, Royce Parker, looked downright relieved. Dominique felt frustrated. She didn't need to be distracted and decided to keep her mind on what was going on in her courtroom and not on the man making her entire body feel heated. And from the way he was looking at her, she had a feeling he wasn't going anywhere anytime soon.

She shuddered and drew in a deep breath. That was not a comforting thought.

After banging her gavel Dominique said, "Court is adjourned until nine-thirty in the morning." She stood and exited the courtroom, quickly heading for her chambers. Just as she had assumed he would, Jordan had remained through the entire court session. It had been close to impossible to ignore him. And whenever she did happen to glance his way, he was always staring at her. Had her complexion been lighter than nut brown, it would have been obvious to everyone that she had literally been in a heated flush throughout the entire proceedings.

Holding her head down as she walked, she wondered what in the world she was going to do. She made a sound of agitated disgust when she reached the area where her chambers were located. What on earth would she do if he decided to show up in her courtroom again tomorrow?

"How did things go today?"

Dominique didn't look up as she responded to Ruth, "Not so good," and kept walking in deep thought toward the door to her chambers.

"Judge Kincaid, please wait up!"

Dominique's head lifted in surprise and she quickly whirled around, trying to ignore the way her heart was pounding fast and furious in her chest.

"What are you doing here, Jordan?" Dominique asked softly as her eyes lit on his face.

Jordan's brow lifted at the not-so-simple question that was asked in a somewhat shaky voice. It was all he could do to keep from reaching out and touching her when he came to a full stop in front of her. Since she had come directly from the courtroom, she hadn't taken the time to take her robe off. An image of how she had looked that last morning he had seen her filled his mind. She'd been hot, sweaty, and delectable, as well as sexy as hell. Even now, with a robe covering her, she still was. It didn't take much to dredge up the basic primal appetite he seemed to have around her. Which was the main reason he was holding his briefcase in front of him.

"Jordan?"

The lips that said his name looked soft and sweet, and he couldn't help but wonder how they would feel pressed against his.

"You didn't show up yesterday morning, Dominique."

Very slowly Dominique forced her gaze away from his, and then she noticed Ruth sitting at her desk watching them intently. She groaned softly. Her entire family would definitely hear about this, starting with her grandmother. Swallowing hard, she returned her gaze to Jordan.

"I would rather that we talked privately in my chambers."

Jordan nodded. "Yeah, that's not a bad idea."

Dominique's head tilted as she looked up at him. She then wondered whether inviting him into her chambers had been a smart move on her part. They would be alone and she barely knew him. All she knew about him was that his name was Jordan, he liked to jog, and he got turned on easily, since she was definitely not the type of woman to cause any man to come down with an immediate case of lust. That was Michelle's forte.

She inwardly sighed. Now that she had suggested that they talk privately in her chambers, she couldn't back out. Instead of saying anything she turned and began walking the last few feet to her door, knowing Jordan was following. She heard him take the time to speak to Ruth.

"Do you want me to hold your calls, Your Honor?"

With a sigh Dominique turned around, slightly annoyed with Ruth. She could read her like a book. "No, don't hold my calls, and when Michelle arrives please send her in."

"I'm sure you'll want me to announce her first," Ruth said in an amused voice, as though she were sharing some joke with herself.

"That won't be necessary."

"You're sure?"

"Positive."

"All right," Ruth said, sounding as if she wasn't convinced that would be a good idea.

Dominique narrowed her gaze at Ruth. What did she expect her and Jordan to do behind closed doors? Get naked? She opened her mouth to say something, but snapped it shut when she realized it would be useless to say anything. Jordan was a man, and according to her family, she needed one.

She was so drawn into those thoughts that she didn't notice that Jordan was reaching around her until he opened the door. He had leaned in close and she breathed in his scent. The manly warmth of it was stimulating. She looked up at him and cleared her throat. "Thanks."

"Don't mention it."

As soon as Dominique walked into her chambers she immediately felt the walls closing in around her. And when she heard Jordan pull the door shut behind them, she suddenly felt heat rush through her body. She whirled around, determined to get this over with. "The reason I didn't come to the park yesterday morning was because I thought it was best that I didn't."

"Why? Because there's a raw, primal sexuality that flows between us? Are you going to deny feeling it?"

Dominique nodded her head. She would deny it because she had to. "I'm not the type of woman to incite uncontrollable passion in a man."

"I've got some pretty *hard* evidence that indicates otherwise," he said, frowning. His eyes bored into hers.

Dominique tensed when he took a step toward her. She automatically took a step backward and then blurted out the question that had been on her mind since seeing him in the courtroom. "What is your interest in Danah Fairchild?"

He eyed her consideringly for a moment before responding. "I don't have one."

Dominique raised an arched brow. "Then why were you in my courtroom?" She narrowed her eyes. "Are you a reporter?"

He raised his eyebrows at the sting he heard in her voice. He then remembered what Royce had told him about how the newspapers had printed news of her aborted wedding. Evidently news reporters were not her favorite people. "No, I'm not a reporter. I'm an attorney."

"An attorney?"

"Yes, for Smith, Hammond, and Rowe." He saw the look on her face and quickly lifted a hand, cutting off the words he knew she was about to say. I'm not involved with the Fairchild case in any way, so being here with you in your chambers is not unethical, and there is no conflict of interest. No harm's been done."

As far as Dominique was concerned his last statement was somewhat debatable, especially when every time she looked at him her body temperature rose. It wouldn't be long before she blew a fuse. There was no doubt in her mind that she was definitely in harm's way, and she intended to remove herself from that situation. But first she needed to know a few things.

"When did you move into the area?"

"A couple of months ago."

"From where?"

"New York."

"You were born and raised there?"

"No. I attended Morehouse in Atlanta, then moved to New York to attend Columbia University Law School. I'm originally from London."

She raised a brow. "England?"

He chuckled. "No, London, Ohio. It's a small town not far from Columbus."

"Oh." She then asked, "I assume you aren't married?"

"No, I'm divorced."

She let her breath out on a sigh, not knowing why she was glad to hear he was single when she had no plans to get involved with him.

"So are you going jogging in the morning?" he asked her.

"No."

"I'm sorry if you think I came on too strong but I

can't help that everything about you turns me on, Dominique.

Dominique tried not to let his words get to her but found they were getting to her anyway. She wasn't a size ten like Michelle, but was comfortable with her full size-fourteen figure. It was one she was proud of and worked hard to keep toned. His dark eyes looked fiercely serious and his strong mouth looked as if it were capable of devouring her. She had to agree with what he said about there being raw, primal sexuality between them. And it had to be a once-in-a-lifetime feeling; she was quite certain of that. What other explanation could there be?

"Will you be at the park in the morning?"

His voice was so quiet and calm, he could have been asking her for the time of day. He took another step toward her, and every nerve in her body went on alert.

"Say you'll be there, Dominique."

She shuddered, drawing in a deep breath. No one, absolutely no one, said her name like he did. He had the kind of voice that could sink into every pore of her body and turn her bones to mush. Before she could say anything, his hand reached out and cupped her under her chin, lifting her face to his. She was aware of everything about him, his size, his strength, and his scent. It was all-male, robust, and earthy rolled up into one.

His look was intense when he said, "I know we don't really know each other, but don't, please don't be afraid of me. I will not hurt you." Then his look turned intimate. "There is this thing between us, Dominique. And it has been there from the first. I felt it then and I feel it now. And I believe that you do, too. Admit it."

She swallowed, refusing to admit anything. "I don't want to become involved with you or anyone."

"That's not the vibe I picked up from you that morning we ran together."

She could just imagine what vibe he had picked up that morning. She had deliberately gone to the park hoping to see him. She had definitely been a woman on the prowl.

"My actions that morning went against my better judgment and were a mistake."

"No," he said gently. "It wasn't a mistake. But there was something I didn't get the chance to do before you ran off."

"What?"

"This."

Before she could take her next breath, he leaned down and touched his lips to hers. It was a kiss that robbed her of her senses. He took things slowly, teasing her mouth to interact with his, and it wasn't a lost effort. It was a good thing his arms had moved to her waist to support her, or she would have fallen to her knees the moment his tongue entered her mouth and began mating sensuously with hers. She closed her eyes, and whatever strength she had left literally drained from her body, but he held on to her tightly as he tasted her and she tasted him. She had often wondered about his taste since meeting him, and now she knew, and doubted she would ever forget it.

No kiss, Dominique thought, had ever made her feel this dazed, this crazed. Red-hot passion ignited the flames of desire blazing through her. Every stroke of his tongue against hers worked incredible magic.

Then he took the kiss from slow to deep, and she returned it in a way she had never done with another man, and that included Kenneth. He captured her tongue with his and held it as he sucked on it, making her heart pound and deliriously drenching every part of her with such extreme pleasure that she actually heard herself whimper and moan.

Somewhere in the back of her mind, she picked up on the fact that his hands were fumbling with her hair knotted on top of her head. Then she felt her hair fall to her shoulders and his fingers raking through the curls. Moments later those same hands moved boldly down her body to her bottom, bringing her snugly against his erection, letting her feel the long, hard length of it pressed against her belly. The feel of him sharpened every sense she had, and little by little she became disoriented by it all. Even with clothes on they seemed to be a perfect fit. She didn't want to think how they would feel together with their clothes off.

But she did think about it. And the thought made her feel bold and reckless. She knew she would regret her actions later, but at this very minute the only thing that seemed important was that he was a man and she was a woman. She tightened her arms around his neck and pressed herself closer as an incredible case of hot lust consumed her.

"Harrumph!"

The clearing of someone's throat shattered the moment. Jordan and Dominique broke off their kiss, panting, barely able to breathe air into their lungs. She blinked twice to get everything, including her mind, back in focus.

Michelle was standing by the door with her arms crossed over her chest and a smirky grin on her face. Dominique stiffened as she watched her sister's gaze skim over them. She was still wearing her black robe, although it was bunched up and twisted. And her hair was no longer in a neat knot on top of her head.

A part of Dominique wanted to hide from her sister's close scrutiny. But Jordan's arms were still around her waist, holding her tight against him, and after feeling his hard erection still pressing against her, she understood why.

She had a feeling that Michelle understood as well. The grin she wore got smirkier. Then she said, "Hmmm, I must say, Dominique, it's about time you decided to let your hair down."

Five

Dominique inwardly groaned. The last thing she needed was Michelle being a smart-mouth, and from the amused expression on her sister's face, she was being entertained at her and Jordan's expense.

"Michelle," she said, glaring at her sister. "Don't you believe in knocking?"

Michelle shrugged, not bothered by Dominique's apparent anger. "Sure I do. However, according to Ruth, you said I didn't have to be announced, so I assumed that meant I could just walk in. Had I known you and this gorgeous hunk were engaging in such important business, I would definitely have knocked first." Her smile widened. "But I'll be more than happy to step back outside awhile and chat with Ruth while the two of you finish up what you were doing."

No, no no. The last thing she needed was Michelle

hanging around and chatting with Ruth. "Maybe you should go on home and call me later tonight," she suggested.

"And miss the chance to meet this guy? Are you crazy!"

Dominique raised eyes to the ceiling, asking for strength and tolerance. At the moment she could very well kill her sister. Seeing no other choice, she made introductions. "Jordan, this is my sister, Michelle."

"Hi, Michelle."

"Oh, my, you sound just as sexy as you look."

A husky chuckle came from deep within Jordan's throat. "Thanks."

Dominique groaned. "Go away, Michelle. Now," she said warningly. She glanced up at Jordan. He was smiling, but so far he wasn't drooling, like most men did whenever they saw Michelle.

"Oh, all right," Michelle said with a pretend pout. "I'll be waiting outside." And with that last statement she opened the door and eased it closed behind her.

Dominique stepped away from Jordan and walked over to her desk. She wondered if she could pay Michelle to keep quiet about today. Chances were that even now she was spilling her guts to Ruth.

"That's your sister?"

Jordan's question interrupted her thoughts. She met his gaze and saw an amused expression on his face. "So I'm told, although I wonder at times. All I know is that when I was two years old my parents brought her home from the hospital, and she's been a thorn in my side ever since."

He chuckled. "No, I don't think so. It's obvious the two of you are close."

She gave him a startled look. "How could you tell that?"

His smile widened. "Because my brother and I act the same way. Although we get on each other's nerves at times, we're very close."

"Does he still live in London, Ohio?"

"No. We moved away from home when we left for college, but since we're a pretty close family, we usually go home for the holidays as well as other times in between. My parents are doing fine and are in good health, but they claim they need to see us every once in a while."

She nodded, wondering if his brother looked anything like him. "What's your brother's name? How old is he?"

"His name is Auburn, and he is three years younger than me. He's a doctor living in Atlanta."

Dominique lifted a curious brow. "And how old are you?"

"I'm thirty-five." He tilted his head and smiled at her. "So there you have the history of the Prescott brothers."

Dominique blinked. "Prescott?"

"Yes, Prescott," he said, recalling that he hadn't shared his last name with her until now.

"Jordan Prescott." Dominique let the name roll slowly off her lips, liking the sound of it. In fact she liked the sound of it too much. Her gaze met his again, and for an instant she froze. Less than ten minutes ago she had gotten the kiss of her life from him, and now, at this very moment, those memories were attacking her better senses. Everything about him was overwhelming: the way he kissed, the way he was built, his strength, his scent . . . and, she thought, as her gaze dropped to his midsection, even his erection. She couldn't believe that after all this time it hadn't gone down.

Taking a deep breath, she clamored to get her thoughts in order. "Look, Jordan, I have to talk to my sister before she does too much damage with her wagging tongue." Quickly crossing the room, she picked up his briefcase off the floor and handed it to him. "I suggest that you continue to use this as a shield for now."

He chuckled in a low, sexy way as he took the briefcase from her hand. "And later?"

"Later I suggest you take a cold shower."

Jordan didn't hold back his mirth when he laughed. It was a deep, rumbling sound that did crazy, intimate things to Dominique's insides. "Yes, I guess that would work. And what about tomorrow?"

"Tomorrow?" she asked.

"Yes, tomorrow. Will you meet me at the park in the morning?"

Dominique knew she shouldn't consider doing such a thing, but she *was* considering it. "Will you be able to keep yourself under control?"

Jordan grinned. "Hey, you can't hold me responsible when you're the reason I'm behaving this way. It's not my fault that I find you so incredibly sexy."

His words made Dominique's pulse rate quicken and filled her with a pleasure she had never felt before. "Yes, I'll be at the park in the morning."

"And you won't stand me up again?" he asked, drawing her closer to him.

For once Dominique knew she would not back out. Maybe her family and Ruth were right: It was time to finally put Kenneth and his betrayal behind her and really start living again. "No, I'll be there."

He leaned over and gently kissed her lips. "Then I'll see you in the morning."

She nodded and watched as he crossed the room and walked out the door.

Michelle's eyes widened. "So you're really going to have an affair with him?"

Dominique rolled her eyes, hoping no one else in the restaurant had heard Michelle's outburst. "If that's your way of asking if I'm going to be sleeping in his bed tomorrow night, the answer is no. What it means is that I've agreed to go jogging with him again in the morning. Then I'll see how things progress from there once we get to know each other better."

"But you're not interested in anything long-term and serious?"

"Right. I don't want anything long-term and serious."

Michelle took a sip of her soda. "I don't know, Dom; not everyone is into recreational sex."

"Recreational sex?"

"Yes, sex with no strings attached as long as the partner is safe. That's just not your style. You're the kind of woman destined to love any man you sleep with. To you sex and love go hand in hand. You're definitely not into having sex just for the fun of it."

Dominique cocked a brow. *Sex for the fun of it?* That sounded pretty much like another name for casual sex to her. "Is that the kind of sex you're into these days?"

"Are you kidding? Who's having sex these days?" Michelle asked, sounding totally frustrated. "I haven't even slept with a man in over six months. Not since I told Marcus to go to hell and carry his interfering mama with him. Like I said, I have issues to work out before I become involved with anyone else." She leaned back in her chair. "Now, getting back to Jordan. Did you say he has a brother?"

"Yes, and he's a doctor in Atlanta." Dominique raised a dark brow. "Why?"

"Ummm, no reason. Just curious."

Dominique sharpened her gaze. Her sister was never "just curious" about anything. She was downright nosy. "Is there anything or anyone else you're "just curious" about?"

Michelle smiled sheepishly. "Well, now that you've mentioned it, there is someone else. That well-dressed, extremely sharp, very good-looking brother who's one of Danah Fairchild's attorneys. Am I to understand that he works at the same law firm as Jordan?"

Dominique knew Michelle was referring to Royce Parker. "Yes." She couldn't help but smile. Parker had been impressive in the courtroom today. His legal skills had been exemplary. However, she wasn't stupid. His finesse as an attorney had nothing to do with her sister's interest. Shaking her head, Dominique glanced down at her watch. "I have to get to bed early tonight. And Michelle, I prefer if you didn't say anything to the family just yet. I don't want them getting their hopes up. It will be hard for them to understand that Jordan won't be a permanent fixture in my life."

"Too late. Ruth has already told Gramma. She was talking to her on the phone when we left."

Dominique raised her eyes to the ceiling. "Doesn't Gramma have better things to do with her time than gossip with Ruth?"

Michelle shook her head. "Not on the days Grampa goes to his Masonic lodge meetings. It's my guess that Mom and Dad know by now, too."

"Is there such a thing as privacy in our family?"

"No. So if you start sleeping with Jordan, I suggest you play it safe and stay overnight at his place. You never know when someone in the family might unexpectedly pop up." She smiled wickedly. "Like I did today. It's a good thing I interrupted things when I did. Five minutes longer and he would have had you stretched out on your desk."

Dominique's color darkened. "No, he would not have."

"Wanna bet?"

Dominique shook her head. No, she didn't want to bet. In fact, she didn't want to talk about it anymore. Glancing around she caught the waiter's attention and motioned for their check. She and Michelle made it a point to dine out together most Wednesday nights. And occasionally on Wednesdays they would join their parents and grandparents at church for dinner prior to the start of prayer meeting.

Later, as she drove toward home, Dominique smiled as she wondered if Jordan had taken a cold shower as she had suggested.

"Please tell me you're kidding, man. Tell me Judge Kincaid is not your mystery lady."

Jordan leaned back in his chair and looked across the room at Royce, who was apparently in shock over the news he had just delivered. He smiled and sipped his beer, deciding not to answer his friend's question just yet. He felt refreshed after taking a cold shower. Refreshed and in a good mood.

"Jordan?"

Jordan tipped his beer to Royce and smiled. "You heard me right. The Honorable D. Kincaid is the same woman who's been making me hot and bothered for the past two weeks."

"Damn. And you're going to pursue her?"

Jordan raised his eyes to the ceiling. "Royce, I've been pursuing her ever since I first saw her."

"But that was before you knew she was a judge, man."

"So what does that have to do with anything?"

"Need I remind you that after your divorce from Paula, you swore you would never get involved with another woman with a career in law?"

Jordan blinked at him, remembering. "Umm, I did say that, didn't I?"

"Yes, in fact you were pretty damn adamant about it."

Jordan nodded. Yes, he had been. "What I said was that I would never *marry* a woman who has a career in law again. There's no way this thing with Dominique will ever get that serious."

"It won't?"

"No. What I'm dealing with here is a unique case of lust. She has everything I like on a woman; big hips, big breasts, big legs and it's obvious that she's also big on intelligence. I'm really hot for her, man."

"So what you want from her is a short-term, meaningless affair?"

Jordan frowned. The way Royce said it made his intentions sound dishonorable. "I want the same thing you want from the women you date."

"Sex. A good time. And more sex?"

Jordan shook his head. He'd always enjoyed sex like any other man, but Royce considered it a national pastime, right up there with baseball and apple pie. "Well, yeah, but I prefer staying with the same woman a lot longer than you do, Royce. I'd rather not change women as often as I change my shirts."

Royce smiled. "If you stay with the same woman too long they start to get clingy, just like those shirts will get if you don't throw a Bounty in the dryer with them. Then you'll have one hell of a mess on your hands."

Jordan took another sip of his beer and met Royce's gaze. "Does Judge Kincaid look like the clingy type?"

Royce thought on Jordan's question for a minute and then said, "No." Seconds later he added, "But any woman can turn into the clingy type, Jordan."

Jordan shrugged. "Then it's up to me to be honest and up-front so she'll know what to expect. All I want from her is something solid and exclusive."

"Solid and exclusive?"

"Yes. Solid enough to know that we understand what we want out of the relationship, and exclusive to the point that while the two of us are dating, we won't be seeing other people."

"For how long?"

"Until either of us feels it's time to move on."

Royce nodded. "Those conditions seem fair."

Jordan leaned back in his chair and took another sip of beer. He hoped Dominique thought they seemed fair as well.

Six

Jordan's gaze fastened on the woman who was slowly walking toward him. Throughout the night he had thought about her, thinking about the kiss they had shared and anticipating when he would see her again.

As he continued to look at her, he wondered just what was there about her that elicited such profound lust from him. He decided it could be a number of things, like her walk. She moved in a way that looked more like she was actually gliding than walking. But then it may have been the gentle sway of her voluptuous hips, or the bouncy fullness of her large breasts. Whatever it was, she definitely had his attention.

He sighed, fascinated by the way the early morning light captured her nut-brown features and her full figure. She was wearing a pair of jogging shorts and a large T-shirt, but neither could block from his mind the allurement of the body they covered. Her hair was pinned up in a knot like it had been yesterday. And he knew he would be tempted to let it down and run his fingers through each dark, thick, and glossy strand.

He felt his body harden. Just that quickly he wanted her with a desperation that no longer surprised or annoyed him. And to be quite honest, it no longer bothered him that he lacked control where she was concerned. After all, she was seductive and enticing, and his body appreciated everything about her. But this morning he had taken necessary measures, since his body seemed to have a mind of its own. Instead of wearing running shorts as he normally did, he had worn loose-fitting sweats. They did a good job of not flagrantly revealing a certain body part.

He glanced down at his watch. She was early. But then, he thought with a smile, so was he. He wondered if that meant they had been eager to see each other. He breathed in the early morning air. It was a perfect morning, he thought, because the person he considered the perfect woman was less than five feet away.

"Good morning, Jordan."

"Good morning, Dominique." Up close he couldn't help but appreciate her features that were contained in the round shape of her face. Her mouth was curved into a warm smile, and delicately arched eyebrows crowned a pair of the most beautiful dark eyes he had ever seen. Then there were her high cheekbones and straight nose. Everything about her totally disarmed him.

"Are you ready to run?" she asked expectantly.

Jordan thought that her low and throaty voice was hot enough to warm his blood. And she was staring up at him with eyes so captivating it nearly took his breath away to look into them. His gaze slowly moved from her eyes to her mouth, and he couldn't help but remember just how good that mouth had tasted.

"No, not yet," he finally answered, taking her hand in his.

He had chosen this particular spot to meet her because the limbs of the huge oak tree blocked from view anyone standing directly under it. Dominique offered no resistance when he gently pulled her under the shadows of a large overhanging branch.

"First, I've got to taste you again," was all he said just seconds before his mouth came down on hers.

Dominique automatically lifted her arms around Jordan's neck the moment his lips touched hers. He captured her tongue and drew it into his mouth. Blood gushed to her head, making her feel dizzy as his tongue began mating with hers. Urgent need raced up her spine and clouded her senses except for two—taste and smell. She was mesmerized by his delicious taste and entranced by his masculine scent.

They broke off the kiss when they heard the approach of other joggers. Panting, Dominique leaned against Jordan to get her breath back and wondered if she would ever breathe normally again. When the joggers passed she glanced up at him, her expression dazed and her lips still parted. "I can't believe we just did that," she whispered, speaking of their torrid, stolen kiss that still had her head spinning.

He took a deep breath and responded, "When it comes to you and me, I can believe anything." He released his arms from around her waist. "Come on; let's start jogging."

Dominique took another deep breath and shook her head. "I don't think I can, since I have no breath left. You took my breath away."

He leaned down and gently placed a kiss on her lips. "That about makes us even, because you took my breath away the very first time I laid eyes on you, sweetheart."

Dominique stared up at him. Jordan always said nice things to her and gave her compliments, which was something Kenneth had never done. Jordan had a way of making her feel special, all woman and sexy. She was smart enough to know that some men were

capable of delivering just any line to a woman if it
would get them from point A to point B. But whenever Jordan spoke, there was always a deep sincerity
in his voice, as though he really meant what he was
saying.

She started to say something in the way of a thank-
you, but he didn't let her. Instead he took her hand
in his and together they began jogging. And once
again he slowed his pace to keep up with hers.

Bending over with his hands on his knees, Jordan
began taking deep, slow breaths. They had jogged an
extra thirty minutes, and although he was sweaty and
hot, his body felt good, as it usually did after a
workout.

He glanced over at Dominique, who was also bent
over and breathing deeply. Her eyes were closed
and a few loose strands of hair had come undone
and were stuck to the perspiration on her face. He
wondered just how her heated and damp skin would
taste on his tongue. He was tempted to cover the
distance between them and begin lapping her up to
find out.

He closed his eyes when he felt his body get harder.
He forced himself to take another slow, deep breath
as his nostrils flared and his mind became tormented
with vivid images of the two of them in his bed naked
and making love in the wildest kinds of ways.

Slowly, still struggling for breath, as well as for san-
ity, he opened his eyes and straightened his body. She
had already straightened and was staring at him. In
that instant, at that moment, he felt the same awareness and connection he'd felt when their gazes had
met yesterday across the span of the courtroom.

Warmth that he was beginning to get used to began increasing in slow degrees and sluggishly expanded to every part of his body. He had never been this caught up, bewitched, enchanted, and fascinated by a woman. Not even with Paula.

He sucked in a deep breath, feeling the effect of Dominique's gaze as if it were actually touching him, and he could tell she was as aware of the magnetism between them as he was. And also, like him, she was powerless against it.

"You're ready to go?" he finally asked, hoping conversation would at least soften the sexual tension surrounding them.

"Yes."

He reached out and took her hand. "Come on. I'll walk you home."

In silence they walked the three blocks to the condos where she lived, holding hands.

"I don't live far from here," he finally said after they had walked through the gated entrance and she had exchanged greetings with the guardsman on duty.

She glanced up at him. He was smiling, and she wondered what he'd found amusing. "Really? Where do you live?"

"Three blocks away from the park."

She stopped walking. "You live here? In this same complex?" she asked as her eyes widened in surprise.

"Yes." His smile deepened. "It seems we're neighbors. Now isn't that a coincidence?"

His voice, she noted, sounded husky and sexually charged. The sound of it sizzled along her every nerve ending. She saw their being neighbors more as a convenience than a coincidence, and could tell by the look he was giving her that so did he.

She sighed when they reached her front door. Although she was tempted to invite him in, she decided it would not be a good idea. Too much sexual current was flowing between them, and she had a feeling that if they were alone they would overcharge and end up galvanized. Besides, she needed time to deal with this latest bit of news that he was her neighbor.

"What are you doing tonight?"

"Having dinner with my family."

"And tomorrow?"

"I'm a Big Sister to a little girl whom I promised to take to a movie."

He nodded. "Then how about having breakfast with me Saturday morning at my place?"

She swallowed. "Breakfast? Saturday morning? Your place?"

He chuckled. "Yes, that was the gist of my invitation."

She didn't say anything for the longest while, then asked, "What time?"

"Whenever you get there. I get up and jog around the same time I usually do each morning, and should be back home and showered by eight."

Dominique thought of all the reasons she shouldn't go to his place for breakfast, the main one being that anytime the two of them were alone things tended to get out of control. A part of her wanted a little excitement in her life, but still she knew she had to be cautious with everything that she did.

"Okay, I'll join you Saturday morning for breakfast, but only if you let me bring something."

"All right, you can bring the orange juice."

She smiled. "Orange juice it is."

*   *   *

"You came alone?"

Dominique couldn't help but smile when she leaned forward to place a kiss on her grandmother's cheek. Every Thursday the family got together for dinner at her grandparents' home. "Yes, of course I came alone. Why is that so surprising?"

Before she could walk away and join the rest of the family in the living room, Constance Kincaid caught hold of her oldest granddaughter's wrist. "Wait just a minute, young lady. Where is the young man I've been hearing so much about?"

"And what young man is that?"

"The one Ruth claims could pass for Sidney Poitier's grandson."

Dominique couldn't help but grin. Everyone, including her grandfather, knew of her grandmother's fascination with the movie star, which had spanned well over fifty years. So for her to believe any man could resemble Mr. Poitier was definitely an honor.

Deciding not to pretend she didn't know who her grandmother was referring to, she said, "I have no idea where he is, Gramma. I don't keep up with him and he doesn't keep up with me."

Her grandmother released her wrist with a frown on her face. "And just what sort of relationship is that?"

"None. Contrary to what you may have been told, Jordan Prescott and I are not an item."

"Then what are you?"

"Acquaintances."

Constance Kincaid snorted. "Acquaintances don't carry on the way I heard the two of you were doing in your chambers, young lady."

Dominique raised her eyes to the ceiling. Evidently

it had been too much to hope that for once Michelle would keep her lips zipped. " You can't believe everything you hear, especially if it comes from Michelle."

"Ruth backed up her story."

"That doesn't surprise me. Now, if you're through with your little interrogation, may I go join the others?"

A few hours later, Dominique thought that if another person asked her about her relationship with Jordan, she would scream. She tried convincing herself that their questions were understandable, since she hadn't shown any interest in a man in over a year, but enough was enough. Heaven forbid if they found out Jordan was her neighbor and that he had invited her to breakfast at his place Saturday morning. She couldn't help but smile. It was a secret she would share with no one, especially with her mouthy sister.

"Is there any reason you've washed that same plate five times?"

Dominique quickly glanced down at the plate she had in the sudsy dishwater. "Oops, I guess my mind was elsewhere," she said, finally rinsing the plate and handing it to Michelle to dry. As part of the Thursday-night dinner ritual, she and Michelle always washed and dried the dishes, since they never contributed to the cooking of any of the food. She and her sister were of the same mind that if you couldn't microwave it, why bother?

Michelle threw down her dish towel. "Okay, sis, 'fess up. What is it that you're not telling me?"

"A lot, since you talk too friggin' much."

"Everyone would have found out anyway. Do you honestly think Ruth didn't know what was going on in your chambers?"

Dominique glared at her sister. "Maybe. But it wasn't your place to give her an account of anything."

"And I didn't. It's not my fault she drew her own conclusions." Michelle giggled. "But you have to admit, there *was* a lot of action going on in your chambers. Jordan Prescott was really getting down on your mouth."

Dominique rolled her eyes. "I really don't want to discuss him with you."

Michelle nodded. "Suit yourself. But will you answer one question for me, please? I promise to leave you alone if you do."

"And what question is that?"

"When will I get to meet his brother?"

Seven

Jordan, slightly damp from his shower, had put on a pair of jeans and was pulling his T-shirt over his head when the doorbell sounded. A warm, heated feeling settled in his stomach when he realized Dominique had arrived for breakfast.

As he moved toward the door he told himself to stop worrying about how things would pan out between them. Her acceptance of his invitation to breakfast had both surprised and delighted him, and he didn't want to do anything that would make her regret coming. He had discovered that complete and total honesty between them was the key. She knew he wanted her, and how much. However, it was just as important to him that she understood what he didn't want, which was a serious enough relationship that would put the thought of marriage on any woman's mind. He had been there and had done that, and had no intentions of going there again.

He opened the door and before he could utter a greeting, he found himself helplessly staring at her. She was breathtaking and enticing. His gaze, of its own accord, scanned the length of her body. She was wearing a pair of jeans that fit tight over the lushness of her full hips. Her T-shirt for once was not a size too large but was a perfect fit that managed to keep her voluptuous breasts in place. However, it did nothing to hide the protruding nipples pressed against it. He wondered how he was supposed to sit across from her at the breakfast table and concentrate on his food and not on her chest.

"Are you going to invite me in, Jordan?"

His gaze was drawn away from her chest to her face, and he felt like a complete idiot for having stood there devouring her with his eyes the way he had. But he was a man and some things couldn't be helped, like a man's reaction to a sexy woman. "Yes, I'm going to invite you in, but I need to warn you that you look good enough to eat," he said in a husky voice that willed her to say something to such a bold statement. His muscles pulled tight in his stomach when she smiled.

"Then it's a good thing I'm not on the menu this morning, isn't it?"

"Hmm," he said, tilting his head and giving her a slow, considering look. "Adding you to the menu would be easy enough."

Dominique felt excitement roil inside of her as she met Jordan's gaze, hot and expectant. She sucked in an unsteady breath as she read his thoughts completely. From the first he had wanted her and hadn't hid that fact. Neither had he been coy or manipulating in his pursuit. Instead he had been up-front in letting her know what he wanted. And in his own straightforward way of saying things and speaking jut what was on his mind, intimate or otherwise, he was letting her know that this morning would be no different. Once she crossed the threshold into his home she would be at her own risk. Although she believed he wouldn't force her to do anything she didn't want to do, she was pretty convinced that he had every intention of talking, feeling, or tasting his way into her panties and subsequently into his bed. If she allowed it, she would be his breakfast, lunch, and dinner. A delicious shudder raced through her at the mere thought of that.

And it didn't help matters that he was standing before her simply oozing sexuality. It should be against the law what his body did to a pair of jeans and a T-shirt. Scandalous at best. Tantalizing at worst. It was obvious he had recently taken a shower. Parts of his skin were still damp, and he smelled incredibly clean, manly, and arousing.

Her gaze was drawn to his midsection. The tight denim of Jordan's jeans didn't give much room, and his erection was indiscreetly bulging against the zipper, straining for release, as if it expected to be freed from its torment any minute now. She was tempted to reach out and stroke it, to let it know the feel of her hand, her fingers, and her touch.

She blinked, surprised at what she had been thinking. She normally didn't have such wanton thoughts. She was a commitment-seeking type of woman who much preferred a serious and steady relationship with a man. But a part of her cruelly reminded her that a serious and steady relationship was what she thought she'd had with Kenneth, and how wrong she had been. Maybe it was time for her to take a whole new approach to life. And judging from how often Jordan had invaded her dreams since she'd met him, he was just what she needed to get things moving in that direction. Suddenly the thought of engaging in recreational sex wasn't such a bad idea.

Her heart began thumping wildly in her chest. It was a foregone conclusion that eventually they would sleep together. She knew it, and she had a feeling that he knew it as well. She was no longer averse to an affair of shared passion just as long as she felt comfortable with the person and they both knew it was a relationship that wouldn't go anywhere.

"So can I add you to the menu this morning?"

This morning! That would be rushing things a bit. It had been a little over a year since Kenneth, and she needed time to get used to the idea of sharing a bed with someone again. Dominique inhaled a deep breath, returned her gaze to Jordan's face, and managed to say, "No, not this morning."

His gaze burned into hers. He stepped outside the door to stand directly in front of her. They stood so close they were almost toe to toe. "But some other morning?" he whispered, his voice ultrasexy and disturbingly raw.

She only hesitated briefly before saying, "Yes, some other morning."

They stood silently looking at each other for a long moment. His face suddenly became tense and the look in his eyes turned serious. "I don't want us to do anything until you're absolutely sure you're ready. But do know one thing, Dominique. For me this isn't a game, so don't tease and don't promise anything you won't deliver." He took a step back to once again stand in the doorway, letting her know what he expected and that the decision was hers.

A nervous shiver passed through Dominique. She wondered if she would be able to meet his expectations when the time came. His words made her realize just what she was getting herself into, and since he hadn't let her inside his home, he was still offering her an out.

But she didn't want an out. He had awakened feelings in her that she wanted to explore with him. In a few months she would turn thirty, and it was time she started enjoying life to the fullest. And she had a feeling he wasn't interested in a serious involvement any more than she. But she had to be sure.

"I'm not interested in any type of serious involvement with anyone, Jordan."

He lifted a brow, glad to hear that. "Neither am I."

"All I'm interested in is recreational sex."

He lifted another brow. That was a new one on him. "Recreational sex?"

She nodded. "Yes. Sex for enjoyment, but I want an exclusive partner for as long as there's interest on both sides."

Jordan shook his head. What she was proposing was just what he had in mind. "Recreational sex sounds like a winner to me."

"All right." She pushed a lock of hair back from her face and then said, "I won't tease and I won't promise anything I won't deliver."

Apparently satisfied with her answer, and feeling they had probably wasted enough time already, Jordan took her hand, tugged her inside his home, and closed the door behind them.

Eight

The urge to taste Dominique rushed through Jordan the moment he had her inside his home. Now that she was inside his domain he felt primal and possessive. And although they had reached an understanding that nothing would happen between them that morning, that didn't mean he couldn't push the envelope as far as he could.

"Here's the orange juice."

He blinked. "What?"

She lifted the brown paper bag she held in her hand. It was a bag he was noticing for the first time. "Oh, thanks," he said. Taking it from her he walked across the room to place it on the breakfast bar that separated his living room from his kitchen.

Dominique glanced around and noted that the setup of their condos was similar, though his was somewhat larger. His living room had a window that provided a clear view of one of the two lakes in the complex. "You have a beautiful view of the lake," she said, walking over to the window and looking out. "It looks so peaceful."

"It is peaceful. I spend a lot of my time out on the patio reading."

She inhaled deeply when she realized he had come to stand directly behind her. His voice sounded deeper and huskier than before. She also noted that his breathing had thickened. Very slowly she turned to face him, knowing what they both wanted. She couldn't stop herself from reaching up and placing her arms around his neck.

Desire-filled dark eyes looked down at her as he placed both hands on her waist and gently pulled her closer to him. She smiled, thinking the feel of his erection against her felt nice. Just as nice as the feel of her breasts pressing against his chest.

"Thanks for inviting me to breakfast, Jordan."

His husky chuckle intensified the already heated sensation that ran down her spine. "I haven't fed you yet."

His gaze lowered to her lips, and she felt him get even harder against her belly. "But you will, as soon as you finish kissing me," she whispered.

The moment his mouth touched hers, she felt her entire body stir and shiver. He began eating away at her mouth like a starving man, nibbling, licking, and sucking. Pleasure and heat began flowing from their joined mouths and going straight up to her head, then moved lower to settle between her legs. She squeezed her pelvic muscles and whimpered when she felt him, hard and huge, pressed against her.

Her whimpers intensified when Jordan began kissing her in another way altogether, taking his tongue and thrusting in and out of her mouth in the same rhythm with which he was grinding against the lower part of her body. He was nearly driving her insane. It was as if he were sending the message to her that if he couldn't get a piece of her one way, he wasn't averse to trying another. Either way, he intended to get his fill.

Knowing that if she didn't take control and pull

back they would eventually end up naked on the living room floor, she broke off the kiss. Panting furiously, she rested her head against his chest as she tried to catch her breath.

His breathing, she noted, was just as hard and deep as hers. He tightened his arms around her as he fought for control. "Sorry," he whispered, and his hot breath close to her ear made her shiver. "I enjoyed tasting you so much that I got carried away."

She lifted her head and looked up at him. "No apology needed. I know the feeling, since I was right there with you." She placed her head back on his chest, wondering how long she would be able to hold out without letting him make love to her.

"Do you want me to show you around before I feed you?"

She lifted her head again and looked up at him. "Just as long as you don't have an ulterior motive for doing so."

He chuckled in a low, sexy voice. "In a way I do. Walking around will give me time to calm down. It's pure hell in these jeans."

Dominique laughed as she shook her head. "Do you talk this way to all the women you date?"

He shook his head. "No. Actually I haven't started dating since moving here, and I talk that way to you only because I've never felt this sort of chemistry before with another woman." And that included his ex-wife. He wondered how he could explain that he had been married for four years and that they had never spoken intimately, not even while making love.

"Why do you feel comfortable talking that way to me?"

He didn't respond. At least not for a few seconds. And when he did so, he studied her and then asked, "Does my talking that way bother you?"

She shook her head. "I have to admit that the first time you did it I was taken aback. No man had ever openly said such things to me before. But then I found that I rather liked it. It's not as if you're saying anything crude or vulgar. Between us it's stimulating, intimate, and deeply personal." And to her it really was. To exchange conversation so personal somehow made her feel they were a close couple who had shared intimacies for years.

Jordan smiled, glad that was how she saw things. "That's the way I feel about it too. For some reason, talking that way with you seems natural, and in no way is it out of disrespect. If anything, it's my way of expressing how I feel in the most blatant way I know how. Like I said, I've never had this sort of chemistry with another woman. And I want you to know just how much I want to make love to you." He took her hand in his. "Come on and let me show you around. There's one particular room I really want you to see."

She lifted a brow as he led her out of the living room toward the back of his home. "And what room is that?"

He smiled. "It's not the room you think. It's an extra bedroom that I made into a workout room."

Dominique glanced around. The room was set up like a fitness center and had every piece of exercise equipment she could imagine. "Wow, this is super."

"Thanks. It saves me time and money. I don't have to join a gym for a good workout, and I can exercise anytime I want."

She looked at the state-of-the-art treadmill. "With something like this at your fingertips, why bother going out jogging?"

"Because I enjoy breathing in fresh air each day. The only time I use the treadmill is when the weather is bad outside."

She nodded. "I like staying toned and thought about joining a health spa but never got around to doing so."

"And now you don't have to. You can use my equipment anytime."

"I can?"

"Sure. In fact, if you want to come by tomorrow I can get you started on a few of the easier pieces, the ones I consider the bare essentials for any workout program."

Dominique frowned thoughtfully. "Tomorrow won't be a good day. I'm driving my grandmother to Daytona to visit a friend after church."

He nodded. "I know how hectic your schedule is during the week with the Fairchild case. What about next Saturday? We can do breakfast again here, and afterward we can spend an hour or so working out."

"I hate for you to do breakfast two Saturdays in a row. The only way I'll go along with it is if you let me prepare dinner at my place Tuesday night."

He smiled. "Sure, I'd like that." He took her hand in his. "Come on and let me show you the rest of the place before I feed you."

Dominique took a sip of coffee and stared over the rim of the cup at Jordan. His back was to her as he stood at the kitchen counter putting the finishing touches on their pancakes. Even wearing something domestic like an apron, he still exuded sensuality and raw male energy. It was the kind that made her pulse race.

To say she had been surprised at his cooking skills would be an understatement. She had watched while he whipped together some of the fluffiest scrambled eggs she had ever seen and fried the bacon to a delicious crisp. On top of all of that, he had just finished making a batch of pancakes.

He had explained that he and his brother knew how to cook, something Lori Prescott had required of her sons. While preparing breakfast he had shared some more interesting tidbits about his family.

"What are you smiling about?"

She set her cup down as he placed the plate of food in front of her. She met his gaze when he came and sat across from her at the table. "I was just thinking about Michelle. She would love meeting your brother if he ever came to town."

He lifted a brow. "You think so?"

She chuckled. "Trust me, I know so. She almost died when she found out you had one."

Jordan shook his head, grinning. "It's hard to believe she's your sister. From what you've told me, she sounds like a rebel."

"And that's putting it mildly. During our teen years there was never a dull moment at our house. She gave my parents plenty of grief while growing up. She resisted authority of any kind, and still does in a way. She has trouble keeping a boyfriend because she's too domineering and bossy. She has this thing about always wanting to be in control."

"Then it should be interesting if she were to meet Auburn, because they are two of a kind."

Dominique nodded. "You didn't drool."

Jordan paused in taking a sip of his coffee and looked at her bemusedly. "Excuse me?"

"You didn't drool. Most men drool when they meet Michelle. You smiled at her but you didn't drool. Even Kenneth drooled when he first saw her."

"Kenneth?"

"Yes, my ex-fiancé."

Jordan frowned. As far as he was concerned that should have told her she needed to dump the guy. "Different things attract a man to a woman. I never was one to go after the tall, slender, model-size woman."

Dominique found that interesting. "Really? I thought most men were attracted to those types."

He shrugged. "Not me. I like healthy-looking women, women with meat on their bones." He smiled. "Nothing turns me on quicker than seeing voluptuous hips, thighs, and breasts." He looked at her intently. "Like yours. They definitely arouse me."

Dominique couldn't help but smile. "Thanks."

After a few moments of silence she said, "Your ex-wife. Was she a full-size woman?"

He looked at her as though it were taking his brain a while to comprehend what she was asking him. Then he said, "Yes."

"Do I remind you of her?"

"No. Other than size the two of you are completely different."

"In what way?"

"You may take things seriously but you also know when to smile and lighten up. She didn't. She was a family practice attorney who didn't know how to leave things at the office. She would bring home a lot of emotional baggage from the cases she handled."

Dominique tilted her head. The tone of his voice sounded bitter. "And that came between the two of you?"

"Yes. She didn't know how to let go and change her role from attorney to wife. You're a judge. However, not once have we talked about any of your court cases. You know where your role as Judge Kincaid ends and your role as Dominique Kincaid, the woman, begins."

She nodded. "Being a judge is my job and not my life."

"Yeah, well, Paula never learned to differentiate the two, and it eventually ended our marriage. I have no desire to marry another attorney again."

Dominique regretted that he felt that way. "It's not that way with everyone. Both my parents are attorneys."

He lifted a brow. "They are?"

"Yes. They met in law school and have worked together ever since. They get along great at work and at home and have a good marriage. It's my belief that an individual's profession has nothing to do with whether or not they make their marriage work. It's how much you're willing to sacrifice to make that marriage succeed."

Jordan nodded. "Your ex-fiancé. Was he an attorney?"

"No. Kenneth was a college professor. He taught history at UCF."

"What's the reason the two of you broke up?" He already knew what Royce had told him but he wanted to hear it from her.

Dominique didn't say anything for the longest time; then she spoke. "Kenneth said I had gotten so caught up in wedding plans that I stopped giving him the attention he needed. And it was during that time that he became involved with another woman. She was someone who moved into his apartment complex."

She took a sip of coffee before continuing. She found Jordan easy to talk to. "According to him it was only a one-night stand. Although that may have been true, the woman got pregnant. He decided to tell me about her a week before our wedding, and only because she threatened to come to the wedding and make a scene unless he gave her enough money to start over in Texas somewhere. He actually had the nerve to ask my parents to loan him the money, and had expected me to continue on with our wedding." She shook her head in disgust. "It never occurred to him that I would call off the wedding because of what he had done. After all, he felt everything was my fault."

Jordan snorted angrily. "And I guess you zipped down his pants and forced him to stick his *thing* into the other woman as well. Did it ever occur to him that he had betrayed you in the worst possible way?"

The depth of Jordan's anger surprised Dominique, and a part of her was touched it was on her behalf. "No, he didn't see it that way."

"Then he was a fool."

She shook her had sadly. "He still is one. He honestly thinks we'll get back together and eventually marry."

Jordan's chest tightened with some strange emotion he had never felt before. Abruptly, he asked, "Why does he think that? Have you given him reason to think the two of you will be getting back together?"

She lifted a brow at the hardness in his voice. "No.

Like I said, he's a fool. There's no way he and I will ever get back together."

Jordan nodded, unwilling at the moment to question why he was glad to hear that her ex-fiancé didn't stand a chance with her again.

Nine

Three days later Dominique sat in her courtroom rubbing the bridge of her nose in frustration. She looked at the two men who were nervously staring back at her. "Please approach the bench. The both of you."

When they stood directly in front of her, she said, "The two of you have really tried my patience today, and I refuse to let either of you turn my courtroom into a circus any longer. A woman is on trial for her life and I expect you to behave like the professionals you are or you will find yourselves in contempt of court."

Both men nodded. Neither was eager to pay a contempt-of-court fine. "Now, then, shall we continue?"

As they walked away she glanced at her watch. It was three o'clock already. The day had dragged by only because the prosecution and the defense had relentlessly bickered with each other, and had refused to give an inch. She had interjected so much that her throat was raw.

She sighed angrily. She had looked forward to preparing dinner for Jordan tonight, and now from the looks of things there was no way she would make it home at a decent time. And on top of that, the prosecution had come up with some new evidence she needed to review to determine whether it was admissible. During one of the short recesses, she had left a message on Jordan's answering machine explaining her situation.

She had seen Jordan that morning when they had jogged, but she hadn't known the trial would go beyond the scheduled time.

A moment later, while a witness on the stand was going over what had happened the day that Lee Fairchild had gotten killed, Dominique felt goose bumps form on her arms. She looked up to see Jordan, dressed in a tailored business suit and looking like he belonged on the cover of a magazine, enter her courtroom and take a seat. When their gazes connected she felt her heart beginning to beat so fast that she had to take several deep breaths. She finally broke eye contact before she literally passed out from the all-too-familiar sensuous heat that was flooding through her body.

It didn't seem fair, all these new sensations she was feeling. And as if that weren't bad enough, she often found herself fantasizing about him during the day and dreaming about him at night.

Taking another deep breath, she turned her full concentration back to what was going on in her courtroom.

Jordan was glad he had finished all his work for that day and was able to swing by the courthouse. He sat in the back and watched Dominique. What Royce had told him was true. She was tough but fair. He leaned back and settled comfortably in his seat finding her utterly fascinating. As he sat there and watched her, his imagination got wild. He remembered when he had kissed her at his place on Saturday and how his tongue had thrust in and out of her mouth over and over, nearly ravishing it. In fact, he had actually tried leaving his mark stamped somewhere, everywhere in her mouth. He couldn't imagine a more enticing and delectable spot to place his brand.

He inhaled deeply, feeling as if he were on fire, and looked at her. She was staring hot and heatedly right back at him. He liked that.

He also liked the fact that she was no pushover. Nor was she easily swayed into doing something she didn't feel comfortable doing. He would have given almost anything for them to have slept together at his place Saturday morning before breakfast, after breakfast—the entire day. But she hadn't been ready. As hot as he had made her for him, she had held back because she hadn't felt fully comfortable with the situation yet. He was more than willing to give her time, just as long as she didn't play games with him. And he felt fairly certain that she wasn't playing games. She wanted him as much as he wanted her, but by nature she was a cautious person who didn't immediately take anything at face value. Hell, considering what she did for a living, he couldn't very well blame her.

But the truth of the matter was that he liked her. He liked her a hell of a lot. He could name over a hundred things about her that literally turned him on big-time, and without very much effort. There was no doubt in his mind that they would be good together in bed. But he was enjoying her out of bed as well.

He knew without a doubt that Judge Dominique Kincaid, the woman, was definitely getting to him.

Dominique glanced at her watch. It was nine o'clock and she was still in her chambers going over pages and pages of legal documentation regarding the Fairchild case. She had convinced Ruth to go home hours ago, knowing it would well be past eleven before she would finally finish what she was doing.

She leaned back in her chair. She was getting a little hungry and thought about calling Michelle to bring her something to eat from a fast-food restaurant. She was surprised Ruth hadn't asked her about dinner or offered to order something for her before she'd left.

She glanced toward her chamber door when she heard a soft knock, wondering who it could be. The courthouse was usually empty this time of night, since most everyone had left for home. The only people around were the security staff and the maintenance crew. "Come in."

Her mouth went dry and her heart began beating wildly in her chest when Jordan appeared in the doorway. From the way he was dressed, wearing a pair of jeans and a chambray shirt, it was obvious he had gone home and changed clothes.

She couldn't stop her gaze from wandering up and down the full magnificent length of him. Whenever he was moving about he was temptation in motion, and whenever he was standing still, as he was doing now while leaning against the doorjamb, he was stationary sex appeal. The man was definitely all of that and a bag of chips. A big bag of chips. The spicy-hot kind.

As she got her wits back she noticed he held two things in his hand—his briefcase and a huge white paper bag. The aroma of food suddenly flooded her chambers. "Jordan? What are you doing here? Didn't you get my message about dinner at my place being canceled?"

His smile immediately ignited every female part of her body. Her breasts suddenly felt tender, and the area between her legs got warm. With shaking fingers she placed the papers she had been reading aside.

"Yes, I got it and completely understood. I called and spoke to Ruth a few hours ago and she mentioned that chances were you would be staying late tonight. So instead of you feeding me, I decided the decent thing to do, *Your Honor,* was feed you."

Dominique thought of the breakfast he had prepared for her that past Saturday. "You've fed me once this week. I already owe you a meal."

"I'm not keeping tabs, Dominique. Besides, all I did tonight was order takeout at Sharkeys."

She raised a brow. "When did Sharkeys start doing takeout?"

His smile widened and she felt it all the way to her toes. "Actually they don't. Someone I know has connections and arranged things for me."

"Oh."

He walked into her chambers, closing the door behind him with his foot. "So I'm ordering you to take a break and eat."

Because she was hungry, he really didn't have to order her twice. She stood to move the papers off her desk. "I really appreciate this. I was just thinking about calling Michelle and asking her to bring me something. You're a lifesaver."

He placed the food on her desk. "No, I'm not. I would have used any excuse to keep our date tonight."

She lifted her head to stare at him. The thought that he had wanted to spend the evening with her touched her. "You're sharing dinner with me?"

He grinned. "Yes, and don't worry: I brought enough, if you're feeling somewhat greedy and concerned with sharing."

She chuckled as she pulled the containers from the bag. "No, that's not it. In fact, I'd like the company."

"Good. And afterward while you read whatever it is you have to read, I have some papers I need to read as well."

She lifted a brow. "You're sticking around after we eat?"

"Yes. I don't like the idea of you going to your car late at night alone, so I plan to stay here, then walk you out."

Dominique smiled, once again touched by his concern. "I've worked late at night many times. The parking lot is well lit and there's security on duty. I'll be fine."

"I'm making sure of it, Dominique."

"Thanks." She tried to remember whether Kenneth had ever bothered to show up at the courthouse late at night, concerned for her safety, and couldn't think of a single time he had done so.

While they ate they talked about everything other than work. He listened while she told him about her parents and grandparents and how her grandfather's family had once owned most of the land surrounding International Drive.

"It's amazing when I hear people talk about what a small town Orlando used to be before Disney World came to town. It doesn't sound like the same place."

Jordan nodded. "London is still pretty much a small

town. Hell, it's so small there's a man who delivers milk each day, and the doctor still makes house calls on occasion. It's country but pleasant. More and more of the young people are moving back home to escape the rat race of the big cities."

Later, after disposing of their garbage, Jordan took a seat on the sofa that rested on the other side of the room and pulled out the papers he'd brought along from his briefcase. Dominique resumed reading the legal papers about the Fairchild case.

She thought it was nice having him share her space and wasn't at all bothered by it. After reading for what seemed like hours, she lifted her head to rotate her stiff neck. She glanced across the room at Jordan and smiled. As if he'd known she was looking at him, he lifted his head from the papers he was reading and smiled back. Her heart began beating so fast for a moment she thought she had forgotten how to breathe. Finally, when she remembered, she broke eye contact and lowered her gaze to begin reading again.

An hour or so later Dominique read the last sentence on the page. Her eyes felt tired and strained. Glancing at the crystal clock on her desk, a gift from her parents, she noted that the hour was past eleven. It was much later than she had intended to stay.

"All finished?"

She glanced over in Jordan's direction. "Yes, what about you?"

"Yes, I'm done."

She stood. "It won't take me long to get everything together to leave."

"Take your time."

She was putting the last of the papers in her briefcase when she felt his presence directly behind her.

"I meant to tell you the other day, before I got kind of sidetracked, that you have nice chambers."

"Thanks." She sighed as she slowly turned around, and couldn't help it when she automatically leaned forward, parting her lips.

He couldn't help it either when he leaned down and captured her mouth, taking hold of her waist and pulling her closer. He couldn't think of a better way to end the evening than to take his fill of her like this, especially since she wasn't quite ready for the next level yet.

Deciding it was time to end the kiss before he was tempted to spread her out on her desk, Jordan pulled back and smiled when he saw that her lips were still damp from the taste of him. "Dominique," he whispered.

She lifted her gaze up to his. "Yes?"

"Are you going jogging with me in the morning?" he asked in a voice filled with the same lust she felt.

"Yes."

He was watching her intently. "And on Saturday morning, will you join me at my place for a workout and breakfast?"

Her eyes were glazed with seductive heat. "Are you sure you want to feed me again?"

"Yes, I'm sure."

"And during the workout, are you going to teach me all the essentials I need to know?"

Jordan inhaled deeply, thinking about all the things he wanted to teach her, to show her, and to experience with her. "Yes," he whispered, bringing her back close to him and liking the way she felt in his arms. "I'm teaching you everything you need to know, and first we'll start off by getting you familiar with the bare essentials."

Ten

Dominique knew she was in trouble the minute Jordan opened the door Saturday morning. She quickly dragged in a deep, calming breath. He was standing before her dressed in an outlandishly sexy pair of gym shorts and a short tank top. It was the same top he had worn once before that stopped just above his navel. Her gave automatically went to the small, sexy indention in his ultratight belly. Her gaze was further drawn to the line of curly hair that grew from his navel and became lost in the waistband of his shorts.

"You're ready, Dominique?"

She swallowed and lifted her gaze to his and stupidly asked, "For what?"

He crossed his arms and leaned against the doorjamb, completely at ease and acting as if a dense woman appearing on his doorstep at eight in the morning were the norm.

"For a workout and breakfast—in that order," he said, grinning at her.

"Yes, I'm ready," she said, wishing his mouth didn't look so darn enticing. She had gotten a dose of him three times that week when they had gone jogging together, and when he had unexpectedly shown up in her chambers Tuesday night. And all three times when they had kissed, his taste had consumed her senses. When he moved aside she walked in.

"Good. We can go ahead and get started," he said, leading her down the hallway.

When they entered the workout room she glanced around, again admiring all the equipment Jordan owned. The treadmill was stationed in one corner of the room and a heavy-duty stair climber was sitting in the other. He also had a multi-purpose weight bench, a magnetic exercise bike, as well as a bi-level dumbbell rack.

She walked over to the exercise bike, to take a closer look. When she turned around she swallowed when she saw him checking out what she was wearing, a pair of nylon shorts and midriff top.

Dominique looked down at herself before meeting his gaze again. The length of the shorts was more revealing than she usually wore, and she wondered if she made a mistake in putting them on. "Is what I'm wearing okay?" she asked quietly, when he continued to stare at her.

Jordan shook his head thinking that she looked incredibly sexy. Her thighs were even better looking than he had originally imagined. After that first day when they had gone jogging, she had started wearing sweats like him. Now, up close, he was seeing her bare legs and thighs. They were smooth and sleek, stacked and thick—just the way he liked.

"This is what I want you to try out today," he finally recovered enough to say. "The key to the whole process is not to overdo it."

"Are you saying that too much of anything isn't good for you?"

Jordan smiled, thinking that couldn't be all true because he couldn't imagine too much sex from her being anything but good. "Too much exercising is. You don't want to tear any muscle tissue."

She nodded. She definitely didn't want to do that.

"Come over here for a second. I want you to see what you're going to start with first. It's what I call the Bare Essential."

She crossed the room and saw a huge piece of equipment that reminded her of the Total Gym that Chuck Norris advertised on television. "The Bare Essential?"

"Yes. I consider it the ultimate necessity. This baby alone can give your body the complete workout it needs," he said, smiling.

She raised an arched brow. "If that's true, then why do you need this other stuff?"

He smiled. "Because it's always good to have variety, and each one of them serves a purpose. After a while your body gets used to the same muscles getting worked, so you should switch equipment every so often. But for now this is the one we'll concentrate on."

She lifted a brow. "We?"

Chuckling, he said, "Yes. I've appointed myself your personal trainer."

Her personal trainer? Dominique didn't know quite what to think of that. She had assumed he would show her the best equipment to use, then leave her on her own. "Do you think I really need a personal trainer?" she asked, saying the words on a sigh.

His eyes got a devilish glint in them. "Yes, for a while you do, and I'm putting myself at your disposal."

She didn't want to think about what that entailed.

"Today I want us to concentrate on your heart rate."

She blinked when Jordan's voice intruded into her thoughts. She nodded, thinking there was nothing wrong with her heart rate except for whenever he was around. Then it always managed to race out of control. "Why are you concerned about my heart rate?"

"Because monitoring a person's heart rate while they're exercising takes the guesswork out of how much of a workout they can endure. Some people can't take the intensity of a vigorous workout." He lifted a brow. "You don't have heart problems, do you?"

Not before I met you, she thought. Instead she answered, "No, as far as I know, I'm as fit as a horse."

"Good. Before we get started, I want us to do a series of warm-up exercises."

Dominique nodded. She knew the importance of warming up before starting any strenuous workout.

"Let's do a few jumping jacks."

Minutes later, barely able to catch her breath, Dominique discovered that Jordan's definition of "a few" was slightly different from hers. She usually did about twenty-five and called it a day; however, he was still going strong at 125. He had left her behind when they had reached sixty. The rest of the time she had watched him. There was definitely something stimulating about a nicely built man jumping up and down while throwing his hands together over his head. It emphasized his strong legs and just how tight and firm his thighs and butt were. Then there was the sweat that had begun forming on his body, slowly drenching the skin under his tank top and traveling down toward the wispy curly hair under his navel, then trickling lower into the waistband of his shorts. Watching the path the sweat was flowing down fascinated her.

"Dominique?"

He had called her name twice before she'd realized he had been speaking to her. She quickly glanced up to his face. "Huh, yes?"

His gaze suddenly became glued to her mouth, and her lips automatically parted under his close scrutiny. "Yes, Jordan?" she repeated.

He shook his head as if to clear his mind. "Let's do some leg lifts," he said, getting down on the floor. "It's important in a general warm-up to concentrate on those specific muscles you intend to work."

She nodded and joined him on a huge mat. He had told her that the carpeting installed in this particular room had a thicker padding than the rest of the house for added cushioning.

"I thought you might find it more fun to do this type of warm-up with music. That way it will feel like you're dancing more than exercising. And I think *Flashdance* will do the trick." He reached over and pushed the button on a nearby CD player. "Now, then, let's get started."

Dominique placed her body in position, following Jordan's lead. Moments later the music kicked into gear. The melody started off slow and easy, allowing them to do a few body stretches. Then gradually Irene Cara's voice brought the song into a rousing tempo. Jordan coaxed her to move with the music, in tune with the beat.

She began lifting her legs to the sound of the invigorating music. And when the song reached a throbbing, galvanizing pitch, she became energized along with it and kicked her legs higher and faster, maintaining the fast-paced rhythm the music projected. Jordan was right: It felt more like dancing than exercising. She was so into what she was doing that she failed to notice that Jordan had stopped and was watching her.

Jordan sat back, mesmerized, spellbound. With his breath caught in his throat he watched the way Dominique moved, fluid, graceful, and seductive. Her legs, big and strong, lifted and kicked to the vigorous beat of *Flashdance*. The only thing he could think of while watching her was having those big, strong legs wrapped tight around him while he was buried deep inside of her.

She must have finally felt him watching her, because as the music begin winding down, so did she. Their gazes met and held and he was hard-pressed to keep his hands from reaching out and touching her all over.

"What's next?" she asked softly, clearing her throat and breaking the silence when the music ended. She glanced away and looked across the room at the piece of equipment he had shown her earlier. "Should I try that out now?"

Jordan nodded as he tried to gain control. He grabbed a towel off a nearby rack and tossed it to her, then watched as she wiped the perspiration from her face, hands, and chest. When she handed the towel back, without thinking he brought the towel to his face and breathed deeply, inhaling her scent.

Dominique watched as the image of what he had just done filled her brain, making her hot all over. In that instant she knew, without a doubt, that there was no way she would leave today without having been made love to by him.

Slowly, struggling with her breath from that realization, she stood and walked over to the piece of equipment he called Bare Essential. Easing her body onto the vinyl-padded glide board, she placed her hips at a comfortable angle. Leaning back in a reclining position, she grabbed hold of the hand cables. It was then that she noticed Jordan had come to stand by her side.

"We'll take it slowly," he said huskily. "I want you to breathe in deeply while I count."

"How many times?" she asked, trying not to look at him. The sexual chemistry between them was beginning to ignite in a way it had never done before. She felt it and knew he felt it too. Her skin began to get warm and tingly, and every part of her was on the edge of anticipation. Even the air surrounding them crackled, seemed to have thickened, and was thrumming with sensuous heat.

"Let's try fifty for starters. I want you to slowly lift your hips up and then back down into position. The strain will tone your thighs and buttocks." *Not that they need much more toning,* he thought. As far as he was concerned, they were already perfect.

Dominique sucked in a quick breath when he reached out and touched her, merely adjusting the cables to make sure they fit securely within her hands.

He looked down at her, and the darkness of his eyes made heat stain her cheeks. Her breasts began to tingle and the area between her legs began to throb. His gaze transmitted passion that actually made her insides tremble. "You ready?"

She nodded. "Yes."

He began counting. "One . . . two . . . three . . ."

As he counted she closed her eyes and used her body weight to lift up her hips—as far as they could go—and then ease them back down, while keeping her knees slightly bent and her legs at an angle. At first the movement was difficult, strenuous. But she was determined to endure. She felt her muscles tighten, her pelvis clench, and her knee joints strengthen. And the area between her legs felt synergized.

"Seven . . . eight . . . nine . . ."

As he continued counting Jordan watched her breasts stretch and tighten with each movement she made. Her nipples began puckering against the resistance. His gaze moved lower. Her shorts strained against the continuous aerobic motion, forcing the garment to ride high on her hips, exposing more of her smooth flesh.

He sucked air into his lungs as his gaze then came to rest on the area between her legs. The way she was lifting her hips—up and down, back and forth—looked seductive as hell, like some sort of mating ritual. An immediate need to have her—to get inside of her body—took full control.

"Seventeen . . . eighteen . . . nineteen . . ."

Without missing a beat in counting, and without giving much thought to what he was doing, Jordan pulled the tank top over his head and tossed it to the floor.

"Twenty-four . . . twenty-five . . . twenty-six . . ."

He then pushed his shorts down his legs, taking a condom out of the pocket before tossing them aside.

"Thirty . . . thirty-one . . . thirty-two . . ."

He eased the condom slowly and deliberately over his erection, then glanced over at Dominique. Her eyes were still closed. She didn't have a clue as to what he was doing.

"Thirty-eight . . . thirty-nine . . . forty . . ."

His body hardened when he noticed the hair that had escaped the single braid on her head began getting damp with perspiration. It didn't surprise him that something as basic as sweat was fueling his sexual appetite. He had an urge to know the taste of her damp skin on his tongue.

"Forty-five . . . forty-six . . . forty-seven . . ."

He inhaled a deep breath, wanting to know how the movements of her hips felt under him while he was planted deep inside of her.

"Fifty."

In that instant she released the cable, relaxed her body, and slowly opened her eyes. She looked over at him and her gaze locked on his naked body. He watched as she sucked in a deep breath at the same time that her eyes became hot with surprise, then awareness.

Without saying a word, he walked over to her and lifted his leg to straddle both her and the equipment. "Take a deep breath, baby," he said softly. "Inhale and then exhale."

Slowly, with her gaze still glued to his naked body, she did as he instructed. Eyes simmering in lust looked down at her, and for the space of a heartbeat, neither of them said anything. Words were the last thing on their minds.

When the silence became a heated mist that began closing in on them, he spoke in a low, intimate, and erotic voice, leaning down toward her, and at the same time reaching his hand down to gently cup the area between her legs. "I want you."

His deep, throaty, sexy voice, as well as the words he had spoken, caused heat to gather where he had placed his hand. Dominique automatically reached her arms up to encircle his neck. This was the show of acceptance Jordan needed. He lowered his mouth to hers with a hunger that could not be denied. Any control he had was gone.

He sucked her tongue into his mouth at the same time his hand left the area between her legs and moved higher, seeking out her breasts. Pushing her top aside and releasing the front hook of her bra, his hands trembled when he touched her bare breasts, sliding over her nipples and feeling them harden under his touch.

Breaking the kiss he pulled her top over her head and her bra along with it, and got his first view of her naked breasts. "Mercy." The word was a guttural sound from his lips as his eyes feasted upon her. Her breasts were large, ripe, and delicious. Like a starving man, his mouth immediately went straight to them and began licking and sucking.

"Jordan . . ."

He heard his name whispered from Dominique's lips on a quavering moan as his tongue greedily tasted each swollen nipple. His hand then moved down lower and slipped into the waistband of her shorts and panties until it came into contact with the very essence of her. She felt hot, slick, and wet.

"Oh, baby," he said hoarsely, inhaling deeply the full scent of her. It was the unique feminine scent of a woman in heat. His nostrils flared and his tongue trembled inside his mouth, aching to taste her.

"Lift up. I want you naked," he said softly, breaking their kiss as his hand gently pulled down her shorts and panties, then tossed them on the floor near his clothes. His eyes blazed a trail down her nude body, appreciating everything he saw.

He dipped his head and his mouth went back to her breasts before slowly moving lower. He intended to make her as out of control as he was.

"Jordan!" Dominique bit back another groan. He was making her body feel things it had never felt before. Naughty but nice. Insatiable. Seductively his. She was becoming sexually insane. A mass of heated, sensual bliss. Then, when she thought there was no way she could handle any more, as his fingers took over and thoughts of anything and everything except the sensations she felt vanished from her mind, her world suddenly exploded into a thousand pieces. She cried out her pleasure and he kissed the sound from her lips.

"Your body is about to get the ultimate workout," he whispered when she slowly began coming back down to earth. "Just do like you did before and lift your hips each time I give the count," he said seductively, his warm breath close to her ear.

She nodded, unable to speak. Jordan's intimate loving of her had left her speechless, breathless. It had been incredible. Earth-shattering.

"Look at me, baby."

And she did.

"Keep your eyes on me," he whispered. "Open your legs as wide as they can go for me. I've got something to give you."

She continued looking at him while she did what he said. Her body began feeling heated all over again the moment she felt him, large, thick, and hot, slip inside of her. It was a tight fit, and he moved slowly, deeply, to connect their bodies in the most elemental way.

"Ahh," he growled huskily as he continued to push forward. "That's it, just relax."

Everything inside Dominique felt wonderful, and erotic images of what was taking place down below infused her mind. "Jordan," she whispered hoarsely, automatically moving her hips, wanting him.

He stilled her movements with his hands. "Not yet, baby. Otherwise I could hurt you. I want you just that much. Don't move until I start counting."

"Like before?"

"Yes."

"Just as many?"

"More, if you can handle it. But when you get tired, I'll take over."

She nodded.

He began counting again. "One . . . two . . . three . . ."

On each count, she lifted her hips, bringing him deeper into her body, stretching herself inside in a way she didn't think possible. And when she pulled back, inch by inch, almost bringing him out of her, he automatically thrust his hips downward to stay connected.

"Ten . . . eleven . . . twelve . . ."

Each count meant another stroke, another thrust, another earth-shattering passionate moment.

"Twenty-one . . . twenty-two . . . twenty-three . . ."

Dominique didn't have the strength to take any more—the pleasure was too great—and she felt her body getting ready to explode again. He evidently felt it too and took over. Reaching down, he placed his hand under her hips to lift her, locking their bodies together.

"Wrap your legs around me, baby," he whispered seconds before he began thrusting with increased speed. His entire body focused on hers as he brought her to another climax—the second, and not long after that, the third.

He continued to ride her, not letting up nor letting her down. Her legs were wrapped around him, keeping her body locked in place as he made love to her over and over again.

Jordan's nostrils flared as they inhaled the scent of sex, and he knew at that moment, without any doubt, that this wasn't just lust. He'd been in lust before, but never had it made him this crazy, this uncontrolled, this desperate. It was as if he could not get enough of her, and he wondered if he ever would.

That was the main thought on his mind when he felt his body become engulfed by a sea of turbulent waves, taking him under. He felt himself drowning and wondered if he would survive. But if he had to die, this was certainly the way to go, while he was still tightly embedded inside of her—to the hilt. When he came, the force of his climax was so strong he felt his entire body convulse. He yelled out her name, not caring if the entire city of Orlando heard him.

And as he gathered her in his arms as aftershocks continued to ram through him, he knew in that space of time that she had become his bare essential; his ultimate necessity.

She called it recreational sex. But now his mind was calling it was something else entirely.

Eleven

It was near noon when Jordan opened his eyes. He blinked, then smiled at the feel of the soft, feminine body snuggled next to him in his bed. His leg was thrown over hers, their bodies still connected. He intended to stay inside of her for as long as he could.

Jordan tightened his arms around Dominique. After

they had made love in the workout room, they had showered, then had gotten in his bed, where they had made love again twice, possibly three times, before falling asleep. They never got around to eating breakfast. Making love was the only thing on their minds, and they had mated like rabbits.

Now he was hungry after having worked up an appetite. But a part of him didn't want to disconnect their bodies just yet.

His gaze roamed over the part of her not covered by his bedspread. She was still naked and her breasts were visible. He thought of the baby who would one day suck her breasts.

His baby.

He drew in a deep, sharp breath at the implication, that he was planning for her to have *his* baby. He had been extremely careful today and felt reasonably sure she had not gotten pregnant. But he had all intentions of getting her pregnant one day . . . after they had gotten married.

He shook his head, not believing the way his thoughts were going. He was a man who had sworn he would never marry again, and he hadn't counted on falling in love a second time. But he had.

How was he to know that one day he would meet a woman by the name of Dominique Kincaid? No one had warned him of the dangers of sexual chemistry and how powerful it could be, or the chance of lust turning into love. And he certainly hadn't known that he possessed such an insatiable appetite. He could stay in bed and make love to her for the rest of the day, the night, the week, the year. Hell, he felt himself getting hard just thinking about the fact that he was inside of her while she slept; which wasn't smart, since he hadn't taken off the last condom he'd used. He needed to go to the bathroom and discard it and put on another one before he did something really stupid, like deciding to make love to her without using one.

Regretting having to do so, he eased out of her, slipped out of bed, and headed for the bathroom. A short while later he returned and got back into bed. She was still asleep and didn't budge an inch when he gathered her close into his arms. Shifting her legs apart he eased himself back inside of her.

He tried not to groan at how good the connection felt. It was a tight fit. Snug. And even in sleep her body was hot. He wondered whether, if he began moving just a little bit, if she would wake up. He smiled, deciding to try it and see.

He moved his hips once, twice, then again, gently pumping into her. He turned and buried his face into her neck, feeling the need to lick her somewhere and deciding it would be there. He licked her again and again, then gently sucked on her soft skin, nipping at it with his teeth, not caring that he would probably leave a visible mark on her neck. The thought of branding her as his woman sent a wave of passionate possession through him.

"Jordan?"

His name came out of her mouth in a hoarse, sluggish whisper, and with a soft groan he pulled her closer into his arms as he continued to pump inside her in a smooth, steady rhythm.

"Yeah, baby?"

Slowly she opened her eyes to meet his. They were soft from sleep. She drew in a deep breath when she felt him moving in and out of her. "What are you doing?" she asked in a voice that sounded drowsy, yet a bit overwhelmed.

"Do you have to ask?" he answered, amused, as he pushed deeper and deeper inside of her each time.

A dark tint slashed across Dominique's cheek and she sucked in a deep breath. She felt her body awakening in pure sexual pleasure with the feel of him inside of her. "You haven't gotten enough?" she asked, amazed as she thought of the number of times they had made love already.

"I don't think there is such a word as 'enough' where you are concerned, baby," he said as his gaze focused on her lips and saw them quiver into a smile.

"Rather greedy, aren't you?"

Jordan chuckled. "You make me feel that way."

Never in her life had she awakened to find a man already in the process of making love to her. "I like that," she said, smiling.

Without missing a beat Jordan shifted positions and moved on top of her. Cupping her buttocks in his hand he lifted her to wrap her legs around himself.

Dominique moved her hips to meet his strokes. They were coming faster and stronger. He kissed her, thrusting his tongue in and out of her mouth.

"Dominique." Jordan moaned her name, and his body shuddered at the same time he felt her climax. The force of it shook him everywhere, and he drew in a deep, satisfied breath as sensation after sensation rammed through him. And he knew at that moment that he loved her with every part of his body, and he intended to tell her so.

He wanted her to know that this wasn't about recreational sex any longer. And if he was true to himself he would admit that it never had been. He had fallen hard for her the first time he had seen her. What other reason would he have for being so intense about having her?

Smiling, he noted that she had gone back to sleep with him buried deep inside of her. He decided to tell her how he felt as soon as she woke back up. At that moment he heard the sound of his doorbell and remembered he was expecting a courier to deliver a package. He quickly eased out of bed, wanting Dominique to get all the rest she deserved.

Dominique stirred and woke up to an empty bed and the aroma of something cooking, and whatever it was, it certainly smelled delicious. She rolled over and looked around, realizing that she was still at Jordan's house and in his bed.

She smiled. How many times had they made love that day? Five? Six? Seven? Who was counting? Her smile widened when she remembered that he had been the one counting earlier that day . . . in the workout room.

Groaning, she felt the need to bury her head under the pillow when she thought of what they had done on that piece of equipment. It had been simply shameless, but she had enjoyed every single minute of it. In fact, she would just love doing it again, but some other time, definitely not today. Her body felt too sore.

She grinned, liking the feel of the soreness and the reason for it. Making love with Jordan had been fun, fulfilling, just plain incredible, and she hoped he felt the same way. She intended to have many more such moments with him.

She frowned when a thought suddenly occurred to her. Would he still want her now that they had slept together? And if so, for how long? All they had agreed on was recreational sex. Was that all he wanted from her?

She inhaled deeply, not wanting to think about it. She would savor the moment as long as it lasted, and when he was ready for things to end, she would walk away with her memories. No, she thought, shaking her head. She would walk away with more than memories. At some point in time he had managed to capture a piece of her heart. He would never know she had fallen in love with him. She had finally accepted that she loved him the moment he had slipped inside of her. It was then that she had realized that Michelle had been right: She was the kind of woman destined to love any man she slept with. To her, sex and love went hand in hand.

Slipping out of bed she retrieved her gym bag off the floor, wincing slightly at the soreness between her legs. She would take a hot bath, change into some more clothes and find out just what Jordan was cooking in the kitchen.

Jordan glanced down at the report a courier had delivered. He was ecstatic. The private investigator he had hired had gotten the information that was needed to prove that his client's suspicions were true and his wife had been cheating on him. In fact she still was, although she was fighting the divorce and claiming to be the faithful wife. Getting the proof showing otherwise had taken longer than Jordan had anticipated, but it had been well worth the wait. The photographs were pretty damn damaging, and as far as he was concerned the investigator had hit gold. Over the past three months she had done nothing but give her husband as well as his attorneys hell with her intent on remaining Mrs. Harrison Phillips.

He checked his watch, needing to call Preston Fulton, the attorney who was his backup on the case. Jordan was sure that Preston would be glad to know what he had discovered about the over-sexed Annie Phillips, and hopefully, pretty soon they, as well as Harrison Phillips, would see the last of her.

Dominique felt totally refreshed as she left Jordan's bedroom and walked into the kitchen. His back was to her while he talked on the phone.

"Yeah, man, she was something else. I got just what I wanted and all I can say is that it was well worth the wait. It wouldn't bother me in the least if I don't see her again after today."

Shocked at what Jordan was saying, she stared at his back. Her mouth opened but nothing came out as anger, hurt and humiliation washed over her. He was bragging about what had happened between them to whomever he was talking to on the phone.

She backed up slowly as tears came into her eyes. Quickly going back into his bedroom she gathered her things together and tossed them into her gym bag. Leaving his bedroom moments later, she noticed he was no longer on the phone but was now outside on his patio, staring out at the lake. Was he out there gloating about how easy she had been? As tears streamed down her face she turned to leave. Before opening the door she scribbled a note on a sheet of paper and left it on his coffee table. She then walked out the door.

* * *

Jordan checked his watch, deciding to go wake Dominique. The food he had fixed for her had gotten cold. He had expected her to be up and about hours ago. Only an almost dead person slept that long, although he knew she was probably pretty damn tired from all the physical activities that they had shared that day.

He walked into his bedroom and noticed the bed was neatly made up. Thinking she was in the bathroom he knocked on the door. When he didn't get a response he pushed the door open and went in. She wasn't there.

Walking back out into his bedroom he glanced around the room. Where was she? He walked through each room in his house and didn't find her anywhere and had to finally reach the conclusion that she had left without saying anything. Why?

He went into the living room and sat down. It was then that he saw the note she had scribbled and left on the table. Her handwriting was legible and the message she had written was crystal clear: *Go to hell! Dominique.*

He felt anger consume him when he read the handwritten note again, thinking there had to be a mistake. What was the meaning of it? She had a lot of explaining to do when he saw her. He had warned her that he was not into playing games.

Grabbing his car keys off the table he walked out the door. He intended to confront her and find out just what the hell was going on. And she'd better have a damn good reason for sneaking out and leaving such a hateful message.

* * *

Michelle checked her clock when she heard the knocking at her door. It was late afternoon. She had just come in from shopping and had gotten into bed, determined to take a nap before getting dressed for the party she planned to attend later that night. Shoving the covers aside she slipped out of bed. She hoped it wasn't her ex-boyfriend. He was the last person she wanted to see.

She snatched the door open to find her sister standing there. And from the way Dominique looked it was obvious that she was upset and had been crying. A lot.

"Dom? What's wrong? What has happened?"

Michelle angrily paced her living room. She stopped long enough to glare at her sister, who was sitting on the sofa sniffling.

"What do you mean, you won't tell me what happened? The hell you won't, Dominique," she said in frustration. "You have the nerve to show up on my doorstep, looking like a war-torn puppy and with a hickey on the side of your neck the size of a baseball, and walking so stiff that if I didn't know better I'd think you've been involved in some damn sex marathon, and—"

Michelle stopped talking in midsentence. She suddenly studied her sister. *Oh, mercy,* she thought as she watched the way Dominique suddenly became nervous under her close scrutiny. "You did do it! You slept with that guy, didn't you?"

Dominique glared at Michelle. "That is none of your business."

Michelle glared back. "I'm making it my business, since you decided to come here instead of going home." A horrible thought then flashed through her mind combined with a look of sheer mortification. "Oh, my goodness! What did he do? Force you into performing some sort of kinky sex?"

"Michelle," Dominique chided gently, remembering just how dramatic her sister could get. While she and her sister were growing up, her parents and grandparents always referred to Michelle as the drama queen. "Jordan did not force me to do anything I didn't want to do."

"But you're admitting that the two of you did do something kinky?"

Dominique tipped her head back and stared at the ceiling. *Lord, please give me strength.* She then looked back at Michelle. She refused to think of what she and Jordan had done in the workout room as kinky. If the two of them never spoke again, she would still always think of that time as something pretty damn special. "No, we did not do anything kinky."

"But you are admitting to having slept with him today?"

Knowing Michelle was like a dog with a bone who wouldn't let up until her curiosity or nosiness was appeased, she said, "Yes, Jordan and I slept together."

"And?"

Dominique squeezed her eyes shut, wishing she didn't have to tell Michelle anything, but knowing deep down that she wanted to tell someone, and like it or not, her sister was also her best friend. She opened her eyes. "And he bragged about it afterward to someone on the phone."

Michelle's eyes widened. "You mean he actually had loose lips?" she asked in astonishment. "He's actually the type to kiss and tell—or in this case, one who bangs then sings?"

At Dominique's nod Michelle became livid. "How dare he! The dog! Who did he call? The *Tattler*?"

Dominique raised a dark brow. The *Tattler* was their local tabloid that exploited everybody's business. They had done a hatchet job on her last year when she had called off her wedding to Kenneth. Within twenty-four hours everyone in Orlando and the surrounding counties knew that Kenneth had screwed around on her. "No, I believe that he was talking to another guy."

Michelle snorted. "Probably that good-looking attorney friend of his named Royce Parker. The two of them were probably comparing notes about the women they screwed today."

Dominique sighed, deciding she had told Michelle enough and didn't want to talk about it any longer. "Look, I'm not in the mood to go back home tonight. Do you have a problem with my spending the night over here?"

"Of course not. If you want me to I can change my plans and not go to Chimeka's house-warming party."

Dominique shook her head. "No, you should go. I'll be fine. Besides, I want to be alone for a while."

"Are you sure?"

"Yes. Just promise me you won't say anything to the family about this."

"Of course I won't, Dom. Is there anything you need?"

Fresh tears appeared in Dominique's eyes, although she tried fighting them back. She had sworn after Kenneth that no other man would make her cry. She looked over at her sister sadly. "I could really use a hug right now."

Michelle quickly crossed the room and gave Dominique the hug she needed.

Twelve

Jordan crawled in bed that night madder than hell. He had gone directly to Dominique's house after reading her note, only to discover she wasn't there. He had sat in his car for over five hours waiting for her to come home and she never did. In fact, he had just returned from her place and she still wasn't there. His anger had started turning into worry.

He had called directory assistance to obtain her sister's phone number, only to be told the home phone number for Michelle Kincaid was unlisted. In a frantic moment he had called Royce, who within minutes had gotten Michelle's private number from a woman he used to date who worked for the phone company.

He had called Dominique's sister's home, only to be royally told off by Michelle once he had identified himself. She had told him the same thing Dominique had written on the note, "Go to hell," but that was only after she had called him a number of not-so-nice names. With an order that he not call back, she had hung up on him.

He was so angry he was seeing fire. Come hell or high water, he intended to get to the bottom of what was going on. Starting first thing in the morning he would camp out on Dominique's doorstep if he had to. She had to come home at some point in time. She couldn't stay away forever.

As he moved around in his bed trying to find a

comfortable spot, he breathed into his lungs her feminine scent that now drenched his bed linens. The smell
of sex still lingered in the air. They had made love
too many times that day in his bedroom for it not to.
For a while it had seemed as if he were superglued
between her legs. No sooner had they recovered from
one orgasm then they had started working on another.
Hell, at one point he'd even had a few multiple ones,
which was something that had never happened to him
before. But being inside of Dominique's snug, tight,
and hot body had almost driven him insane.

He shook his head, thrown for an emotional loop.
What could have possibly gone wrong? Had she awakened and regretted what they had done? No, that
couldn't be right, because he knew for a fact that she
had enjoyed their lovemaking as much as he had.

Had it been the number of times that they had
made love? Had the realization scared her senseless
when she'd taken the time to think about it? They
had made love more times in one day than some married couples did all year. But he hadn't forced her,
and again, she seemed to have enjoyed it as much as
he did, so that excuse wouldn't wash with him.

He sighed deeply as he stared up at the ceiling. He
knew her body had to be sore. Did she blame him for
that? He levered himself up on his side and thought
about it. He had been rather greedy, but again, she
could have stopped him at any time. Besides, even if
that was the reason she had left—so he wouldn't make
love to her any more that day—that was no reason to
write what she did on that note. The words she had
written seemed so out of character for her. A part of
him knew she must have really been driven by a high
degree of anger to write such a thing. And the question was, Just what in the hell was she mad about?

He remembered Royce telling him once how a woman had gotten really mad at him about finding another woman's undies under his bed. Since no other woman had ever shared this bed, or had even been in his bedroom, for that matter, he felt certain she hadn't found another woman's underwear or anything else that could have set her off.

Finally finding a comfortable position in bed, he stopped fighting against the sleep he needed. He loved Dominique and he had to believe that no matter what the problem was between them, it could be worked out.

Early the next morning Jordan arrived at Dominique's apartment. He breathed a sigh of relief when he saw her car. As far as he was concerned, she had a lot of explaining to do. Since he had called her practically all night, he could only assume she had just gotten home.

He hadn't gotten much sleep last night and was irritated as hell. And on top of that, he hadn't been able to eat, which had him agitated as sin. For a Prescott, a combination of irritation and agitation was deadly. So the way he saw it, Dominique had better have a lot to say in her defense and most of it had better sound good.

He knocked on the door and it was snatched open immediately.

"Michelle, I told you that I would be—"

She stopped talking in mid-sentence when she saw it was him and not her sister. Not waiting for her to invite him in, just in case she had a mind not to, he walked in and ignored the way she slammed the door shut behind him. "I don't like disappearing acts, Dominique," he said gruffly, turning to face her and trying to keep the anger simmering inside of him under control. "You owe me an explanation."

"I don't owe you anything and I want you to leave."

"Not until you tell me why you left without saying you were gone and then leave me such a hateful note."

Dominique placed her hand on her hips. "You better be glad that's all I left."

Scowling, Jordan lifted a dark brow. "When did you become such a hellion?"

"About the same time you became a damn jerk."

Slowly, still struggling to keep his anger under control, he stared at her for the longest time without saying anything. She stared right back.

A few moments later, he sighed in frustration. They weren't getting anywhere. "Dominique, I—"

"What are you doing here, Jordan?" she interrupted whatever he was about to say as she tried to hold on to her composure. "Haven't you done enough?"

Her questions had a staggering effect. Jordan studied and wondered if all their lovemaking yesterday had sent her to the emergency room or something. Had making love to her all those times with such intensity hurt her in some way physically?

Not knowing the answer to that question he leaned forward and asked softly. "Did I hurt you yesterday?" His voice filled with the same deep concern that was reflected in his eyes. He lifted his hand to gently rub his finger across her cheek.

Dominique drew in a shuddering breath from his touch, mesmerized by the intensity of his care and concern. Thinking he was referring to the phone call she had overheard, she responded quietly. "How could you think you had not hurt me?"

The distress and regret in his features were evident with her response. "You were at the hospital all this time?"

Dominique's eyes glittered in confusion. "The hospital?"

"Yes?"

"Why would I have gone to the hospital?"

Now it was Jordan's time to look confused. "You just said I had hurt you."

Dominique shook her head. Clearly they weren't on the same page. "Just what kind of hurt are you talking about?"

Jordan lifted a brow. "What kind of hurt are you talking about?"

Dominique glared at him. "Like you don't know," she snapped.

Jordan shook his head in frustration. "I don't know, Dominique."

"Then I suggest you go home and try to figure it out."

Jordan met her glare. "I'm not going anywhere until we get this cleared up," he snapped, finally losing it. "You and I are going to talk."

Dominique crossed her arms over her chest. "We have nothing to say."

"The hell we don't," Jordan said, crossing his arms over his chest as well.

"Oh, for pete's sake, why can't you—"

She never finished her statement because Jordan pulled her into his arms and began kissing her, and her treacherous body let him; and actually enjoyed it as his tongue mated with hers.

When he finally ended the kiss, she regained her senses and tried pulling away from him.

"I'm not letting you go. We're having this out, baby. Here and now. I'm not going to lose another night's sleep or miss another meal because of you."

"Oh, your conscience is bothering you now, huh?" she snapped.

"Among other things," he said thinking of how his body was aching for her.

She noted his arousal and lifted her chin and glared at him. "You're nothing but an animal."

He leaned against the door with his arms crossed over his chest. "Then I guess that makes you an animal's woman."

"I am not your woman!"

"Oh, yes you are. My brand is all over you, sweetheart. Have you taken a good look at your neck lately? And I'm sure if you were to take off your clothes you would find a number of other such marks over your body."

Dominique stared at him, her face flush. "And to think that I thought you were special."

He heard the pain as well as the disappointment in her voice and it cut him to the core. "And I thought you were special, too. I still do. I think you are very special. Nothing and no one will ever change my thinking on that."

Dominique turned away from him, refusing to let him see the tears that had come into her eyes. But she knew she had not been quick enough and that he had seen them anyway. She suddenly felt the heat of him directly behind her.

Wanting him to know that she knew the truth she turned to him and looked up at him, not caring that he saw the hurt in her features. "If you thought I was so special why did you tell?"

Very gently he asked. "Why did I tell what?"

"Why did you tell what we did?"

For the longest time he looked at her, trying to figure out what she was talking about then said. "I didn't tell anyone what we did. It was private and between us."

A single tear dropped from her eye. "I heard you, Jordan. I heard you talking on the phone. I heard what you said."

For the life of him Jordan still didn't have a clue as to what she was talking about. He crossed his arms over his chest and stared down at her, studying the tears in her eyes. "Okay, if you heard then tell me what I said."

Dominique closed her eyes as the memory of his words brought her more pain. Moments later she opened them. If he wanted to play dumb he would do so by himself. "You know what you said."

He reached out and gently pulled her to him. "No, sweetheart, honestly I don't."

Dominique glared at him. "Then by all means let me refresh your memory. You told whomever it was that you were talking with on the phone while standing in your kitchen that, and I quote as best I can . . . she was something else and I got just what I wanted and it was well worth the wait and that it wouldn't bother you in the least if you didn't see me again."

Jordan frowned but didn't say anything. He kept looking at Dominique. In fact he went so far as to tilt his head to the side as he continued to stare at her. When he still didn't say anything, she said. "Does that ring any bells now?"

"Yes."

He watched as her shoulders drooped. "And after

eavesdropping on that conversation, only part of it I might add, you assumed I was discussing you?" he asked quietly.

"Yes, weren't you?"

"No."

The flutter that suddenly appeared in her chest, almost stole her voice. "No?"

"No."

"And you expect me to believe that?"

"Yes. Had you hung around yesterday instead of jumping to your own conclusions, you would have known the person I was talking to on the phone was another attorney who is working on the same case that I am. The person I was talking about was a client's wife who has been a pain in the rear-end. For the past six months she's been fighting the petition for divorce and denying her husband's claim that she was having an affair. Well, information I received yesterday from a courier while you were asleep indicated she'd been lying through her teeth and wasting all of our time. All I was doing was letting this other attorney know that from the photographs my private investigator had given me, that the woman was something else; and saying it was well worth the wait, merely meant that I had been waiting to expose her for the adulterer she was; and saying that it wouldn't bother me in the least if I never saw her again meant just that, considering all the hell she's put my client through."

Dominique swallowed. She hated admitting it but his explanation was plausible. "And it wasn't about me?"

That single question, after what he'd just explained, set him off. "I just said it wasn't, Dominique. In fact, I'm highly pissed that you would think that I would tell anyone about what we did. What kind of person do you think I am? You certainly don't hold me in high esteem."

She could see the hurt in his eyes and it took her back. It also made her realize that she had been wrong about him. "Well, what was I to think?"

He moved closer to her. "You were to think, after everything that we shared, that I could not in no way say those things about you. But instead you lumped me into the same category as your ex-fiancé and took your role as judge to the hilt by being both judge and jury. And personally, I don't appreciate your doing that."

"Jordan, I—"

"No, I think you've said enough and it's nice to know what you think of me." He turned to leave.

"Jordan, wait!" When he stopped walking but didn't turn around she said. "I'm sorry, I made a mistake. I jumped to the wrong conclusions. It's hard for me to accept things at face value sometimes. I overreacted when I should not have."

He turned around. "No, you shouldn't have."

"It's hard for me to trust men."

"I can see that. But I'm not just any man, Dominique. I'm the man who became a part of you yesterday in the most elemental way. The man who had to talk himself out of deliberately getting you pregnant, and last but not least, I'm the man who loves you."

Dominique froze in place. Her gaze searched his. "You love me?"

"Yes, but I guess you're not going to believe that either. You're going to tell me that you don't believe anyone can fall in love with another person that quickly."

New tears burned Dominique's eyes. "No, I'm not going to tell you that because it happened to me."

When she saw the uplifting of his brow she said. "I love you, too, Jordan. That's why I hurt so bad when I thought all I was to you was a conquest to boast about."

Jordan reached out and pulled her into his arms. "You were wrong, baby. But I guess when I think about it, I can't expect you to trust me blindly since we haven't really spent a lot of time together. I suggest we fix that. I want us to start spending more time together, building a stronger relationship between us so nothing like this will happen again."

He leaned over and placed a gentle kiss on her lips. "I love you, I want to marry you and I want you to have my baby. Do you think that's asking for too much?"

She smiled as pure happiness shone on her face. "No, that's not asking for too much."

"Good, because I consider those things the bare essentials."

Dominique reached up and wrapped her arms around his neck. "And I consider those things a part of every woman's dream."

When he lowered his head to hers they sealed their love with a kiss.

Epilogue

"Do you realize that in less than an hour you will be a married woman? I am so happy for you, Dom."

Dominique smiled at Michelle as she put the finishing touches on her makeup. A little more than a month after their disagreement she and Jordan were getting married, having decided not to wait, since they wanted to be together.

Instead of planning something elaborate they had both decided to do things simply with a private ceremony of family and close friends. Michelle was her maid of honor, and Royce Parker was Jordan's best man.

Dominique looked across the room at her sister. "Thanks. I'm pretty happy about everything, too. Jordan is everything I've ever wanted in a man." She then lifted a brow at her sister. "I couldn't help but notice you and Royce Parker last night. The two of you couldn't keep your eyes off each other."

Michelle didn't try to hide her grin. "Oh, so you noticed?"

Dominique nodded her head. "Of course I noticed."

Knowing Michelle wasn't going to tell her anything until she was good and ready, Dominique stood and walked over to the closet to get her dress. It was an off-white tea-length gown. According to her mother and grandmother who had been with her when she'd made the purchase, the dress had been made just for her. She smiled. In a few minutes she would become united with the man she loved.

Jordan ignored the room filled with people as his gaze, his thoughts, and every single part of him concentrated on the woman walking toward him. She was beautiful; stunning. *His.*

He smiled with all the emotions his body could produce. And the warmth of love and appreciation that shone in his eyes sent a silent message to her. He intended to love her forever because to him she was everything essential.

STRICTLY BUSINESS

BUSINESS

Y Francis Ray

To women who live large and enjoy every exciting moment of it, and to those who are still trying to find their way.

One

After driving for two days, stopping only for gas and food, Garret McKnight pulled up in front of his new home in Dallas, Texas, on a Sunday afternoon. Too weary to get out of his truck, much less climb the stairs to his second-floor apartment, he leaned his head back against the leather seat and closed his eyes.

He shouldn't have pushed himself so hard, but he'd had little choice. He was meeting Clifford Jones, owner of Jones Business Strategy, at nine the next morning. With the business Jones promised to throw his way, and Garret's own leads, his company, Installation by Design, could double its profit margin within a year.

Office buildings in the Dallas/Fort Worth area were cropping up faster than mushrooms after a spring rain. They needed up-to-the-minute workstations installed quickly and efficiently, and Garret and his crew of fifty-one, in his unbiased opinion, were the best around. Most of them were already settled in the area, and the rest, like Garret, were making the final move from Las Vegas this weekend. By the time he met with Clifford Jones, all his men would be in Dallas and ready to get started.

The roar of a powerful engine and the slamming of a door had him opening one eye. A woman in a smart black pantsuit with a cropped jacket had him opening the other eye. *Nice.* He watched the sway of her rounded hips as she climbed the stairs, and his weariness fell away. She had a lush, curvy figure. He idly wondered if her face looked as good as the rest of her.

His musing was interrupted by the sudden screech of tires, then the sound of running footsteps. "Monica, wait!" A slender man in a gray suit rushed by the driver's side of Garret's truck and caught up with the woman on the stairs. "Monica, please listen!"

She whirled on the stairs one rung up from the man. To Garret's delight she was beautiful . . . and spitting mad. "Bryan, there is nothing you could possibly say that I'd want to hear."

"You misunderstood. She meant nothing to me."

Monica *tsk*ed. "Do I look like a fool to you?"

Not from where I'm sitting, Garret thought. *You've got a body that makes a man glad he's a man.*

"I care for you, Monica."

"Before an hour ago, I might have believed that lie." She folded her arms over her voluptuous breasts. "I never want to see you again."

Unashamedly Garret braced his hands on the steering wheel and leaned forward, craning his neck so he could see upward through the windshield.

"It was just a dance," Bryan tried to explain.

With obvious disbelief, Monica threw her hands up in the air. "What you two were doing on the floor could hardly be called dancing. I suppose you'll try to tell me that instead of kissing, you were trying to resuscitate her."

Garret chuckled. *You tell him, pretty. Guys like that are the reason guys like me have such a hard time getting women to trust us. Obviously he's another fool who didn't appreciate what he had.*

"Please listen," Bryan pleaded. "I care about you."

"Say that one more time and I'll be tempted to do something you'll be sorry for."

His head snapped back as if he was surprised by her response. "You can't end this. Your parents are expecting us for dinner tonight. Your father and I do business together!"

"Watch me." She turned to leave.

He caught her arm, fear and desperation in his voice. "Your father could ruin me if he called the company! He's one of our biggest customers."

Garret's eyes narrowed.

Monica glanced at her arm, then at Bryan. "Take your hand off me."

"Monica, be reasonable!"

"Let me go."

"I refuse to believe you'd end it over a kiss that meant nothing to me."

"My arm."

That's it. Garret got out of the truck and started toward the stairs. *Three strikes and you're out, buddy.* "Is there a problem, miss?"

Monica never looked away from Bryan. "Thank you, but I can handle it. Bryan. Now."

"I'd do as she says if I were you," Garret said, stopping directly behind the man.

Bryan threw an irritated look over his shoulder, saw the broad shoulders of a man who outweighed him by thirty pounds and was probably five inches taller, then brought his angry gaze back to Monica. He released her arm and brushed by the man on the way down the stairs. At the bottom of the stairs, he looked back up and said, "I'll go, but women your size can't be choosy."

Monica's eyes widened at the vicious taut. Her embarrassed gaze jerked toward Garret.

Garret cursed under his breath and turned toward Bryan, but he was already running toward his Lincoln's still-open door. Hopping in, he roared off. When Garret whirled back, Monica was gone.

"Bryan Owens is a fool, and what does that say about me for dating him for six weeks?" Monica fumed as she stalked through her second-floor apartment to her bedroom. At least she now realized what kind of man he was. If she hadn't passed the jazz club on the way home, seen his car, and decided to stop, she might have never known.

Her hands trembling with unleashed fury, she undid the silver buttons on her jacket. To think she had planned to buy him a silk shirt and tie when she went to Rome for her twenty-eighth birthday in eight weeks. He'd said he'd hoped she didn't forget him with all the Italian men after her. What guff! She'd been a total idiot!

Remembering the stranger on the stairs, she paused in pulling off her slacks. *Dark and dangerous* had been her fleeting impression of him. She was unsure if it was because of the sensual huskiness of his voice or the full beard. He'd certainly been built. The muscles beneath his white T-shirt were well-defined. He would have made mincemeat out of Bryan.

Screwing up her face, she went to her closet. He might have helped her, but Monica hoped she never saw him again. She didn't need a reminder of her stupidity and one of the most embarrassing moments of her life.

On the way to her closet, she passed the trifold mirror on her triple dresser. Immediately she stopped, and then walked closer. She wore only her black lace bra and thigh-high panties. It was all out there, and it was all good.

She wasn't a toothpick. She was a curvaceous woman, but that didn't mean she wasn't feminine or intelligent or loving or loyal, or lacking in any of the other qualities that other women not of her largeness possessed. Star Jones had proved that women with their proportions had it going on. Bryan was a fool if he didn't understand that.

Monica's mouth curved into a smile. She put her hand on her ample hip. She was a solid size twenty-two, but she took care of herself and she looked damn good. Her size was as much a part of her as her caramel skin color or the texture of her baby-fine hair. "Bryan, you'll never know what you missed."

Smiling, she continued to the bathroom to take a bath and get dressed for dinner at her parents' house. Alone. She shook her head. She'd let another man get away. Her mother would worry; her father would want to know if Bryan had gotten out of hand. She'd answer their questions with three little words: He was stupid.

Monday morning Monica grabbed her purse and briefcase, and hurried for the front door. Mondays had always been her least favorite day. Hence, once she began working with her father's company and discovering others felt the same, she'd started bringing goodies for the break room to get the week off to a better start.

Today she planned on bagels, but the shop where she wanted to pick them up was twenty minutes out of her way. As usual she was cutting it close.

Closing her door, her head down, she started for the stairs and bumped into a warm, immovable object. Strong, work-roughened hands closed with inexplicable gentleness on her upper forearms. "Whoa."

Monica heard the laughter in the deep voice that unexpectedly sent tingling sensations tripping down her spine. She lifted her head, an apology already forming on her lips. Her eyes widened. It was the stranger from the day before.

He smiled easily down at her, as if they'd shared laughter before. "Late for work, huh?"

"I . . . yes," she sputtered.

His dark head tilted toward the door behind him. "I moved in last night. Looks like we're neighbors."

"Neighbors," she parroted. Life couldn't have such a perverse sense of humor.

Startling white teeth flashed in a dark, sinfully handsome face. He extended his right hand; his left remained on her arm. "Garret McKnight."

Monica belatedly realized he'd been holding her all along and she hadn't felt the least bit annoyed or afraid that a stranger held her. She shifted slightly and the hand immediately fell away.

"Carla."

His mustache curved slightly upward. She had the distinct impression he wanted to laugh. Her mouth tightened in annoyance. "Somehow you don't look like a Carla," he said.

"Be that as it may. Good-bye." She held up the

handbag in one hand and the briefcase in the other as her excuse not to shake his hand. They were not going to be new best friends. Even now, she felt like tucking her head and slinking away in embarrassment. "I'm sure you'll be very happy here."

She hurried away, feeling him watching her every step of the way.

"Monica, your father wants to see you in his office," Bridget said.

"Please tell him to give me a second and then I'll be there," Monica told her father's secretary. She hung up the phone and continued to flip the pages of the contract she'd received that morning. It was just as she and the head of purchasing for Miller Enterprise had discussed. When she dropped the signed contracts off that afternoon, it would be the biggest furniture sale of her career.

Standing, she left her office and headed down the hallway, tastefully decorated by her mother with framed African-American art and potted plants. Entering her father's outer office, she waved to Bridget and continued into his office without knocking.

Her father and the man beside him were standing in front of an open bookcase with their backs to her. Her brow puckered. There was something oddly disturbing about the man. Perhaps it was his size.

Her father weighed in at two-fifty and stood six-five in his size-thirteen bare feet. He usually dwarfed most men, yet this stranger, who was at least three inches shorter and sixty pounds lighter, held his own. His shoulders were wide beneath his white shirt, his legs long and muscular in sharply creased khaki pants. Even motionless he exuded a raw power.

"You wanted to see me, Daddy?"

Her father turned and so did the man with him. The smile on Monica's face died. Embarrassment heated her cheeks. "You!"

Clifford Jones's heavy brows bunched. He glanced questioningly from one to the other. "Monica, have you and Garret met before?"

Monica could think of no plausible answer that wouldn't let her father know she had stretched the truth last night to explain Bryan's absence. By the time she'd arrived at her parents' home, she'd managed to cool down even more and had decided telling them that Bryan was stupid would raise too much speculation. Instead she'd told them that she and Bryan had decided they wanted different things out of life. Fortunately, her niece and nephew had been there with their parents, Monica's older sister and her husband, John, and her parents had spent the evening doting on their grandchildren.

"Monica?" her father prompted when she didn't say anything.

Garret's midnight-black eyes twinkled mischievously. "I didn't think Carla fit."

"Carla?" her father said, obviously puzzled.

Garret's lips twitched. "When we met this morning your daughter knew only that I was her neighbor. A young woman living alone can't be too careful."

Smooth, Monica thought, but then Bryan had been a glib talker as well.

"Perhaps we should try the introductions again." Garret extended his wide-palmed hand. "Garret McKnight."

With her father watching, she had no recourse. "Monica Jones." She expected a killer grip or a limp handshake. What she got was gentleness and a flash of awareness as his hand closed over hers. Her eyes widened and she quickly withdrew her hand, but not before she saw the identical awareness in his eyes.

"Garret, I'm glad you were able to get the apartment," her father said into the heavy silence. "Monica told me about the vacancy."

"Thank you, Monica. I hope I can call you Monica," Garret said.

"Of course you can," Clifford Jones answered for his daughter, then took his seat behind his desk. "We're informal around here."

Garret continued to stare at her with those fathomless black eyes of his. Monica felt a strange fluttering in her stomach. That would teach her to skip breakfast. "Sure."

"Thank you, Monica."

Was it her imagination or had his voice really dropped to a sensual croon? The palm of the hand he'd held tingled. Time to put an end to whatever craziness was going on with her. She faced her father. "You wanted to see me?"

"Yes, and I must say Garret and you living next door to each other couldn't have worked out better." He leaned forward and braced his arms on his desk. "I've just given Garret's company the exclusive contract to install our furniture. You two will be working very closely together. Starting today."

Her attention jerked toward Garret. It was going from bad to worse. "How can you have enough certified installers if you just moved here?"

"My men and I have been living in efficiencies for the past month. We did the Meadowbrook offices and Park City on time and without a hitch."

She frowned. Both were big contracts with 100 and 125 units respectively. Their firm bought the furniture and workstations directly from the manufacturer but they contracted out for the installations. "Simpson Installations was hired for those projects."

Garret folded his arms across his wide chest. "I subcontracted the job. Seems he lost his workers."

"You stole his crew?" she asked in disbelief and outrage.

His eyes flashed. All lazy indulgence disappeared. His arms dropped to his side. "I quit Simpson and started my own firm. The men followed. I make my own way or not at all. I don't climb up on the back of anyone."

She flushed and thought of Bryan. That was exactly what he had tried to do in dating her. He was the sales rep for one of their major suppliers of office furniture.

"I have nothing but praise for Garret's work, and I admire his ethics," her father said, obviously trying to pacify him. "He could have stayed in Las Vegas and taken all of Simpson's business. The man didn't take care of his company. Garret was the one we called when there was a problem. Simpson would hire him back in a heartbeat. He's good, Monica."

Her father had certainly leaped to his defense. He liked him. He hadn't cared two hoots and a holler about Bryan. "I apologize if it seems I questioned your character."

"Accepted. As I said, you don't know me, but you will," he said softly.

Her brows bunched. She got the distinct impression his last words were a promise.

Her father nodded his graying head. "You're right

about that. Monica is the best salesperson we have," he said proudly. "She's the main reason you'll be busy. She sold that two-hundred-unit office job I was telling you about."

Monica waited for disbelief to flash across Garret's face the same way it had Bryan's when she'd purchased the furniture from him. Garret surprised her again. "Beauty and brains. A winning combination."

Monica lips tightened despite her father's chuckle. She wasn't letting another man they did business with charm her. "Nice meeting you, Mr. McKnight—"

"Garret, please."

"Garret," she said through clenched teeth, then said to her father, "I was just checking the contracts for Miller Enterprise. I'd better get back to them."

His round face looked thoughtful. "Can you be free by four?"

"I don't see a problem with that," she said, moving toward the door, very aware that Garret's attention was on her.

"Good, then you and Garret can meet Scott Peters at the site on McKinney."

"What!"

"He's getting anxious about the installations," Garret told her. "He called while I was here and I suggested I could meet him and go over his specifications. Your father thought it would be a good idea if a rep from his company accompanied me."

It was logical. Scott had needed his hand held since the contracts had been signed. They were on target, but every other aspect of the opening of the rental office property he managed had hit one snafu after the other. She wanted to send someone else, but she had made the sale, was vice president of the company,

and had always put their firm before her personal
feelings.

She wasn't afraid of any man. "I'll meet you there."

Garret inclined his head. "See you then."

Monica left the room feeling a prickling awareness
every step of the way.

Two

The white brick, eight-story office building Scott Peters managed was on lower McKinney Avenue near
downtown Dallas. Old and new money were evident
in the trendy boutiques, chic restaurants, and upscale
town homes lining the street. Luxury cars vied with
the only cable car service in the city for the right of
way on the cobbled street. Office buildings here were
sedate, parking at a premium, and the grounds well
maintained. Location here meant you had arrived.

Grabbing her day planner, Monica got out of her
black Cherokee. Her usual decisive steps lacked their
briskness as she crossed the parking lot on the ground
floor of the building. She wasn't looking forward to
this meeting, and she didn't have to think long to
know the reason: Garret McKnight. He disturbed her,
and it wasn't just because of the situation with Bryan.

Opening the glass door to the back entrance of the
building, she immediately saw Scott and Garret. Scott,
short and balding, prowled the black-and-white-tiled
floor like an expectant father. Garret, a zipped folder
in his right hand, leaned casually against the empty

receptionist's desk. Before she could do more than cross the threshold, Garret turned to her. Her stomach did a backflip.

Scott threw a look at her, shook his head, and then continued to pace. "Hi, Monica. Looks like my luck is holding steady."

"What's the matter?" Monica asked, stoically keeping her attention on the building manager.

He stopped. "The elevators won't work."

Instead of a bank of elevators to her left, she saw the empty shaft and strings of heavy cable. The medical offices they were installing furniture in were on the fifth floor. "I can come back tomorrow."

"I can't," Scott said, stuffing his hands into the pants of his navy blue suit. "I'm flying out tonight to San Francisco. My wife will divorce me if I cancel another vacation."

"There's always the stairs," Garret said quietly.

"Five floors," Scott said with a tinge of horror in his voice.

"I can check the specifications by myself, then come back down," Garret said. "You and Monica can wait here."

"I sold the units. I should go with you," Monica said.

Garret's gaze lazily drifted over her short-sleeved mint-green dress to her three-inch pumps. "In those shoes?"

Her chin lifted. She'd worn heels since she was fourteen. Her mother loved shoes and had passed the passion onto her daughters. "Yes."

His dark head tilted as he studied her a brief moment longer. Then, as if coming to a decision, he said, "It's an unnecessary climb, but it's your decision."

"It is, isn't it?" Monica gritted out a smile.

Scott grimaced. "If you two are going, I guess I'll go. I want to double-check the measurements with you. The office manager for the doctor's office is in Rome until next week, so the responsibility was passed on to me."

Monica's eyes lit. "I'm going there for my birthday. The trip is a present from my parents. I can't wait." She sighed dreamily. "The coliseums, the grottoes, the architecture."

"The shopping," Garret added with a grin.

She finally looked at him. "Have you been there?"

"Not yet," he said, and then turned to Scott. "If you'll lead the way, Monica and I will bring up the rear."

Not looking the least bit thrilled by the prospect of climbing five flights of stairs, Scott headed for the stairwell. Monica followed. She'd gone only a few steps up the stairs before the hair on the nape of her neck prickled. She slowed, and then glanced behind her. Garret smiled innocently up at her.

The wording he'd used came back to her: *bring up the rear.* Her eyes narrowed accusingly. He was staring at her behind. She'd left the long mint-green jacket to her dress in her car.

"If you've changed your mind, Monica, I understand," Scott said, his voice concerned. "This will be quite a climb for you."

The insinuation was that she couldn't make it because she was a woman of substance. "Lead the way."

Loosening his silk tie, Scott continued up the stairs. Monica followed, her mind on Garret instead of the stairs. Every now and then she'd turn to try to catch him looking at her, but she never succeeded.

"I need to rest," Scott said as they reached the fourth-floor landing. "You aren't tired?"

He was looking at Monica. She looked at Garret. "Are you tired?"

"I was about to ask that we stop." Exhaling loudly, Garret brushed his hand slowly across his forehead, looking no more tired than if he'd crossed the street. "I'm glad we only have one more flight to go."

Monica's eyes widened in disbelief at the obvious lie; then an instant later she realized Garret was trying to let Scott save face. *Talk about men and their fragile egos.* But he was an important client. "I could use a rest."

"Guess this is our exercise for the day," Scott said as he began to climb again.

Garret came up beside Monica and took her arm. "From where I'm looking, you're in pretty good shape."

She glared at him. "You've been looking at my hips."

"No," he said, his mouth curved into the most devastating smile she'd ever seen. Then he leaned over and whispered in her ear, "I've been looking at your hips *and* your legs."

Her eyes widened at his boldness; her body shivered as his warm breath caressed her ear. She'd tell him off just as soon as the client was out of hearing range. But as they continued up the stairs she became aware of the close proximity of their bodies, the heat and hardness of his sending an oddly tingling sensation spiraling through her.

She concentrated on taking a step instead of thinking about the man next to her. She was glad for more than one reason when they reached the fifth floor, and wished desperately for a cooling glass of water.

*   *   *

Garret was a man who knew how to set priorities. On the fifth floor, he'd immediately begun remeasuring and going over the installation plans with Scott, answering his many questions, reassuring him when necessary.

Jones Business Strategy's and Garret's company's reputation were on the line, just as Scott's was. The job would be completed on time and to his satisfaction. Garret would drop by the site daily, and do a final walk-through with Scott for his approval before he submitted the bill. Monica could accompany them. Scott left them in the parking lot, still grumbling about the elevator, but at least he wasn't worried about the installations any longer.

"Very nicely done," Monica said, her arms folded around her day planner as she stood by her car.

"Thank you." Garret glanced at his stainless-steel watch. "It's after five. You're about to go home?"

"Eventually," she said evasively, and reached for the door handle of her Cherokee.

Garret reached it first, but simply held it, trapping her between him and the vehicle. "You're going out with that guy again?"

Monica's chin jutted. "Although it's none of your business, the answer is no."

"He was a fool who didn't appreciate what he had," he told her.

Caught between being flattered and embarrassed all over again, Monica went for bravado. "I don't want to discuss Bryan."

"Good, then how about us?"

She blinked. "Us?"

"You're a beautiful, vivacious woman, and I'd like

to get to know you better over dinner tonight." His brushed his fingertips across her cheek. "Soft, as I thought it would be."

Monica felt her resistance melting. No man had ever touched her with such aching tenderness before, looked at her as if he'd never get enough.

Garret stepped closer, aligning their bodies, his mouth hovering close to hers. "Go out with me."

A car horn blasted near them, breaking the spell he'd woven. She pushed firmly against his wide chest. She was thankful when he straightened. "Dating people you work with isn't a good idea."

"I'd say that all depended on the person. What do you say we discuss it further over a couple of prime ribs tonight?" he cajoled.

"No," she said, getting into the Jeep and hoping she sounded firmer than she felt. "Good-bye, Garret." She closed the door and pulled off.

Monica arrived at her Mediterranean-style apartment building a little after six. She'd looked a long time and debated even longer on whether to buy a house or rent before reaching a decision. Seeing the Meridian apartment home, with its red tile roof and glistening white brick facade, had made her decision easy. With twenty-four-hour maintenance and maid and laundry service, it was like living in a hotel. But she also had the amenities the finest custom home possessed without the bother of a lawn to care for or the hundreds of other bothersome things that her parents and sister had to deal with in their homes.

She had a busy lifestyle with her church, organizations, and job. Apartment life suited her. She'd hate to move.

Grabbing her things, she slid out of the car and then started for the stairs. Perhaps Garret would forget about trying to ask her out. Her mouth twisted. *And pigs fly.* He had a way about him that said he didn't take no easily. Well, he'd have to this time.

She started up the stairs, then abruptly halted as a muscle spasm knifed through the calf of her right leg. Her briefcase tumbled from her hand as she grabbed the railing to keep from falling.

Her eyes shut as she tried to straighten her leg. The spasm intensified. Air hissed though her teeth. Her purse slid off her shoulder to land beside her feet. The white paper sack with her dinner tumbled through the opening of the stairs. She was in too much misery to care.

"Monica, what's the matter?" asked an anxious voice behind her—a voice that she recognized instantly.

"M-muscle spasm," she moaned out.

Wide-palmed hands closed around her calf, and then began to briskly rub from her knee to her ankle. The pain increased.

"No." She bent down to try to push Garret's hands away and almost toppled. "Stop. Please."

"I'm sorry, honey; I've got to loosen up the muscles. Just hang on," Garret told her. "Think of something pleasant. Like walking in the rain with me or dancing beneath the moonlight in my arms."

"I-I'm not going anyplace with you," she said.

"I'm a nice guy," he said, continuing to massage her leg. "My parents think so. I'm the oldest of four and the only boy, so I've been taught how to appreciate a woman. They all live in El Paso."

Monica found herself listening to what he was saying instead of concentrating on the excruciating pain in her leg. "Any chance you might go back?"

"Nope. I like it here." Standing, he slid his arm around her waist. "Time to walk."

Her eyes widened in protest. "It'll hurt!"

"Only for a little while." He already had her handbag slung over his broad shoulder, and her briefcase in his other hand. He helped her down the stairs, taking her weight easily, and then started down to the sidewalk.

Monica had no choice but to follow. Without the support of the handrail, she'd fall. Her arm went around his neck.

"You have sisters and brothers?" he asked.

Monica put her foot down, expecting the crippling pain, but it was only a throbbing ache. "A sister. Ten years older."

"She in the business?" he asked, opening a gate and leading them toward a paved walking path that meandered behind the apartment.

"She and Mama are in academia. Both teach history at the college level." The pain was almost gone.

"So one followed Daddy and one followed Mother."

They passed beneath the cool shade of a mature oak tree. Even at six the temperature remained in the high nineties in June. Perspiration beaded on her forehead. "I've always been a daddy's girl; plus I like being out and meeting new people."

"Really?" he asked, smiling down at her.

She flushed and faced forward. "Most of the time."

"I'll grow on you." They followed the curving path past the occasional flower beds and colorful dwarf shrubs. "You get the contract delivered all right?"

"Yes," she answered, glad he had directed the conversation to a business rather than a personal level. "Work starts in three months. He wants the job done in four weeks."

The sun dipped lower, but neither seemed to notice. "No problem. I've allotted fourteen of my guys to do the job. The rest will be busy with the other assignments I've lined up."

"Then we aren't your only company?" she asked.

"Although your father promised to help any way he could, I'd be a fool to depend on one firm," he said. "Does his offer of assistance bother you?"

"Yes," she answered truthfully.

"Then I'll just have to work on gaining your trust." He stopped and stared down at her. "Starting now."

Monica knew the kiss was coming, debated whether she should evade, then found herself anticipating, then enjoying the softness of his mouth, the rasp of his soft whiskers against her skin.

His arms circled her, drawing her closer while he savored and excited her. His hands caressed the small of her back. "Have dinner with me," he murmured against her lips.

"I can't," she whispered, stepping back.

"I'm a man who has always gone after what he wants," he warned. "At thirty-two I see no reason to change."

Out of his arms, she could think. "Then I'd say that you're long overdue for a reality check. Thank you. Now, may I please have my bag and briefcase?"

Wordlessly Garret handed them over, and then watched her walk away from him. She could run, but she wasn't going to escape.

He pressed his lips together, recalling the heat, the

incredible sweetness of her lips, the glorious weight of her in his arms. No, she wasn't getting away.

He followed, already planning his strategy to wear her resistance down. It wouldn't be easy, but what of value in life was? Probably because of Bryan and stupid guys like him, Monica didn't realize what a fabulous woman she was. Garret was just the man to show her.

He caught up with her at the pool gate, and then walked quietly beside her. "Why a vacation in Rome?"

"I've just always wanted to go there and throw a coin in the Trevi fountain. The city has always seemed a place for love—" Her mouth snapped shut and she sped up.

Tucking the information away, Garret continued beside her. "When are you leaving?"

She shot him a look that clearly said her departure date was none of his business.

"I told Scott you'd check out the building with us when it's completed."

"Eight weeks from yesterday."

That didn't give him much time to work past her defenses, he thought. But he'd always been a man who worked best under pressure.

Reaching the stairs leading to their apartments, he inclined his head toward what was left of her dinner on the ground. "I guess dogs don't like salad greens. What was it?"

"Grilled chicken salad from Mario's."

"I'll go up and get a bag and take care of this."

"Thank you." She started up, then abruptly turned. "I appreciate everything you've done for me, but our association has to be strictly business."

He propped one booted foot on the bottom rung.

"You mean I can't kiss you and feel like I'm holding a little piece of heaven?"

She gulped. "You shouldn't say things like that."

He came up another step until they were eye to eye. "You interest me a great deal. I'm not walking away, and you can't shove me away. Get used to it."

Monica trembled and was unsure of the reason. "You can't threaten me."

"Threatening you is not what I'm after. Loving you until you moan in ecstasy is."

Monica's heart drummed. Her body heated. Turning, she continued up the stairs and into her apartment, her breathing off-kilter.

How could fate have done this to her? All her life she'd wanted a man to look at her the way Garret did, for his touch to make her tingle and forget reason, to hear his voice and have her heart beat faster. It had happened with a man she didn't dare trust. She wasn't letting herself be fooled again.

She pushed away from the door, crossing the oyster-colored carpet of the high-ceilinged living room, sat down on the overstuffed sofa, and glanced around. The furniture was sleek and distinctive, the room uncluttered and spacious. She'd made a home for herself here and was happy. She wasn't moving because of Garret.

Her eyes closed, she leaned her head back against the cushion. She wouldn't let him invade her thoughts. She'd be strong. With her trip coming up, she'd be too busy getting ready to go to think about him. Yet, even as she told herself that, she remembered his avid mouth on her, his gentle hand on her back.

Resistance wasn't going to be easy.

Pushing up from the sofa, she went to the kitchen

and started rambling though her refrigerator, already knowing she'd find nothing to eat. That was why she'd stopped for the grilled chicken salad. Sighing, she headed back to the living room for her purse.

Opening the door, she almost jumped upon seeing a lanky, dark-haired teenager, his hand raised as if he were about to knock. "Yes?"

"Sorry if I scared you, miss. This is for you." Handing her a white paper sack, he turned and hurried toward the staircase.

"Wait," she called, the smell of grilled chicken drifting out of the bag to her. "I didn't order this."

He grinned. "He said to tell you it's to replace the other dinner."

Although she already knew the answer she asked, "Who is *he*?"

"Your new neighbor."

Three

The next morning Monica left thirty minutes before her usual time. It wasn't difficult. She'd slept poorly. Garret had quickly become a complication she didn't need. No matter how hard she tried to resist the unwanted attraction to him, it did no good.

Her mouth twisted wryly as she sat behind her desk in her office. Besides great lips, he had fabulous hands. She'd been in too much pain to pay attention to those hands when her leg had been cramping. But then he'd kissed her and he'd held her so tenderly while his hands stroked her, excited her, made her feel special. And scared. She'd been determined to keep her distance, and then he'd sent dinner.

The gesture had been impossibly sweet, almost romantic. It would have been rude not to have called and thanked him. But once she heard his voice, she vividly recalled his mouth, his hands. Hot shivers had raced down her spine. Her palms had grown damp.

She'd quickly gotten off the phone, but that hadn't kept her thoughts from him. He was there every time she twisted and fought with the bedcovers. If she reacted so strongly to his voice, the last thing she needed or wanted was to see him in person.

And he was still invading her thoughts. She hunched further over her desk. She was going to get through these specs so she could meet with her client. The absurd attraction to Garret would pass.

After all, she wasn't a dreamer like her mother and sister, who let their hearts rule them. Monica, like her father, was practical. They based their decisions on facts, not something as immeasurable as emotions.

However, that heretofore irrefutable truth wasn't helping her with her present situation. Her experience with men in romantic situations was limited. Although she had lots of friends, male and female, she'd never dated very much. Too many men expected a woman to fall into bed with them two seconds after they met.

Bryan hadn't pushed in that area, and she'd been fooled into thinking that meant he cared. What he cared about was her buying power. Garret wouldn't have to push, but it was yet to be determined what he wanted. No man had ever put her into a tailspin before, and she wasn't letting it happen now.

Monica kept that thought all morning and into the afternoon as she returned phone calls, scheduled appointments, and tackled what seemed like never-ending paperwork. At six-ten that evening, she grabbed her purse and briefcase. After a quick stop at the grocery store, she was heading home.

An hour later she trudged up the stairs with her purse, briefcase, and the first of two bags of groceries. On occasions like these she regretted living on the second floor, but she'd wanted a balcony with the coveted view of the downtown Dallas skyline, and that meant the second floor.

After putting away the perishables, she went back down the stairs, opened the back of the Cherokee and leaned in to get the last bag. No matter how she stretched, her fingertips kept only grazing the top of the brown paper sack. The bag girl had shoved it against the backseat. Hitching up her black pant leg, Monica crawled in.

"Hello, Monica."

The deep voice floated over her. She froze with her behind up in the air, her hand reaching. *Why am I doomed to be embarrassed or aroused by this man?*

"I haven't been home long myself. I came back downstairs to get my folder I left in the truck," Garret drawled. "Can I help?"

Monica felt like butting her head against the floor of the car. "No, thank you."

"Been grocery shopping, I see," he said in a conversational tone. "My mother and sisters came down last weekend and stocked up for me."

Deciding he wasn't going away, Monica grabbed the paper bag and pulled it toward her.

"Let me help." She gasped as Garret leaned in, his

big, muscled body brushing against hers, and circled the bag with his arm. "I'll take this on up, unless you want help getting down."

"No, thank you."

Whistling, he turned away. Monica sneaked a peek to see him carrying the bag of fruit and vegetables toward the stairs. She scrambled out of the Jeep and straightened her blouse. Perhaps moving wasn't such a bad idea after all.

Closing the hatch, she started up the stairs, but when she reached the landing she didn't see the bag of groceries in front of her door. Trying to remember that he had helped her and fed her, and that he was an employee, she knocked briskly on his door.

"Come in."

She did. Curiosity overrode indignation, and she gazed around the surprisingly neat apartment. He'd gone for chocolate leather with cream accents. The state-of-the-art computer and workstation in the corner of the room were expected. Soft music drifted from the stereo in the dark oak entertainment center.

A few steps inside, a delicious aroma drifted to her. Her stomach remembered she'd worked through lunch. "If I can have my groceries, I'll be on my way and let you get to your dinner."

"Your groceries are in here," he called out from the kitchen. "I don't want to leave this."

Since men who cooked were an unknown quantity to her—her father and brother-in-law certainly didn't—she found herself more interested in what Garret was doing than in her groceries. He was at the stove, stirring asparagus, broccoli, and carrots in a wok. Three flounder fillets covered with chopped onions and red and green peppers were sizzling on the oven-top grill. "You cook?"

He flashed her a grin, then gave his attention back to the food. "I get tired of eating out. Last year I was gone a total of eight months. I eat so much junk food I try to do better when I'm at home."

"I feel the same way," she said.

"Imagine that. We have something in common," he said easily. "Do you mind turning over the fish?"

Monica picked up the spatula and nudged the fish, a frown working itself across her brow. "How did you do this so fast?"

"Like setting my clothes out the night before, I get things ready for dinner if I plan to be home. Do a little precooking, if necessary. But I don't deserve all the credit. My mother and sisters have the food labeled with directions and instructions." He nodded toward a plain black notebook. "My safety net. Would you like a glass of wine? It's in the refrigerator. Glasses in the cabinet next to the sink. I can tell you about Quick Care."

Monica, who had been thinking it would be another hour before she ate, snapped her attention back to Garret. Quick Care was a chain of clinics specializing in emergency care. They had offices all over the city. The firm was an old client of her father's. "Did everything go all right?"

"Like a dream. We'll probably finish the two new facilities ahead of schedule." He eyed the fish.

Monica dutifully turned the meat over. "It smells delicious."

"Tastes good, too."

Opening the refrigerator, she found that indeed it was well stocked. Getting the wine, she poured two glasses and handed one to Garret.

Instead of taking it in his hand, he leaned over and put his lips to the glass. Automatically she tilted it so

he could drink. His gaze met hers and she felt a frisson
of awareness spear through her.

"Never tasted better." Returning to his cooking, he
related how the installations had gone. Gradually
Monica's nerves settled. She heard the pride in his
voice when he spoke of his crew, his dedication and
determination that the job was done well. Her father
had been right: He had a strong work ethic.

Garret dumped the vegetables into a white bowl,
then slid the fish onto a platter and took both to the
round glass-topped dinette.

"I should be going," she said, edging toward her
groceries.

"Stay and eat. I have plenty." Taking two plates
from the cabinet, he set them on the table as well.
"I'd enjoy the company. Hope you don't mind plastic utensils."

"Your flatware didn't get packed?"

He grinned boyishly. "I hate washing dishes and I
forget to run the dishwasher. Bad combination. If you
weren't here, I'd be eating off a paper plate."

Monica picked up the heavy blue stoneware. "We
have something else in common."

He grinned.

Dinner was wonderful. Garret was easy to talk to
and be with. If only he didn't work for them she'd
seriously look forward to seeing where their attraction
would lead. With a suppressed sigh, Monica got up to
help clear the table. "You're a great cook. I'll help
you with the dishes."

He took the serving dishes out of her hands. "Even
I can manage this amount."

She promptly took them back. "*We* can manage."

They quickly cleaned up the kitchen together. She was almost reluctant to leave. She couldn't remember when she'd had such an enjoyable evening with a man. Picking up her groceries, she headed for the door. "Thanks again for feeding me two nights in a row."

"Thank you for making the end of my day so enjoyable."

She blushed. "Good night."

"Good night."

She walked to her door, opened it, and then looked back. He was still there watching her. Darkness had fallen. Light spilled from his apartment. He was a gorgeous hunk of man. The beard lent him a dangerous quality that made her feel almost reckless. No woman could probably keep him, but it would be an interesting ride while it lasted.

"Go on inside, Monica, before I forget about good intentions and remember the taste of your mouth on mine."

She went, but once inside she licked her lips.

The next morning Monica left for work at her regular time. Her pace was leisurely and self-assured as she went down the stairs to her car. She didn't even glance toward Garret's door.

She'd given herself a good talking-to. She was an intelligent, twenty-seven-, almost twenty-eight-year-old, independent woman. Hiding from or avoiding a man, as her maternal grandmother would say, didn't show her at her best. Last night while in the bathtub, she'd figured out the reason he appealed to her: She was suffering from rebound, and his rescuing of her had soothed her bruised spirit.

Getting into her Cherokee, she smiled. There was

no need to be concerned about Garret. She had it all under control.

It was barely seven Wednesday morning when Garret pulled up in front of his office in a strip shopping center in southeast Dallas. The only cars in the lot were those in front of the doughnut shop at the corner.

Unlocking the door, he went straight to the large bulletin board in his office. Listed on it were the seven installations in progress, the men assigned, the total number of units finished, and the number that remained.

He kept a sharp eye on the progress of each job, and he personally checked on each every other day. He didn't watch his men. He was there if they or the customer needed him. Being available wasn't something his ex-boss had made a habit of, and he'd lived to regret it. Garret never took his fledging business for granted. He paid bills and his employees first, not himself. He was in the black and he planned to stay that way.

Nodding his satisfaction that everything was on or ahead of schedule, Garret took his seat behind his desk and went over the contracts Clifford Jones had sent by messenger the day before. Garret leaned back in his leather chair. Although he knew it had been a long shot, he'd hoped Monica might deliver them. Disappointed when she hadn't, he'd gone home. She was still on his mind when he had gone back downstairs for his folder and seen her with her hips up in the air in her Cherokee.

His mouth twisted wryly. He really should have left, but he hadn't been able to resist admiring the view. He'd stuck his hands in his pockets to keep from doing something that would have gotten his face slapped. Dinner had proven that she wasn't as immune to him as she'd like to pretend, but she was fighting the attraction.

He wasn't egocentric, had certainly struck out a few times before, had shrugged and walked away. But he wasn't walking away this time.

Monica's lush body had piqued his interest the second he'd seen her walk past his truck that first day. Her face had captured his attention. Her unshakable spirit earned his respect. The lady wasn't a pushover. The entire combination of who and what she was appealed to him.

He looked at the schedule. He'd be chasing his tail for the next couple of days, so she was safe for the time being. Not being able to follow up on last night was unfortunate, but it couldn't be helped.

The last thing he wanted to do was give Monica or her father a reason to regret their association. No one had to tell him that he had to prove himself with her. Trust was a major factor to her, personally and professionally. But Garret had always accomplished what he set out to do.

This time it would be no different with Monica.

Four

Friday morning, Monica walked into the break room for a cup of coffee. "Hello, Bridget," she called, going to the carafe.

"Morning," Bridget returned. "Bryan Owens called

three times yesterday. He says it's very important you call him."

Monica finished pouring the decaffeinated coffee into her mug, aware that Bridget, who stood beside her, watched her closely. In her mid-sixties and as sharp as they came, Bridget had been her father's secretary since he started the company fifteen years ago. Bridget's loyalty lay with her father. Clifford's was with his family. If Bridget suspected for a second that Bryan had used Monica to further his own bank account, her father would hear about it.

"I'll call him." Monica sipped her coffee, her face a careful mask. He'd also left messages on her home answering machine pleading for her forgiveness. Thank goodness he'd already had a business trip to Nashville planned this week and wasn't due back until the weekend.

Bridget added sugar and cream to her own coffee. "You decide if you're going to use his company or Sanders for Colfax?"

"I haven't decided." With everything within her, she wished she could dismiss Bryan's bid. She couldn't. He might be unprincipled. She wasn't. She'd give his bid due consideration, although it galled her to do so. She'd have to decide soon. She had a meeting Monday morning with the business manager of Colfax, an electronics firm. If they went to contract it would top her last sale.

Bridget nodded her frosted head of hair. "In the three months he's been Middleton's rep, I've never heard him sound so rattled. Whatever the reason you two broke up Sunday, he wants to work things out."

Monica's hands tightened around her mug. What he wanted was for her to accept his bid for Colfax's 230 units. "I'll try to call today," Monica said, glad they were alone. Then she turned . . . and wanted to dissolve into a puddle and flow down the drain in the sink behind her.

Garret, his dark gaze riveted on her, stood just inside the doorway. From the hard look on his face Monica realized he'd heard enough of the conversation to know she'd been used.

"Good morning, Bridget. Monica."

"Good morning, Garret," Bridget greeted him with a smile. "Clifford isn't here. He had a dental appointment this morning."

Garret's gaze centered on Monica. "I came to see Monica."

Bridget flickered a glance between the two—Monica tense, Garret purposeful—then cleared her throat and said, "Well, I'd better get back to work."

Monica thought of following until Garret stepped out of the doorway to allow Bridget to pass, then closed the door and leaned against it. Unease swept through her. He didn't look like a man bent on seduction. He looked more like a man ready to vent his anger; with that powerful body of his, he could do a lot of damage.

"I thought you said you weren't going out with him again?"

The harshly spoken question surprised, then annoyed her. "I don't have to answer to you."

He was across the room in three long strides and towered over her. "Is he the reason you won't go out with me?"

Monica tried to feel outrage at his proprietary action. But it was difficult as she gazed up into the darkest, most beautiful eyes she'd ever seen, midnight black fringed with thick, velvety lashes. "I made a mistake with Bryan. I won't make another one."

"Mistakes don't taste like this."

His mouth fastened on hers. The persuasive gentleness undid her; the thoroughness of his tongue inside the warmth of her mouth excited her. He had the strength to take, but he used seduction, luring her to follow, to forget, to lose herself in his arms, in this kiss, in him.

Monica obeyed the demand with a passion she was unaware she possessed. She forgot to be embarrassed, to be outraged. There was only this moment, this man who took her places she'd never been before, never thought existed.

Garret felt the edges of reality blur and fought for control. No woman, no kiss had ever undone him as this woman, this kiss had. Knowing that if he didn't stop soon, he wouldn't be able to, he lifted his head. His breathing ragged, he stared down into her face flushed with passion. Her eyes were closed, her lips moist and trembling.

Seconds later her sooty lashes fluttered and then lifted, revealing dazed chocolate-brown eyes. He felt a swift possessiveness he'd never experienced before. His hand cupped her cheek with exquisite tenderness. "You're a beautiful, intelligent woman. Don't throw away what we could have."

Monica shut her eyes again, and then shook her head. "I won't be ruled by mere physical attraction."

"It's more than that and you know it," he said fiercely. "Or we would have been in bed by now."

Her eyes popped open. She pushed out of his arms. "Just go."

He stared down at her. "This isn't over."

Monica watched him stalk across the room, yank the door open, then leave. If he came near her again she'd . . . run like crazy.

Garret got to his truck, but couldn't go any farther. He braced his hands on the sun-warmed hood. Becoming angry with her wasn't going to get her to go out with him. He never raised his voice to a woman. Well, except for his sisters, and that was to be expected.

What got to him so badly was that she reacted so passionately, yet refused to open her mind, her heart. He was a man who wanted—no, demanded—it all, because he'd give just as much. He grimaced. He knew that. Monica didn't. What she did know was that the last man she'd trusted had betrayed her.

Rage swept through Garret as he remembered Bryan's last words to Monica, the hurt embarrassment on her face. She had a right to be cautious. He'd just have to be patient enough to show her that with him she didn't have to be. He reentered the gray, single-story building.

Hoping she hadn't left the break room, he went there first. He pushed the door open. She was in the same spot he'd left her. Her head came up. Dark eyes widened.

"I'm sorry," he said, letting the door close. He silently cursed himself for putting that wary look on her face. He was no better than Bryan. "I have no excuse. Your spirit attracted me initially. I can't get upset if you use that same spirit to disagree with me. If you'd give me five minutes of your time, I'd like to explain."

"I won't change my mind," she told him quietly, watching him cautiously.

"Five minutes," he repeated. "Your father trusts

me, and you can too. If you still don't want to go out
with me after you hear what I have to say, it will be
strictly business between us from now on."

His words should have made her glad, yet somehow
they didn't. The door behind him opened and Vickie
Turner, their marketing director, came in.

Vivacious and pretty in a slim magenta dress that
fitted her shapely figure perfectly, Vickie barely
glanced at Monica as she greeted her before returning
her full, interested attention to Garret. Vickie loved
men, loved the attention they couldn't seem to help
bestowing upon her.

Monica introduced them and watched Vickie almost
preen. She had a way of drawing men to her. Garret
didn't seem immune to her charm as he shook hands
with her, smiled down at her. Her dark head barely
came to the middle of his wide chest. And worse,
Monica couldn't fit one thigh into the size-six dress
Vickie had on.

The uncharacteristic thought brought Monica up
short. She never compared herself to other women,
and certainly not to their shape. She was her father's
daughter in all things. Just as she'd inherited his mathematical skills that allowed her to breeze through advanced calculus in the seventh grade, she inherited her
lush body from his side of the family. She'd always
been proud and accepting of both traits. Neither Garret nor any other man would make her doubt herself.

"If you'll excuse me, I was about to go to my office,"
Monica said, finally moving away from the counter.

Garret immediately brought the full force of his
gaze to bear on Monica. "I'll go with you. We
haven't finished."

Vickie arched a delicate brow. Men didn't usually
walk away from her.

Monica experienced a lightening of her spirits. Garret wanted to be with her. "See you later, Vickie."

"Of course. I hope to see you again, Garret," Vickie said, obviously not willing to concede defeat.

"I'm sure we will," Garret said politely, then followed Monica out of the room and down the hall.

Her body really knew how to fill out a dress. She had a curvy figure that, thank goodness, she didn't always hide behind baggy clothes or long jackets. Today she had on a lemon yellow straight dress. He'd like to lay her down in sunshine, slowly take off the dress, then let the sun and his body warm her skin.

Monica stopped at her door, and then turned to glare at him. "Stop that!"

Garret stuck his hands in his pockets. "Sorry."

Inside her office, Monica went behind her desk and sat down. It was done as much to get off her shaking legs and to put some distance between her and Garret as it was to remind him that she was in charge. "Five minutes."

Garret didn't plan to waste a second. "Both my parents were the first in their families to get a college degree. It wasn't easy for them or my grandparents, who were factory workers. I grew up knowing the value of an education and hard work. I had a paper route from the time I was seven until I was fifteen. I never missed a delivery except when my family was on vacation. I still had chores at home, schoolwork, sports, and extracurricular activities. I never let one slide for the other."

His hands came out of his pockets and he extended them to her. Calluses laced his palms. "I'm not afraid of hard work or going after what I want."

Monica folded her hands on her desk at that last remark and gulped.

"I got into installation the summer of my junior year in college, when a couple of guys from my old dorm needed help. Then I was young enough to enjoy traveling and sleeping in a hotel, but I also saw the potential." He came around the desk.

Monica felt compelled to meet his gaze.

"I worked, saved, learned about the business and how to keep the customer and the employees happy. When Simpson started being lax, I warned him several times. He liked going to the casinos in Vegas more than taking care of his business. He threw away his company. I didn't steal it from him."

She saw no duplicity in his eyes. "I believe you."

"I don't know any other way but to go all-out for what I want." The intensity of his gaze sharpened. He placed his hands on the arms of her chair and twisted it toward him. Her knees bumped his legs. "I want you."

Monica's breath stalled.

"It's not a passing interest. I'm not trendy. I've had the same truck for ten years. The newest thing in my apartment is my computer. I keep what I have."

Her heart drummed.

"We can go as slowly as you'd like." He leaned closer. His warm breath fanned her face.

She inhaled and tasted the coffee he'd had that morning. She wanted to taste him. She shook her head and turned away.

Strong fingers beneath her chin brought her head back around. "Take a chance. You won't be sorry."

She teetered on the brink. He sounded and looked so sincere. Still . . . "If you didn't work for my father, it might be different."

"If I didn't work for your father, we wouldn't have

met," he pointed out. "If I subcontracted your father's business, would you go out with me then?"

Her eyes widened in alarm. "You can't do that," she told him, sure that it hadn't been an idle statement. "Your company earned those contracts."

The back of his hand brushed fleetingly against her cheek. "Besides being beautiful and intelligent, you're fair and compassionate. Any guy would jump at the chance to go out with you."

She wanted to believe.

The yearning must have shown in her face, because he hunkered down in front of her and took her hands in his, his thumb grazing across the back of hers. "You set the rules. You decide where we go. Tell me anything but to walk away. I can't do that."

She swallowed, and then took a tiny step toward what she wanted. "Well . . . ah . . . a lot of us here get together the end of the month at La Casa, a Tex-Mex restaurant on Oak Lawn, not far from downtown." She moistened her lips. His hot gaze followed.

Clearing her throat, she continued. "We usually get there around seven for dinner and drinks. Maybe we could start tonight, getting to know each other."

"You won't be sorry." His hands gently squeezed hers. "I may be a little late, but I'll be there. I want to finish the Nelson project today."

Ron Nelson had an investment firm and was one of their most exacting and exasperating clients. "Then why aren't you there?"

"Because I had to take care of something even more important." He placed a tender kiss in each of her palms, then stood. "Look for me."

Then he was gone.

* * *

La Casa was a favorite watering hole for the business set to get together. The tables were wood, the floor bare, and the walls adobe. They served the best enchiladas in town, the best margaritas in the state. After a long, stressful day at work, that was enough of a recommendation for the working class to come and wind down.

It was what had drawn Monica and the rest of her coworkers. That was usually enough, but not tonight. She nibbled absently on a chip and kept her eye on the front door. Tonight Garret consumed her thoughts.

It was a heady experience for any woman to be the object of a desirable man's attention. Garret was more than desirable. He made her salivate. But that could also lead to trouble.

She hadn't lost a moment of sleep over Bryan's betrayal. She'd berated herself for her poor judgment, then moved on. This afternoon she'd called and left him a message on his voice mail with exactly those words. But if Garret was playing with her emotions, she wasn't exactly sure how she'd react.

"Oh, my goodness! It's Garret!"

Monica heard the excitement in Vickie's voice the moment she spotted Garret entering the restaurant. He'd changed from jeans and a navy blue polo shirt with the logo of his company on the front to black dress slacks and a white shirt. The full beard gave him a sexy, dangerous look.

"He's looking this way," Vickie cried, lifting her hand and waving. Garret waved back and started toward them.

Garret had gone only a short distance when Monica realized Vickie wasn't the only woman watching him.

Despite being powerfully built, he moved with an easy grace that bespoke self-assurance and confidence of his place in the universe. He'd let few things sway him from his goal.

Monica realized something else just as quickly: The other women might be watching Garret, but he was watching her. She experienced a delicious thrill of pleasure at the knowledge.

"Garret, it's great seeing you again," Vickie purred when he neared. "If you're not meeting anyone, please join us."

"He's meeting me," Monica said, then could have bitten off her tongue at the possessiveness in her voice. Apparently the twelve people sitting with her heard it too, because their eyes bounced between Monica, Garret, and Vickie.

Garret paused by Vickie, who was taken aback. "Thank you. You're as warm as your smile."

Vickie beamed with pleasure.

Garret moved to the head of the table, where Monica sat, her lower lip caught between her teeth. She might regret her outburst, but he didn't. She cared.

He pulled an empty chair up beside her and sat. Their arms brushed against each other. She trembled, but didn't move away. *Progress.* "Good evening, Monica."

"Hello," she said, a bit flustered; then she introduced him to the other people at the table.

"Would you like a menu, sir?" asked a waitress in a white off-the-shoulder blouse and short black skirt.

He gave a nod toward Monica. "I'll have what she's having."

The waiter left and the table became quiet as people kept throwing glances at him. He picked up a chip and dipped it into the bowl of salsa near Monica's plate. "Hot and spicy. Just the way I like it."

He watched her again as he put the chip into his mouth. His eyes were dark and intense, with an almost tangible promise in them, as though he'd savor and enjoy her the same way. Heat shot through her.

She quickly reached for her margarita. What would he do to a woman to take her to the heights of passion if she gave him free rein of her body?

What *wouldn't* he do might be a better question. She gulped more margarita.

"Thanks for inviting me. I had a good time," Garret said as he stood beside Monica while she unlocked the door to her apartment.

Finished, she turned to him, then nervously ran the tip of her tongue across her lower lip. "You're welcome."

Garret took pity on her. "We're getting to know each other, remember? We're in no rush."

"The way you look at me says a whole lot more. Like you could gobble me up," she finished in an embarrassed rush.

Unrepentant, he grinned. "That about sums it up," he said, then sobered. "I can't help how I feel. I enjoy looking at you."

Below them Monica heard cars pass, people talking, but the sound was muted, as if it were miles away. "Or do you enjoy looking at women, period?" she asked, holding her breath, waiting for his answer.

He stepped closer until their bodies touched, thigh to thigh, breast to chest. "You can answer that yourself. Who had my undivided attention tonight, or anytime we're together?" he asked softly.

"I do." The answer came out in a shaky whisper.

His hands cupped her face. "Right the first time. You're the woman I want to be with." His mouth brushed softly against hers; then he stepped back. "Can I see you tomorrow?"

It took a moment for Monica's scrambled brain to register the question. "I-I'm taking my niece and nephew to the circus. Their parents have an afternoon just for themselves every couple of months."

"Sounds like a great idea. Mind if I tag along? I haven't been to the circus in years," he said. "I could make runs to the concession stand; then, too, you wouldn't have to take both of them to the bathroom if one had to go."

"How did you know about the bathroom?" she asked. They always did, and they always got into an argument about it.

He laughed. "I told you I had sisters. If I had gotten on their last nerve that day or any other time, one or the other would ask to go to the bathroom just at the good part of the movie. I learned not to tick them off when we were going out."

"Sounds like they're smart."

"They are," Garret said proudly. "Two are electrical engineers; Cyria, the youngest, is a biochemist."

His loved his family. They had something else in common. Another link. "Is your truck large enough or should we take my car?" Monica asked.

Five

Garret's Silverado had cab seats. Like his apartment, the truck was clean and well cared for. The polished black finish gleamed in the hot Dallas sun. "Your truck looks new," Monica commented as he helped her inside. She'd already given him the address and directions to her sister's house in Oak Cliff.

"I take care of my possessions."

She looked at him over her shoulder. "I'm beginning to see that."

"Headway," he said, then shut the door and went around to his side and got in. Fastening his seat belt, he pulled off.

Monica noticed his strong hands on the steering wheel, the flex of the muscles in his thigh as he braked or shifted gears. She enjoyed looking at him too, and she wasn't going to berate herself or him for doing so again. "Did you finish the Nelson job?"

"Yes." He braked at a signal light. "I still have the key. I'll take you over tomorrow if you'd like. I notified Nelson and he already came over."

She twisted in the seat toward him. Nelson would think nothing of having them reinstall or modify a unit. "How did it go?"

Garret eased through the green light before answering. "He was pleased. He said with office buildings going up in record numbers I stand to make a small fortune. Gave me his card to invest my money."

"You must have made quite an impression," she said, delighted. "He's quite good, and selective with his investment firm, I hear. Are you going to hire him?"

Garret hit the ramp to the freeway with a burst of speed. "Not anytime soon. I don't have any play money. The payroll for fifty-one employees in the field plus two in the office takes a king-size bite out of the hefty checks companies like your father's send me."

"You're all right, aren't you?" she asked, unexpectedly worried.

His gaze briefly left the freeway as his hand closed reassuringly over hers. "Don't worry. I'm fine. I haven't missed a payroll or a payment yet, and I don't intend to. Now, tell me about your niece and nephew."

Monica studied his strong profile for a long moment to affirm that he wasn't just talking to keep her from worrying. It was difficult to tell with his beard, but she didn't think she detected any anxiety.

Slowly she relaxed against the soft leather seat. "Aaron is nine. Thea is five," Monica began, relating anecdotes about the rambunctious pair.

It was only as they exited the freeway twenty minutes later that she realized her first concern had been the stability of Garret's business, not fear that he was trying to use her. His had been to reassure her, and when that failed, he'd tried to distract her. He'd done the same thing climbing the stairs of the office building, and when her leg was cramping.

She wasn't Garret's possession by a long shot, but she couldn't deny the warmth his caring caused.

"Monica, if you let him get away, you should have your brain examined," Deborah said in the kitchen where she'd dragged her baby sister from the den to get the scoop. "To quote my students, he's yummy."

Deborah, slender and lovely with a heart as big as Texas, was a romantic. Monica loved her dearly. "We're just getting to know each other."

"Hmmm," Deborah said. "If the looks he's given you were any hotter, you'd incinerate."

Monica blushed. "He said he couldn't help it."

Deborah screamed and hugged Monica. "I knew it. I just knew it."

Seconds later two worried men followed by two wide-eyed children burst into the kitchen. Luckily the doorway was wide enough to allow the broad-shouldered men through at the same time. Their gaze swept the spacious blue-and-green kitchen as if looking for danger, then settled on the women by the island.

"What happened?" John, Deborah's husband, asked.

"Are you all right?" Garret wanted to know.

Monica tucked her head. Her cheeks were hot.

Deborah pushed her shoulder-length braids behind her ears, then slung her arm casually around her baby sister's shoulders. "Everything is just perfect. We were just celebrating." Her gaze zeroed in on Garret, who was staring at Monica with a worried frown. "So, Garret, tell us about yourself. Your family? Your intentions?"

Monica's head snapped up. "Deb!" she said in a hiss.

Garret laughed. "Honorable, I assure you."

John shook his head of microtwist curls. "What comes into her mind comes out. She told me she loved me after the third date in grad school, then said she'd wait until I was sure."

Garret wondered if last night could be considered a date, then asked, "What did you say?"

John's strong ebony face creased into a smile. "I asked her what took her so long. I knew after the first date."

Deborah and John met midway across the spacious kitchen beneath the skylight. He kissed her bronzed cheek.

"Aunt M, can we please go now? They're about to start." Nine-year-old Aaron folded his arms across the colorful jersey of his favorite NFL team and shot his parents a disgruntled look.

"I want a hug, too," five-year-old Thea, in braids, declared.

Her parents leaned down and hugged their youngest between them. Her brown eyes sparkled. Monica glanced up and into Garret's eyes, and wondered why her stomach felt funny.

"Aunt M," Aaron said, his back firmly toward his parents in case they were still kissing. He sighed long and hard. "Can we go?"

Garret put his hand on the boy's thin shoulder. "In about seven years you'll understand."

Aaron gave Garret a shrewd look, then glanced at his aunt. "You two aren't going to be doing anything like that at the circus, are you?"

"Aaron!" his parents cried in embarrassment.

"Aaron!" his sister said because her parents had and she didn't want to be left out.

"Aaron!" Monica said, her cheeks warm again.

Garret considered the question as seriously as it was asked. "I promise I'll do my best not to."

"My dad says a man never breaks his promise," Aaron, all of four feet and weighing sixty-two pounds soaking wet with his tennis shoes on, said solemnly.

"He's right. That is one of the two things a man never does."

"What's the other?" Aaron asked.

"Give up," Garret answered.

The circus was nonstop fun. The children's eyes were as big as saucers as they watched the trapeze artists triple-somersault past each other to catch the swing on the opposite side, a young woman put her arm in a lion's mouth, a man place his head beneath an elephant's foot.

Thea wanted one of the trick poodles to take home. Aaron opted for the barebacked rider's beautiful black stallion. Since it was a special day, Monica let them gorge on popcorn, hot dogs, and cotton candy.

Leaving American Airline Center almost three hours later, Aaron and Thea just had to have a souvenir book, sweatshirts, and a cannon-shaped gun that spat sparkles instead of a human. Sharing was not an option. Monica's protests and trying to pay for the items met with a firm no from Garret, as had all the other times she'd tried to pay for anything.

"Garret, I was taking the children to the circus, not you," she said as they walked with the throng of people heading to their cars. She held Aaron's hand. Garret carried an exhausted Thea, her arms clamped trustingly around his neck. "You didn't let me pay for anything."

"I wanted to do it. They're great kids."

"I should have paid," she protested.

His hand curved around her shoulder. "Stop arguing or you'll make me break my promise to Aaron, and he'll lose all respect for me."

Aaron, who had been shooting his gun, glanced up.

"I guess since you bought us all this super stuff, you can if you want." He obviously didn't see the appeal.

Monica's eyes widened. She clamped her mouth shut.

"Thanks, Aaron. Since she stopped arguing, I'll wait until later."

Later.

Monica couldn't get that word out of her head as Garret drove the children home, or as they relaxed over a quiet dinner by the pool with her sister and husband after Aaron and Thea had gone to bed.

"You're all right?" Garret asked.

"Guess I'm a little tired," she answered.

He got up immediately. "Why didn't you say so? I'll take you home."

Monica refused to make eye contact with her sister. She stood when Garret's hand closed around the white rattan chair she sat in. "Good night, Deb. John. Thanks for dinner."

"We're the ones who should be thanking you," Deborah said, rising also. "The children had a wonderful time."

Garret extended his hand to John as he rounded the table. "Thanks. Dinner was great, and you have two precious children."

"We think so. Glad you agree." John and Deborah walked Garret and Monica to the door, and then waved good-night as Garret pulled away from the curb in front of their two-story white colonial home.

"You're sure you're just tired?" Garret asked before they had gone half a block.

Monica leaned her head back against the seat and closed her eyes. "Yes, please don't worry."

He couldn't help being concerned. She'd enjoyed the circus as much as the kids. She'd shrieked and looked though her fingers during most of the trapeze act. She'd been as taken with the poodles as Thea had. It was only after they left that she'd grown quiet.

Keeping the truck barely under the speed limit, he maneuvered through the cars on the freeway and thought of what had happened afterward. The answer hit.

He'd been teasing her about kissing her. Was it anticipation or dread that caused her to become quiet and contemplative? He'd give a lot to have the answer.

"If you don't want me to kiss you good-night, I won't," Garret said as he parked and unbuckled his seat belt. "You're running this show."

The interior of the cab was dark. The light from the black wrought-iron lamp by the stairs couldn't pierce the darkness where his truck sat. Monica didn't think it was an accident that Garret had chosen to park so far away. She unbuckled her seat belt.

"Monica." His voice, like a velvet glove, stroked her senses.

In her opinion, at her age she was too old to play games. "That's not what worries me."

Gently his hands settled on her shoulders and he turned her to him. "What does?"

"How much I enjoy it when you kiss me," she said softly. "I don't want you to be a lie."

"I'm not." His lips brushed across hers. "Trust me. I'm not."

Monica's lips warmed under the teasing assault of Garret's mouth. Denial was impossible. She went into his arms, following his lead, holding nothing back.

Her full capitulation snapped his control. The kiss abruptly changed from gentle to ravenous. Their tongues tangled, dueled. Passion built quickly. Her soft, fragrant body pressing against his was sweet torture.

His hand found the lush roundness of her breast. They groaned together. His nimble fingers undid the buttons of her magenta-colored blouse, found her skin, silky smooth beneath. He couldn't seem to get enough of her mouth or of touching her. He wanted her beneath him, crying out his name.

The beams of a car lit the interior of the cab. He jumped, hitting his elbow on the steering wheel, then went still when he saw Monica, her blouse completely undone, her eyes wide and staring at him. "I'm sorry. I didn't mean for this to happen."

His hands shaking, he began rebuttoning her blouse. He kept his eyes on the task. He was afraid to look at her and see the condemnation in her eyes. She'd trusted him, and he'd almost made love to her in his truck. He hadn't acted so irresponsibly since he was in high school. "You deserve so much better than this. Please believe me when I say it won't happen again."

He finally looked at her, and felt like the lowest life-form. Her head was bowed as if she were ashamed. He couldn't blame her. "I'll walk you to your door."

Silence.

Cursing his stupidity and lack of control, he went around to the passenger side and opened her door. Her head still down, she slid out.

"Monica, please say something."

Shaking her head, she remained silent.

Lightly touching her elbow, he walked her down the sidewalk, then up the stairs. It was both the shortest and the longest walk he'd ever taken. With each step he wanted to stop and hold her, to go down on his knees and ask for forgiveness. Each step took her out of his life that much faster.

He stopped in front of her apartment. "Monica, it won't happen again."

Head bowed, she pulled her key from her purse. Her hand trembled so badly she couldn't get it into the lock.

"Let me." He held out his hand, palm up. She probably didn't want him touching her any more than necessary. After a long moment, the keys dropped into his hand.

The bolt shot home. Opening the door, he held out the key. Like him, she held her hand palm out.

His hand fisted briefly around the keys; then he placed them in her hand. "If you can ever forgive me, I'll be waiting."

Monica walked though the door. She turned and slowly lifted her head. "You don't have to wait."

Six

"What?" Garret couldn't believe his ears.

"You don't have to wait," she repeated, still not looking at him.

He started toward her. She glanced up sharply, then backed up and dropped her head again. His heart sank.

"Maybe you should close the door first," she requested softly.

Without taking his eyes off her, he reached behind him and pushed the door shut. Slowly he went to her. Thank goodness, this time she didn't back away. "You aren't angry with me?"

Her gaze was steadfastly locked on the center of his chambray shirt. "I admit I thought you had planned it at first because of where you parked, until I noticed your hands were shaking when you . . . you buttoned my blouse. You were trying to take care of me."

"You were upset after we left the circus. I wanted to talk to you about it, but I was afraid you'd hurry into your apartment and leave me at the door." Frustration shimmered in his voice. "What happened was unplanned."

"I know." Down went her head again.

It came to him at once. When Monica was angry she let people know it. There was something else going on here. His gaze narrowed as he looked at the top of her head of short black curls, her slumped shoulders, and her fingers fidgeting with the gold clasp of her handbag.

The pieces tumbled into place. Embarrassment, not anger. If she were embarrassed that would have to mean . . .

He lifted her chin with a hand that wasn't quite steady. In her beautiful face traces of discomfiture remained, but so did the passion that had held them both in its grip. "You've never been with a man before, have you?"

She bit her lip. "No."

"Oh, baby, then I'm doubly sorry." He pulled her into his arms, kissed her hair, and wondered how he was going to keep it together with a virgin who pushed every button he had.

She shuddered once, then worked her way out of his arms. Her smile was overly bright. "I hope we can still be friends."

He frowned. "I don't understand. I thought you weren't angry with me."

"I'm not." Her smile wobbled. "We both understood from the first that you wanted more than friendship. Inexperienced women usually make men run or go rabid. I don't think I'd like putting you in either category. So it will be strictly business from now on."

"Which one of us don't you trust this time?" Garret asked, and watched her gaze skitter away.

A baby chick alone with a hungry wolf. She probably had no idea how much power her reaction had given him or the deep responsibility he felt.

Her eyes widened as he went to her and gathered her in his arms. "I'd be lying through my teeth if I said I didn't want to make love to you, kiss every luscious inch of your body, then start all over again."

"Garret," she whispered, her body trembling against his. "I don't want this."

"Yes, you do; you're just scared." His fingertips grazed her cheek. "I told you I'm in this for the long haul. I'm not going anyplace."

"I don't want you to be a lie."

The softly murmured words sank even more deeply than the first time she'd said them in his truck. Now he understood their full implication and her fear. "I'm not." He stepped back. "What time do you want to check out the Nelson place?"

Her hand swept through her curls. "Are you sure about this?"

"Very."

"One should be fine," she said slowly.

"Then there's just one more thing we have to settle before I say good-night." He smiled when she stumbled back.

"You're going to kiss me," she said, the words an accusation.

"And we're both going to enjoy it. Consider it another step in establishing trust. It would be impossible to be around you and not touch you." His eyes darkened. "Come here, Monica."

She shook her head.

"Come here."

She wanted to go, and that scared her. Garret had the ability to take her out of herself, make his will her own. She'd never experienced that before. She realized why she'd never given the boys or men she'd dated a second thought after they broke up. It was because they'd never touched anything within her. But from the moment she'd heard Garret's deep voice there had been a connection that grew stronger each time she heard his voice or saw him.

Now she understood the sweet madness the women at the office talked about when they became sexually excited. Nothing else mattered but the clawing need that consumed them. She didn't know if she could control that compulsion or trust Garret not to take advantage of her.

"Monica, you're safe with me. I'll never go any further than you want. I promise."

He wouldn't come to her; that she also understood. She had to be the one to trust. Her practical mind told her Garret and these new feelings of sexual awareness were an unknown quantity and to tread carefully, but her heart took a leap of faith and believed.

She took one step, then another, until their bodies touched. "If one button comes undone you're in trouble."

"I'll keep that in mind." His mouth met hers, not to stay, but to tease, taste, nibble, then slide away, only to return and repeat the sweet torment. It was an enticing dance that lured and invited her to join in. She did, running the tip of her tongue across the seam of his mouth, suckling his lower lip. His mouth fastened possessively on hers and playtime ceased.

His tongue was boldly erotic, a conqueror sweeping all in its path. She was helpless to resist. But as she surrendered, she found that that there were no victors. Each shared the pleasure of their mouths joined, their bodies straining to get closer.

She felt herself sinking, losing herself; she whimpered in protest even as her fingers tightened to bring him closer.

He heard her and eased back with an iron will until a mere wisp of air separated them. "Lady, what you do to me."

Her breathing labored, her body heated and pulsing with unmet need, she said, "Ditto."

Laughing, he picked her up, smacked her on her kiss-swollen lips, then set her down. "I'll see you at one tomorrow."

Monica put her hand to her booming heart as the door closed, then sank down on the arm of the sofa. The man kissed like a dream, looked good enough to gulp whole, and picked her up as if she were weightless. He was definitely trouble, and until she left for Rome she was going to stop worrying and enjoy every deliciously wicked moment.

*   *   *

Garret arrived promptly at one dressed in tan slacks, a white shirt, and a tobacco-brown jacket. His dark gaze swept over her like silent fingers. "You always look beautiful."

"Thank you. You look good yourself." She'd worn lavender linen pants with a matching unconstructed jacket and Lycra top. Grabbing her purse, she was out the door. Hand in hand they went down the steps. It was a bright, clear day. Monica felt the sun on her face and smiled.

"So he's why you haven't returned my calls."

She went still, then jerked around to see Bryan, his face sullen. She couldn't remember why she ever thought he was attractive, even though he was perfectly groomed and dressed in an expensive double-breasted suit. He was such a user.

Garret stepped between them. "I'd advise you to leave while you can still do so under your own power."

Bryan's eyebrows shot up. "You can't threaten me."

Garret leaned closer. "That was a prediction, not a threat."

Eyes petrified, Bryan stumbled back. "This is between Monica and me. I earned that contract and she knows it."

"I won't ask you again," Garret said, his voice deadly quiet.

Monica had always fought her own battles. She touched Garret's rigid arm and stepped forward. "I have to be able to trust my supplier. I can't trust you."

Bryan's brown eyes narrowed with anger. "You're just angry because I was with another woman who's shapely and doesn't look like—"

Garret's fist plowed into Bryan's thin face. His

head snapped back. Before he could topple over, Garret grabbed his crisp white shirt and pulled him up. "Listen, and listen good. You come near Monica again, or do or say anything to upset her, and there won't be a hole deep enough for you to hide in to get away from me—and I won't stop with one punch. Understand?"

Weakly, Bryan nodded.

Glancing in the direction he'd come from, Garret saw the Lincoln Bryan had driven the first time. Ignoring the few curious onlookers, he led the unsteady man to the car, fished in his pocket for the keys, then activated the lock and put him inside.

"Make life easy on yourself and stay away from Monica." Slamming the door, Garret turned just in time to see Monica go inside her apartment. Behind him Bryan was shouting obscenities as he started the car and drove away.

Monica wouldn't answer the door or the phone. Worried, Garret resorted to leaving threats on her answering machine. "If you don't answer the door this time when I come over, I'm going to call your sister, then your parents. I mean it."

Hanging up the phone, he took a few calming breaths, then went to Monica's door and knocked. "Monica, the next call is to your family."

He heard the dead bolt slide back, the lock click. The door slowly opened. He stepped inside expecting to find Monica teary-eyed. Her chocolate-brown eyes were clear, her cheeks void of tearstains. She'd changed into black stretch pants and an oversize white blouse. "You're all right?" Garret asked, not quite convinced.

"Yes, so you don't have to call anyone. Now I'd like to get back to reading."

Garret closed the door. "What were you reading?"

"Garret. I'm busy."

"No, you're not; you're hiding." He met her glare head-on. "We had a date to go look at the Nelson job."

She folded her arms across her chest. "Forgive me, but I don't feel like going out."

"Go get your purse so we can go."

"Garret, I'm not going anyplace." Turning away from him, she took a seat on the sofa and picked up a paperback. "You can let yourself out."

She was stubborn, but so was he. He took a seat beside her and peered at the pages. "Italian/English dictionary. Getting ready for your trip?"

Monica lowered the book, then stared at him imperiously. "Yes. Do you mind?"

"As a matter of fact I do. I was looking forward to spending the afternoon with you." He leaned closer to her. "A woman's promise is just as important as a man's. I'm holding you to it."

"I'd rather stay at home."

"Suit yourself." He plucked the book from her hand, his fingertip raking across the second pearl button of her blouse. His eyes on her, he moved closer. "I hear Italian guys like to pinch. I can see you slugging one."

"You're coming very close to getting a demonstration."

He grinned. "I'm not the pinching type." His finger continued to toy with the button of her blouse. "Any rules about these coming undone this time?"

"Stop that," she said, but her voice was breathless.

The button slipped free. "You didn't sound all that sure to me."

"I—I'm sure." At least, she wanted to be.

"Do you know how tempting you are? How you take my breath away?"

She stared deep into his eyes, then closed hers. "Reassuring me again, Garret?"

"Telling you the truth." He licked her lips. She jumped, her eyes wide and startled.

Another button slipped free. "All you have to do is look."

As if compelled she stared down as his large, dark hand freed a fourth button to expose the rounded swell of her breasts.

"Beautiful," he whispered, his lips brushing just above her white lacy bra. "I wish you could see yourself with my eyes; then you'd believe."

Air became harder to draw in. Monica felt her bones dissolving. "What are you doing to me?"

"Showing you what I see." His tongue took the place of his mouth, tracing the fullness.

Her breasts were heavy. Achy. Needy.

"Tell me you believe." His teeth nipped through the lacy material.

Words were impossible.

Transfixed, she watched his head move down her stomach, his teeth and tongue paying homage to her heated skin. His hot tongue dipped into her navel.

With a shuddering moan, she reached for him, drawing him back up until their faces were inches apart. Dark, intense eyes stared at her. "Tell me you believe."

"I believe," she whispered.

He kissed her, pressing her down on the sofa, his

hard body covering her like a hot blanket. It was a long, long time before he lifted his head. "I was kind of hoping that you wouldn't give in quite so soon."

Her arms twined around his neck. She'd be smart enough this time to just enjoy the moment and not think about anything permanent. "We can always pretend I still need convincing."

Smiling, he stood, pulled her up, then began rebuttoning her blouse. "I'm getting pretty good at this."

"Yes, you are," she said softly.

He glanced up. Her smile was openly beguiling. "Come on, let's get out of here."

They stopped by the Nelson office first. Garret and his crew had done a wonderful job, and she told him so. The next stop was his office. She was surprised and pleased that he wanted her to see it. As he showed her around, she was impressed by his organizational skills and the number of projects he had going.

He talked openly of his plans to build his business, and then expand to Atlanta. As they left his office late that afternoon, there wasn't a doubt in her mind that he'd do everything he'd set out to do.

"What do you want to eat?" he asked, helping her into his truck.

"Surprise me."

He chose a Japanese restaurant. Their fingers laced, they strolled across an arched wooden bridge lit by swaying lanterns. In the startlingly clear water below they saw the flash of colorful, foot-long fish. Inside they removed their shoes and dined on chicken teriyaki and shrimp tempura. She'd never felt more relaxed or appreciated.

Back at her apartment, she invited him in. "Thank you for not letting me hide."

He sat beside her on the sofa, his grin pure wickedness. "I enjoyed every second."

She blushed, but didn't look away. "So did I."

Garret sobered and touched her cheek. "I don't think a coward like Bryan will bother you again, but if he comes by the office, let your father handle it."

"I have to do it," she said, then continued as anger swept across his face. "Twice he's gotten away with trying to take a petty swipe at me. When he doesn't get the contract, he's going to think it's because of our breaking up and not because of his lack of integrity. He'll show up."

"I could call your father."

Her hand rested on his wide chest. "You won't because you understand that I have to do this by myself."

Garret's warm hand circled the back of her neck. "If you come away with one hair out of place, he's mine."

She shivered at the fierceness of his gaze. "He threw me off balance twice; it won't happen a third time." Her voice matched Garret's angry gaze.

He nodded in satisfaction. "Call me after you've torn a strip off his sorry hide."

"Count on it." His confidence in her meant a lot.

Reluctantly he came to his feet. "I'd better let you get some rest."

She didn't want him to go. It surprised her how much. "Thanks. I had a wonderful time."

"I'll probably get in late tomorrow evening, but do you want to come over for dinner?" he asked at the door.

"Why don't you come over here? It's about time I repaid you for all the meals you've fed me."

"I'd like that." He leaned over without touching her, and gently kissed her. "Good night."

"Good night," she said, and closed the door with a dreamy smile on her face.

Seven

Monday morning found Monica rushing again. She'd had a restless night thinking of Garret. He excited her, thrilled her. She'd never met anyone so thoughtful or caring. He made a mockery of her plan not to let him get close to her, and although she was delighted he had, she still planned to tread carefully.

Stepping into her bone-colored heels, she grabbed her purse and briefcase and headed out of the apartment. Opening the door she saw a bloodred long-stemmed rose tied to the outside doorknob with a red satin ribbon. A white card fluttered in the early morning breeze.

Her briefcase and purse hit the floor. Her shaking fingers lifted the card. *I miss you.* A little thrill swept through her. Untying the flower, she lifted the lush bloom to her nose even as she walked out on the landing, her gaze searching for his black truck. It wasn't there.

Picking her things up, she closed the door. Sniffing her rose, she headed for the stairs. The nearest place to buy flowers at this time of morning was at least five miles away. He'd have had heavy traffic both ways. His actions went beyond thoughtful and bordered on pure romantic.

He certainly knew how to please a woman . . . in all things. He was a wonderful man. It was a good thing that she left in seven weeks or she might be tempted to really start caring about him.

Monica worked all day to catch up after being late that morning. It was past two and she was still scrambling. She'd barely found the time to call Garret and thank him for the flower.

Pen poised over the ordering sheet, she let her mind wander as her gaze drifted to the rose in a bud vase Vickie had loaned her. Her comment that at least one of them had gotten him had Monica blushing and stammering. The sophisticated Vickie had laughed.

The tip of Monica's finger brushed across the soft petal. Garret's beard was just as soft.

Abruptly the door opened. Frowning, she glanced up and saw Bryan. His angry face didn't frighten her in the least. "Say what you have to say; then leave. I'm busy."

The door slammed shut. He stalked across the room and glared at her across her desk. "My boss just called to chew me out about my losing the contract. He also said you asked for another rep."

Casually she leaned back in her chair. "Since I've become so offensive to you, Bryan, I'd thought you'd welcome our not working together."

Her straightforward attack obviously caught him off guard. "I was just angry."

She folded her hands. "I wasn't. I made a logical decision based on your actions. You have no one to blame but yourself. I don't want to work with you or see you ever again." She rocked forward and picked up her pen. "You know the way out."

"You can't do this to me! Your father is one of my biggest accounts!" he said.

"You did it to yourself." She came to her feet, walked around the desk, and opened the door. "You may have time to waste, but I don't."

"Why, you—"

"Say it and you'll regret it more than I ever will," she said, her voice sharp and cutting.

He stared at her a long minute, then stalked past her. She swung the door shut. "Prick."

The door opened and the receptionist, two male salesmen, and Vickie came in. They looked worried.

"I thought I should get someone, Monica," Gina, the receptionist, explained. "I knew he hadn't gotten the contract and he looked angry when he passed my desk."

"You did right, Gina, but I'm fine."

"Losing you and the contract must have smarted," Vickie said. "But who would pick Bryan over Garret?"

"Who indeed." Monica took the way out Vickie offered. "I don't want my father or Bridget getting wind of this."

The men saluted. The receptionist smiled shyly. They all left except Vickie.

"Yes?" Monica said casually, hoping they hadn't been able to distinguish what she and Bryan had said.

"I just *have* to ask this," Vickie said.

"Yes?"

"Is his mouth as wicked as it looks?"

Monica blinked, then smiled.

"Damn. Thought so."

Monica's smile turned into a smug grin. "If you go near him I'll have to pull your hair out by its roots."

"From the way he was looking at you Friday night, I don't think you have to worry about his straying. You got yourself a winner, Monica."

Her smile faded as the door shut. She didn't have him and she didn't want him. Did she?

Garret wasn't pleased that Monica hadn't called him, and he let her know it loud and clear that night in her living room. "I warned him about going near you. Where is his office?"

Her back to him, Monica sifted though her CDs in front of her entertainment center. She was glad she had waited to tell him until they finished dinner. "Whitney or Janet?"

"He shouldn't have bothered you."

"Maybe Barry." She slipped the disk in and the incredible, sexy voice of Barry White came out of the speakers.

"You aren't listening to me, are you?" Garret said, hands pressing into his lean hips, his long, muscular legs braced apart.

"Every word." She swayed to the music, the red silk caftan she was wearing swirling around her ankles. "I just think we could spend our time engaged in pursuits more enjoyable than discussing Bryan." She shimmied down, then came back up.

"More enjoyable pursuits, you say." Garret shoved Bryan to the back of his mind and focused on Monica's every movement.

Her hands in the air, she snapped her fingers in tune to the pulsating beat. She glanced provocatively over her shoulder. "Infinitely."

His hands circled her waist. He swayed with her. Leaning his head down, he rubbed his whiskered cheek against her chin. She purred. He kissed her ear. She shivered.

"I might be persuaded to forget," he said in a growl.

"Thought so."

Garret took care of his own, and regardless of what Monica thought, he wasn't going to let Bryan get away with trying to intimidate and badger her again. Monica might not want to give him Bryan's address, but Bryan's home office in Atlanta was only too happy to give the information.

Locating Bryan's office in a glistening gold high-rise near the tollway, Garret entered without knocking. The other man glanced up, gasped, and grabbed the phone. "Security. Get up here now!"

"They won't get here in time," Garret warned, crossing to him.

Bryan dropped the phone. Rising, his hands stretched outward, he backed against the glass windows behind him. "Stay away from me."

"You made this trip necessary, not me." Garret planted his hands on the desk and stared at the quaking man in front of him. "I warned you not to get in Monica's face, and you did anyway." He straightened. "The only reason you don't need medical care now is that she wants to handle it, and I want her to know I have confidence in her ability to do so. But know this: You're a walking miracle. Three strikes and you're out in my book. Monica is giving you another chance. Blow it and nothing either of you can say will save you."

The door burst open and two armed security guards rushed in. "What is it, Mr. Owens?" one of the guards asked in a breathless rush. "Is this man bothering you?"

Garret didn't even glance their way. "They won't always be around."

Bryan swallowed. Perspiration beaded on his head.

"Mr. Owens?" the guard asked as they flanked Garret.

"I won't ask you again," Garret said in a deadly quiet tone.

"All right. All right," Bryan blabbered.

"Good thinking." Turning, Garret nodded politely to the two men. "Gentlemen."

Pleased with the outcome of the meeting, Garret went to the elevator. On the way down, the chrome door opened on the fifth floor. Directly in front of him was a travel agency. Through the glass he saw posters of London, Paris, and Rome. A young couple chatting excitedly about their trip stepped on.

The mild satisfaction Garret felt earlier faded. Monica was leaving him soon. It didn't matter that he was taking a flight out the next day for a job in Memphis. He missed her already.

Coming off the elevator, he punched in her office number on his cell phone. Just the sound of her voice eased his sudden loneliness. He pushed the glass door open and walked into the warm morning sun. Her voice made him feel even warmer. "What are you doing for lunch?"

Laughter drifted to him through the line. "Having it with you, apparently."

He chuckled. At times they understood each other so well. "I'll pick up some sandwiches and be there around twelve."

"See you then."

He hung up and got inside his truck. She wasn't gone

yet, and he was going to make sure that, while she was here, he spent as much time with her as possible.

Monica kept telling herself it was just a simple luncheon date, but she'd been excited since Garret had called. He simply put a smile on her face. She'd cleared the small lamp table in her office and set it with paper plates and plastic utensils from the break room. The roses he'd placed on her door for the past two days were the centerpiece. Their knees bumped, their faces were no more than two feet apart, and she'd never felt more alive.

"You certainly are inventive at this," Garret remarked, then took a bite out of his turkey-ham sub.

"Thank you." Monica nibbled a chip.

"I saw a travel agent today and thought about your trip," he said casually. "You still excited?"

Her smile faltering, Monica picked up her soft drink. "Of course."

"You don't look like it."

Because I'll be leaving you, she thought, and then shook her head. What was the matter with her? She'd wanted to go on this trip for nine years. "Long past couple of days," she finally said, then began wrapping up the sandwich she'd taken only a couple of bites from.

"What's the matter?"

"I guess I'm not hungry." She put her turkey sandwich back into the sack. The chips and cookie followed.

"Me either," Garret said, then reached across the table and covered her hand with his. "I'll call."

"You'll hardly know I'm gone," she said, trying to sound casual, but her voice shook.

"I'll know." His hand tightened on hers.

Determined to keep their relationship light, she pulled her hand back. "Thanks for lunch, but you'd better get out of here and go to work."

He didn't move. "We're still on for the movies tonight?"

"Yes. Of course."

"See you then." Standing, he brushed a fleeting kiss across her forehead.

Her eyelids drifted shut. When she opened them the door was closing behind him.

The instant Monica opened her door to Garret that night, she went into his arms. His mouth unerringly found hers, trembling and sweet. There was as much desperation as there was passion in the kiss. Lifting his head, he shoved the door closed behind him with one hand, and kept the other around Monica's waist.

"You ready?"

Her fingertips gently touched his lips. "What if we stayed here?"

"Anytime I can keep you to myself, I'm all for it."

"You certainly are good for a woman's ego," she said, leading him across the room to a game table.

"The only woman I'm interested in is you," he said, taking a seat in front of a Scrabble board. "What are the stakes?"

About to sit, Monica stopped and gazed up at him. "What do you suggest?"

He grinned devilishly, then eyed the buttons on her ecru blouse.

She blushed. "G-Garret!"

"All right, I'll be good. We'll play for pennies."

Monica took her seat and tried to tell herself she wasn't disappointed.

*   *   *

Garret couldn't seem to get enough of Monica. He'd been dating her for almost five weeks, but each time they parted he couldn't wait to see her again. She haunted his thoughts.

They hadn't been intimate, but had come darn close a couple of times. When she trembled with desire in his arms, he felt both weak and powerful. He never tried to push her into going further. He discovered he enjoyed holding her, talking with her, or watching her try to cheat her way out of a game of Scrabble just as much as the intense occasions when desire raced through his veins.

He respected her decision even if he did go to sleep hard and wake up harder. At least she was with him. In two weeks she'd leave for Rome. Just thinking about her being that far away from him for ten days made his gut ache.

Nodding to the receptionist, he continued down the hall to Monica's office. He should be across town finishing up a job. No woman had ever kept him from his company. He rapped on the door.

"Come in."

Looking delicious in a pretty sky-blue pantsuit, she stood in front of her desk. On top of it was a tall crystal vase filled with the roses he'd given her each weekday since they had started dating. The ones he gave her on the weekend were in a vase in her apartment. "I think a couple of them need to go to rose heaven."

She looked up. Her eyes lit. His chest tightened.

"I can't bear to throw one away." She placed the folder in her hand on the desk. "What brings you here?"

"Two reasons. The first is that I forgot to ask what kind of movie you wanted me to rent for us to watch tonight."

"You choose. The second?"

"I couldn't stay away." His hands were around her waist before he realized it. "Why can't I get enough of you?" He didn't wait for an answer. He kissed her thoroughly, as if he'd find what he sought in the heated sweetness of her mouth. Neither heard the door open.

"Monica!"

Garret whirled. Monica jumped and scrambled out of his arms. "Mama."

Eight

Alice Jones, fashionable in a mocha silk shantung pantsuit, not an auburn hair out of place, stared frostily at the man who'd been all over her daughter. "And you are . . . ?"

"Garret McKnight. I work for your husband's company." He extended his hand. She didn't even glance at it.

"I'd like to speak with my daughter. Alone."

Garret and Monica traded worried glances. "Mrs. Jones, Monica and I have been seeing each other."

Her arched brow lifted in an imperious gesture her history students had come to dread. "And that is the reason for what I've just witnessed?"

"No, ma'am," Garret rushed to say. "That's not what I meant at all. I apologize."

"You have nothing to apologize for," Monica said, stepping beside him. "We were just kissing."

"You're vulnerable after your recent breakup with Bryan," her mother pointed out. "I won't have any man take advantage of you."

Garret's jaw clenched.

Monica's eyes narrowed.

"Mr. McKnight?" Alice opened the door wider.

"You're going to be all right?" Garret asked Monica.

She smiled to take the worry from his face. "She's just worried."

Garret kissed her on the forehead and ignored the hiss behind him. "See you tonight. I'll pick up the popcorn."

"It's a date."

He stopped when he was directly beside Mrs. Jones's rigid figure. "You don't know anything about me, and in your place I'd be concerned too, but I care about Monica. I'd never do anything to hurt her."

"Words are easy," was Mrs. Jones's comeback.

"You don't trust any easier than Monica." He reached into his shirt pocket and handed her his business card. "You can ask Clifford about me, or, if you want, you can check up on me. I have nothing to hide."

Alice closed the door behind him. "So Aaron was right."

"Aaron?"

Alice crossed to Monica. "He said you and this Garret were looking all dreamy-eyed at each other, just like his parents. Monica, I don't want you to get hurt on the rebound."

"Oh, Mama. I guess I should have told you the truth about Bryan."

Instantly alert, Alice placed her hand on her daughter's arm. "What is it? What happened?"

"Sit down. You aren't going to like it." Monica told her mother everything.

With each word, Alice Jones's anger grew. Alice was slender and shapely, as was her eldest child. She'd despaired when Monica's body rounded. It had taken Alice's full-figured sisters-in-law, who were very happy and secure in themselves, to help Alice realize she was doing more harm than good by trying to restrict Monica's caloric intake or talking about her weight all the time.

Did she want a happy child with some heft to her or a neurotic string bean? The answer had been easy. She'd thrown away the calorie counter and concentrated on helping Monica learn the importance of good eating habits and exercise. She was proud of both her daughters.

"Wasn't his company up for a large contract?" Alice asked.

"Yes." Monica leaned back against her desk and folded her arms. "They didn't get it. I won't do business with anyone so unscrupulous or mean-spirited."

"Which brings us back to Garret." Alice looked at her daughter shrewdly. "He's the reason you haven't stayed long when you visited lately?"

Monica's face softened. "We have so much fun together just doing nothing, or watching movies, like we're doing tonight. He makes me laugh. I feel beautiful, invincible when I'm with him. I'm sad when I'm away from him and deliriously happy when we're together. I've never felt that way before."

"You're in love with him," Alice said, shocked and worried.

Monica started. "No. I just like him. I don't want to be serious about anyone until I'm at least thirty."

Alice studied her daughter for a moment longer, then came to her feet. "You picked up your trip packet from the travel agent yet?"

"No." Monica's arms fell to her sides. "They close early on Friday, and Garret and I have plans for tomorrow."

"Garret again. Perhaps this trip is coming at a good time."

"Mama, Garret is nothing like Bryan," Monica said, mild exasperation in her voice.

"But you didn't think Bryan was that way until he showed his true colors. What if Garret is the same?"

"He isn't," Monica defended him. "I respect you, Mama, but I won't have you say bad things about Garret."

Alice's shrewd eyes narrowed. "I have to get back to campus."

"You're going to tell Daddy, aren't you." It was a statement, not a question.

"Your father and I have never kept any secrets from each other," her mother replied.

Monica chewed on her lip. "He wasn't too happy when Deborah and John became serious."

"But you're not serious, so you have nothing to be worried about. Good-bye, Monica," Alice said, and left.

Monica rounded her desk and plopped onto her chair, wondering why her mother's words weren't reassuring.

Garret looked up from screwing a bolt into a desk and saw Clifford Jones. The older man wasn't smiling.

Garret came to his feet and stuck the screwdriver into his tool belt. "I'll be back in a few minutes, fellows."

He crossed the furniture-cluttered office. "I expected you thirty minutes ago."

"Tie-up on the freeway. Where can we talk?"

Without another word, Garret led Clifford to the last room off the empty corridor. His company had been hired to install all the workstations for Metroplex Realtors, which would take up the entire third floor.

"All right, what's going on between you and Monica?" Clifford asked, his hands braced on his hips.

Garret had hoped the meeting would be civilized, but he wasn't counting on it. It certainly hadn't gotten off to a good start. "We like each other and we've been going out," Garret answered truthfully, aware that that wasn't what Clifford wanted to hear.

"I won't have my baby girl used."

Garret held on to his temper by sheer force of will. "And what is that supposed to mean?"

Clifford didn't back down. "I won't have another man like Bryan around my daughter. My wife told me what he did. I'd call his boss if it wouldn't get out and embarrass Monica."

"If he says anything about Monica he'll answer to me, and this time he won't get off with just a punch, regardless of what Monica wants," Garret said, his body taut.

A speculative gleam in his dark brown eyes, Clifford dropped his hand to his sides. "You gave him a good one, Monica said."

"He hurt her," Garret explained, the memory still having the power to send rage pulsing through his veins.

"Guess I found out what I came for."

"What?" Garret said, trying to pull back from his anger. "What are you talking about?"

Clifford gave Garret a slap on the back that almost toppled him. "A man who'll fight for my daughter wouldn't hurt her. Should have known I didn't have to worry about you."

"I wouldn't harm Monica."

"No, you wouldn't," Clifford said in agreement, nodding his graying head. "You wouldn't lead her on in a relationship that's going nowhere except the bedroom."

Garret's jaw dropped. Clifford merely smiled and walked away.

Alice rushed to her husband the moment he exited the rose marble office building. "What happened?"

"You're right; he cares about her."

"I knew it!" she cried. "While I was waiting I called Deborah, and she thinks so too. Oh, do you think they'll get married?"

"Garret looked more angry than ready to propose when I left him," Clifford said, a hint of satisfaction in his voice.

"Clifford, you didn't scare him away, did you?"

He snorted. "He impressed me as the kind who doesn't scare easily."

"He's possessive and protective of Monica." Alice sighed dreamily. "It's so sweet and romantic."

Clifford took his wife's arm and led her to her car in the parking lot in front of the towering building. She'd followed behind his Cherokee. "Deborah picked a good man. I intend to make darn sure my baby girl does the same."

"They may have picked each other out, but I don't think either realizes it yet."

His gaze glinted like polished steel. "Then he'd better watch what he does with my little girl."

"The same way you watched what you did with me?" she asked sweetly.

"Alice!" he admonished, jerking his head around to see if anyone had heard.

Opening the door to the black Jaguar, she slid inside. "I'm going to find Deborah the instant I get back on campus."

He leaned down to the open window. "I almost hope you're wrong."

"I'm not. Monica's dreading going to Rome, and it's all because of Garret." The car's engine came alive with a polite rumble. "Don't worry. It'll all work out, and if you're still moody tonight, I have ways of taking your mind off it."

His grin was slow. "I'll be home early."

"I'll be waiting." She drove off with a flourish.

Clifford watched her go, still grinning, until he thought of Monica and Garret, and about his courting days with Alice. His father-in-law had been right: Payback was a son of a gun.

Monica was waiting for her father when he arrived an hour later at his office.

"What did you and Garret talk about?"

"Now, baby—"

"Daddy, I'm not a baby. I'm a grown woman. Like I told Mama, I respect you both, but this is my life."

"I don't want you hurt again with a user like Bryan."

"Bryan barely kissed me. I know why now, and I can only be thankful."

A muscle jerked in her father's jaw. "Garret may be all right, but I'm glad you two will have some breathing room when you go to Rome."

"I'm thinking about not going," she said, the idea gaining merit with every second that ticked by. After her mother had gone, Monica had thought a lot about her relationship with Garret. It hadn't taken her long to realize why she missed him so when they were apart, or why she let him go further than any other man she'd dated.

"I wouldn't make that decision until you've heard what I have to say."

Monica whirled around to see Garret. Her heart pounded. "You *want* me to go?"

Before he could answer, Alice and Deborah rushed in. Both were panting. "What's going on? What's happening?" Alice asked.

"Right on time. Thanks for coming," Garret said, closing the door behind them. "I have something to say to all of you."

All stared at him.

"Deborah, first, thank you for allowing me to see Monica without judging me."

Her face impassive, Deborah nodded.

Garret's gaze rested first on Clifford, then on Alice. "I can't say the same for your parents, but then I realize they love Monica and want to protect her. But I think they forget that they have an intelligent daughter who can take care of herself."

"Of course she can!" Clifford snapped.

"Then let her do it," Garret said just as quickly. "Monica," he said, his warm gaze on her.

"Yes?" she answered barely above a whisper.

Smiling, he took her hands and found them cold and trembling. "What can I say except that I'd hoped to put this off for a little longer, but your parents' interference has made that impossible."

Alice and Clifford spluttered.

Garret ignored them. "Plus your trip will keep us apart, so I wanted you to know how I felt before you left."

"W-what?"

"I love you."

Deborah shouted.

Tears formed in Monica's eyes. She found speech impossible.

"I went by the travel agency after your father left. I can get a seat on the plane on one condition."

"You're not going with her!" Clifford shouted. Both Alice and Deborah shushed him.

Monica ignored him. "What about your job?"

"Already taken care of. Now, my question is"—he stepped closer—"will you marry me and take the trip with me as our honeymoon?"

Monica's heart soared even as she felt her knees give out.

Garret caught her. "Honey, I know you're still learning to trust me, but I love you. I promise to take care of you and cherish you for the rest of my life. I have a check in my pocket to pay your parents back for your trip. All I want from you is your love."

"Garret."

"Yes, what is it, honey?"

"Will you stop talking and kiss me so I can say yes?"

"He didn't ask me yet." Clifford pouted.

Garret kissed Monica gently on the lips. "Yes."

Clifford wouldn't be silenced. "John asked me. You have to ask me."

With Monica secure in his arms, Garret said, "Do I have your permission, Mr. Jones, to have Monica's hand in marriage, to love and to cherish her all the days of my life?"

Clifford drew out the moment until his wife and daughters glared at him. "Yes."

Monica hugged her parents. "It seems I owe you thanks instead of the chewing-out I was prepared to give. I didn't realize how much I loved him until I was faced with leaving him and possibly losing him to another woman."

"You'll never lose me," Garrett said. "I told you, I'm here for the long haul."

She smiled up at him, her heart in her eyes. "Yes, you did, and I'll never doubt you again. You've shown me what real love is." She turned to her father. "Now I'm taking the rest of the day off so Garret and I can plan a quiet wedding."

"Monica, you can't do that! You deserve a big wedding," her mother cried.

"Yes, she does, and she'll have it." Garret gently pulled Monica into his arms. "My mother and sisters will be delighted to help. I figure, between the people we've met in our jobs, it won't be difficult to get what we need. With your obvious sense of style and taste, Mrs. Jones, it will be a wedding we both can remember."

"You definitely have possibilities," Alice said with a pleased smile.

"I try," Garret replied with a smile. "Come on, honey, let's go back to your place and strategize."

Clifford watched them go with a worried frown. "Strategize, my Aunt Fannie."

"Isn't she lucky to have found a man who loves her so much?" Deborah said, smiling after them.

Clifford hugged a sniffling Alice to him and draped his other arm around Deborah. "She sure is. Just like you were."

Monica and Garret got a lot of kissing in that day, but they also planned. They enlisted the help of friends and family to ensure that the wedding would come off without a hitch.

Two days before their Sunday-afternoon flight for Rome, Garret and Monica were married in a beautiful evening ceremony. The soft scent of vanilla candles and fresh flowers filled the packed church. Monica, radiant in a white tea-length gown, stood beside Garret in his black tuxedo. Neither faltered as they repeated their vows.

Afterward limousines ferried the newlyweds and guests to the romantic reception on the rooftop of a downtown hotel, where white-coated waiters and a buffet of roast beef, grilled chicken, and smoked salmon waited. White tapered candles flickered atop the white linen tablecloths on each round table.

Overhead the full moon looked close enough to touch, but the bride and groom seemed to notice only each other. No one was particularly surprised when they left early.

Unlocking the door of the bridal suite he'd arranged for, Garret picked Monica up and carried her inside, kicking the door shut behind him. He didn't put her down until he had feasted on her lips. But even then he kept her within the circle of his arms.

"I love you so much," he said, staring down at her.

"I love you, too," she replied, her voice a bit shaky. "I guess I'd better go change."

Garret smiled devilishly. "If you need any help with buttons, just call."

Monica turned and lifted her short veil. "As a matter of fact, I do."

Chuckling warmly, Garret undid the six buttons, kissing her skin as he unfastened each one. He did the same when he unbuttoned those at her wrist. "You need help with the dress?"

Her body trembling, her heart drumming, Monica nodded.

In seconds the silk chiffon gown lay askew on a chair and Monica stood before him in a white bustier, lace panties, and white hose. "I knew you'd be beautiful," he said.

His kiss started at the corner of her mouth; then he worked his way downward to the snap of the garter of each stocking. By the time he had pulled the sheer hose from her legs Monica could barely stand.

"G-Garret, do you think we could continue this in bed?"

"We can try to get there," he said, kissing her thigh before rising and taking her into his arms.

They made it . . . just. On the king-size bed Garrett fought to get his clothes off. With Monica's clothes he took his time. He was intoxicated by the taste of her skin.

Monica quickly discovered that she loved the flex and play of Garret's muscles beneath her hand, that passion made modesty impossible. Naked, she gloried in the heat and hardness of his body on hers. She had always thought his mouth and hands were spectacular. Now they stroked and teased until she ached with wanting.

"I'll love you always, Monica," Garret said as he brought them together.

Monica felt pressure, then pleasure as Garret made them one. She followed the pace he set as if they had been made just for each other. Seconds before they came apart in each other's arms, she realized that they had been.

Later, replete, she lay snuggled next to Garret. Angling her head, she kissed his chin. "Is this the reason you wanted us to have two days alone before we left?"

He smiled down at her. Taking her left hand, he kissed the hand-engraved platinum wedding band circled with diamonds on her third finger. "The only thing I want to see for the next forty-eight hours is my wife. Hopefully by the time we reach Rome I'll have enough restraint to let you out of bed, but I wouldn't count on it."

She grinned wickedly. "If your performance gets any better, I may not let *you* out either."

Quickly he rolled on top of her. "Why don't we just see?"

And they did. Again and again.

About the Authors

Blackboard bestselling author **Rochelle Alers** has published thirty titles since her 1988 debut novel, *Careless Whispers*. Cofounder of Women Writers of Color and Readers Plus, Rochelle is the proud recipient of the first Vivian Stephens Career Achievement Award for Excellence in Romance Novel Writing. Additional awards include: Arabesque Book Club, Favorite Author; Romance In Color, Author of the Year; six EMMA and two Gold Pen Awards. A native New Yorker, she now resides in a picturesque fishing village on Long Island. Visit her Web site at www.rochellealers.com.

Donna Hill began her career in 1987. Since that time she has had seventeen published novels to her credit, and her short stories are included in ten anthologies. Three of her novels have been adapted for television. She has been featured in *Essence,* the *New York Daily News, USA Today, Today's Black Woman,* and *Black Enterprise,* among many others. She has appeared on numerous radio and television stations across the country, and her work has appeared on several bestseller lists. She has received several awards for her body of work, as well as commendations for her community service. She continues to work full-time as a public relations associate for the Queens Borough Public Library system, and organizes author-centered events and workshops through her coowned editorial and promotions company, Imagenouveau Literary Services. Donna lives in Brooklyn with her family. *Rhythms* is her most recent release for St. Martin's Press. Her next novel is entitled *An Ordinary Woman*. You may contact Donna via her Web site at www.donnahill.com.

Brenda Jackson lives in the city where she was born, Jacksonville, Florida, and has a Bachelor of Science degree in Business Administration from Jacksonville University. She has been married for thirty years to her high school sweetheart, and they have two sons, ages twenty-five and twenty-three. She is also a member of the First Coast Chapter of Romance Writers of America, and is a founding member of the national chapter of Women Writers of Color. Brenda has received numerous awards for her books including the prestigious Vivian Stephens Award for Excellence in Romance Writing 2001 and the EMMA Award for Author of the Year in 2000 and 2001.

Bare Essentials is her sixteenth publication.

Visit her Web site at www.brendajackson.net.

You can also write to her at P.O. Box 28267, Jacksonville, Florida 32226. She loves hearing from her readers.

Francis Ray is a native Texan and lives with her husband and daughter in Dallas. A graduate of Texas Woman's University, she is a school nurse practitioner with the Dallas Independent School District. She was nominated in 1999 and 2000 for the Distinguished Alumni Award. Ms. Ray's titles consistently make bestseller lists in *Blackboard* and *Essence* magazines. *Incognito,* her sixth title, was the first made-for-TV movie for BET. She has written twelve single titles and for six anthologies. Two books and two anthologies are scheduled for 2003. Awards include *Romantic Times* Career Achievement, EMMA, and the Golden Pen. *The Turning Point,* her first mainstream novel, is a finalist for the prestigious HOLT Medallion Award. At the release event for *The Turning Point,* she established The Turning Point Legal Defense Fund to assist women of domestic violence in restructuring their lives. With the release of her second mainstream novel, national bestseller *I Know Who Holds Tomorrow,* Ms. Ray has pledged to continue that effort. Visit her Web site at www.francisray.com.

NOW AVAILABLE IN TRADE

VENISE BERRY

a novel

Colored Sugar Water

By the Author of the *Blackboard* Bestseller *All of Me*

DUTTON